SHA'KERT
End of Night

ISHMAEL A. SOLEDAD

Temple Dark Books

Sha'Kert: End of Night
First Edition Paperback
Copyright © Ishmael A. Soledad 2021

Cover art by Bekka Björke
www.thebekkaffect.com

Cover design & Typesetting by Temple Dark Books
Temple Dark Publications, Ltd.
www.templedarkbooks.com

The Author asserts the moral right to
be identified as the author of this work

ISBN: 978-1-8382594-0-2

Acknowledgements

The author expresses his appreciation and gratitude to all those whose assistance, in various ways, contributed to making this book possible, especially and explicitly to the following: CJ Dotson, Gaia, The Gatekeeper, Samone Johnson, Charlotte Kane, Fred Maillardet, and Tea S Massey, for reasons known to each of them.

On The Old Order Amish
Creating Menno Stoll

The Old Order Amish trace their roots back to the sixteenth-century Protestant Reformation in German-speaking Europe. Doctrinal differences led to schisms that, by 1694, culminated in the formation of what we term 'the Amish'. From 1736 they began migrating to North America to escape persecution. In 1937 the last European congregation dissolved. By 2012 there were over 275,000 Amish scattered across thirty-one states in North America.

There is no single Amish church or community, rather a spectrum centred around common, core characteristics. The quasi-German dialect *Pennsylvania Dutch* is their mother tongue, with English spoken as a second language. Highly patriarchal, they live in church districts or *communities* of twenty to forty Amish families. Leading simple, farming lives, they accept change only where it does not compromise their beliefs. With formal schooling ending at thirteen, they have as little interaction as possible with broader society (*the world*) and the non-Amish that inhabit it (the *English*). To the Amish the world, the English, and everything that goes with it only leads them away from the life they believe God wants them to live.

Church membership (the *gmay*) is gained by baptism into the church as an adult. With beliefs inseparable from each and every part of their lives, and founded on the *Bible* as God's word, each *gmay* develops a set of rules – *ordnung* – governing day to day life, dress, behaviour, and practices. Breaking the *ordnung* leads to reproval and, in the most extreme instances, *shunning*, the absolute social, spiritual, and business isolation of a person from the *gmay*. Of all Amish groups, the Old Order Amish are the most conservative; with the greatest level of separation from the world, they are the least liable to change.

So why base Menno Stoll and his community on the Old Order Amish? Although certainly no idyll, their lives recall a quieter, simpler, and slower existence centred on faith, family, work, and community. Although guarding themselves continually against the influence of the world, they are compassionate and caring to those within it. Yet to see them as some archetype of the 'stoic frontier farmer' is to sell them short; they are subject to the same hopes, desires, and fears as the rest of humanity. As sixteenth century anachronisms in a modern world their survival, let alone prosperity, is testament to their strength of character. How this could play out one, two, or three hundred years into the future fascinates me.

At its heart, *Sha'Kert* is not a story of good versus evil, but of people thrust together into the unknown, acting out their lives in what they believe is in their best interests. I could think of no better foil than the Old Order Amish, and no better way to highlight the inevitable conflict that arises.

Ishmael A. Soledad, October 2020

Prologue

BARE ROCK GLISTENS, small pools of water hide in crevices to ripple and shudder before a biting wind. The mountain soars – a harsh, naked crown, proud and exposed under a leaden sky challenging any who would dare scale it and stand and stare into the abyss of snowbound valleys and jagged ice-capped ranges.

On an old world, a new thing is born. Three hundred pairs of eyes stare at a naked figure. He stands a gaunt, racked frame; I easily trace lines that mark bone and sinew, joints puffed and raw under goose-pimpled skin. Patchwork scars run over folds of flesh, across dirt-worn skin perhaps once white, perhaps coffee – now uniform gray. One calloused hand grips a rough staff, the other balances against the gale's desire to fling him to the valley floor. A knotted rope of greasy hair sways, its smaller twin graces his face. He stands steady on the edge of cracked and flaking rock, his presence alone enough to meet the challenge of the wind, the cold, the distant eyes.

From the left, a hand reaches out, grabs his hair; he arches back, body taut. From the right, a knife, the blood-stained haft and pitted blade exuding primal danger. Hair pulled tighter, higher, he balances on the balls of his feet, calves strung tight and back erect, staff falling as both arms stretch out.

The knife rises, hesitates momentarily as the hand tightens its grip, then descends deliberately to the nape of his exposed neck.

1

Part I: Earth

Chapter One

Greg

I JERK UPRIGHT, the sheet falls from my sweat-stained shoulders. I can taste the air, feel the chill through my feet. I am the figure, but the rest? My mind knows I'm at home, but my arms reach for the comfort of the bedroom wall on one side, my wife on the other. I am here, she is here, the room is here. Above me the clock winks quarter of three to remind me nightmare and reality are different. The nightmare's gone, and with it any chance of sleep.

Lou stirs, mumbles as dreams break the surface. I slide to the end of the bed, take one step, and close the partition noiselessly behind me. Pen's is ajar; it's hard to tell where she ends and the toy penguin starts. I resist the urge to go in, stand watch over her. I lower myself into my favorite chair and flick the apartment walls clear. The lights from a city of four hundred twenty million people burn away my nightmare.

How can she think it's beautiful? Long ago I thought it was opportunity, the noise and movement invitation to grow and integrate, chance and fortune calling me; but it's proven a mocking caricature of promises made but always held out of reach in that dim gray boundary between truth and lie. It's frustration, a zoo, an assaulting, demanding presence that requires constant effort to keep at bay. But now I want to tear down the walls, let its raucous scream join the cacophony of light to overwhelm me.

As the city changed, so did my nightmare. At first fears not only of death but of the open, the cold, of a sky stretched horizon to horizon unbroken by a single structure, any sign of humanity. Yet as the city changed, the emptiness moved to saving grace and desire, my fears crystallized in open nakedness, fault lines written clear, unshielded before everyone to view, examine, judge. Then, now, to this.

I turn to Pen's space; city lights paint stained glass from floor to ceiling. Another crack, the unfairness of a six-year-old suffering ailments no one can diagnose. A better parent would have helped her, a richer one bought salvation, but I am neither. Tomorrow may tell – an answer, perhaps a solution.

A wisp of auburn hair brushes across my face. Lou leans over, wraps her arms around me. "Pretty, isn't it?"

"Better than daylight."

"She'll be fine, don't worry."

"Hopefully, it's over tomorrow."

"Nightmares?"

"Yeah, sorry I woke you."

"It's just worry."

"No, it's always there."

She sits on the arm of the chair, looks into my eyes. "The knife?"

"There's something else, Lou, something on the fringe that keeps skipping away."

"Which is?"

"When that knife falls, before I wake up, I feel it's the end but also the beginning, sort of both rolled together. It's not the dying that terrifies me, or the uncertainty, but…"

"What?"

"I know it's my choice, my decision. Like I volunteered to be a human sacrifice."

"Want to know what I think?"

"I have a choice?"

"No. Penny's illness is playing with your mind. The Greg Robertson I know doesn't dream of suicide." She stands, flicks the walls opaque and holds out her hand. "Come back to bed. If you can't sleep, we'll find another way to take your mind off the dream."

I sit in a six by six-meter clearing in the depths of the Black Forest, cradle my morning espresso like gold. With three walls set to Schwartz Wald, the illusion is only broken by Lou in her leotard and Pen with her penguin. They commandeer half the fourth wall each; Lou's broadcasts the *MorningSize* show, Pen's the *Doctor Dora Discovery* channel.

It's easy enough to ignore Lou; Pen shoves her penguin in my face. "Dad, can we take Mister Fishy?"

"Do you remember Miss Growly?"

"Uh huh."

"What happened when you took her out?"

"She died."

I can almost see the shower of foam as the toy lion exploded under the mag-lev's debris catcher. "Where is she now?"

Pen looks up, confused. "Don't know."

I pull her in with one hand, tickle her with the other. "Her guts are across the railway, all over the path, all over the people in the station."

She squeals.

"You want to add Mister Fishy's guts, too? Lion guts, penguin guts, lion guts, penguin guts." The wall flickers to window.

"If you two are quite finished, we need to get ready," Lou says. I pause in mock obedience, whisper in Pen's ear, "Say 'yes, Mummy'."

3

"Yes, Mummy," Pen repeats loudly. As she scuttles away to find her shoes, I settle back, resume my coffee.

"That's both of you, not just one."

I don't like hospitals, no matter how presented or packaged. You only come here if you or someone you know is sick, and as far as life expectancy goes, they barely beat the morgue. Many years ago, they tried to re-label them as health centers, scattering random dieticians and exercise machines here and there. All that's gone now, all save the furniture and décor. Glass, plasteel and ceramic walls and floors, memory latex and bamboo furniture, windows of smart glass. It gives a clean, harsh, up to the minute feel that's clinically cold and unwelcoming. They've tried harder for the children, cartoon decorations on the walls, gentle rainbow pastel-colored beds and chairs.

The specialist's office mirrors the rest, tries for cozy friendliness and safe nonchalance – it fails. The four large chairs arranged in a perfect circle unsettle me; I drag a chair next to Lou's, draw an inquisitive tilt of the head from the specialist AI. Pen sits on the floor, absorbed in the animal parade on her VR headset.

Doctor Lee's expression shifts from bored familiarity to mild concern. "You still comfortable with daughter remaining? We have very good crèche, she could wait until we finish."

"No, she'll only be curious later."

"As you like. This is specialist AI Laia, she's new addition, childhood disease specialist. She runs tests and analysis on your daughter."

How can a gender be assigned to a thin, dull chrome AI? Like all AIs I've met, it's face is utterly androgynous; I can't think of them as anything but 'it'. Their perfect, accent free speech doesn't help.

"We know what is wrong. Penny has a serious but treatable condition," Laia says. Lou's grip on my hand tightens. "Normal cells produce wastes then flush them out through the body. Penny's cells do not work properly. The wastes build up slowly over time which leads to her eyesight, concentration, behavior, and personality problems."

"Does it have a name?"

"It is called Batten disease. Penny has the CLN3-R variant."

"You said it can be treated."

"There is more. The lack of concentration, eyesight and personality problems are only symptoms. If untreated CLN3-R is fatal by age ten. In plain terms Penny's cells are poisoning her and, if left untreated, will kill her in three years."

It takes a second to register; Laia's words echo perfectly formed, dispassionate, clear in my mind. Pen sits silently, back to me, ramrod straight. The knot in my stomach grows. "You're sure? There's no chance you got it wrong?"

4

"No probability for error exists. Results have been checked, peer-reviewed and examined. Concurrent diagnoses received from thirty specialist AIs."

I sink a little lower in the chair. Lou's grip tightens, her shoulder's heavier, voice shakes. "Where did she pick it up? Is it something in the air, the water?"

"It is not environmental. It is inherited from the child's parents through an error in a specific chromosome. If only one parent has the faulty chromosome, their children do not inherit the condition. If they both have the faulty chromosome, the child is guaranteed to inherit the condition."

Pen's taken off the headset. The room recedes, a strange detachment grows in me. Lou starts to shake, small jerks transmitted through my shoulder: "We gave this to Penny?"

"Yes, and to all your future children. With CLN3-R it is a certainty."

"You said it can be cured."

"We can go in, reprogram the child's cell structure and chromosomes. We can do this only before they reach a certain level of physical development, around seven years of age. As Penny is a little ahead for her age group, we estimate we have seven months at most to start treatment," Laia says.

"So, we're just in time, Doctor Lee?"

"Yes, Louise. It's complex new procedure but successful, no pain. She'll be with us for month, unconscious stasis, while nanites operate. She won't know thing, go to sleep dying six-year-old, wake up perfectly healthy nearly seven-year-old."

"When can you start?"

"Tomorrow, next week, soon as you want. We have space and capacity. There is one problem. Procedure is not on the list."

"Sorry?"

"Is not on health benefits list. Is new technique, not fully through trials. Works properly, waiting certification."

"So?"

"Until certification not on list. Not on list, no public funding, no insurance cover. Is full fee paying, not all up front not all at once, there are payment cycles, but still full fees."

"Money's no issue."

"I understand, but don't ignore anything that makes burden easier." Doctor Lee touches his tablet, sends across a dense table of figures. He grimaces, almost apologetically. "I've broken cost of treatment into components, obtained estimate from all other hospitals in district. Our options are keen."

Lou's nails dig deep, the room grows colder. The numbers are impossible, obscene.

"We try to keep numbers as low as possible. There are people here who help, perhaps little time, day or two, talk it through?"

"Yes, yes, thank you."

"A few days' delay has no impact. Laia will help make arrangements and provide you with summary of Penny's condition."

Lou pulls the harness tighter than usual, binds us in lockstep as we emerge from the hospital level. Out as one into the tidal flow of people, we retrace our steps along moving pavements, belts, escalators, and the rare mad dash to avoid open sky and putrid smells. I see nothing, feel nothing but numbing cold to replace my usual unease and revulsion. I'm on autopilot towed behind her, left foot right foot head down and go. Lou'd normally beat an erratic path from one display to another, vendor to vendor to chat about nothing and everything but now she drives us on, one arm on me, one threaded through Pen's harness.

The numbers finally register in the mag-lev for home, crushed into a family corner seat held steady by the press of bodies. It's more money than we will earn in thirty years. Pen tugs my trouser leg. She hasn't said a word since the hospital. "Dad, the man said I'm going to die. Am I?"

"No honey, the man's stupid. You are not going to die."

"Good. Mummy can't do her exercises without me."

Lou's head drives into the nape of my neck.

I sink into the couch empty and exhausted. Dusk casts cold, sterile shadows through the apartment; the sun seems beaten, cowed as it struggles to push light through thick polluted air.

Lou lingers at Pen's partition. Shoulders slumped, she stares at Pen as if the act itself can tear the guilty chromosomes from her body, cleanse her by telekinesis. The couch moves, Lou's feet join mine on the window ledge.

"How do we do it?"

"Some of the numbers aren't right, Greg. We could get it done in other places, foreign clinics maybe. Sometimes they're good."

"That brings it to…?"

"Four-fifths their lowest number. Makes it a little bit impossible, not totally impossible."

"If we sell everything, that's maybe a fifth, we'd have enough for the down payment. But the rest? We need to show it all up front, no questions asked."

"Have to beg, borrow, call in every favor, everyone we know. Perhaps we can get close."

"I'm not even sure we could raise it if we indentured ourselves for life. And who'd lend it? They don't give that much to the likes of us."

"Maybe if you were a bit higher up."

"What? Hold on, Lou, that's not fair."

"You let them push you down when you're better than them."

"I've done okay."

"You don't advertise yourself, don't go hard enough."

"I'm not educated like the rest. You know it makes it harder."

"You made it that way. You were the one that got kicked out. You can't blame anyone else."

I'd never told anyone the whole story. All they'd ever seen was the vid headlines. It still burns after ten years but I've sworn no one will ever know beyond those involved. Not even her. "I'm not making excuses, I'm only saying. Right now, what matters is getting the money to save Pen."

"I know, I didn't mean anything, it might've made it easier, that's all."

"No matter what, we'll raise it. Six month's just so tight."

"It'll be hard, but we can get there."

"Exactly. Somehow."

Dusk fades to silent evening, the city lights beat the glow of rising threeships into submission. One hundred fifty levels below, beltwalks and mag-levs snake like trails of multicolored fireflies.

"Did you catch the rest of the info dump, Lou?"

"Which part?"

"Us. Batten's disease. Kids."

"Not totally."

"We can't have any more kids."

"You think the government's going to revoke our license?"

"Every child we have is guaranteed to get Batten's disease. We can't have any more, Pen's it." I don't need to see her face, feel her tense. Giving Pen a brother or sister is at the heart of Lou's plans.

"No. No, that's not right."

"There's more. You can have kids with anyone. It's only if someone else has the same variant it causes trouble. Lou, the male gene's the trigger. It's me, I'm the problem."

"You? You're telling me you've not only sentenced Penny to death, but any other children we could have, killed off our family? You can't be that paranoid."

"It's got nothing to do with what I think. It's a fact."

"How can you be so narcissistic? This isn't about you, it's about Penny."

"Pen's all I'm worried about, you and her. It's simply facts."

"Facts, is it? Well, what do you suggest?"

"If I can't, I mean, if you wanted to –"

"You want me to go breed with someone else, get some sperm donor loser to impregnate me?"

"The next contract cycle's up soon, I wouldn't stop you."

"You'd load that onto me, make me wear it?"

"I'm being honest."

"No, it's about you and your self-pity."

"It's about maturity, being realistic."

"You want maturity? We got Penny into this, we'll get her out and that's all there is to it. You damn well stick out what you started!"

Mister Fishy bounces off Lou's head, comes to rest upside down at my feet. Pen stands arms crossed, tear-streaked face. "Don't shout!"

Louise reaches back, points one finger. "Don't throw your toys! Pick it up right now or it goes in the disposal!"

Lips quivering, Pen bursts into tears. Lou's by Pen's side instantly. "I'm sorry, we didn't mean to shout."

"Don't like it when you shout."

"We're tired, cranky. Even parents get cranky."

"Don't hate me?"

"No, no, how could we? We love you."

"Still like Dad?"

"Of course I do, silly."

We sit on the floor, Pen between us. It's simpler to stay than get her into bed, so we lie down and huddle together.

"Greg, the things I said, I didn't mean them."

"I know. Same here."

"We'll get through it, right? We'll make it?"

"Yeah, for sure. One step, one thing at a time. We'll be fine."

My nightmare returns in force, played out against a sickening blood red sky.

Chapter Two

Louise

EVERYTHING IS NOMINAL, it all ticks along smoothly like most days. I recline my chair to the point where tiredness does not quite overwhelm the need to stay on top of the information flow. The gerontology feeds are lumpy; ordinarily, I'd reset the framework – today, I'll make do with simple smoothing. It's a huge effort to stay on top of the basics, keep up with the boards, let alone improve them. Hone in on the reds, Louise, put out the bushfires and let the smoldering threats remain until they, too, warrant attention. It's a rookie's board, mainly green, a touch of orange, a sliver of red. On par for the job but for me an abysmal shortfall. For the first time I don't care; it's all been thrust solidly back to the banal, the irrelevant.

The bottom left screen flames purple then silver as Clara's face pops up. It's months since we've been on site together, shift changes and work from home conspiring against us.

"Okay, Louise, you're here, I'm here, it's lunch…so let's go."

"I can't, I've got five percent reds and –"

"And I've assigned Adam to cover both of us. Two minutes at reception, okay?" and her face winks off. Clara's a force of nature, although exactly which one, I'm not sure.

Clara leads the way up forty levels and out past the edge of the building to McDsGlass. I look down through crystal clear polycarbonate to human and vehicle traffic clogging the streets, lift my gaze across the city to distant mountains beneath an unbroken mocha curtain.

We elbow our way to a booth overlooking the heliport corridor, take the last two empty seats from a pair of salary men. A tiltwing shoots up, a giant silver dragonfly ascending through a swirling cloud of gnat-like drones. The city is alive, vibrant and connected; my mood starts to lift.

The smartglass phases, RosieMac's face appears. "Bonjour, Clara Daynez. QueenMac, KrispFries, low sodium cola?"

"Please."

The image flickers. "Buenas tardes, Louise Hierro. We have missed your company. A soy grill wrap, FibreFries and TripleDip chocolate sundae with fudge. Your meals will be two minutes."

I lose myself in small talk and the view. So many people, so many stories, but to me only one matters. Does everyone feel like this sometimes, connected but separated? The service tone pulls me back. "Your meals," RosieMac announces as the plates descend to the booth, "and a complimentary green tea and chamomile boost for Louise Hierro. McDsGlass takes our family's wellbeing seriously. Happy days!"

I stare nonplussed at the cup in front of me. "A freebie? I must look awful."

"Like shit, but better than I would. It's not going well, is it?"

"Better than we expected but it looks shaky. I don't think we can do it."

"You're not giving up?"

"What? No, of course not! But what they want Clara, it's so much."

"How close are you?"

"We've called in all the favors, set up the socialnet fundraisers, worked out what we can get if we sell it all. But it's nowhere near enough."

"How's Penny?"

"She knows, Clara, she absolutely knows what's going on but she doesn't say, doesn't let on. She's so well behaved lately, even when we argue she tries to be good."

"And you and Greg?"

A gust pushes against the window, drones shift like a frightened school of fish – first with the wind, then against it, silver flakes caught in an insistent tide. How is it with me and Greg? How could it be? Clara's got no idea, she hasn't been here, hasn't felt useless her child dying despite her, because of her. I jam the spoon into the chocolate fudge, stuff the overloaded cargo in my mouth. "Some days it's great, sometimes it feels like it's the two of us against the world. Mainly we tear each other apart, it hurts like hell but I just don't care. We gave this to her, Clara, it's both our faults but there's times I believe him, I really believe he's responsible."

"You can't, you're a reasonable person and Greg didn't mean to do this. None of the pre-contract checks would show it, how could either of you know?"

I plunge the spoon down, send drops of topping onto the smartglass. It cleans itself; two towelettes and a box of tissues appear next to me. "I know, but it doesn't help. He still thinks it, still blames himself. I see it in his eyes when he thinks I'm not looking, emptiness like he's failed us. Do you know what he said?"

"What?"

"The idiot suggested I forget contract renewal and find someone else, someone without the gene, with money. Can you believe it?"

"You know something, I can. To him it's probably a logical choice if it gets Penny cured. It's not the twenty-first century, hun. I mean, if you've told him about your family, it's probably the only option he could come up with."

"He doesn't know all of it."

"I'm going to light a few more candles for you. You're going to need them."

"Add a minor miracle to a major miracle."

"How long have you got left?"

"Four months if they're right, but it's possible out to a year, a year and a half, but it's a lower chance of success."

10

"Now, don't think of it, we'll get there. What's next?"

"Well, we've scared off most of our friends and what's left of the relatives, the socialnet fundraisers have gone quiet, so now it's the banks and loan sharks. Anyone and anything with money."

"We've started the 'miss a cup help the kid' fund. We're all putting in, it's a little bit from everyone, maybe it'll make a difference."

"I didn't know."

"It's no more than you'd do for us. We have to stick together. Anyway, we've also made you work for it."

"What?"

"Those double shift schedules you've been given? You can thank Jimmy and his first contract cycle partner." Clara spreads out a towelette. She points to my half empty glass of green tea. "Anyway, let's have a little fun. Finish that off and tip the leaves here."

I tip the leaves out and nearly clip a bot as it tries to scurry away with the towelette. I drop the leftover FibreFries to the floor in the hope they will keep the bot at bay, at least for a while.

Clara twists the towelette one way, then the other, accompanied by occasional 'hums' and 'has'. I can't make anything of it but Clara takes it seriously, even if she pretends it's all a bit of a joke. She gives the towelette one final twist, turns it to me. "There, that's interesting."

"Looks like modern art."

"No, go around in a circle, clockwise, outside to inside. See these? Shapes like a house, a spade, an 'm'. These mean good fortune, money, success. Told you it would be fine."

I can barely make out the shapes, but right in the middle, quite clearly, there's something else. "What about this?"

"What about what?"

"There, in the middle."

"That's the far future, don't worry about that."

"But what is it? It looks like a snake wrapped around a mountain. You can't have missed that."

"No, of course not. It's just a silly game, a bit of fun, forget it."

"Come on, Clara, play to the end."

"Well, it's nothing, it's never exact, there's many interpretations." Clara scrunches the towelette, drops it to the waiting bot. "Look at it one way, a snake means enmity or trouble, and a mountain a journey, a very hard one. Look at it another and they both mean starting over, shedding the old and moving on. Depends."

We make our way to the exit. "Thanks, Clara."

Clara trails behind, watches the bot devour and process the discarded towelette. "Any time hun, any time."

THE AUDIO CRACKLES: "Upload immediate, Greg Robertson." I shift in my seat to find the exact balance between support and comfort, tighten my restraints, adjust the airflow, and reinitialize the neural interface.

A wireframe representation of the city replaces my bare white cubicle, leaves me to float omniscient and omnipresent in the construct. Across the frame, endless pearl strings glow pale blue, occasional yellow-orange, in places pure white. One light changes from pale blue to red. The framework shoots past to halt at the pulsing light, diagnostic outputs behind me, live feed overhead, systems schematics below, unresponsive audio surveillance unit in front. Live view exposes no obvious damage, a review of the last ten seconds no sign of interference, accidental or otherwise.

The schematics flash through me, nominals overlaid with actuals, layer by layer, micron by micron. A yellow-black barred section slowly pirouettes. Maintenance schedules, install dates, failure rates and probabilities for the integrated circuit emerge, each examined, each noted. A simple failure, before scheduled replacement but not outside norms – it's an annoyance rather than an issue. I pull up inventory and asset control, check for a replacement, supervising AI, and repair bot. Tagged, logged, and scheduled, the burning red light of unit failure is replaced by the white strobe of maintenance.

Time check gives me a little room, I flip to live view. The city falls until I stop at the two hundred eightieth level, the limit of Enforcement surveillance assets. Above me, the government enclave disappears into the brown dome of pollutants; below, the steel gray city, a continuous field of cubes and boxes joined haphazardly, an undulating carpet of barely contained mayhem. Neither drags me back here, rather what lies between. The horizons beckon, emptiness between what humanity has built below and the price paid above. To one side low mountaintops, to another the faint shimmer of ocean; but always too far away, beyond the limits of my city, my prison.

The city reverts to wireframe and rises to meet me. Even two seconds can be too long, a unit could fail unnoticed; thankfully not this time.

A ripple to one side announces my replacement's arrival. Quick protocol exchange and I swap the city for my cubicle. At least the job's busy enough to keep me distracted, stop my mind from wandering too much. I step down and straighten my shirt. I have an appointment to keep.

"Mister Robertson, please come in, sit down." I take the extended hand. "I'm Tony, the area rep."

A figure next to Tony leans across. "Jonathon. Pleased to meet you."

12

I sit nervously. The room feels unusual, but they seem open, keen enough, particularly Tony who reminds me of an old-time real estate agent. They should be glad to see me – after all, I'm here to beg. Nobody goes to the Enforcement Benevolent Fund if they can avoid it; only when every other option is gone. They have money and lots of it, never turn anyone away in exchange for ruinously high interest rates, ironclad liens, and weighty administration fees. It's said the only thing that separates the Fund from an extortion racket are their badges. I smile warmly.

"So, we have your details, all the information we need." Tony turns his tablet off, makes a show of placing it on the edge of the desk, out of the way. "A quick recap if I may, of your application. The amount is for an operation on your daughter, and you offer security over your total assets and income streams."

"Yes. Whatever it would take to service the loan."

"Certainly, in matters like these there are few constraints. Your recent credit history is very active, unfortunately all unsuccessful. I take it we are your last choice?"

I shift uncomfortably. "Well, yes, that's true, it's not that the Fund is –"

"That's quite alright, most of our customers follow the same path. They could save themselves a great deal of frustration if they came to us first. Allow me to be frank, Mister Robertson. The amount you have asked for is...significant, in truth the largest request I have seen, by a wide margin. For this you offer security of low value together with an extended...a greatly extended...payment horizon."

"We're good risks, our histories are clean with no defaults, no judgments, early payments on everything."

"Which is all well and good with lesser amounts, but this? The Fund is not unsympathetic, Mister Robertson. I'm touched by your plight. However, I have a duty to the Fund members, a requirement not to overstep our already generous and flexible conditions." He puts the tablet away. The gentle click as the drawer locks is a thunderclap. "Unfortunately, Mister Robinson, the Fund is unable to grant your application. We cannot provide you with the amount you request. I am sorry."

I half expected it, months of the same message conditioning me, but it still feels bitter. My voice is faint, defeated, forced to civility by the faint hope that, in slightly better circumstances, I could find myself here again. "Thank you for at least considering it."

"Don't think all your options are closed. I invited Jonathon here not to watch your last hope dashed but rather knowing he may have an arrangement that can help. I will leave you to talk in private."

It dawns on me; the room's devoid of screens, monitoring devices, any of the usual surveillance assets. Bitterness changes to wariness as clean cut, bespectacled Jonathon takes on a different perspective. "We can get Penny the treatment she needs, Greg."

13

"How? The Fund has already said 'No', and we offered them everything."

"We're not interested in what you offered. It has no value."

"What does?"

"Knowledge. Information. Schedules."

"I don't like where this is going."

"And I don't think you have a choice. How long has it been since the diagnosis? Four months? All that time and effort, you and Louise, and you find yourself in front of these sharks?" Jonathon places his glasses on the desk. "Greg, for everything you've done and everything that's been promised, how much have you raised?"

"Twenty, maybe twenty-five percent."

"No. Try eighteen. It's not going to increase, no one will give you another cent."

"We've still got time."

"No, I'm telling you. I'm telling you there's no money, no more for Penny. You're not stupid. You know who I'm with, and if I tell you there's no more, you can believe me."

I fight my anger, hold back the urge to throttle him. Of course, it's crystal clear now; room with no surveillance, links to the Fund, and if they say there's no more money they can probably do it. I grit my teeth, force the words out. "Why do you want to kill Pen?"

"Oh please, Greg, don't be naïve. We're not interested in your daughter. I'm a family man, too. My son Tsuen is the same age as Penny. Why would I want to kill a child?"

"Then why?"

"Because you have something we want. If you didn't, Penny would be as good as dead. You could never raise that amount and even if by some miracle you did, you would still have to get by us to get her treated. Be thankful you are of some value."

"What do you want?"

"Nothing more than for you to do your job, and every so often provide a little information. The surveillance unit maintenance schedules, nothing unusual, merely times and duration for places we may be interested in."

"That's it?"

"That's it."

"And you'll give me the money, all of it?"

"No. We'll cure her. Money's only a vehicle, an avenue to control what really matters. Make no mistake, accept the offer and Penny starts treatment inside forty-eight hours. Treatment overseen by Doctor Lee and Laia."

"You own them?"

"Let us say we have an arrangement. Penny will be treated and cured by the best. We live by our word and die by it if necessary."

14

I'm in turmoil; boxed in again. I want to run, dive into a screaming rage, or simply fold under the weight of my conflicted emotions and impotence. Above it all the possibility, the certainty of treatment overwhelms me. "I'll have to...I mean, Lou...I can't by myself."

"Of course, this is a family decision. Louise is wrong you know, Penny has barely a month left. After that, it will be too late." Jonathon stands. "We do not make these offers lightly. Consider carefully, it's your daughter's life. I will call you tonight for a decision." He opens the door part way, turns. "One last thing. We only offer once. To decline is considered impolite, a slight we overlook. To return later and ask again is an insult, something that cannot be ignored."

I make the belt ride home alone, silent and pensive in the tightly packed mob. Does it matter, does it make any difference where it comes from as long as it cures her? We're prepared to trade away our lives anyway, is this anything other? The more I think the less the price, the easier the decision. Maintenance schedules. Information about what would happen anyway regardless of me or anybody else. All that remains is to convince Lou.

PENNY TROTS OFF down the hall. A few minutes alone is welcome, an entire day of mother-daughter time's precious but draining. Well, now the Jaskins will feel it for a few hours, seven children in one apartment for the pod play date.

I had sisters, a brother, I never needed scheduled 'interaction' time while it lasted. The old feelings rise; damn him, damn what he took from me! Dead and paid his debt to society but what about me, what about Penny, what about everything stripped from her because of him?

A pair of pink pompom socks lie on the floor. Typical Greg, his turn to keep it in order and it's half done. I crush the socks on top of Mister Fishy in the dirty clothes chute. It's not fair on Penny, stuffed animals and imaginary horses are no fair trade for other children. No child should be restricted to a pod, a single class, a handful of friends. What child deserves a hyper-vigilant parent to watch their every move, every step? Unfair, but the way it was, the way it is. Would I let Penny go unwatched, fall into another old man's grass? Of course not.

I turn to the bare expanse of our six-by-six apartment. Partitions stowed, everything in its place, a picture of minimalist heaven. Even at my worst it's never been like this, a draconian order imposed on what I can control while what really matters unravels. I go to the wall, bring up the exercise net: "*Hello, Louise Hierro. Live group or simulation?*"

"Live group."

"*Your desired level?*"

"Nine."

15

The young face is replaced by a hard, pock-marked scowl carved into a tattooed head. "Well, well. Louise Hierro. Just look at you, about time you were back. Ladies, we have a backslider among us." The face is matched by a rock-hard lean body in sweat-drenched shorts and top. Five holograms spring up around me, projections of the current live group. "I promise you this will hurt. Think you can slack off and I won't know? I see it written all over your thighs, butter ball. All of you, now, drop down and give me fifty, and quickly."

An hour and a half later I crack, bend over hands on knees, clothes soaked. One by one the holograms kneel, fall over, or collapse spreadeagled on their backs before they wink out. "Next time, Louise Hierro, I am going to give you a real workout, and even more if I see you at McDsGlass again. Mother knows and mother sees."

I've nearly recovered when Greg walks in. He looks tired, pensive. "The Punisher?" he asks.

"Just finished."

"I see. That sort of day."

"How did it go. Did they accept it?"

"No. I mean...yes, no. The Fund knocked us back."

They were our last real hope, everything else long shots or desperation. The room slowly recedes as my chest tightens: "Oh."

"But there was this other person, Jonathon, says he can help."

"Help? How?"

"He can get Doctor Lee to treat Pen. He's going to call, ask what we've decided."

"'What we've decided?' You didn't say 'yes'?"

"No, I didn't say anything. It's not quite so simple."

How could he? Months fighting rejection and despair, our daughter dying and when someone makes the offer we need he doesn't grab it with both hands? "Take it she lives, reject it she dies. What's so difficult about that?"

"They want something. They don't care about money or the apartment, they want something else."

"Well, give it to them."

"But you don't know what they're asking."

I feel it inside, hope swamped by panic and anger. What's wrong with him? We've offered everything to everyone for this and he's worried about what they want? It doesn't matter, it's worth it whatever it is. All I hear, all I know is they can give my baby her life back. "Honey, look at me. You can fix her, make her better. They can, can't they, it's true?"

"Yes, yes, they can."

"So why can't you say 'yes'? They can have anything, anything at all."

"They want information, some internal schedules."

"So, give it to them."

16

He smiles. It seems forced but it's still a smile. "I had to make sure you were happy with it."

"Happy? It's wonderful! I'm going to tell Penny."

I'm nearly at the door when the phone chimes. The window flickers to a beak-nosed face behind wire-rimmed glasses. "Hello, Jonathon," Greg says, "I've talked it over with Lou and…"

Chapter Three

Henry

I WAKE SLOWLY, let my eyes adjust to the darkness. A sliver of moon peeks between the curtains, casts faint light across the bed to my pocket watch on the post – 2 a.m. The silence is broken only by the gentle buzz of Luke's breath. I wait, count. I am patient.

The floor is cold under my bare feet. I move carefully to the doorway, avoid the loose board to the left, Isaac's bed to the right. I pull the door flap, slip out, let it fall back to close my brothers from me. I stop at the stairs. No noise, my parents and sisters still sleep. I reach into the wooden clothes box, move aside winter coats and breeches until my hands find the bag I put there yesterday. I lift out a white shirt, pants, socks. I dress quickly, check for my shoes, Melville, small roll of notes, pen knife. Satisfied, I hoist the bag onto my shoulder.

I head to the kitchen, take the note from my pocket, and place it at the head of the table. It will wait there untouched till morning, no one will dare disturb it until Father sits for breakfast. I know what he will think, what he will say; it's better like this.

I step onto the porch, close the door on my old life to face an uncertain future. The city lights are an amber haze that encircles our house, the farms, my world for seventeen years. A ring of concrete and steel towers in the distance; the array of the forces of evil, Father would say, the tide of the world washing in.

I put my shoes on slowly, deliberately. Off the porch then one mile down our dirt track, another mile along the graveled one-laner to the black top, the boundary between two worlds. The bus will take me into the city; by dawn, I will be gone and this place only a memory. I make my way to the steps. The boards complain gently, there's a rustle to my left.

"Henry?" Mom. I turn. She must have waited all night on the porch bench, huddled in a worn gray hand-me-down blanket. Her hair's down, bonnet at her feet. "Where are you going?"

The moonlight's faint, the city lights strong. I see her face creased, worried. She knows, she just hasn't told herself.

"I'm leaving."

Her face ripples apprehension to fear, fear to horror. She controls it; the quaver in her voice betrays her. "No. No you can't."

"You knew one day I would."

"I won't let you."

I tried to tell her many times, but she wouldn't listen. Coming to my eighteenth they wanted me baptized, a committed member shackled and controlled. I'm not ready for it, maybe I never will be.

"It's choking me, Mom. I can't live the way they want me to."

"The way God wants you to."

"How can god change his mind one week to the next? Last month the buggies are only black, this month gray's okay. It makes no sense."

"The guidance is there to keep us separate, apart from the English...and you'd go to them? The world has nothing but horror and evil."

"No, there's more, something that's not here."

"What else can there be?"

"School, Mom. I want to learn, go to high school, maybe college one day."

"Nothing good ever comes of worldly learning. I should know. We only need the basics, everything is in the Bible." Her lips draw tight, eyes narrow, head shakes. "You kept that book she gave you, didn't you?"

A pang of guilt goes as quickly as it came. Moby Dick and Typee prod me through the bag, a worn volume when received; now dog-eared and falling apart. "Yes."

"Didn't we teach you? Don't you know it only takes the smallest thing to open the door? You should have sent it back when we told you, but what's done is done." She pulls the blanket tight. "You can stay here, go to school in the city." She seems frail, an old woman trying to avoid the inevitable, desperate to hold onto her first-born. I sit, put one arm around her thin frame: "It won't work. Father would never allow it."

"It will hurt him if you up and disappear."

"Father? I don't think so."

"You don't know everything about him. What son does? It will, you know. He won't show it to you or anyone, even me, just keep it inside. But I know."

"If I stay, I'll only go later. It will hurt more, cause more pain. I'm not going to be like Ezra Wittmer, back and forth, back and forth until I'm shunned. This way at least I can still come by. Sometimes. Maybe."

"And this won't hurt me? I won't let you see me cry but cry I will when you're gone. I won't be able to sleep for wondering how you are, how the world's pulling you away, if you're safe."

"Don't worry, I've a job waiting, a small one to get me through school. And a place to stay, a place with a family, I'll be fine."

"Will I see you again?"

"I'm not going to the ends of the Earth. I'll only be two hours away, it's hardly anything. I don't hate you, but I can't live like this. Do you want me to visit sometimes?"

"Of course, but your father might find it difficult."

"I can work around that. If you want me to visit, I will. I promise I'll never move too far away, so you always know where I am. But I can never move back." I kiss the top of her head. She stays rigid, silent. I stand, pick up my bag. "I left a note on the kitchen table. Father won't like it but at least he won't be left to wonder. Goodbye, Mom."

She stares at me, tears my heart out. This is why I wanted to sneak out, what I tried to avoid, why most Amish boys leave like thieves in the night. Not for the sternness of their fathers, not the judgment and gossip of their neighbors, but the breaking of their mothers' hearts. She half raises one arm; it falls back as if changing its mind. "Goodbye, Henry."

I hang my head and walk away; my shoes know the way, the soft sigh of dirt underfoot breaks the silence. I pause at the rise for one last look. Mom sits still under the blanket. From their bedroom window a solitary gas light throws my father's silhouette at me. It wavers, then the house sinks back into darkness.

Chapter Four

Menno

IT IS A GOOD DAY, warm and mild with a gentle breeze across the paddock. I lift the stoneware jug to my lips, drink exactly two mouthfuls of cold water and place it back under the cherry tree. Coffee swirls run before the wind to taunt the faint yellow disc somewhere above. Hardly sunshine, hardly a sky. Once, many years ago, I saw it briefly, incandescent in a patch of blue, even that now faded memory. I check the rig, the set of leather on the team, then kneel for clevis and jointer. I dig my hand into the sod, pull out a fist full of dirt; it dribbles out, a cascade of dark brown – rich, warm, pungent. As close as a man can get to God this side of the grave. I stand, reach for plow and reins. A flick, a word of encouragement, and the team resumes the steady march to turn paddock to furrowed field. A good day's work will see it finished and I can move closer in, away from the edge, away from the black top.

I grew immune to spectators long ago, learned the futility of asking them not to photograph, to respect my beliefs; I now content myself with prayer as I close in on them. I keep my eyes down; I scanned the cars and English for the first few weeks, but the face I sought remained hidden or was simply not there. I reach the boundary, turn the team, start the next furrow.

Farming gives a man peace, patience, a different pace to life and time to think. Necessarily alone, a blessing when things are good, in times like these it sits heavy, a curse on a troubled mind. I push the thoughts away, begin the deep toned intonation of *O Gott Vater Wir Loben Dich*, carry the ancient hymn out past the horses, through the fields. The horses move in time to the slow rhythmic tune, peace returns as I let the words wash over, sink through. Line follows line through my voice, line follows line on the ground, the land changes yet again as it has for generations.

"Menno! Menno!" Freda stands under the cherry tree and waves, blanket on the ground, lunch spread out. "I thought it was a good day for a picnic. Help speed your day, remove you from the English quickly."

The gray arc gleams, an ever-present reminder. From here it soars into the air, from the black top I need to lean back to see where it ends. "There are more than last year, all with their cars, tablets, cameras. Every year more, every year closer." The grayness stares back smugly, plumes of white-rust smoke here and there, tangled thickets of silver antennae and satellite dishes cluster limpet-like to its sides. A dull thrum announces the arrival of a tiltwing over the boundary as it disappears into the gray maw. The city hums with so-called life but it is death, eternal death to the unwitting. "He is in there somewhere. Where did we fail, Freda?"

21

"He came this morning after you left. He's staying with Ben Lutz."

Mennonites? It could be worse. "Maybe there is hope. Perhaps God's mercy will soon bring him home."

"Mahlon wouldn't talk to him, walked out as he walked in, but Luke seems eager to know, asked many questions. I'm afraid for him, too."

"We cannot chain them at home, we can bring them up properly and pray but, in the end, it is between them and God."

"Menno, he had cigarettes." She spits the words as if the Devil himself formed them. "I could smell it on his clothes and hair. What next, alcohol and cards? What if Luke gets that way, too?"

It tore my mother's heart out when David left. Even after these years, I see the tears, the doubt and fear in my father's eyes each time I left the house, each day until my baptism. Until then, nothing is written in stone, nothing unforgivable, no one without hope. "I did not follow David. Luke does not have to follow Henry." Perhaps it is the warmth, perhaps the company; I tarry, open a little more. "We all feel it more, the world, the pressure. Lester and George's land taxes have gone up again. I am sure our notice will show the same. It is getting harder to make it work."

"The other day Ruth was saying Omar's thinking of selling up, taking a factory job. Hard enough as it is, harder still just married."

"Temptation of the world, easier and easier. Bring up children the right way, the Godly way, teach them the value of hard work on a farm and the world offers them ten times as much for half the effort. They are being lost, slowly but surely. How many this year?"

"Four, if you count Henry. Then there's Minister Genaamd's passing last month."

"At least that will be fixed soon enough." I sweep my arm across the horizon. "This is not liable to change, only to grow."

"It reminds me of the martyrs."

"How?"

"The world turning against them, the rejection, the persecution. The slow strangling of communities, falling away and then the righteous standing strong in the face of it all, faithful to death." Freda folds the blanket, packs the remnants back into the basket. "I'll have supper ready early tonight, don't be late."

I stand, brush a few loose crumbs to the grass, watch her walk away. A perfect choice twenty years ago, a perfect choice now, a gift of the perfect helpmate from God. It humbled me then, it still does. The burden is heavy, the need to be a true, upright Christian husband, lead the house as Christ does his church; it is the least I can do and even in this, I fall short too often. If anyone has failed Henry, it is me, and it is up to me to set it to rights.

I resume deep in thought, thoughts of martyrs, testing, church history. They were called to be a peculiar people, to suffer for their faith, so there was no

22

surprise or shock for the martyrs, for the fact of the world set against them. Now there is relative peace, the shift from open persecution to the subtlety and nuance of the call of the world.

I am no martyr; my faith is not strong enough to stand that test. I would flee, leave the old world for the new with my family. We are not like the martyrs of old but like the others, encircled by the world and its temptations; but for us there is no place to go.

The crowds have left, gone back to the world and their televisors and screens and liquor, back to their homes. I still think it strange, the few English I once talked to said they found my simple life, faith, and rejection of today unsettling, perhaps confronting. Every bird has its nest, and they have returned to theirs.

They may think me uneducated, but I am no fool. The gray circle is not the end of the city but the start, the start of the globe-straddling metropolis humanity created and inhabits like battery hens in gilded cages. Here and there it is broken for agricultural combines, fisheries, insurmountable terrain or private reserves and, in ever-declining numbers, holdouts like us, people true to the old ways, struggling under failing and wavering laws. There is no doubt we are being pushed out as greedy eyes covet our land, stack bills and circumstance against us. It is not our way to fight back but to endure as examples, turn the other cheek as Christ taught, knowing full well the second blow will come. Doubtless if I miss one bill, make one payment a penny short, they will take it all.

It stays with me on the walk home; an idea forms, grows slowly in my subconscious then peeks out through supper. It is outrageous, unheard of, yet starts to gain a life of its own. Was not the new world as unsettling for the original church? To use boats, to travel with the fear of falling off the edge of the world? What is distance now, anyway?

By the time the plates are cleared, I have decided. It is not even a possibility, merely an idea, but I know who can tell me if it has any chance. I become aware of the Bible in front of me, Isaac's expectant gaze, the rest of the family's stares. It is unlike me to forget the evening reading. "Luke, on Monday, you will take care of your brothers and sisters. Mother and I will be in town all day."

Freda gives me a quizzical gaze but says nothing.

"Before we begin, we should pray for tomorrow, that God chooses a good and righteous minister for his flock."

And in particular, and especially, that it is not me. Please not me.

Time drags by; the day is warm, the Yutzy's barn homely, Bishop Jesse's voice monotonous. If not for the hard bench, the dig of nails into palms, I would have dozed off hours ago. It will not do, today of all days.

I glance up, tear my gaze from my knees. Freda stares back across the room with barely concealed worry. It is reflected across the hundred and twenty of us, the sixty or so church members in a tense, burdensome air. Each married woman wonders, fears; could my husband be the one? Today someone will replace Genaamd, chosen to be minister, to have the burden of shepherd added to them, their family, their wife. For no recompense. Without pause. For life.

For eight hours we brood through the hymns, the sermons, the foot washing, the brief pause for lunch as the married men become more withdrawn. Now, as communion closes and Bishop Jesse inexorably wends his way to the moment, the silence grows to trepidation. If called, none can reject it. To say 'No' is to turn your back on the church; that can only lead to shunning, total and complete exile.

It does not matter. I know, I had known since the call was made for this service it would be me. I recall a conversation a lifetime ago on a similar Sunday with a shocked, white-faced young man, married only two months and ordained minister. My question is forgotten but his answer is still clear. 'I knew, I knew it would be me,' Jesse replied, repeated years later as he was called from minister to bishop. My conviction is as strong, the knowledge as deep. It does not matter, nothing can change it, an hour or so and the lot will fall to me.

The monotone falters then resumes in a quieter, restrained fashion: "...as shepherd of our church community, our gmay, an overseer must be above reproach, the husband of but one wife..."

The call to ordination starts with First Timothy articulated slowly, clearly; draws the standards for nomination, standards each member knows, each has heard before. With Henry gone to the world, maybe I fall short, perhaps I fail, but my hope is stillborn. It does not matter. It will be me.

"...we will now receive your votes..."

Bishop Jesse and the deacon enter a side-room, close the door until a crack is left and in that crack an ear. Old Ezra stands, makes his way to the door. A pause, a whispered phrase and he returns. As he sits, the next oldest makes his way to the door, a process repeated from oldest to youngest male member, then oldest to youngest female member, until all the baptized have whispered a name in that ear.

My turn arrives. It does not matter. I toy with the idea of whispering my own name but that would be pride, would bring condemnation and reproval. "Cephas Miller."

The door closes as the last member comes back. Bishop Jesse emerges, takes four songbooks from the bench, moves back behind the door. The congregation stirs. Four books. Four names. In one of those songbooks a small slip of paper is placed, the books closed, the lots cast.

A small droplet lands on my hand. Cephas' brow is covered in sweat, his tension plain as he rocks back and forth, eyes shut. I know what he thinks, know he ponders his chances if his name is called. Brother, it does not matter.

The deacon emerges with four songbooks, each tied shut with string. Once arranged on a bench, Bishop Jesse turns to face the congregation.

"There are four brothers in the lot. David Lambright, Cephas Miller, Daniel Yoder, Menno Stoll. Come, take a book and kneel."

We kneel in a line, wait with songbooks in outstretched hands. The others stare down as if force of will can remove that slip of paper, expunge the burden. My gaze fixes on Bishop Jesse. It does not matter. It will be me.

Jesse unties the book in David's hands. Nothing. Cephas tenses, Daniel starts to shake; one chance in three.

Cephas places his book into Jesse's hands, Jesse unties the string slowly. He shakes his head. Nothing. Cephas barely suppresses a sigh, his wife Mae not so successful, the sound magnified in the torpid silence of the barn.

Daniel's shaking grows; one chance in two, he must be thinking, one chance in two. I catch Jesse's gaze. He knows. I want to laugh, scream at the inevitability, the absolute certainty of it all. The mounting reality of the burden crushes my desire. It does not matter. I know. Jesse knows. It will be me.

Jesse pries the songbook from Daniel. He considers for a moment, then places the book on the bench. He turns to Daniel, shakes his head. Nothing.

Daniel slumps against me, I put an arm around him, help steady him. A keening rises from behind, her voice known but strange, a sound I dread will become familiar.

I place my songbook carefully into Jesse's hands. Jesse pulls the string, takes one step back. With a small sigh, Jesse reveals a slip of white paper nestled in the cover.

"The lot is cast into the lap, but the whole disposing thereof is of the Lord. Brother Menno Stoll is chosen."

I do not hear the words of ordination as I stand, condolences from the other three and welcome from the deacon lost to me. I am a man whose son has abandoned the faith; a man whose mind is slowly being turned to leaving; and God has chosen me as shepherd of his flock.

Suddenly it is over. The congregation thins until I stand alone to stare forwards, accept reality. I turn, Freda red-eyed and droop-shouldered, children close. I feign a smile, walk back across the divide to my family.

I let Luke drive the buggy home, children up front as we make our way through the patchwork of houses and fields. Freda and I sit on the back, stare at the landscape. Life will never be the same, the troubles of the gmay and everyone in it are now mine; and my troubles are hers.

The steel gray arc glares down to taunt me. You lose your son to me and you would shepherd these? I will bleed your youth away, steal your land and the gmay from your grasp.

It does not matter. I know beyond a doubt. It is me, and I am chosen. Henry will return and the gmay will continue.

Chapter Five

Greg

I TURN THE DIAL DOWN, give the pan a final stir, then put the lid back. Another ordinary night at home with the family, another one I wouldn't change for the world. Pen's partition walls blaze with fluorescent anime figures, part of her ancient history school project. Like any other seven-year-old, she studies as hard as she can, tries to please herself when she's able. Except most seven-year-olds don't get within months of a death sentence. Since the treatment, she's been transformed, and each day I'm more aware of what I nearly lost. I still pay, will pay for decades, but it has fallen into a routine; now I hardly give it a thought.

I slide onto the couch next to Lou. She ignores me, headband logged in and virtuvacing. Not as good as a real trip, but as most of the places don't exist anymore, there's no choice. We used to take these trips together but lately she's started going by herself; or, more to the point, with someone else. I bring the wall up to see. She's in some place called Spain. Why she likes being chased by large ugly animals is beyond me.

I flip to the newsfeed, settle back. A human announcer tonight, a change even if she is augmented: *"...majority seven to nine decision the full bench..."*

Lou moves closer, grabs my hand.

"Welcome back. Good trip?"

"Oh yeah, you should've been there."

"...grant AIs the right to voluntary euthanasia..."

"Clara the clairvoyant there, too?"

"Don't be mean, Greg. She's a nice person and if you don't want to socialize, then who else do I go with?"

"...united Right to Life Advocates, appeal..."

"I know, she's a little, well, eccentric, don't you think?"

"If you mean she has an open mind, then maybe, but it makes her different, not weird."

"...refused to comment. In developments closer to home, Dandenong Enforcement confirm last week's..."

"Shhh, Lou."

"What?"

"...appear not to have been random..."

"I need to watch this."

"...citizens, but targeted three underworld figures known to Enforcement. The execution-style hits carried out between 21:00 and 21:10..."

My chest tightens. Lou flexes her fingers, complains against my grip.

"…levels twenty-four and twenty-five of the Bunggles residential sector. Enforcement officials are following several leads but, hampered by lack of surveillance data…"

I silence the screen.

"What's wrong?"

"I know about the murders."

"Of course you do, you work for Enforcement."

"No Lou, I mean I'm part of it."

"Don't be ridiculous. You aren't responsible for criminals getting killed."

"You remember Jonathon?"

"Yes, he wanted some information."

I never told her the whole story, exactly what Jonathon had wanted and how often. Or what followed. And she'd never asked, never wanted to know. We'd both shoved it to the back of our minds – me the knowing, she the lack of it – overtaken by Pen's recovery. "He wanted to know when the surveillance units went down for maintenance. For the whole city."

"I don't see –"

"Not once, Lou. Every couple of weeks for the past eight months I've sent him the schedules."

"Well that…that…means nothing. You told me there's multiple units, overlapping coverage. That's not how it was there."

"He called me two weeks ago, told me to take all the surveillance units in that part of the Bunggles offline for three minutes."

"Oh, no."

"I'd no choice. They own me for Pen. When it was schedules it was different, but now this? There's no way out. I've saddled us to the Triad."

"Triad?"

"The Fund's in deep with them and now we are too, probably forever."

She broods, face stone, gaze rigid. Her shoulders relax, a smile forms. "It doesn't matter. We had no choice. He was our last hope and he knew it."

"Exactly, it was either him or…or, well you know."

"So, it makes no difference. There was no other choice, no other way."

"I'd do it again in a heartbeat. Even knowing this."

"Exactly. So what if three criminals die to keep my baby alive? It's worth it, more than worth it."

I realize I'd known it would turn out like this the moment I was left alone with Jonathon. I didn't like it then, I don't like it now, but it makes no difference. Even if it goes against everything I think I am. Lou's gone from shock to acceptance in seconds; she'd probably pull the trigger herself on the three of them and not bat an eyelid. "So now we stay calm, see it through. We'll be fine."

She puts her hand on my knee. "Yes, we'll be fine."

27

The hot plate hisses and spits violently as the pan boils over, burns down to a dark, tarry mess.

I CLOSE THE door behind the last of them. I called the gmay to discuss, or rather to tell them, what my family will do; and to make one final appeal. It is no secret, I have been open and careful not to keep secrets, show pride in special knowledge. To the gmay's credit all sixty members are here. Even Bishop Jesse, who feels the idea is both ill-conceived and breaks the gmay's ordnung, the rules we live by.

It is a tight fit with the benches in place; men and guests pack into the main room, women spill out to the kitchen, children elsewhere. A blanket of black hats and plain bonnets is broken only by suits to the front, denim jeans and a checked jacket to the back. It has been over a year since I saw him, yet the world has taken its toll. Henry has hair below the shoulder, a moustache and no beard and is, if possible, thinner than the night he left. Why is he here? True, he lives with Denae and her family, and now seems to work with Elliott, but surely he knows how this will turn out?

I sit next to Elliott and Denae at the front, patient as Bishop Jesse commits the meeting. I stare out the window behind him; a row of black buggies shines in the afternoon light, the saloon flyvver at the end breaks the symmetry of boxes. How many will commit? How many will remain in a few hours?

I stand, turn to face the room. "It is no secret my family is leaving to seek a better place to live, bring up our children, to stay on the land. I have asked Mister Tring and Miss Martin here to provide details and invite any who wish to come with us to indicate." Elliott and Denae stand next to me. "After they have talked and taken your questions, we will discuss it as a gmay."

I resume my seat. I was dismayed when Denae arrived in a pants suit; even though we know the English are sinful, a woman in man's clothes can easily disturb some. I hope Elliott will do most of the talking. I saw Henry discuss something with him earlier. Thankfully, after the introductions, Denae simply hands out some papers and sits, while Elliott begins: "We've summarized the core facts on the flimsies Denae's given out. Our firm has worked with you for a number of years, but I must say Mister Menno's request was, ah, was rather unique. In the end, it is possible, and from a purely economic viewpoint is well worth while, and that is how we have approached it. The, ah, spiritual or moral aspects are obviously your own."

Denae hands Elliott a flimsy. He points to a solitary chart: "This is based on an average eighty-acre farm here in your community, in the best of circumstances. The red line...this one," indicating a steep curve, "represents costs, given everything we know. Now this one," pointing to a blue horizontal line, "represents gross farm returns."

Elliott pauses to let it sink in. "In the simplest of terms, it means if you stay here, you will be bankrupt in three, maybe four years."

There is no reaction save a few gentle nods.

"In our opinion, you have three options. First, pray for a miracle or, I think, a series of them. I don't say that lightly. The numbers are correct and will not change – they are in fact optimistic. Second option, give up farming and your lands to obtain other work. This is what your, ah, other communities have done. The other option, the one outlined on the other side, the one Mister Menno asked us to explore, is to leave and continue on elsewhere. The numbers indicate…"

It takes Elliott the better part of an hour, uninterrupted, to go through the details. The questions that come back are, as I expected, to the point and precise. Not for nothing our reputation as good farmers and shrewd businessmen.

"When you say a little colder, how much?"

"Perhaps fourteen, maybe fifteen degrees in winter, hardly noticeable."

"The hundred acres a person, how'd they work that out?"

"It's based on the number of people in each household over thirteen years of age."

"And it's free?"

"Yes, completely. Don't forget the, ah, tax holiday. This government goes out of its way to attract and keep migrants, to make it easy and, I would add, they view you as, ah, as the perfect migrants."

"Mister Tring, there is still one thing I do not understand. Why?"

"Why what, Bishop Jesse?"

"If it is as lucrative as your figures suggest, and I've no reason to doubt them, why isn't there a line of people waiting to go?"

"The simple truth? No one wants to go. It is everything that we, the 'English' as you call us, don't want. It's untamed, sparsely populated, and empty, and lacks all the comforts and conveniences we have here. It's at the bottom of everyone's list but fits your requirements perfectly."

"You've not mentioned how far this, this…what's it called again?"

"Juuttua."

"Yes, how far this Juuttua is."

"My apologies. It is, I think, three thousand eight hundred light years away."

"It's going to take a while to get there."

"Oh no, quite the opposite. In total three, maybe four hours. You'll be asleep for most of it."

The room falls silent as I stand. "Thank you. You too, Miss Martin. If you could give us some time? Freda will offer you coffee while you wait."

Elliott and Denae shuffle out with Freda and the women. Henry hesitates then slips out after them. I don't have to wait long for Bishop Jesse to start. "I didn't like this idea before and I like it less now, Menno. It's not right."

"How is keeping my family together not right?"

"You heard him, it's four thousand years away. It's too far. You'd split the gmay with no chance of fellowship or support."

"Distance is no issue. When we left the persecutions of the old world, some also said the new world was too far, forever separated. It did not stop them then, we do not condemn them for it, and it saved the gmay."

"No chance for fellowship, no chance to return? They could, you won't be able to. More to the point, travelling in a spaceship? That's hardly separation from the world."

"It's not different from using the bus," Cephas says. "We shouldn't own a bus but we can use a bus, even hire a driver. We're not buying one, are we, Menno? I mean a spaceship."

"No, of course not, Cephas. It is nothing more than a necessary tool. There is no ordnung about it."

"The ordnung are more," Bishop Jesse says. "They are the way of submission and humility, our traditions to keep stable in the face of change. It's not easily changed, brother, and care needs to be taken that humility is not lost or pride arises."

"I am no wiser than any here, I respect the traditions and voice of the gmay. I have thought it over prayerfully, sought your views, all before today. It is not lightly I came to this decision. It is simply my only choice." I make my way to the window. The steel gray band shimmers, lazy columns of dark gray smoke above. "This has taken one son, lured him in even against my prayers, our efforts, the love of the gmay. Every day it draws closer, calls to our children, tempts us to go there, work there, be part of it. The evil one is subtle, and his work surrounds us day and night."

I move back, stand between the benches. "I still have five children to bring up. Do I stand by and watch them grow in the shadow of evil, never to be baptized? If I do nothing, I should rightly be condemned; would you condemn me for trying?"

The silence hangs heavy.

"That is why I must go, why I must take my family. Why I ask if any will go with us. In the end it is simply what we have always done. Move on, set up a new community, a fresh gmay to avoid the world, let us live as God intends."

I am drained. It has been a battle to have the discussion, dissent is not my desire. It could be no more than us, maybe Omar, perhaps Cephas.

Omar, the youngest of the married men, stands. "It's why Ruth and I are going. We can't get by unless I get a job in the city and that's not how it should be. We don't want our children, when we have them, bought up surrounded by the world."

"We'll go, too." Cephas says. "Mae feels worried and unhappy. It's a chance to make life what it should be."

Some heads nod, some shake. Bishop Jesse turns to face me: "So, that's three families, maybe more. We will stay here where God put us, as others will. No one can condemn a man for trying, and the gmay will place no sanction on anyone who leaves. All we will give you are our blessings and prayers. A year ago, when the lot fell to you, I said there would be times we would disagree. This is one of them, and perhaps it is best for you to leave. But remember. You were ordained for life, and going does not change that. Whatever God has in store for you on Juuttua, you are their minister for life."

I embrace him, watch him leave. The room empties, some to the kitchen, some to the front door. Children wander past on the way to the chickens. Horses are untied, buggies turned around. Small columns of dust make their way down the road, turn off here and there for home.

I step through to the kitchen. A dozen and a half faces stare back; hope, fear and expectation written on them all. Nine families. I smile to myself. I am going with a community, a gmay of my own.

Elliott looks relaxed, seated at the end of the kitchen table with everyone clustered around. He consults his tablet. "It was always going to be enough with your family of six, Mister Menno, and now with sixty, well, there will be more generous terms. It's a sizeable migrant group for Juuttua, your land assignment will be one hundred forty acres per person."

Henry peers past Denae. "It's sixty-one."

"Oh? You've decided, then. Fine, even better, sixty-one it is."

Freda looks at me, turns away. Had she known? It would be like her. Everyone else takes it in stride, it is our way, at least in public, to remain calm. At least that incredible distance will not lie between us. I turn back to Elliot and Cephas.

"Yes, Mister Cephas, there are weight limits but you can take as many of your tools and household goods that fit," Elliott says. "It's part of the incentives, they want you there and productive, not to be stranded without any way of farming."

"What does it look like?"

"Well it's a standard threeship spindle. It's a little, ah, difficult to quite describe the shape."

"No, I mean the land, our new home."

"Of course. I don't have great images of the exact plots themselves, but we have good ones of Juuttua." Elliott turns to me. "They are projections, are they allowed?"

"As long as you or Miss Martin operate it."

Denae taps one carefully manicured fingernail on her tablet. Two globes, each about a yard across, appear in the air above the table. She points to the larger one, a dull, pockmarked ball-bearing. "Earth. The flecks of green are agriculture, blue ocean reserves and aquaculture, polar regions in white. Everything else is the city." She spins the globe, expands one area. "Your community, twenty-six to twenty-nine family units, depending on definition, total area just over two thousand two hundred acres." Less than half a dozen small points of light wink on. "Other communities with the same religious affiliation."

She moves Earth aside, pulls across the other globe. Whites, greens, and blues dominate, here and there dull yellow and ochre-red. "So, Juuttua, smaller than Earth but not that you will notice. Seventy to seventy-two percent ocean, two main land masses, one at the South Pole under at least a mile of ice."

Denae points to a familiar peanut-shaped patch of deep brown, green, and white that stretches from below the equator, over the North Pole and part way down the other side. She points to a tiny spot of silver on the lower portion. "Your destination is here. One city, rather a settlement of two hundred thousand on the tropical shoreline. Otherwise, small centers of up to five thousand people scattered within a few hundred miles." She moves her finger halfway to the pole. "Your area, heavy forest and grassed plains far enough away for your purposes but close to transport lines. Nearest settlement two hundred miles away, leaves enough expansion room to purchase additional acreage. Given around ten family units, we're looking at approximately seven thousand acres granted."

She leaves the globes to rotate above the table. It is a stark contrast, the dull glow of a sinful world against the earth-tones of a new and unsullied one. It will be many generations until my gmay will need to think of leaving. The faces around me tell the same story; knowledge is one thing, to see it so starkly contrasted another.

"It seems strange we can take seed stock," Omar says, "but not horses and chickens."

"It is regrettable but there are, ah, health issues that mean it is not possible. The, ah, process of the journey requires every living being to be in the cabins, asleep for the transfer."

"Oh."

"There are animals on Juuttua – horses, pigs, chickens, all the usual ones. They were taken as embryos and hatched there, so there is a supply of their descendants. You will be able to purchase what you need, and with hard currency you will find it inexpensive."

Denae leafs through a dozen identical, neatly bound sheaves of paper. "There's space in the agreement to specify the livestock you need. If you complete it, I will make sure you get what you require at a fair price."

Elliott glances at his watch. "It's been a good, productive day. It's time we were getting back. Is there anything else?"

Freda coughs. "There is one thing. I have a large supply, we all do, of preserves and pickles and such. I guess these we can't take?"

"Of course you can. The only restrictions aside from the obvious safety ones are maximum weight and living animals." Elliott stands. "We should let you good folk go home. If you could make sure you each have a copy of the papers from Denae? Excellent."

I stand, walk them to the door. "Elliott, Denae, thank you for your time."

"A pleasure, Mister Menno, and a unique one. Twelve to eighteen months will see all sixty-one of you on Juuttua. I was a little concerned when it was your family alone, but ten families, a little ready-made community, that sounds much better. Henry, are you coming back with us?"

"Yes, could you wait a minute?"

Now that it is only the three of us, and Henry is close, I note subtle changes. He has an air, an attitude closer to English than Amish. Perhaps submissiveness and humility have been replaced by arrogance? Puffed up in knowledge and pride, original sin, the way of the world. Henry of all people knows how I feel, what I think, so why come here?

"Father."

"Henry. It has been a while."

"Over a year."

"How have you been?"

"Well enough. I'm not here to come back home."

"It seems like a lot of trouble to tell me what you will not do."

"I'm coming with you to Juuttua. If you want me to."

"You have made it clear you are only responsible to yourself, so how can I stop you? Why are you coming?"

"I promised Mom I wouldn't be far away. I'm not going to stay with you or be a farmer. I'll be in the city." He turns, walks off without a backward glance.

"Freda, when did you know about this?"

"Tonight, when he told Elliott. He made me that promise the night he left."

"At least in that he keeps his word."

"There's still hope."

"As long as he is alive, yes, there is still hope."

There is still worship on Sunday, a sermon to prepare and maybe deliver, members to guide, counsel, and chastise. My mind wanders away from Sunday to the months and years ahead as I read through Ephesians Chapter Five.

I have an empty planet to go to. I have my family and nine others, my gmay, with me. And Henry.

"HAPPY BIRTHDAY OUR Penny, Happy Birthday to you."

33

Pen aims a breath at the candles, extinguishes seven. One refuses to go out, gutters as she starts to run out of wind. I lean across, one deft puff and the eighth candle sends a spiral of fawn smoke into the air. The cake divides itself into nineteen evenly weighted slices, each too much, too rich. Four layers, rainbow-colored frosting and what appears to be part of a marzipan penguin foot stare back at me. The foot slides down the slab to leave a raspberry peanut butter chocolate stripe in its wake. Lou'll get the Punisher back for both of us, might as well make it worthwhile. I take a large bite as the pod descends back into the chaos of nine sugar-powered children.

We dropped the partitions across six apartments, Pen's party a welcome excuse to socialize. Pen's party, so it's her call on the layout. She made two sides transparent, giving a thirty-meter-wide view across the city; the other two sides she christened 'underwater land'. An ocean stacked with fish, dolphins, enormous seahorses, mermaids and, of course, penguins. I can't shake the feeling I'm inside some gigantic, lopsided fishbowl, and at any moment all of us will be washed out to the city below.

Lou tries to balance a drink and plate on one flipper and gesticulate with the other. This year it's her turn to dress up. Pen went through the horse stage when it was mine – eight hours on all fours as a pony had been quite enough. I'm sure I still have the bruises. I make my way to the far corner and the relative safety of the adults. It doesn't last long.

"Dad, Mum, come on." Pen has Lou by one flipper, grabs me in her other hand: "I already got Heidi and Jamal. I need you, too."

"What for?"

"It was your idea, Greg. You can't get out of it."

I feign half-hearted resistance. "Oh no, I can't be seen with children or penguins, it's a security breach."

"Shut up, you idiot, behave for your daughter."

The bot raises a three-sided screen as we near: "*You want enhanced gangsta again, birthday girl?*"

"No, old time now." Pen says.

"*Okie dokey, oldie moldy. Stand still.*"

I wrap an arm around Pen's waist, lift her up so her face is next to mine. Pen swings her arms around both our necks.

"*Nicey, nicey. Now let's see smiles, smiles, I can't see teeth, Daddy-man, where's your teeth?*"

"I'll show you teeth, you plastic parrot, when I bite your –"

"Greg!"

"*Atta boy Daddy-man, Mummy's the boss. Big smiles, little kissy kissy and three, two, one.*"

Three rapid clicks, a whirr, and the screen folds. My back twinges, Pen's nearly to the point I can't do that anymore.

The bot stirs, disgorges three identical photostrips from its mouth. *"And done. Happy birthday girl."*

Pen grabs them eagerly. "Yeah, two hundred percent plus."

She shoves one copy into my hands, one into Lou's, then darts back into the knot of children.

They look like old photo booth shots at museums, from the black and white to the frames and Kodak logo. Three photos, the first one nice, natural, boring vanilla. In the second, we managed to kiss Pen on the cheek at the same time, to her pretend discomfort. Pen had stuck a finger up each of our noses in the final one, wicked grin on her face. A shot for the ages, probably what she had in mind all along. "She's your daughter."

"Your idea, Greg, don't forget it."

"Never again."

"Fair enough."

"I'm keeping this for her first serious partner, let them know what they're in for."

"Mine? For the grandkids. I can wait that long for revenge."

The pod chimes. *"Greg. Incoming call."*

"Message or delay."

"Options unavailable. Enforcement."

Lou shrugs, waddles away. I raise a small privacy field. Work – not unusual, but as always ill-timed, something minor or irrelevant that can wait. "Accept." It takes a second to recognize the face. The ebony skin, square jaw, and deep gray eyes are singular, if unexpected. "Santosh?"

"Greg. How are you?"

"Fine. How long's it been? Ten, twelve years?"

"We need to talk. I'm in the sector tomorrow, we should meet."

"Well sure, I can get an hour or so, Lou would –"

"No. Just us, and don't worry about signing in."

A time and address come over. The first seeds of doubt creep into my mind. "What's this about?"

"How's Penny coming along?"

"Great, why wouldn't she?"

"Doctor Lee's a hard man to get at short notice. Expensive but the best."

My legs grow numb, my gaze locks to his impassive stare. "Santosh, what's this about?"

"Don't miss that appointment Greg, don't be even one minute late." His face winks out. The screen darkens, his business card glows as my stomach knots:

SANTOSH KUMARA
ENFORCEMENT
LEAD INVESTIGATOR, INTERNAL FRAUD

The privacy field lowers. I'm oblivious to the laughter and conversation around me. The card, that finger of accusation, hangs in my mind's eye.

"Are you alright Greg? You look like you've seen a ghost."

"They know, Lou."

"What?"

"It's over. They know."

Chapter Six

Greg

I DESCEND INTO the bowels of the city. It's oppressive – merely the knowledge of being in the tenth sub-level with two hundred or more of city, flesh and bone bearing down lends a claustrophobic tinge to the air. It's the lack of windows, knowing from the fiftieth down it's all city – wall-to-wall city – that plays with my mind. Walls set to exterior views from further up, sequences of non-existent fields and oceans, funneled light and cool circulated air can't fool my subconscious. Ten years ago, it was only the fortieth level down that was like this. How long until they reach my place?

I decided last night to try and bluster my way through. I have no idea how much or how little Santosh knows and I'm not going to make his job any easier. Privacy breaches happen all the time.

I find the café easily enough, a thin sliver of light sandwiched between two bento bars; neon lights scream breakfast specials. Because, or perhaps in spite, of its neighbors, the café sports an ancient chalkboard and tattered red and white awning. I barely have time to settle in when Santosh arrives. We are the only ones here. The girl behind the counter steps outside, locks the door.

"You did the right thing, Greg."

"It's not like I was given a choice. Hell of a way to keep in touch. How's Gloria, Ethan?"

"Fine. You're in deep shit."

"What for?"

"Don't play stupid, I know you and you're not. Want me to spell it out?"

"Spell what out?"

"Maintenance schedules."

"What about them?"

Santosh pushes his chair back, starts to rise. "You know how this goes. You start cooperating or it ends now."

"Alright, alright."

He sits. "So, how many times in eighteen months did you send the sector's maintenance schedules to your handler?"

"So, I send some schedules out now and then, a bit of information. Nothing's down more than two minutes anyway. What can happen in two minutes?"

"Yeah, nothing. Nothing at all...except you gave it to *them*. You know what they were doing to you? Grooming you, compromising you, getting your toe in before your ugly ass. What else did you do for them? Come on, tell me. Say it to my face."

"Say what?"

37

"I'm not playing games. I know what you did, I want you to say it. Say it to me and to yourself."

"Okay, okay."

Santosh glares. "Tell me what they asked you to do that first time six months ago."

"A node, they asked me to drop one node for one minute, that's all."

"What happened in that minute?"

"I don't –"

"Don't bullshit me! We've got your net logs, surveillance data. I know you saw the coverage, so tell me…what happened in that minute?"

"Three people, three criminals were killed."

"Murdered, Greg, murdered because of you. And only two were criminals, one was undercover, one of us. You know what that makes you? An accessory. How many other times have you shut off a node for them?"

"Twice, maybe three, I dunno…I think."

"Five times, five nodes, five shut-offs. Louise ever ask you why you don't watch the feeds anymore?"

"No, no, she's –"

"Well, I do. You don't want to know. You want to stay ignorant. So, let me tell you. Every time you took a node down, someone's been killed. You're responsible, it's your finger on the trigger nine times, and sticking your head in the sand does not make it go away."

My eyes bore a hole in the tabletop, a small patch where the red and white check's worn through to reveal green plastic. Nine. One's Enforcement. One of them is us. I know what we do to our own, no quarter given, the ruthless lust for retribution. I had no choice, I have no choice; anger fights panic as I wait for the hammer-fall.

Santosh points to the street. "You know what this is for, why we keep the barest units below third sub-level, don't even try to get proper coverage? It's balance. They aren't strong enough to take it all, we're not strong enough to wipe them out, so it's an arrangement, second best but manageable." His chair creaks as he gets his breath. "They keep it down here, away from the public, and everyone's happy until some idiot goes and breaks the balance. You know it, I know it, everyone knows it. What happened to you, Greg?"

"What happened? My kid happened!"

"I didn't –"

"What the fuck would you do if it was Ethan going to die, hold hands with Gloria and pick out caskets?"

"I –"

"What would you do if your kid looks at you and asks, 'Daddy, am I going to die?' Sit back and let her? Nine, ten, a hundred, a thousand I don't care…she was not going to die."

38

"There must have been another way, something else."

"Want to find out who your friends are? Try this. And where were you when I was begging the Enforcement network? You didn't even put your hand in your pocket. Like the rest of them. Everyone ran, the government had nothing, couldn't get near it until they came around."

"You knew what it meant, where it would lead. What happened to the principled guy I went to Uni with? That Greg would have found another way."

"He's dead. You know where principles got me, back then. And don't give me that old line, don't you forget who dragged your ass out of the fire and took the fall."

"I never have. If I didn't owe you, I'd be the first calling for your blood, but after this we're square. You know how this should end."

"Prison, a few years perhaps."

"You're an accessory to nine counts of murder. You know how this works. You killed one of our own, civilian laws don't apply. We'll make an example out of you."

"It's worth it for Pen."

"Well, that's a problem, too."

"What?"

"It's not only you, it's all three of you. You got Penny's treatment as payment. We'll reverse it, set her back to how she was."

"No, no you can't."

Santosh slides his tablet across. "We've already made out the charges, depositions and briefs. There's no appeal. You'll hang, Penny will get back her CLN3-R, and Louise will get five to ten as an accessory after the fact."

The tablet glares at me. It's damning. The judge, the prosecution, both have reputations. They'll sentence Pen back to a lingering horrid death; Lou'll be torn apart in prison or worse.

"Unless."

"Unless?"

"Unless you do as I say. All of this, to sentence and revert, it's all done in public. We can't afford you, Greg. We can't afford one more public humiliation. We're nobody's friend, the public don't trust us, government barely tolerates us, the criminals laugh at us. Half want to feed you and your family to the wolves, half want to bury you so none of this comes to light. Fortunately for you, they listen to me and I still owe you."

"So?"

"So, late tomorrow you'll get a job offer. It's a slightly higher grade in a dead-end place where you'll disappear for life. You and your family will be out of sight permanently. Accept the job offer, this sinks out of existence. Knock it back, take your chances with the courts."

"That's it?"

"One other thing. It's a job lot. The three of you go – you, Penny, Louise – or it's no deal. If one stays, you all get prosecuted. If one ever comes back, you all get prosecuted."

"I don't have much choice."

"I wouldn't look at it like that. If it weren't for me, you'd be in chains before you got to blow out the candles."

"Don't worry about tomorrow. I'll take whatever it is now." I don't look at the tablet, press my thumb to the screen.

"Done. They'll send the details across later but remember all three of you need to go."

"Don't worry, I'll make sure. One thing…where is it I'm going?"

"Does it matter?"

"No. But I'll need to tell Lou."

"You'll like it. I've seen your jaunts in the grid, I know you like space." The girl re-enters the café, busies herself behind the counter.

"Thanks Santosh, it's –"

"Don't. We're even. I don't want to see you or hear your name again. You and your family are dead to me."

Santosh walks to the door. He stops, turns. "The place. Look it up. It's called Juuttua."

I MADE IT a telework day, half-heartedly stayed at home as I waited for Greg or, if it went as he expected, the call to let me know he was in custody. Three hours. I've no idea how I'll last through seven more. I drain my second coffee.

The door opens, he walks in: "They know everything, Lou."

"You didn't tell them?"

"Didn't have to. Santosh had it all, more than I knew. You remember those three that were killed? One was Enforcement, one of our guys."

"No. No, it couldn't be."

"I saw the evidence Lou. He was one of us."

"He could be lying, making it up."

"No, it's true. You know what they want to do? They want to give Pen back Batten's disease. They want to kill her."

"They can't! No one in their right mind would do it."

"They can and they do. There's no appeal, no nothing. They've already got it lined up, done everything except sign the convictions."

"I won't let them take her."

"He offered me a deal. There's a place they'll send us to so they don't have to go public. In exchange, they won't do anything to us, anything to Pen."

"So, they don't kill her, just get rid of her father?"

40

"Listen, Lou, will you calm down? It's not me, it's us, the deal is that the three of us go. You, me, Pen."

What does he mean, 'us'? Penny's done nothing, I've done nothing, he's the one that made the deal. "Why all of us, you're the one handing out schedules."

"They've got you as an accessory after the fact, and Pen's an embarrassment to them. We all go. If any of us stay we all go to prison or worse. It's all they offered, and if it weren't for Santosh, we'd have no choice at all."

"It's not fair, Greg, not fair on me or Penny."

"And you think I like it? Pushed into a corner and shoved around again? First the Triad, now this – no choice in any of it. Don't think you're not part of it. You didn't put up much of a fight when they offered, and you said you'd do anything."

"I still don't think it's fair. I have to give up my apartment, my friends…Penny will have to make new ones and you know the trouble she has. Then there's the job – I'll have to get a transfer if they have a branch at…where are they sending us, Greg?"

He's dropped his gaze, put his fingers on the bridge of his nose.

"Where are you taking me? Not the Northern Hemisphere? You can't be serious, it's a backwater. Have you any idea what those people are like?"

"It's not there, Lou."

"Well, where then?"

"It's called Juuttua."

"Where on Earth's that? I've never heard of it."

"It's not on Earth. It's just Juuttua."

"Not on…oh no, you haven't? House!"

"*Louise Hierro, can I help?*"

"Where's Juuttua?"

"*Juuttua. Ecliptic line through galactic core, distance three thousand seven hundred forty-two light years.*"

"Across the other side of the galaxy? You're taking me to the end of the universe?"

"*Correction, Louise Hierro. Current estimate –*"

"House literal off and shut up!" Damn him, he cut a deal like that? I can feel the anxiety, the childhood nightmare rise. "Tell me it's developed, Greg. Tell me it's not some damned jungle or sandpit hell I'm going to."

He fidgets, plays with his fingers, eyes darting. He only ever gets like that when he lies. "It's getting there, it's…it's in demand, Lou. We're lucky to get it, it's on everyone's list."

"I know you're lying, why can't you just tell me?"

"We can't change it. We're stuck with it."

"House!"

"*Louise Hie–*"

"What's Juuttua like?"

41

"*Size 0.83 Earth standard, orbit –*"

"No. Population, industry, main cities."

"*Capital city of Juuttua is Faith. Main employment agriculture seventy-two percent, industry twenty percent, services eight percent. Population three hundred fifteen thousand, net growth half one percent per annum.*"

"Three hundred fifteen thousand? It's empty, there's nobody on it! House, screen right capital city, screen left main land mass." The window splits, aerial view of Faith to one side, topographic map overlay on satellite imagery to the other.

I start to shake, my head throbs, throat tightens. The city is patchwork blocks scattered on a green-brown carpet beside an expanse of light blue. I zoom in, each block an apartment complex arranged in rows along broad boulevards. Do these people actually travel outside to go between sectors? I see the scale at the bottom. It can't be right, it's impossible. I zoom in more, the apartment complexes change to individual dwellings, each separate, not a part of a pod or a sector.

Two stick-figures emerge from one and walk away. These people have to go outside to go anywhere, have to walk the dirty earth, breathe unfiltered air, stand under the empty sky. Alone. I'm seven again, on that roof, the old man, the grass, the empty vulnerability. I close the image, turn away from the wall. Greg's in front of me, guilt and concern all over his face.

"I'm sorry, Lou. If there was any other way…"

"You know what I'm like, how could you? I don't know if I can. All that empty, all that space."

"It's either that or Pen dies. We've no choice."

"You could have at least told me first."

"How? There's no good way, you know that. Look, if they can do it, you can. We'll find a way, okay?"

"I'm not happy, Greg, not at all."

"We've got each other, we've got Pen. That's enough."

"Yeah. We've got Penny."

Greg stays silent, pulls away. The guilt's gone, concern takes its place. "I have to do one more thing."

"What? You said we've no choice, we have to go."

"If we go, jump on the first threeship, they'll know. We'd be as good as dead. I have to go see Jonathon, see if they'll let us."

As Greg leaves Penny comes home: "Hey Mum, was that Dad?"

"Yes honey, he has some errands."

Penny laughs. "He looks like an old man."

I drift away as Penny chatters on about her day, her school, her friends. I'm condemned to that forsaken rock because of a deal he made. He's dragged me and Penny in even though we've done nothing. Penny is safe, that's the main thing. Greg, well…Greg's another matter.

Chapter Seven

Greg

JONATHON GLOWERS AS he leads me across the courtyard. Pebbles crunch underfoot as we tramp through open space toward a single wooden door. I'm acutely aware of two discreet, but obviously armed, men in the corners and the old-style mechanical lock on the door. Getting in was tricky; getting out, if they don't want me to go, will be impossible.

Jonathon pauses, jabs a finger in my chest. "One last time, don't do this. You're better off taking your chances with the courts."

"As I said, I don't have a choice. If I go and don't tell, then my family's as good as dead. If I stay, my family's as good as dead."

"And you go in there, you'll go home in pieces. You want to do it, then fine...it's no problem of mine. One bit of advice. Nobody, and I mean nobody, tells her what to do. You beg."

I follow him into a bare room. Two high-backed wooden chairs face each other across a concrete floor. He points to one. "Sit. Wait until you're called." Jonathon moves through the curtain on the opposite side.

The room's small, chair hard. Cold seeps through my clothes, occasional goosebump on my arm. I imagine lines of penitents filing in one door and out the other, all seeking an audience, some granted, some not. Like the mandarins of old but harsher, clinical, perhaps random.

The curtain parts. A bent old Asian cleaning lady painfully makes her way to the other chair. I ignore her. She studies me over horn-rimmed glasses. "Haven't seen you before. Called you, has she?"

I give a feeble smile.

"You invited yourself?" she says. "No one comes unless called." She seems harmless, if nosey. I'm being kept waiting deliberately, a game. Maybe talking will calm me a little. "I'm in trouble."

"Who isn't?"

"No, real trouble. Trouble outside, trouble here, trouble at home."

"So?"

I shrug. "I've got to leave, if I don't tell them, well..."

"Ah, you owe them. How much?"

"My daughter's life."

"You have big trouble. You should stay, pay it back. They have long arms and long memories."

"So do the people who are making me go."

"So, you come to tell them you are running out?"

"I thought I was, but now I'll have to ask, maybe beg. It doesn't matter, I don't matter. Just my daughter."

"Ah." She stares at me for a few minutes, as if she can see through me. It's a disturbing gaze, enquiring, measured, one I can't meet; I shift nervously.

She steps down from the chair, no longer stooped but straight-backed, hard-faced. She takes two brisk steps to the curtain and turns to face me. "No more charades, Mister Robertson, we continue this inside." Jonathon appears by her side instantly.

Jonathon waits until she is past him before he ushers me through into the largest enclosed space I've ever seen. A vaulted ceiling four levels above displays a partly clouded blue sky. Manicured trees and shrubs encircle the room; and inside those, neatly trimmed roses. There are real birds in the trees. A stream runs the length of the room, bubbles over a small rocky outcrop. It's the stuff of dreams. If it's designed to intimidate, to put me in my place, it works.

Jonathon pulls me roughly back onto the paved pathway. "Pay attention. Only she may go off the path."

A small push in my back sends me to an open rotunda in the center of the room. She sits on a raised platform, an antique cushioned chair beneath her. Two identical unsmiling figures stand slightly behind her, one to each side. Jonathon stops at the bottom, waves me up. A low, bare wooden stool faces her. I sit uncomfortably, look into her face. She stares back, cleaning lady replaced by cast iron.

"You may address me as 'Ma'am' or 'Miss Xi', as you wish. Jonathon tells me you want to renege on our arrangement. Is this true?"

"Yes, I mean no, Ma'am, it's like I said, like I've told Jonathon. They've found out."

"Yes, yes, I know that, and what they think they can do with you. Where were they when you needed help? Did they treat Penny? No. You had a choice, a choice about loyalty. So why loyalty to them and not to us, Mister Robertson?"

"They'll hang me and kill Pen if I don't."

"And what makes you think we will not do worse?" She relaxes her grip on the chair's arms. "The most disappointing aspect of your behavior is your lack of trust. We own parts of Enforcement, parts of government, places you can't imagine. Santosh fed you the line about 'below third sub-level' as if it's Enforcement's gift to us? We stay below because it suits us now, Mister Robertson, and when it does not suit us, we will go where and how we wish." She shakes her head, scolds me like an idiot child. "Why did you think that even with this we can't help you? You sign your family's lives away too quickly."

The figure to her left bends, whispers at length. Her eyes close, a worried crease makes itself known below graying hair. With a sigh she stands; I follow rapidly as Jonathon flails his arms at me.

"Wait here until I return. I have to attend to another, once that is done, I will decide what to do with you." She hasn't gone more than ten meters when she stops. "Perhaps you should see this. And you, Jonathon. Come."

We follow her into a lift, descend into a harshly lit, stark concrete corridor, barred doors along both sides. Here and there a guard sits limply, animated to attention as she strides into view.

We step inside one door to a brightly lit room. A young girl to the left, wrists bound atop a thin mattress, sobs. She is covered by a thin blanket, her torn skirt and blouse on the floor. A young man stands opposite, bare-chested and smiling, flanked by two towering guards. A smaller man, bald save for one long braid cascading past his shoulder, stands to the right. As Miss Xi enters the room, he bends double, bows until his braid scrapes the floor. The young man tries to step forward, his way barred by the guards' outstretched arms.

"Aunty –"

"Silence." She turns to the bowed figure, voice flat, emotionless. "Li Cun, you allowed this to happen. How?"

"Miss Xi, it is entirely my fault. It is –"

"Stand up and face me."

He stands, face drawn tight with fear.

"What did he tell you?"

"He dismissed me, Miss Xi, told me to leave. When I heard the screams, I came back, tried to prevent him, called you." He bows deeper, lower. "I was not successful."

"I was clear when I instructed you. Was there anything you did not understand?"

His legs, ramrod straight, start to tremble. "No, Miss Xi, nothing."

"I am disappointed in you, Li Cun."

His body shakes, the braid tap dances against the floor.

"One tenth the cost of repair and one tenth the loss from damages are your punishment. That is all. But you are warned – one more episode, one more slip, and I will not be as kind. Forty years of perfection does not permit one error. Do you understand?"

"Yes, yes, Miss Xi, thank you."

"Your work here is not finished. Wait." She turns to the young man. "How can you be so stupid?"

"Aunty, it's fine, no problem. She's here, I'm here, why not? It's not as if anyone cares."

"You have the pick of our boys and girls. I do not stop your stupid perversions for respect of my brother, and you do this? Too many times, I've had –"

"But, Aunty –"

"Do not interrupt me. Do you forget who I am? You forget your place. You forget it all and think our blood covers you." She strides to the bed, pulls the

46

blanket from the girl. With a whimper, the girl tries to burrow her way into the wall. "This is an investment, our business, not a toy for your pleasure. When her father pays, we return her undamaged, untouched, that is the game. Anything else disrespects us, disrespects our business. You would disrespect me?"

"No, Aunty, never."

"I can make nothing from her now, I must mend her and send her back. I, do you hear, I must make amends because of you to keep our respect."

I shrink back into the wall, unsurprised to find Jonathon next to me.

"Do you know what this will cost me? No, of course not, in twenty-five years you have no idea, not even the start. My brother's last issue, you disgrace him. Twice. This stops now."

"Yes, of course, Aunty, it won't happen again."

"Hold him."

The guards tighten their grip; he starts to pale, eyes wide. "Aunty, what is this?"

Her gaze is fixed on him; she extends one arm. "Blade."

Li Cun pulls out a knife, curved blade and dulled handle, places it firmly in her hand. Eyes like saucers, the young man struggles against the guards: "No, no, please Aunty, Miss Xi, no, please."

She hefts the knife once, as if to gauge the weight, the feel, the fit in her hand. She takes one step forward, eyes locked to his, toe to toe. One hand grabs his hair, bends him back. The other brings the knife in unhurried precision across his neck. A red smile opens from ear to ear; Miss Xi stands rigid as his life drains away.

I double over, dry retch. Jonathon grabs me, pulls me up.

Miss Xi turns to Li Cun. "Clean this up. Fix her, repair her, clean her, and return her untouched to her parents. They are now under my protection. Do not fail me."

She turns on her heel, walks out. The lift to the rotunda is made in strained silence. I push back against the wall, place as much space between myself and Miss Xi as possible. Once seated she observes me at length, long and cold, predator to prey. "You understand the lesson, the reasons?"

"Yes, Miss Xi."

"Even with family, it is business. You and your family are simply an asset to me. Or a liability." Her shoulders sag. "What good is your family to me dead? Do not forget I own you, I own Louise, I own Penny. Now and the future, this place and any other. I am tired of bloodshed today, Mister Robertson, so you may leave to this Juuttua. Perhaps it is time for us to expand. We will remain in contact. Do not forget us."

Without waiting for a reply, she turns to the figure on her right. "Escort Mister Robertson home. You will keep an eye on him, ensure his family leaves safely." She closes her eyes dismissively.

I manage a garbled 'thank you' and hurry out the door, back into the city and as far away from Miss Xi as I can.

MISS XI SITS silently for several minutes, Jonathon in attendance. She slowly opens her eyes, stands. "It is too much. Enforcement need to remember who they deal with, their limitations, understand the consequences of overstepping the boundaries."

They walk down the path, Jonathon a respectful and wary step behind.

"Jonathon, what do you think of my actions today?"

He halts, thinks carefully.

"Necessary, but regrettable, Miss Xi. Forced upon you by others."

"Hmm. It is time for you to take on more. You are willing?"

"Of course, yes, Miss Xi."

"Very well. I will send a message, a clear and strong message, to Enforcement. This Robertson family is irrelevant. You will go to the spaceport, find the ship they are leaving on, and ..."

Chapter Eight

Henry

"NO, MISTER MENNO. I'm afraid, ah, I'm afraid that's not at all possible. We've discussed this many times, many times, and it's impossible."

I feel like I've been referee, interpreter and translator the past fourteen months as I run between Elliott and Father, Mom and Denae to clarify this, explain that, smooth over little irritations. Nothing confrontational or even mildly distressing, no more than the thousand and one points of incomprehension when a seventeenth century way of life is confronted by the modern. Like the first year I was out, all confusion and worry.

"Henry?"

"I'm here, Elliott. What's up?"

Elliot points, clearly frustrated, to a gray mare next to a cargo container. "That."

"That, Mister Tring," Menno argues, "is my best buggy driver, the only horse she feels confident with. What good is a buggy to me without a driver, or a wife that cannot attend to her business?"

"But we have arranged four horses for you, Mister Menno. You've bought them and they are waiting for you. They are exactly as, ah, exactly to your requirements."

"They are not Damsel, Mister Tring."

Elliott will never win. The gmay values good animals, my father likewise. What he won't say is that he's had Damsel for eight years and he's grown fond of her. It's not his way to show he's sentimental over tools. Elliott's been careful with his words to the gmay – perhaps a direct approach will work.

"Father, do you know what Damsel will be like when she gets to Juuttua?"

"She will be fine. A little confused, maybe, but fine."

"No, she won't. Elliott's been gentle, but the truth is if you take Damsel she will be a lunatic, out of her mind and dangerous when we get to Juutua. You'll have to put her down."

Father's left eye starts to tic. "Oh."

"Henry is correct, Mister Menno, it is as he says. Believe me, η—space is no place for livestock."

Anything with a brain that is conscious in η—space, even for the blink of an eye, ends up fried. Permanently. Accidents still happen. There's a place, a nice, secluded, gentle place on the other side of the planet that houses twenty former astronauts, sixteen others. No one in polite company discusses it – I told Elliott and Denae not to mention it to the gmay.

"What do you want to do with her?" Menno asks.

"We could take her on as another, ah, sale lot. Forward the proceeds to you once done."

"No, I do not think that is needed. We have money enough." Father glances over his shoulder at Damsel, then past me. "Take her to Bishop Jesse, Henry. Perhaps he would have some use for her. Try not to let your mother see."

I lead Damsel through a small throng of contractors. Placid as usual, she takes it all in stride, another strange ritual from a strange species. No wonder Mom likes her, she's old and too tired to be anything other than gentle and cautious. She was the perfect first horse for the twins. She'll be a perfect fit for Bishop Jesse.

The gmay is unrecognizable, half of it going, half to be transformed. They've nearly finished loading, only the Lehman's to go, ten households plus as much machinery and goods as can be packed into one threeship. Barns torn down, all the homes save the last two used last night, the gmay resembles a jigsaw with a few pieces thrown away. Over where the Luthy's place was, the heat haze from excavators shimmers, machines tear through fields, prepare the ground for multi-level industrial agriculture. The land was snapped up, reputations as good custodians and relatively large lots put prices at a premium. The rest of the gmay was keen to buy but the bidding was ferocious, the prices incredible, the reach too far. The thing Father runs from closes in on everyone else because of him. The calls started after the auctions ended, the others asking, wanting to know if it is still possible. In five years, maybe less, the gmay will not be.

The reaction from the carrier had been entertaining. Amish? In space? They'd nearly been beside themselves. How do you fit them with other passengers? Will they panic? What will they do? Until they crunched the numbers, found they could jam the lot of them and their goods and normal trade cargo in one threeship, a self-contained node. Now, nearly done, only the last few hexagonal containers remain to be filled.

Bishop Jesse leans against his fence, a curious onlooker. He's been true to his word, even supportive, but as the time drew closer, he and the rest of the gmay pulled back as if to reconcile future to present.

"Bishop."

"Henry. Nearly done?"

I point to Damsel. "Father wants you to take care of her."

"Glad he finally saw sense. You're still going, haven't changed your mind?"

"No, Elliott has a friend of a friend. There's a job waiting for me."

"Seems a long way to go when what you left us for is on your doorstep."

"You know I promised Mom."

"Seems to me there's more to it, but you'll have to find that out yourself. Since you're determined, can I get you to do something for me? Just between us."

"Such as?"

"Menno. Keep an eye on him. Here in the gmay, we've had the three of us – myself, Deacon Jimmy and your father. It's a balance, one goes slightly off, the other two bring him back, you know. We're all human, all liable to make mistakes." He frowns, scratches the nape of his neck. "He'll be by himself there, no one to balance him. He needs someone, Henry. That gmay's going to need someone."

"You know I'm not part of it. Anyway, he's got the others. Cephas was in the last lot."

"He's stopped listening, Henry, he's starting not to talk it through. He gets stubborn, sticks to a view, then when he backs down or listens to reason, laughs it off. I'm worried he's forgotten j-o-y, you know, Jesus – Others – Yourself. He's started to turn it on its head. There's no place for that here or there."

"He doesn't listen to me. If anything, he'd do the opposite. It's only because Elliott's put me between them and my going along makes Mom happy that he tolerates me at all."

"Freda listens to you, Henry, and your father listens to her. I know you, I watched you grow, so even if you don't admit it, I know you care for these people. Why you left, why you don't want to be a member is between you and God, but you can't deny you care for them. And if you do, you'll keep an eye on Menno when you can. And if you see something, talk to Freda, that's all."

It's true, I guess. I'd never thought of it. Maybe it's more than Mom but I don't think so. "I can't promise anything."

The bus lights flash, a figure waves both arms above its head.

"Looks like that's it. Time to be going."

"I'll pray things work out, Henry, that it will be blessed."

Chapter Nine

Greg

DRAB AND CLINICAL, you'd think over the years they'd make these places engaging, even relaxing. Everyone's in a rush, some are worried, no one wants to spend five hours in a spaceport lounge, not with kids anyway. I look at Pen, plugged into the net as she soaks up everything. Still too young to know how long it can be.

I'm deflated. I struggle with the shock of understanding what and who I fell in with. I should be happy she's alive, so why the constant churn in my head? Would I change what I had to do to cure here? Of course not, so why keep flogging myself? The line opens up, Lou gives me a sullen jab, shuffles forwards.

And Lou. The tension is now a constant if silent companion – she plays innocent victim perfectly. Of course it's going to be hard on her, to winkle her out of our apartment once there. At least we've got one in a pod and not one of those stand-alone things. They need her skills on Juuttua, the job will help. But it's not only the change, the fear of Juuttua; beneath it there's more, a sharp edge pointed solely at me. Once she's settled in, once she's got her networks sorted out, she'll be fine, she needs a community. Another jab, another shuffle, now only one group in front, a tall man and three kids. Travelling with one young daughter is hard enough, but three?

"Hey Dad, know you can go crazy if you wake up on the flight?" Pen sports a wicked toothy grin, sucks down feeds as fast as they can load. The tiny scar on her temple's nearly healed, a faint pink scratch the only sign of her birthday present. The PermELink wasn't my idea, not at her age, but Lou insisted. As usual, she'd been right. Pen loves it. I feel for the small lump at the base of my neck, again thankful it's disabled for everything but work.

The man at the counter's agitated: "...no, that's not going to work, like I told you..."

I bend until my nose nearly touches Pen's. "No one would notice the difference if you woke up."

"Well I'm gonna set an alarm for you to test it, then you can go live with the other zombies."

"...and I said it's not good enough..."

"That's where you and your friends live, so I'll have good company." Pen giggles, screws her face up as I add, "and it's cheating if you network your next line, Pen."

The man pounds his fist on the counter. "No, you will not! I don't care, if you don't, I will."

The ashen-faced counter girl steps back. She's shorter than Lou, maybe nineteen. Pen moves behind Lou. Something in me falls over; I'm too tired and worried to put up with stupid arguments, I want to get this over with, sit down and go.

I speak quietly, gently. "Problem?"

The man turns, glares down at me. "None of your business."

"It is my business, you're stressing my daughter."

"It will be now, idiot. One or two of you…I don't care, I'm not standing for it."

"Calm down. What sort of example are you to your kids?"

Red faced he steps forward, bunches one fist. "Don't tell me how to behave or I'll –"

I bring up my Enforcement ID. It hovers bright silver and blue in front of him.

"I'm, I mean, it's no problem, really."

"It's no problem really, Sir."

"Yes, ah, no problem at all, Sir."

"Your name?"

"Steve."

I go to the counter. Steve's daughters peer out between his legs. "That's better, Steve. Tell me slowly, what's the problem?"

"They want to split us up, three seats on one threeship and one on another. I can't have my girls away from me."

I look at the counter girl expectantly. "He's nearly last to check in. We've had to split them but the threeships go to the same place," she says.

"Which is?"

"Juuttua."

Great, I'll see more of this guy. "You've no spare seats anywhere?"

"There's a few stragglers, everyone else has pre-checked or checked in."

Steve points to Pen. "You're a family man, Sir. You've a pretty daughter. Well, I've got three. I can't let them out of my sight, they'll be by themselves or worse yet only one of them, and you know what can happen."

"They will be perfectly safe, Sir," the counter girl says. "We'll keep a close eye on them and after the first hour everyone's asleep."

"You can't guarantee nothing will happen. I mean, two hours is a long time and with a hundred and eighty other people around?" Steve points across the room to a group of people in hats and ankle length skirts. "The flight's full of crazies, I don't want my children near them."

"So, you either go and accept they'll keep an eye on your daughters, or wait until the next one and get there later with the right seats."

"No, no, Sir, I can't wait a month. She's having an operation, she needs us. We can't be late, we have to go today."

I float my ID across to the counter girl. "We seem to be going to the same place. Any chance our seats can help?"

"You're on the Pulsar, Node A. I've one of his children allocated there. His others are on the Pegasus." The counter girl looks at me, a question in her eyes. "I could swap the three seats, but Pegasus is a cargo ship."

"What does that mean?"

"Pulsar is a pure passenger ship, three nodes each seating one hundred and eighty-nine. Pegasus is three-quarters cargo plus sixty-four passengers in one node. No real difference except only two cabin attendants," looking to the hats and skirts across the room, "and you'll be travelling with them. Just them and your family."

"Does that fix it, Steve?"

"Yes Sir, yes, and may I say –"

"Good. Is that okay, Lou?"

"Makes no difference, we're all asleep anyway."

I turn back to the counter girl. "Okay, if you can, it's settled."

"All done. Your family can wait over there for boarding. And you're on the top tier, outward view. Best seats in the house."

We walk away. "Amish," Pen says.

"What is, Pen?"

She stops, gives me Lou's best lecturing pose. "Hmmff. The people in hats and dresses. Amish. You should make your bot active, Dad, don't be so old."

"Why? I've got you."

Lou gives me a strange look.

"And?"

"And what, Greg? Or should I call you 'Sir', too?"

"It wouldn't hurt sometimes. Why the look?"

"I've never seen that side of you."

"Which side?"

"You know, what you did."

"Oh that. Forget it, I guess I'm tired."

IT'S GONE WELL. Another few hours and I'll be on Juuttua. I look across the departure lounge, the small enclave of Father's gmay sits in silence, men to one side, women and children to the other. Strange how what was once normal quickly becomes different, even repellent. The reaction when we arrived at the spaceport was entertaining. At least in here the throng that gawked and followed us has been left behind, but to Father's dismay he will feature in the local news feeds tonight.

Elliott had been candid, declared Juuttua to be 'fit for fourteenth century pilgrims, but the undoubted armpit of the galaxy for modern types'. It makes no difference; here I am, here the gmay, and there the threeships. I watch them through transparent walls, red-green cones nestled below the twentieth level. The glyphs track my eyes, tell me which is what; the Pulsar to the right, in front the Pegasus shimmers in the heat haze. Sleek and compact, Pegasus looks like three cones linked tightly by two doughnuts.

A small commotion at the counter catches my attention but it's over before it starts. A couple and a kid walk over, a man and three girls hurry away to the Pulsar's lounge. I take my feet off the chairs in front. The woman seems nervous, perhaps preoccupied. It's my first time off-world, maybe it's hers. The guy's distracted, relaxed. Our gaze meets and, after a quick nod of acknowledgement, he shuts his eyes.

The kid studies me. "You're not Amish."

Singled out when I was part of them but now, when I'm out of it? The kid's probably bored. "Why?"

"You dress normal, you've got zips and colors."

"I could be in disguise, maybe a new type you don't know about."

"Nope, don't think so. I see your cigarettes. I'll get a snap and look you up in the netbase –"

"Penny! Don't be so rude. Don't bother people you don't know." The woman gives an apologetic smile. "Sorry she annoyed you, she's very inquisitive. It gets the better of her manners."

"It's okay, there's not much to do anyway. I'm Henry."

"I'm Louise, this is Greg. You've already met Penny."

"Yes, Little Miss Curious. You're off to Juuttua?"

"Yes, and you're with the…others?"

I look at the kid. "The real Amish?" I turn to Louise. "Yeah, they're starting a new community and I'm tagging along. My parents are there, Father's the tall one with the salt and pepper beard. I used to be with them but, well, you know."

"Told you he wasn't."

"Shhh, Penny. Do you know anything about the place? We've been a bit rushed, a sudden job offer, I haven't been able to look."

"A little, not much. The city's okay, I guess. Small but it sounds alright. Up north where everyone else is going, it's harsh and cold, but that's what they want. Not me, I won't visit that often."

"Oh, I guess we'll find out when we get there."

The hum of the departure lounge stops, threeships and family fade. It's the eyes that capture me, two dark green jewels that sparkle, smile and dance. Set between a sharp, dark-haired fringe and button nose, they flash at me, eyelids scrunched in amusement. The mouth opens, closes then stays shut; the corners bend up. The face tilts to one side, comes closer. Hair slides past ears that frame eyes now wide in undisguised mirth.

I'm supposed to do something, the pressure in my chest and dry mouth tell me, but those eyes hold me frozen. They draw closer, the mouth moves again.

What is it I'm supposed to do? Breathe, the pain in my chest demands, and while you're at it pick your jaw off the floor.

"...said you are in the flight attendants' space."

The noise of the departure lounge returns. The kid and Louise barely hold back laughter. The eyes, now joined by that voice, don't. I spring up, jump to one side. "I don't, I mean I didn't know. I'm sorry."

The eyes, now attached to a petite frame, sit down in the chair next to the one I just left. She pats the empty chair beside her. "You don't have to get up, you can sit here."

I sit, ramrod straight. I put my hands in my pockets, think better of it and cross my arms, think that too detached so I put them palms down on my knees. The kid giggles, Louise hushes her even as she fights her own laughter.

"Relax, I'm not going to bite. There's still some time before take-off, so you need to be comfy, Mister Sorry."

"I didn't mean to take your seat, I didn't know it was reserved."

She twists, looks up at the red, foot-high, Flight Attendants Only sign. "I should worry your eyesight and hearing are going, but let's put it down to pre-flight nerves, shall we? I'm Kelli, one of two attendants on today's flight. The other's Peter, he's over there with the rest of the group."

She's about two years older than me, those eyes are incredible.

"So, you'd be the Robertson-Hierro party of three, and you had better be Henry Stoll. I've no Mister Sorry on the manifest, so if you're not, I'll have to put you in handcuffs."

"Sounds good to me," I murmur, obviously not quietly enough as Kelli quickly flashes red. "Do you have any questions, anything I can help with?" she asks.

The kid leans across; her tablet shows a large white rocket with brown and white smoke shooting from its tail. "Will we see anything through the smoke?"

"We don't do that anymore, no pouring chemicals out the back. It's like a lift, gentle and smooth, no smoke, a little hum. If you want, you can watch everything."

"Everything?"

"As much as you like. From Earth to the spindleship, spindleship to Juuttua. Except in η-space while you're asleep."

Greg stirs. "That's what I've wanted to ask. Why is η-space so tricky to go through?"

"It's too complex, space and time and everything is mashed together, everything and everywhen is in the same spot. Only the AI can make any sense of it. It's why the spindleship's so ugly. It's not what you think a spaceship should be."

"So, what does the pilot do, sleep through η-space too?"

"Oh, there's no pilot, only the AIs." Louise looks skeptical; Kelli gives her a smile. "I've done this run for three years, the worst problem I've had is running out of coffee."

I cough to get her attention. Somehow, I've got to keep in contact with her. "If we have any more questions or if, ah, if I want to, I mean…"

She gives me a broad grin, puts her hand on my knee just as I'm plugged into the power grid. "Don't worry. You're all on the upper deck and that's my part of the Pegasus." She leans closer, those wide green jewels bore into me. "And you will sit next to me, just in case."

She stands, straightens her skirt. "I should help Peter, he's got his hands full. I'll see you on board shortly." She turns to me. "I think I'll have to keep a close eye on you, Mister Sorry."

I watch her walk away until she's hidden by a small group of bonnets. I turn to see the kid barely a foot away, wicked smile on her face: "You think she's pretty, don't you?"

Louise pulls her back. "Penny! Don't embarrass Henry more than he is."

"But it's true! He looked at her the way Dad sometimes looks at you."

"I'm sorry, Henry. See what I mean about her manners?"

"It's okay, no problem." Damned if the kid's not right.

Chapter Ten

Greg

WE CLEAR THE spaceport and climb past the fifty-level marker. It's like Kelli promised; no noise, no smoke, only the gentle whirr of circulating air and a subtle, barely noticeable push in the seat of my pants. I'm thankful for the unexpected silence, the lack of excited chatter in a vessel packed with sixty-five others. Lou and the Amish took the option to sleep the whole way, Kelli and Henry are locked in earnest private conversation further along. Pen sits between me and Lou, awake and plugged into the ship's feed.

We made the hull in front of us transparent, a three by three-meter window to the world as it scrolls by. It won't disturb their electronically maintained sleep, and it's a vast improvement over the scattered permaports. Like being in the grid with no wireframe, no live view, but this is real.

Apartment windows slide out of view, replaced by the city's undulations and gray tower blocks as small caverns emerge, neon-bathed corridors sunlight never touches. Caverns broaden to canyons to Rift Valleys as the Pegasus gains pace and we leave the two hundred fiftieth level behind, a plain with rare enclave spires that rise in the distance. The base of the clouds draws near, the limit to all I've seen, the point beyond which the grid has not released me.

The cloud engulfs us, gray rivulets instantly torn away as the Pegasus leans to her task, eager to escape the city's clutches. I press forward against my harness in anticipation.

We shoot out, a twisted plume behind us condenses and falls away. The clouds are unbroken cotton wool, a carpet spread horizon to horizon. The sky steals my breath, blues painted on blue, light to dark, azure on navy. Before the hull can adjust, the sun bursts through, proclaims its presence in shafts of iridescent gold to cast black, hard-edged shadows. I've seen vids, know what it is, but under the raw torrent of power I imagine my skin bubbling and frying away.

Below us another threeship punches through, a red green dart chases us as we chase others, a game of tag that ends only at the Atlas two thousand kilometers above.

The horizon bends as we grab the middle, pull it with us as the edges stay nailed fast. Blues deepen, darken to indigo as the glyph tracks us past five thousand kilometers an hour, units and tens a blur as we accelerate, swap indigo for black. All in silence, no vibration, no more than a gentle shove from below.

"Enjoying the view, Mister Robertson?"

"You kidding, Kelli? It's wonderful."

"You've got another hour left."

I know it's commonplace, every hour this scene is played out again and again but for me it's new, for eons before me only a dream. I imagine myself an old-time astronaut, a daredevil strapped atop hundreds of feet of rocket to risk an oxygen–kerosene immolation, crushed to near death for the chance to see, to go for a few hours or a few days and then return knowing there are no more trips, to settle into a disturbed and unfulfilling existence. I watch the coffee-brown Earth shrink, a ball that holds all I know, all I've done, creep down until all is blackness, eternal void.

I feel her rotate. The glyph hovers on the lower edge, relative velocity and distance spin slowly on their journey to zero. For all the expectation fourteen thousand kilometers an hour may hold, I feel nothing. I float against my harness as the glyph climbs the window, enlarges to a disc. I can barely make out the Atlas, an irregular trusswork jumble with ten stubby fingers; one waits for the Pegasus.

"Time to sleep. Can't have my passengers floating about." Kelli touches a small panel behind Pen's seat. "Goodnight, Penny." She moves behind me. "I'll bring you round once we're in orbit over Juuttua."

THE PEGASUS SLIDES along the Atlas' docking arm, halts. Once settled, the yellow glow of the coupling field covers the spindleship and ten docked threeships, ties eleven vessels as one. Without fanfare or fuss the Atlas translates from normal space to η—space.

The yellow glow shimmers, ripples blue-green then winks out. The Atlas collapses in on itself, a dark smudge that vomits threeships until it fades like smoke. One threeship opens as ripe fruit to spit its contents back to normal space. One drops back whole, one as three separate nodes; one tumbles and cartwheels end over end before it dissolves in a million points of light. Others merge until they rest a perverted, multi-armed starfish to fall back an elongated, distorted caricature. The final threeship shudders, blazes white hot then flattens to nothing, to leave no trace that threeships or spindleship had ever been.

The Myths of the Children of Sha'ntwoy

Creation

Before the all, there was emptiness. Before the when, all yesterdays were tomorrows. Before the answers, the questions were not dreamt...

For the emptiness that overflowed, Sha'ntwoy cried; her tears filled the bowl that held the emptiness, and the emptiness became less than the Nothing. And as the emptiness became less and less, so too Sha'ntwoy's tears, until all of Sha'ntwoy was poured out, emptiness upon nothingness from which the All sprang, from which Sha'ntwoy sprang.

But the All did not consume the emptiness completely – the Nothing remained. Sha'ntwoy took the Nothing to fill her heart with part, and to set part outside the All. So, beyond the All, outside the All, the something is Nothing; and beyond the Nothing less than nothing; and in Sha'ntwoy, and all that sprang from her, the Nothing remains in their hearts.

And the All was without order, so she gave the All questions; and the All was without purpose, so she hid the answers in the hard places. And yet was the All without form, so created Sha'ntwoy the stars and the land and the animals from her joy.

Yet a while she cried, for none existed to ask the questions or seek meaning in the beauty and form of her creation. So, Sha'ntwoy called Kert'ankway from her to join with her, and she bore daughters and sons orange, blue, green, yellow, red, black, and white; and as each birthed, Kert'ankway kissed their foreheads, bringing forth red blood as a sign.

'What is this you have given me, that my children are all colors and their blood flows at their birth?' Sha'ntwoy cried.

Kert'ankway soothed her thus, saying, 'As the colors, so the difference between your children; yet the blood I leave to all is red, a symbol that what lies beneath joins them all and binds to us.'

In her sorrow, Sha'ntwoy burdened Kert'ankway, saying, 'In the All, may each man's desire look to woman, and even yet if he rules, may his heart and mind be subject to her.'

And to her children she gave her Nothing in even measure, casting them to the ends of the All, crying, 'May the Nothing within you drive love and dissent in equal measure until you are once more joined to me.'

But her orange children she neither sent out nor shared her Nothing; for they were as she is.

To the orange children, the daughters and sons of Sha'ntwoy and Kert'ankway, are given the songs of the past.

60

Part II: Neueanbruch

Chapter Eleven

Greg

I SPIN NAKED in the void. Ridiculous outstretched arms, spaghetti strands of fused bone and flesh twist and thread in and out of η-space through nearby suns and moons. One eye gazes outward to the universe that surrounds me; the universe my other eye gazes back inwards to the me surrounding me as I twist and fold, watch my eyes watch me watch them. My chest burns with star birth, every heartbeat a big bang, every breath a big crunch, blood the never-ending cycle of cosmic birth, death, rebirth courses through spacetime. Half of one universe sings to me, 'an event has occurred, an event has occurred'; the other half mocks me with the same. Other universes in unison condemn and accuse me, call me by name. 'Mister Robertson', they call as I scream, as my other abuses and derides me; sounds mix, fold me back on myself as the universe drips blood and emptiness.

'Mister Robertson, Mister Robertson,' it cries from everywhere and nowhere, my body now complete, the universe an empty bowl of darkness, blood red before me, ink black behind…

"Wake up, Mister Robertson, please."

It comes from in front, the universe dissolves to a cherry red glow surrounded by a dark orb, space presses hard against my back, my arms, my legs. I hear breath, feel wetness between my arms and hardness; my back and hardness. Where am I, what am I, where is this I should be? Juuttua. Pegasus. Stasis sleep. I feel pins and needles through my backside, legs and arms, the pull of gravity. We must be there, time to wake up.

I prize open my eyes; one sends a cascade of yellow from the corner, the other stretches cobwebs between eyelids. It's all out of focus, a dull red blur. A hand grabs the back of my head, something hot and wet wipes across my face. Kelli stares at me, concern and fear etched into her face. I open my mouth, try to speak but manage only a rough croak.

She hands me a small glass. I drain it in one swallow.

"Thank goodness."

"We here?"

"No. Something's wrong, we need your help."

"What are you talking about?"

61

"You'll be groggy for a few minutes. I'll get you some more water. Look outside – by the time I'm back with Peter, you'll know as much as we do."

The clear hull's unobstructed. My nightmare's followed me. A sullen orange-red sky looks back, a bloated red sun above pink-crimson clouds. The land rolls away through small valleys and hillocks to the horizon, purple-olive grasses punctuated by violet-blue bushes. In the distance to one side stands a forest of orange-trunked trees, to the other foothills of a mountain range. It's a baleful vision; I see no buildings, no structures of any kind, no life. It's not Earth, it's not Juuttua. What is it?

"An event has occurred, an event has occurred."

An amber light flashes forlornly near the speaker. Pen and Lou are still in stasis, Henry wears a childish pucker. It's ghoulish, row after row of salmon-hued faces sit silently, the undead preparing to rejoin the living. I bend, work out knots and kinks, peer out at odd angles to see what else is outside. Not much, a small stream to the far left and what may or may not be peaks on the horizon. I stand, brace against the hull as feeling returns to my legs. I look down the curve of the hull, past the three passenger decks; we're sunk into the ground. I hobble away from the hull as Kelli and Peter come up the stairs.

"Is it normally this bad, Kelli?"

Kelli cancels the speaker, hands me a flask. "Never. We've been out too long."

"So, where are we?"

"We don't know, Mister Robertson."

"What do you mean, you don't know?"

"It's not Earth, not Juuttua, not anywhere I've seen before."

"When will they come get us?"

"I've no idea. The AI can't tell us where we are."

"Well, how long has it taken other times, from being missing to looking?"

"It hasn't, no threeship has ever disappeared. Accidents yes, but only at terminals."

"But we should be close to either end, Earth or Juuttua, so it shouldn't be long, should it? Kelli?"

"I'm afraid that...I mean, Mister Robert–"

"I'm not your dad. Call me Greg and tell me it won't be long."

"I don't think they can find us. I think it happened in η-space."

"Think? What do you mean, you *think*?"

Kelli stares at the floor.

"Okay, Peter, you tell me, what does she mean?"

"The AI always wakes the attendants first. When we woke up, two others were already up."

"Two what?"

"There were two children already awake but they're, I mean they..."

"They've lost their minds," Kelli says. 'They must've woken up in η-space. They just sit, stare, and drool. I've never lost one before and now I've lost two."

"It's not your fault, Kelli. There must've been an accident, some sort of failure. Where are they?"

"Lower deck, center. They're physically fine, just empty inside."

"All the more reason to get help quicker, get them to medical care."

"It won't help, no one comes back from that," Peter says. "If it went wrong in η-space, we could be anywhere in the universe."

I look from Peter to Kelli. She shakes her head.

"So, we're lost, maybe no one knows about us and we've got two injured children. Apart from that, Kelli?"

"It seems fine, I mean, as much as I can see."

"So why wake me and not everyone else?"

Kelli looks nervously at the other passengers. "I don't know what they'll do, I've never dealt with these people. I thought maybe, you're from Enforcement, you'd have some training or, or, something."

She's lost the poise and confidence from the spaceport, she's as confused and frightened as I am. She thinks I can help with crowd control? Maybe she needs a little push and she'll be right. "Can you leave everyone in stasis?"

"No, we're close to limits, they have to be out in three hours."

I need time to think, to calm down and work out what I'm going to do. Henry said he's related to the Amish, so maybe that will help. But then what? "Fine. Start with Henry, he used to be part of them. But first let's have a look at those two children."

I don't want to see them, I can't help. Kelli and Peter seem too shaken to manage, maybe it has to be me. But what if they want something I don't? I follow Kelli to the lower deck, stand in the middle of three rings of silent bonnets and breeches. The eerie flicker of emergency lights and crimson rays through the permaport casts bloody shadows across the deck.

"Names?"

She points to two small figures. "Amy, Amy and Joseph Lehmann. Twelve and ten."

They sit rigid, eyes wide, breath shallow. A small, perfectly formed drop creeps from the girl's mouth, hesitates on her chin then falls to her sodden dress. I wave my hands in front of them. "Joseph? Amy? Are you there?"

There's no response, nothing I can do and, I suspect, nothing anyone can.

"That's how I found them," Kelli says. "Peter got some water into them, but there's nothing else. They've just stayed like that."

"Let's go wake Henry."

Henry comes around quickly. "The men, whatever you do wake the men before the rest. And Father first, the gmay'll look to him."

63

"Will your dad be right? What's his name?"

"Menno. He'll be fine, we shouldn't get too much trouble out of any of them."

Somehow, I've taken charge. Awake barely five minutes, the initial shock starts to dull as deeper panic rises in me. Peter's calmer, Kelli's shaking, Henry looks stunned. I have to fight the panic, stay calm, keep in control. Activity helps, it always does. "Kelli. Where's Menno?"

"Lower deck, opposite the Lehmans."

"You and Henry start there, Peter and I will start here. Henry, can you fill Menno in and get him onto the Lehmans?"

"Sounds good."

"Once they know, we have to bring the families round. Is there enough time, Kelli?"

"Should be, it takes two minutes from when you hit the release switch. Punch them all first, we'll worry about rehydration later."

By the time we finish the middle deck, Henry's helping a groggy Menno to his feet. Menno takes one look through the permaport, turns, then goes across to the Lehmans. The other Amish men are much the same; a brief look, a shake of the head and a grimace is as much as any of them give. I scramble up the stairway flask in hand, hit Pen's then Lou's release switches.

Pen revives quickly. I dip the end of my shirt in the water to clear the crust of sleep from Lou's eyes, the hubbub from below underpinned by sporadic sobs.

"We there?"

I put the flask to her lips. "Not yet."

She stands, squints at the red landscape. "Where's this?"

"We're in Hell, Mum."

"Not now, Pen. Lou, there's a problem, we're not sure where we are."

"Not sure?"

"When did you do your first aid refresher?"

"Two months ago."

"Two kids downstairs woke up in η-space. Can you take a look?"

"Of course, but if they –"

Pen pushes between us. "Real zombies! Can I look?"

"Didn't I tell you to quit it, Pen? Don't be so cruel." The air pressure jumps, ocean and jasmine waft up. "They're not zombies and you shouldn't –"

The noise below rises. Henry appears over the edge of the stairwell. "You better get down here, Greg."

"Why?"

"Someone's blown the airlock."

Chapter Twelve

Greg

WE CLUSTER AROUND the open airlock and stare at the strange landscape. It's half an hour since the last one woke, long enough for excitement and shock to dull, the adrenaline rush to seep away, replaced by cold reality or vivid imagination. At least the heavily-scented air is breathable.

We've rearranged ourselves, youngest children and their mothers on the upper and middle decks, the rest of us on the lower. Lou's on the far side, occupied and distracted with the Lehmans; she's doing okay under the circumstances but nearly lost it when first confronted by the view.

I tighten my grip, lean out further until I see the curve of the hull meet the ground. "It disappears about where the paint changes color. It's all missing from there."

Kelli hangs out from her waist. "That's where the drive units start. Guess we've sunk in. I can't see any pieces lying around." She pulls herself in, sits. "Well, we're not going anywhere."

"What about the other two nodes, Kelli?" Henry asks.

"Couldn't see them, we'd have to get out."

"Will the ground take us? We've already gone in what, seven meters?"

"It should be fine. The question is if we should step out."

I point to a rectangle of plasteel about three meters below. "Well, the hatch hasn't sunk, so we should be okay."

"Do we want to have a look? We seem stable," Peter says.

"It's an idea. A quick check, see the rest of the ship."

"Fine, but who? Getting back up might be tricky."

No one speaks, each looks away as if to avoid the question, never mind the answer. Except Kelli – she looks at me. She thinks I'm some sort of Enforcement action man. Well, maybe for a while I need to pretend. I shrug, give a crooked smile. "Okay. I've always wanted to play Armstrong. I'll need company. Henry, you up for it?"

Henry glances at Kelli. "Sure, Greg, just didn't want to stop anyone who was really keen."

I slide out until I hang by my fingertips. "Okay, see you in a sec." I drop the short distance to the ground. It's firm, the purple-olive grass spongy underfoot.

Peter looks down as Henry starts to slide out. "Greg, reach down and touch the hull where it meets the ground."

"It's stone cold. Mean anything?"

"Should be warm, hot even. We've been here a while."

I straighten, look up. "How long would it..." My gaze locks above the Pegasus; I take a few steps back. A mountain range towers like enormous fangs, pink-red snow-covered peaks thrust into the cloud base, rivers of gray-ochre cloud driven hard between them. I become dimly aware of Henry beside me: "How high?"

"No idea, but they're amazing."

"Glad we missed them on the way down."

I tear my gaze away. "Let's be quick and get back in, it's getting cold."

It doesn't take long to see what state the Pegasus is in. With no obvious damage and all three nodes sunk in, Pegasus sits embedded in a small rise surrounded by a grassy plain. Behind the Pegasus, I see the enormous sweep of the mountain range, foothills from horizon to horizon, huge glaciers astride valleys. I make out four peaks, at least four mountains, and hints of more behind on each side.

"Hey, Greg, is this place starting to, ah, feel a little better?"

"Maybe, it's a little less weird, even the redness."

"That's good, isn't it?"

"You know what Kelli thinks."

"We'll be stuck here?"

"For a while. We might have to get used to it, maybe make plans."

"Take a bit of a wander?"

"If I leave it up to them, we could be here a month from now and not know any more. They're looking to me. I guess I'll do what I think needs to be done. You said your dad's their minister?"

"Yeah, for life."

"So, he leads them?"

"Sorta, it's strange. They think taking charge is pride, so no one will. Even church is by consensus or agreement unless it's a biblical thing."

"So, how do we get them involved?"

"Just don't put one of them on the spot. Think of them as, well, as quiet, shy, more reserved than us."

I stare at the mountains, guardians of what lies beyond. To hang around and wait for a group decision doesn't appeal to me. "We need to take a look around. If Kelli's right, it's best done sooner rather than later. We'll need food, water, everything."

The wind's colder, blown straight off the mountains, pink streamers roll down the valley and pass overhead. I hope Kelli's wrong, hope someone finds us, but something tells me she's not. I pull my collar tight, try to keep the chill out. "I'll go first thing tomorrow, take a day or two." I nod at the mountains. "It'll be simple coming back, head towards these. Are you up for it?"

"Yeah, can't let you have all the fun," Henry says.

"Me too."

I turn. Pen's behind me. "How'd you get here?"

"Jumped. When we going?"

"*We*...won't be going anywhere except back inside, and when your mother finds out, you might be there forever."

"Can I still go?"

"No."

"Why?"

I step across, try and fail miserably to give her my best fatherly scowl. No ban or appeal to reason will work. I bend and whisper. "Someone has to take care of Henry's girlfriend while he's away."

She brightens, flashes a cheeky smile at Henry. "I'll do it."

"Good. Let's get inside before it's really cold."

"What did you say to her?"

"Nothing, Henry, don't worry about it."

We clamber in, describe what we found to the rest. I'm not ready to take on the whole responsibility. There's sixty others and I don't own the Pegasus. "What do you think's next, Kelli?"

"I'd say wait until they find us, but I don't think anyone will."

"Surely they will try?" Menno asks.

"Yes, Mister Stoll, but they need some idea of where we are, or at least a signal. I'd have to get to the AI directly."

"How long would it take?"

Peter points above him. "It's near the nose. Have to clear the access hatches, maybe half a day."

"They would take how long, if you can talk to them?"

"One or two days. They've got to get organized, send a spindleship and threeship."

"But if you cannot, then what?"

"Like Kelli said, they won't be able to find us and we'll be stuck here," Peter says.

"We could've landed on a deserted part of the planet, maybe there's someone further away," Henry says.

"So, we are either rescued soon or not at all. Is that right, Kelli?" Menno asks.

"Yes, Mister Stoll, it is."

Menno's not as reserved as Henry said, maybe he's been away from home too long. The group falls into a brooding silence. It's no good, we could sit here for days beating ourselves up, but it won't help. "Kelli, how much food do we have?"

"Hardly anything, Greg, a little water and one meal for each passenger, a few extras, plus some snacks."

"Not enough even if we're rescued soon."

"Depends, how long can you live on one meal?"

"Then rescue or no rescue we need to act as if we're here, by ourselves, permanently."

"What do you suggest?"

"I think we see what the AI says, work out what we have and what we can do with it, and have a better look at where we are as soon as we can." Their faces seem to brighten at the thought of doing something. "Peter, can you handle the AI and try to communicate, find someone?"

"Of course."

"Kelli, can you find out what's on board? Do you have a cargo manifest or something?"

"I could, but there's no list for what's in the holds. It's all passenger cargo in one and I don't know what in the others. I could look through it, take a day or so."

"Menno, are your people able to help?"

"Of course, we are not ones to sit back and watch."

"I thought you weren't. Between us all, we should know in a few days what we're looking at."

Lou looks at me. "What will you do?"

"Henry and I will go out tomorrow, scout around for a day or two, see if anyone's there."

"No, no…you can't. We don't know what's out there."

"That's the point, Lou, we have to find out. If help doesn't come, the sooner we know the better."

Lou's not convinced. It's going to be hard on her – no covered spaces, only emptiness and sky with nowhere to hide. How can I help her? I can't be with her all the time. I move closer, lower my voice to draw them in. "Things might look tough, maybe desperate, but we've got to act like we know what we're doing, at least for the children's peace of mind. We're all scared and all we have is each other. Even if we have no idea, no hope, we have to act like we do."

"It's important to keep positive, keep busy," Kelli says.

"We are in safe hands – if God is for us, nothing can be against us." Menno's comment is met by nods from the surrounding beards.

Lou looks at me across the circle, nods. "Yes, there's too much for the kids to worry about without us as well."

"Good. At least we've got a plan."

The sun's a small sliver on the horizon, the world overtaken by deep maroon. My eyes feel heavy, though I've only been awake a few hours.

Peter barely stifles a yawn. "It's been a long day. Stasis doesn't count as rest. We've all been up for thirteen, maybe fourteen hours, plus this."

"It's getting dark. What do we do about the airlock, Greg?" Kelli asks. "It won't refit."

"I didn't see any animals out there, maybe there's none to bother us. But the cold's a worry."

"We've got some of those foil emergency blankets we could put up. I think they're in the med kits. Should we put someone on guard, just in case?"

"Yeah, maybe a few hours each."

"Henry and me, we'll go first."

"Lou and I will take over from you."

It's useless, black as pitch. I peer intently through a small gap in the blankets. No light, no fire, no stars, only the vague outline of the horizon and the feeble light of one small moon. There's a faint glow behind the Pegasus; perhaps another moon.

It didn't take long for Lou to doze off; I left her to sleep curled up on the upper deck with Pen, far away from the threat of the emptiness, to try and help her settle.

It's not much colder, a distinct dip at sunset but then, after an hour, no more. Cold, not unpleasant or freezing, but it's only the first night of who knows how many.

The glow strengthens, the faint shadow of the Pegasus starts a slow march backwards, shortens as the land starts to brighten. It's silver, an untainted light that changes violet grasses to lavender, our red-green hull to pastels. A dusky tendril hesitates behind the Pegasus, emerges to reveal itself a thick brown arc shattered with black and blue-yellow veins. Inside the arc pinpoints of white light blaze, packed so tight they merge into each other, too many to count. Fingers of black, blue, and yellow run through the whiteness, sometimes behind, sometimes in front. The arc continues to crawl across the sky, fills the heavens as it embraces the horizon. Shadows are deep, black, hard-edged, night brighter than red day.

I sit and watch, lose track of time. Whatever, or wherever, this world is, it's surprising. And beautiful.

Chapter Thirteen

Greg

DAWN IS SOFT, no burst of yellow incandescence to announce the sun; a diffuse glow paints the land rosé, kisses the horizon, and sinks into a red sea of its own creation. What this sun lacks in intensity it makes up for in size. Soft and dusky perhaps, but it still hurts to look at it for more than a moment.

I'm over the shock – I've had time to adjust, my panic harnessed to resolve and curiosity. A little of the harshness has gone; the land is still predominantly red and indigo, but I can make out shades, slight variations in color and tone, pick out dark olive-green plants scattered among black undergrowth. It's cool, the drizzle that heralded sunrise rolled away with the clouds to leave the sun to its work.

It's no surprise to find insects around the landing site, small white-blue dragonflies near the airlock, a line of lemon-green ants across one cargo node. It's good to know we aren't the only life around, but small insects are usually prey for larger ones, insects for animals, and somewhere the food chain has to stop. Hopefully, we won't see that end of it.

The meals have been handed out; the Amish women say they have more food in their cargo, bizarre trophy collections of preserves and pickles. It's funny to think a threeship an interstellar grocery cart, but it's good to know the threat of starvation isn't imminent.

Breakfast wafts over me, familiar scents of stir fry and synthetic duck borne on an alien wind. I've stashed ours away with two spares, foil blankets, and a little water in Pen's crankband backpack. I turn to the Pegasus, the backdrop of mountains. They're all outside near the cargo nodes; Peter and Lou wave from deep inside the Pegasus. It's going to be a hard few days for both of us but it can't be helped.

I wave back, move to Henry. "Okay, here we are. Ideas?"

"I don't want mountain climbing or the woods, in case anything's in there."

Off to the right a red-brown lump rises from the ground. "How about the hill for starters?"

"It's as good as anything. How far, do you think?"

"No idea, I've still no sense of scale or distance." We walk for twenty minutes across undulating ground, firm and springy with damp grasses under foot, the occasional patch of knee-high tufts and flowers. My clothes, designed for the city, are useless; Henry's better equipped in a borrowed pair of barndoor trousers and jumper. I shift the backpack, look back. The Pegasus is gone, only mountain peaks above a field of red and amber.

"Funny feeling, isn't it?"

70

"Huh?"

"Being alone. I got it each time I went back to Mom's. I'd get out of the car, stand on the drive and stare."

"I guess. It's not bad, just different."

"The quiet, too. It could be us and nobody else, you couldn't tell. I used to miss it. Not much else really, only that."

We resume our walk, the silent empty land with us. It's mesmeric, calming after the novelty. Perhaps I can get used to it. "At the spaceport, you said you left home because of your dad."

"Yes."

"But you followed him. Seems odd."

"I guess. Maybe it's different not being there all the time. You know, familiarity and that. You don't look the pioneer type. I wouldn't think Juuttua was on your list."

"We've all got our reasons." The grasses rustle, stalks sway as a bird bursts out with a small animal in its feet. It climbs away; its wings beat a rhythmic, languid pattern as it gives us a disdainful stare. "Bird."

"Big one."

"You see four wings?"

"And feet, two sets of claws at the front, two at the back."

"What do we call it?"

"Whatever you want."

"Condor?"

"Why not? It's big enough."

"Condor it is. You can name the next one."

"As long as it's not the first thing I think of. Couldn't call it what I thought as it jumped out."

The silence imposes itself. I don't feel the need or desire to talk. Perhaps the grassland harbors more life, sudden shifts against the breeze, a rustle or half-glimpsed shadow hints at its presence. Or it could be my imagination, the palette of land and sky is still alien, shadows and crevices hard to identify as I struggle to adapt to perpetual twilight. Both of us have stumbled more than once, so we adopt a bent over, ponderous gait that leaves me more unbalanced, more prone to fall. I straighten, search for condensation trails; there are none. I glance at my watch. Time means nothing; the watch fails to find a localizer so stays fixed at twelve. The stop says it's two hours since we started, four since I set it in motion this morning.

"Rest, Greg?"

"No, I'm okay. How far you think we've gone?"

"Could be five kilometers, I'm not sure. Maybe halfway to the hill."

"Break when we get to it? It'll be four hours by then."

Henry holds up an outstretched palm. "Mid-morning?"

"Close enough. Around midday, then."

"Picnic lunch?"

"Sounds good." The longer I'm out, the more I embrace the openness, the space. Unlike the wire frame, it's real, the horizon at the end of an unbroken empty plain and we the only people on it. Any trace of nervousness or uncertainty leaves me as we crest the hill, gaze at white-capped peaks on the horizon, the lesser brothers of those at our backs. To one side a blue-green line; to the other a dense forest. I sit, stretch my legs out to the rustle of breeze through grass.

"You're getting to like it."

"You could be right."

"Told you it'd grow on you. Where next?"

I swivel my head, point to the blue-green line. "There, towards the break, I think it's an ocean."

"Head back tomorrow?"

"We could go back now. We know the answer, but I'd still like to have a look."

Henry pushes the heat tab, peels the lid from his meal pack. "Empty, right?"

"Yeah. Unless Peter picks something up, we're on our own. At least for the short term."

"Funny, it's not what Father wanted, but I think he'll be pleased. An unknown, empty planet where no one can find you. It's the Amish version of paradise."

"And yours?"

"No, I don't believe in the lack of modern technology and all the rest. But the city wasn't perfect either."

"No place is, not that I've heard. Juuttua wasn't. Not that we'll know."

"You think we'll be stuck here."

"I've got this feeling –" A shadow falls. An animal taller than either of us and as broad across the shoulders lumbers to a stop, lowers its head to chew on a tuft of deep lilac grass. One of three crescent-shaped horns massages Henry's thigh as a pair of large, moist eyes look at me. The grass consumed, it turns, deposits a large steaming mound at Henry's feet, then moves off. "What do you make of that?"

"Just glad it was a grass eater."

"Your turn, Henry."

"What?"

"A name."

"Oh, yeah. Bison?"

"Bison it is."

We reach the ocean without trouble or incident, grasses become smaller and sparser until they give way to a beach of fine brown sand. Tracks betray the presence of small animals, five- and six-toed, serpentine trails, others frenzied, uncoordinated. For a while we walk next to the line of pink foam, but the harsh slope of the beach grows tiresome, so we retreat to where the grasses stop. Small yellow-orange birds spring up as we pass; others fly in front, small silver fish in their beaks. I watch them with interest, their deliberate flight. Startled, disturbed, none seem scared or distressed. Some fly close, others towards us. Like the condor, like the bison; here we are, two strange creatures that walk among them, and they are unafraid.

A wide river mouth opens to the ocean and stops our progress. Too wide to cross, we follow it inland. The air turns cold, light dims as the breeze gains the strength to send a chill through my shirt. The stopwatch reads ten hours, eight since we started. Perhaps twenty kilometers – it's enough. A small outcrop of rock close by beckons, holds small hope of protection from the elements. "What say we call it a day? We could bed down over there."

"Good idea, I'm tired and thirsty." Henry drops to his knees next to the river, cups his hands and drinks deeply.

"Are you nuts?"

"What?"

"You've got no idea what's in that, what it might do to you."

"It's not like there's a choice. There's not enough water in the threeship, so in a day or two we'll have to. Why not now, why not me as a guinea pig?"

"No reason, I guess, but you could've warned me."

GREG AND HENRY head away. I smile as best I can, try to put on a strong face. It's all I can do not to scream, run to the far wall, and cower away from the open horror in front of me. Why did he go with him? Any of the others could have gone. He should be here to help me, be with me, so I don't have to face it alone. He gets me into this, then abandons me to it? My arm and eyes hurt; they're nearly out of sight and I still wave like an idiot. No one notices. Kelli stares after Henry, Peter reads a flimsy in front of me. "Should be fine, but it's a tight fit. You good for small spaces, Louise?"

"Yes, no problems there."

Peter leads the way to the upper deck, hands me a plastic card. "Access cards. Can't get to anything without two of these and two people, sort of a failsafe thing. Not that we could do much, anyway." A few deft touches and a small yellow panel opens, a ladder slides down. "Up we go."

He climbs up and moves right, I follow to the left. There's barely enough room for us to squeeze in, my head's against the bulkhead and he's bent to fit. He points to a small red square in front of my nose. "When I tell you, put the card against that. Ready? Okay, on three – one, two, three."

A section of bulkhead turns from steel gray to a light green touch screen. I can't make out the contents, Peter starts a series of taps and slides. "AI interface, not everything, only what we might need on a flight. We can't get it to do anything, it only gives out information." He pauses, brow furrowed. "It's nearly dead, hardly any power left. Must've drained somehow, these things last ages."

I twist and bend, try to see and keep the card in the red square.

"Don't worry about that now, Louise. Shuffle over so you can see. Now let's start with where."

The screen flickers, flashes **UNKNOWN** in green.

"Okay, let's try last known reference point," Peter says.

UNKNOWN

"So, it doesn't know?"

"Perhaps, or perhaps this place isn't on the map."

"Can it tell us how we got here?"

"I don't think so, that's probably too detailed for this interface. I can ask it where the Atlas and other threeships are."

A few taps and the screen lights up. A series of names scrolls across, I recognize Pulsar and Atlas among the list.

DESTROYED: CAUSE UNKNOWN flashes up against each one.

"All of them, all gone?"

"You sure, Peter? Maybe it's wrong."

"No, if it says destroyed, it means it. It must have happened in η-space...maybe, whatever those two kids...if it happened there, if it was in η-space...there's no chance, they're all..."

"So, why didn't we –"

"I can't tell from this! I'm not...I'm sorry, I just...I can't, someone else could dig into the AI, but...I don't...two thousand people? All of them..."

"You knew people on the other threeships?"

"A little. We rotate but, yeah, I know them. My kids, my partner, he was supposed to be on this run, but they went home early."

"Juuttua?"

"Yeah, that's home."

"So, it could've been much worse for you."

"Well, yes, much worse."

"But he's okay, your kids are okay. We've only ourselves to worry about."

It seems to bring him around, pull him back. "We're here, but where is here?"

"Are there any signals, radio or whatever?"

He touches the screen, perfectly flat lines appear. "Nothing. The AI would have sent out a distress call when we landed. It should have been answered by now."

"How long does it take to get an answer?"

"Hours, a day at most. It gets routed through η-space, then they reply."

"So, how long have we been here?"

"Maybe a day, but how long's a day here? The AI can give us the flight time, it might give us an idea." He dismisses the list, the screen hesitates before a single paragraph hovers in front of us:

SUBJECTIVE FLIGHT TIME [SHIP]: 01D – 18H – 28M

"Two days isn't too bad, is it? They could still be getting back to us."

"It's possible, Louise, but it seems a bit long."

A second paragraph appears, flashes twice then settles under the first:

OBJECTIVE FLIGHT TIME [EARTH]: 448Y – 06M – 02W – 02D – 14H – 08M

"What does that mean? Peter, what does that mean?"

He turns slowly, ashen-faced. "It means we're totally alone."

Chapter Fourteen

Louise

WE RE-SEAL THE panel and clamber down, sit as it sinks in.

"As far as the universe is concerned, Louise, we've been gone for four hundred fifty years. They've probably forgotten we exist."

"How? First it says two days, then four hundred years. I don't feel four hundred fifty."

"If it happened in η-space, if the problem started there and we were thrown away from the Atlas, it's possible. We could end up anywhere, anywhen."

"So, why the future? Why not the past?"

"Even in η—space, time only goes one way. We've gone forward not back."

"Why'd we end up here?"

"Chance, randomly spat out into normal space, then the AI went into landing mode. Could've come out in a sun, middle of nowhere, even back at Earth."

"So, it's luck, luck we survived, luck we popped out here, luck we made it down."

"Yeah, exactly. If it weren't, we'd be dead."

"Wait till the others hear about this."

He leans forward, eyes strained, face taut and dour. "We can't tell them."

"What?"

"No signal and no name for this place might be fine, but four hundred fifty years? It's not –"

"Why? They've the right, you can't –"

"It's not something they need to know now."

"You can't be serious?"

"Your partner and kid are alive, but all your friends, relatives, workmates have lived and died, as have their kids and their kids and theirs. Every single person you ever knew or saw back on Earth are dust, each place changed utterly and you missed it all."

"I know, but –"

"And my kids, any grandkids if I ever had any, are dead and gone, I never got to see any of it, if they fell in love, matured, whatever, and I have to deal with that and being stuck here. It'll be bad enough for us, but sixty others? There's going to be enough pain without this."

I'd lost contact with my family decades ago, so they're dead to me, anyway. But this, the absolute certainty everyone's gone? Clara's dead, everyone in the Center's dust? Grief threatens to overwhelm me, I nearly lose it as memories flood back, visions of Adam, Clara, kids' birthday parties, lunch at McDsGlass, Friday nights at Skartz. "Maybe you're right, but it still doesn't feel right."

"It won't be forever. Once we're settled, once we're on our feet, then we tell them. But not now, okay?"

My mind wanders to Greg, the two of us; I realize our marriage contract ended hundreds of years ago. Or did it? Which is right, Earth time or our time? Does it matter?

"Okay, Louise?"

"Huh?"

"What do you think?"

"About what?"

"We tell them later. Make it our secret. For now."

"Yes, yes of course."

A small bonneted head appears in the stairwell. "Peter, Kelli's looking for you." The three of us descend to the hatch. I'm still preoccupied as Peter jumps out; I nearly follow then shrink back, flatten myself against the far wall.

The Amish woman looks at me, concern on her face. "What's the matter, you hurt?"

I scrunch my eyes, try to dispel the outside, the empty space on empty space. Greg should be here to help but he's not, even though he promised. The vision of the empty stays with me so I stare at the floor, try to replace one with the other. "I'm not hurt, I can't...I mean, I can't go out there."

The Amish woman looks out cautiously, leans back in. A flicker of understanding runs across her face. "Oh, you don't like open spaces."

"I've got this fear, I can't stand them, I hate the open."

"How did you manage back home?"

"I never could. If I had to, Greg was there. I know there's nothing to worry about, but I can't help it. You wouldn't understand."

She cocks her head, folds her arms. "Now, wouldn't I? What makes you say that?"

"You're out there and not worried. You're all farmers in huge empty fields, so how could you?"

"I do go out and I have to, but that doesn't mean I'm still not scared. It's less than it was but I always have been, ever since I can remember."

I look at her. She's barely one hundred forty centimeters tall but suddenly she's steel, the toughest thing I've seen. "How?"

"How? Simple, I don't have a choice. An Amish girl can't hide in a house all her life and cows don't milk themselves. Anyway, if it's the cross that God has given me, I have no choice but to bear it."

"I don't have that sort of faith."

She steps across, links her arm through mine and nurses me to the hatchway. "Now, you see, you don't have to. I'll stay with you until he gets back and whenever you need."

"Thank you, but I really don't think –"

"There's no choice, sooner or later you'll have to. Anyway, if you look, it's not a big open empty. It's just a bigger box than the one you're in."

"You're kidding me."

"Oh no, it's all boxes, bigger and bigger ones, houses to worlds to universes. The sky's the lid, the ground the floor, the mountains the wall. It's really tiny if you want it to be."

I bend forward slowly, the cold grabs my stomach. Okay, sky roof, dirt floor. I can pretend a little, maybe a little, it's just bigger, just a bigger box. My breath's rapid, shallow, I try to slow it, breathe deeper, slower. It seems to help. I look steadily at the ground below the hatch. Maybe later, I'll try the horizon, maybe later. The arm in mine tightens.

"You see, you look like a strong person. I'm sure you can."

"Maybe you're right. I'm sorry, I don't know your name."

"Freda. Freda Stoll, Louise."

"Freda, yes, I think you're right, maybe I can."

"Now, take your time, tell me when you want to go out and we'll go, no rush."

We edge out slowly, stand on the surface close to the Pegasus' hatch until I gather the strength – eyes fixed on the ground and arm locked to Freda's – to creep around the base. I nearly lose it twice, the sudden cry of a bird pulls my gaze skywards, a slight stumble nearly separates me from her. By the time we're near the first cargo node, I'm able to look across the immense gulf between it and the passenger node; by the time we reach the second cargo node, my shaking's nearly gone and I can peek at the horizon. Through it all, Freda stays linked arm in arm, sometimes quiet, sometimes encouraging, always patient. I feel calmer and safer with her than I do with Greg.

Kelli and Peter are in earnest discussion with Menno under a yawning cargo bay door; the cluster of bonnets and hats occasionally nod, sometimes shake. Peter sees us, beckons us over.

"...moment it's loaded, it belongs to the company until it's delivered," Kelli says.

Menno tugs at his beard. "Yes, that is clear, but it is still not right."

"Only if we're not entitled and we don't compensate them." Kelli levels the tablet, places her thumb print next to Peter's. "I'll enter into the ship's log that we've requisitioned it and, when we're found, today or a hundred years from now, the owners will be paid. Plus interest."

"Down to the last cent?"

"Absolutely, and to the company's account. None of the passengers bear responsibility or liability."

"Good. Let us waste no more time."

The crowd moves to the other cargo node.

"Menno's satisfied?" Freda asks.

"Yes," Kelli replies. "I understand his worries, but it's cleared up."

"What happened?" I ask.

"Menno worried that taking anything other than their cargo was stealing, even parts of the threeship."

"But he's okay?"

"Yes, but now's the hard bit." Kelli points to the open cargo door. "The passenger cargo node opened easily, but the others are jammed tight." The screech of thin metal being torn apart reaches us. One of the Amish removes a short axe from a cargo door. "Then again, maybe it's not so much a problem."

Getting the door open proves the simpler task. The manifest is no help, simply a list of who consigned what cargo. Nothing's designed for manual unloading and nobody feels like scattering the contents of the cargo pod haphazardly on the ground. Peter and two of the Amish eventually settle on squeezing up the central access shaft to break into each container.

Menno disappears, comes back minutes later with loaded arms. I watch him as he hands two blankets to Ruth Lehman, a bat and ball to a group of young children, then leads the older boys toward the forest. "Now, where do you think he's off to?"

"I'd expect he's having a look, trying to keep the young men busy." Freda moves towards the cargo node. "We can make ourselves useful, Louise. I know what's in this one."

I sit in the middle of a rough assortment of bags, boxes and sacks, some open, others neatly stacked; piles of barn door pants, coats, and shawls.

Peter bends over, peers into an open sack. "Looks interesting, what's this?"

"Farewell gifts from the gmay. What size are you?" Freda asks.

"I don't know, normal I guess."

Freda rummages at her feet, hands him a chain knit jumper. "They made enough to last ages, until we got established on Juuttua."

Peter slips it on, the hem falls below his backside, arms clearly too long. "May be no fashion winner, but it's certainly warm. Thank you."

"Should be enough for all of us a few times over. I didn't see any shoes, can't recall if there were any."

I look at Peter, then the horizon, a vain effort to spot Greg. I drop my gaze back to the box at my feet, resume my count of jar lids.

Refugees and castaways all, they don't have a clue how much or how far but simply get on with it, work it out. I haven't heard anything harsh or worried from any of them. Not even from that poor lady and her children. I see her sift through bags at the base of the Pegasus, while Penny chatters at her two children. I've never seen that side of her, she's been there all day, even though she knows they can't hear or speak.

Freda shifts again, a gentle back and forth as she moves. She's stayed with me, not said a thing, simply been there and made no fuss as if it's normal. The same with all of them, they treat me like I'm one of them. I reach up, feel for the bonnet and shawl Naomi gave me to ward off the cold. A small laugh escapes me.

"Well now, that's a better sound out of you."

"I'm halfway to being Amish with all this."

"Perhaps you are." Freda's face catches the last of the sun's rays, soft ruddy glow to one side, the other tinged yellow-blue. Beyond her a small cluster of older boys stoke a fire. Menno and two boys pick their way towards us preceded by the soft, pungent aroma of burnt wood. Other odors tease and encourage as they stop, hold something out to us.

"Mrs. Stoll, Mrs. Hierro, would you like some?"

I look closer – it's a thick branch with an impaled animal, outside dark red-brown, rotund body, seven legs and wings. A gash along one side reveals white-blue flesh. "What is it?"

"We're not sure, but it tastes delicious."

They've eaten a dead animal, a wild one? It hasn't been processed, checked, it looks nothing like food. No, he can't mean it, he can't be serious. My stomach says something else, the smell entices even as the thought repulses.

"The boys caught a few of them. It is perfectly safe. We ate the first hours ago, no trouble apart from wanting more." Menno slices the meat, places it in my palm. "The leg and breast meat you will like."

I stare at the warm flesh, slow drip of purple liquid through my hands. It disgusts and appeals but the smell sharpens my hunger, expands the hole in my stomach. I take a small, cautious bite then as flavor and hunger overtake worry, I devour the rest. I suck the grease from my hands, scraps from bones, shards from between my teeth. I hear Freda tear every last morsel from the small offering.

Darkness settles in, challenged only by the dying fire. I stand close to Freda, still within reach just in case. She's right, it's all boxes in boxes, I can manage somehow. She knows what it's like, understands like Greg can't, has a strength that jumps across to me when I need it. I turn to where I think the hill is.

"They'll be back tomorrow, Louise, he'll be fine."

"Yes. He always is."

Chapter Fifteen

Greg

I POKE MY head through until it hangs from my shoulders, make sure my hands are inside and pull the tab. The foil blanket tightens, seals and shrinks until I'm clad in a silver body suit. It will keep me dry, warm, and reasonably comfortable for as long as I like. Night falls to clear black sky and a faint, familiar glow from one horizon. We lie here, two large sardines on a tomato paste landscape, and look up.

Henry turns to me. "No satellites."

"None I can see, Henry."

"And nothing today."

"No people, buildings, aircraft, ships, garbage, nothing."

"So?"

"So, that's that. We're on our own."

"If it's all like this, yeah, we are."

"I'd like to get a closer look at those other mountains."

"Why?"

"Maybe there's something there, a settlement we can't see."

"It has to be more than a week away. You'd go just in case?"

"If Peter's got nothing, we'll have to, Henry. To make sure."

"I guess it makes sense, sooner rather than later."

"You'd be up for it?"

"Of course."

"Good."

It's not long until I'm alone with my thoughts and Henry's snores. I'm tired, filled with an anticipation and delight I haven't felt since the early days with Lou. It was in me the other night and it drove me here, demanded I stay the extra night when there is no need. Henry knows, he must at least suspect but he snores, sleeps through it. I force myself to stay awake.

The tendrils emerge, the arc teases and pulls the white into view as blue and yellow fingers caress the stars, a coquettish call to my soul as night turns to day. The shadow of my outstretched hand is hard against my breast, my heart against my ribs. The sense of solitude overwhelms, connection to the emptiness and stars all-consuming. It intoxicates and captures me; I am its willing prisoner.

It's closer to night than day when we sight the Pegasus, a red-green dart in a field of violet. I turn to Henry and smile for the first time in hours.

The day's been hard, and I felt every single footstep, every single meter. The night was quiet and restful. We woke early to fresh dew and a mild breeze. Henry seemed no worse off for the previous day's effort but I'm in trouble from the start as my joints protest the hardness and strange angle of the night's bedding. I work most of the kinks out before I try to walk; it only takes two steps until the pain in my feet pulls me down. I take off my shoes and see huge circular patches of swollen skin on my heels and big toes, a sickening assortment along each foot.

"Quite a collection, shame you've no socks." Henry says.

"Socks? What are they?"

Henry pulls up one trouser leg, reveals a black and orange cloth around his ankle. "Old Amish clothes, they don't go for those new things. I keep wearing them from habit." He sits, takes the blankets out and wraps them around my feet. They seal tight from toe to knee. I lock and seal my shoes, take a few cautious steps. "Feels alright."

"Should be fine until they burst, we'll get them properly sorted tonight, find you some better clothes."

"What do you mean, 'burst'?"

"You've never had blisters before?"

"These things? Never."

Henry looks at me in disbelief, then pity. "Don't worry about it, I'll tell you later."

We move along the beach, stick to the tideline where the sand is hard. It helps ease each footstep, a gentle cushion under plasleth shoes.

"You've not done jobs that need muscle, not brains, Greg?"

"Why? It's what bots do. Mind you, we've always stayed in shape, done the programs and checks and all that."

"It's not the same, I spent most my life on that farm. Look." Henry puts his hand next to mine. Mine are soft and smooth; his are lined, patches of hard skin on the fingertips and along the undersides of his fingers. "It's been a while, but I still have the marks. The work changes you, a few blisters are only the start."

"You're full of good news, aren't you?"

"It gets easier after a bit. Anyway, maybe now they've found a signal."

As the day progresses, the pain in my feet is joined by cramps in my legs, tight chest, and a distinct wobble as I walk. Added to my hunger it makes me uncomfortable, irritable, and argumentative. Henry's stubborn refusal to be anything other than fine needles me although I'm careful not to let on. We've a long way to go today and maybe more after.

I concentrate on the land to distract me from my own weakness. It's easier to accept the redness and sky as normal now, nuances of hue and tone are clear. What was long red grass now splits itself into several subtypes, each with its own distinctive color. The wind picks its way along the foreshore this way and that, plucks and twists the blades to send darkened upper faces down, while lighter rouge of the undersides flash toward me as waves of red-brown scurry away.

82

Higher up the beach swirl brown eddies, sands lifted with small insects, birds darting in and out to gather their breakfast. I fancy that out beyond the breakers, beyond the blue-green to the black-olive ocean far away, I see an occasional breach, a flash of pink foam and rippled water.

The rhythm of step after step, crunch of sand and wisp of breeze lulls me, ties me close to the land and further from my tiredness and pain. My skin feels crusty; I touch my tongue to my hand, a strong salty other my reward. The warm sun on my neck, the brace of cool air adds to the natural rhythm. I've no idea of the time of day, nor any inclination to know; it feels out of place, irrelevant. Maybe night, day, sleep, awake are all that's needed, all I need to know. To the front tower the mighty peaks, my constant companions. Perhaps that, too, is enough, enough to simply know and recognize.

Henry pulls me out of my reverie. We stand at the mouth of a narrow, fast river, a series of low waterfalls upstream.

"Do you remember crossing that?" Henry asks.

"Can't say I do. Overshot perhaps?"

"I don't think so." Henry glances at the mountains, the ocean, the sun. "If we follow it inland, I guess we find the Pegasus."

The scrabble up is slippery, the land a gentle slope before us. It's harder going than the beach, hidden ruts and rocks on sometimes sodden, sometimes soft ground drains me until Henry spots the Pegasus.

They've been busy since we left, a fire burns to one side and small piles of objects cluster around the base. There's slow movement on the plains in front, men pace deliberately up and down as if lost in thought. From behind, a rustle – a young boy passes us burdened by pots and pails full of water. The pain in my feet and stomach are forgotten as we hurry after him.

A few figures come to us, among them Lou arm in arm with an Amish woman. How can she manage? I've never seen her out in the open, never mind relaxed, confident. Her embrace is as enthusiastic as it is welcome.

"You look like you're doing well."

"With a little help, yes." Lou sees my silver feet below three-quarter bell bottoms. "You've hurt yourself."

"I've got these things on my feet, they hurt like crazy, but Henry says they'll be fine."

Lou has me in one arm, the Amish woman in the other as we make our way back to the Pegasus. I'm sure it's Menno's wife she's got there.

I think it's chicken soup; it's got a strange taste, it's nearly all water with green strands on a surface slick with grease. Must've started rationing already, had as much luck as we did. I don't care, don't stop to ask as I drain it. I nearly lick off the glaze, glance around furtively but I needn't worry. They're all silent, single-minded as they wolf it down; Menno's got a soup line clear across his beard. Our eyes lock for a moment, he's as tired as me but hides it better. "What did you find, Greg?"

"Nothing." There's no noise, no comments. They expect it, they know it. "We saw animals, birds, life, but no people or signs of them."

"So, the planet is empty?"

"Well, this bit yes, but that's only a day's walk out and back. We'd have to go further, have a better look out past the mountains to know for sure."

"We should have seen lights, heard vehicles or ships if anyone's around," Henry says, "but there was nothing."

"How'd you go, Peter, any signals, messages?"

"Nothing, no one's listening or talking. The AI doesn't know where we are, so I'd say we're totally off the map."

"Is that possible, could we have gone that far?"

"Anything's possible," Kelli says. "Put a foot wrong in η-space, you could be anywhere. And here we are."

Peter's gaze locks on the fire. "Three days. We've been gone three days. Enough for a signal out and back."

Lou gives Peter a strange look. What's with that? "Lou?"

"Penny's bot's dead, it's not linked to the grid."

"What does that mean?" Menno asks.

I turn to him. "It means we're totally on our own, Menno, no one's going to come. We have to make it with what's in the ship and what's around us."

There are nods from Kelli and Peter, slight grimaces from the Amish. The children stay silent as if they understand what the words mean.

I pull the oversized jumper tight, burrow my hands in the sleeves; the heavy coarse fibers tickle but keep me warm. The first stars creep up, still beautiful but somehow more distant. I drift out of the conversation, drift back as Kelli continues.

"...looked at, some seems useful, some's useless electronics."

"All our goods are here. We took Elliott at his word. We brought enough to start ten farms, all the equipment and seeds. We also have some of our best rootstock fruit trees."

"Will they work here?"

"God willing, Kelli, they are modified for Juuttua's cold."

"So, how long until they've grown, until we can eat them?"

"From planting, if everything goes well three, maybe four months for the seed, five or six years for the trees. But we need to get the ground ready first. We have the tools but not the animals. With the animals it could take two weeks, without them, I do not know. Everything needs to be done by hand."

"No one has tilled the land that way to my memory," Cephas says. "We will not know how long it takes until it is done."

84

"If the land is good, perhaps less. If the land is bad then perhaps longer," Menno says.

"Then the sooner we start the better. Tomorrow, Menno?"

"Yes, Cephas, tomorrow."

Four to six months, tomorrow to harvest if things go right. I look around the circle, stop at Kelli. They've worked it out, only one question remains. "How much food do we have, Kelli?"

"Ship's meals are gone, it's whatever's in the cargo. Freda, how much have we got?"

"We think enough for four, maybe five weeks; if we stretch it, perhaps ten. It's all preserves, jams and chutneys and the like, no real food."

It's not enough, not nearly enough, but no one dares say it. It is what it is, the hand we're dealt. The certainty of being alone seems to settle everyone, a plan no matter how much work's involved lifts them. Peter looks tired, withdrawn; he's the first to turn in. One by one, they filter away until seven of us are left to sit and watch the fire die.

The silence intoxicates me even when shared, embers glow below as embers burn above. I love this empty, this quiet, it grows on me as it soaks me away. It takes a will I barely possess not to abandon myself to it, cut everyone off and just be.

"Why were you going to Juuttua, Greg?"

Does he know? No, how can he? There's no possible way. "My job, Menno. A better position, more money."

"A choice, then?"

"Yes, you could say that."

"We had no choice. We were forced."

"I don't understand."

"All we want is to live as God intends, the old way, but the world would not let us." His voice betrays no malice, perhaps a tinge of sadness. "Juuttua was a new start, a chance to live where the temptations of the world were distant, far away from our children."

"So, to you this place must be acceptable?"

"Yes, and more, a chance to build that community under God and, if you wish, for all of you to be a part of it."

"Well, I'm not sure, I've never thought about being Amish. I'm not even sure if I have a religion."

"No, to be Amish is different. We work and live as a community to support each other rather than as families of ones or twos, separate and independent as you do. It is something you may want to consider, at least until we are established. It may be impossible by yourselves."

Is that a threat or a statement of the blindingly obvious? They have everything we need, perhaps it's genuine, a real invitation. Why do I feel like I'm talking to Jonathon? "It sounds sensible to work together, but I'm no farmer."

"It is simple enough." Menno stands, Freda after him. "A quick stroll before sleep. Until tomorrow."

They walk away, disappear behind a cargo node.

"Be careful, Greg. I left the community he led."

"It's not like there's much choice, Henry. We need them to survive. I'm sure there'll be no trouble, and anyway, once it's all established, maybe it won't matter."

"Father can be stubborn, fixed in his own ideas. Amish ministers are known to be strict. He's the only one with any form of authority over them, no matter how soft."

"Thanks for the advice but we'll be fine, we're all adults. No matter how he thinks, we're all in this together, so we're in the same community anyway. It's only a convenience for a while."

WE ROUND THE cargo node, head to mountains silhouetted by a band of stars. Henry and Greg's voices shrink, smothered by the night. We sit, I draw Freda close. There is something about this place, some element that draws and lifts me, an intrigue since I first set foot here but now a certainty. The stars fade, gentle mist rain falls. We remain alone, still; since we emerged from the Pegasus, we have had barely a minute to ourselves, by ourselves. This darkness punctuated by silence fills me. "Do you feel it, Freda?"

"The cold, Menno? A little, the drizzle is nothing."

"No, the rightness of this place."

"It's a harsh but not impossible land."

"We are alone, the sixty of us, a whole planet."

"And Louise's family, Kelli and Peter."

"It is God's gift, a gift no gmay has ever been given, a chance to build a life without the world, with none of the temptation or pressure."

"Perhaps, maybe it is at that."

"No maybe at all. Why else would we be here, with our tools, our seeds, on a planet waiting for us? And there is Henry."

"Henry?"

"Why did he come with us? Why, if not for your prayers?"

"Do you think he will rejoin the gmay?"

"I have no doubt. Here, he will relearn the value of honest work with no world to cloud or confuse, no temptation to waste time on books or tales. It is always the way, with no temptation they stay and grow strong."

"What of Louise and the others? The world may have come with us."

It is perhaps true, a concern, but what can I do? It is of no consequence. It is not my place to tell anyone outside the gmay what to do. "They are only five and are more isolated than us. We have our gmay, God, our ordnung. They only have themselves. They need us more than they know, the world will turn to us in time."

The mist rain clears. We sit and watch the cluster rise above the mountains, the silver light beautiful, a gift deserving a community and people dedicated to God, living the lives He requires. Our homes, our farms, the other gmay were the imperfect past, mere practice for this place prepared for us.

"When the lot fell to you, I was scared, frightened of the responsibility and burden placed on you and the family."

"I know."

"But now we're here, I'm happy you were chosen. Of them all, I know you'll stay strong and humble before God."

It gives me pause. Perhaps she is right, perhaps I was chosen for this. Is it pride or vanity to accept the obvious? I was given the inspiration to go to Juuttua, to lead the others. Is it wrong for the tool in God's hands to acknowledge the fact? No, and I am both humble and willing, chosen, and I should acknowledge the fact. I am here, sole minister and sole authority in the gmay until I decide another is needed.

We rise, drag ourselves away to catch what rest we can. Tomorrow the real work starts, the hard, relentless slog to harvest that farmers have always known, will always know. Here, and with what we have, we will need all the strength and rest we can muster.

Especially the leader. Most importantly their leader.

Chapter Sixteen

Greg

CEPHAS PLACES ONE hand between my shoulder blades and pulls hard on the shoulder strap. A practiced flick secures the buckles, aligns side traces and hip straps.

"Okay, Greg?"

He nearly knocks the wind out of me, jury rigged harness bulky and harsh against my skin. My shirt was transformed to tatters in a day, so I've deliberately gone bare-chested to keep my Amish jumper intact, allow the bitter cold to keep me awake. The breastband under my armpits chafes and constricts, but I know from our first few attempts it's in a better place. It's too large, too bulky, never designed to be used this way. Thankfully, we agree the whips aren't called for. I throw my left arm across Henry's shoulders. "Yep, all good."

Cephas moves behind us, I feel the trace click as it attaches to the plow. Ahead of me to the right the earth is a freshly turned jumble of soil, rocks and plants; to the left the grass stands knee high, a uniform carpet of purple olive. Henry tightens his grip, pulls me closer. More and more these last few days I've felt like an animal, a beast of burden. I push out an off-key chorus from an ancient song concerned with just such a fate.

"What's that?"

I repeat it for Henry's benefit.

"Well, so much for that theory."

The traces tighten, pulls us straight.

"Ready?"

Henry chants a slow 'left-right, left-right' metronome as we set off along the line between turned and untouched earth. The harness, the plow, everything is designed for horses and we are no matched pair. The necessary discipline of left–right is no guarantee of success, the drunken waver and inconsistent depth of each pass testament enough. Here, now, it doesn't matter.

The first step, the lean into the harness and jerk as the blade bites into the sod, is excruciating; the next steps are no better as momentum, however slow, has to be kept up for fear of the jerky stop-start torture of my first attempt. My foot slides too far into the turned earth, my hip strap slides up and down over open welts; I suck breath through clenched teeth as pain shoots through me. I don't break stride. More than necessity, it's pride; I know I am the weakest of them, it drives me to make a lie of the fact. Once each day is done, I crawl into my jumper, into my allocated space on the Pegasus with Lou and Pen to collapse into sleep.

The harness tightens, Henry's weight comes then goes. I see him hobble out of step then regain his rhythm with little fuss. As hard as it is on the inside with the soft dirt, the rocks and rubble on the outer are worse. Cephas' tug on my outside trace reminds me I am off to one side again. Finish this pass, then one more on the outside, and I get two passes behind the plow. Weary arms and hands remind me it's no rest back there. I see women bent over turned earth at the far end, children beside them. I wonder how Lou's getting on.

I PROTESTED MENNO'S decision not to let women near the plows, told him and Cephas their outdated, misogynistic attitude was wrong. He patiently, if condescendingly, explained there were things god intended for men and things god intended for women but, more importantly, with no animals, plowing could not be women's work. I was ready to dig my heels in and fight when I remembered that, for all his biases and misconceptions, Menno knows how to farm. 'If we had animals, you would be plowing,' he said, 'but I will not have any woman in harness.' As I watch Greg stumble and strain, bruises and welts multiplying hourly to fall spent into sleep these past few nights, I'm glad I backed off.

Not that we have it much easier. Penny's in one group of children at the edge of the forest to gather firewood, cut and stack saplings. I was horrified when they gave her an axe, but now it seems normal. Halfway through the day, Penny's group swaps with the other to dig a ditch from the creek to the Pegasus and then to the fields, crude irrigation lined with the rocks we claw from the ground.

The soil is cold, rocky, unforgiving. In the deepest recesses, pools of ice-cold water accumulate, purple-green patches in obsidian black dirt. A hard edge intrudes, I add my hands to Freda's, tear the loose dirt away. We stand, lift the rock between us, carry it to the edge of the field to lie with dozens of others. We return, kneel to extract the smaller stones and pebbles, fill the bucket again. I drive my hands into the soil like I was shown, to find the concealed ones, not only those that present themselves.

Has it only been a few days? I'm always cold, chilled to the bone from the ground, a constant ache in my back and arms. We kneel, surround the furrows like the penitent in worship, bend in supplication from sunrise to sunset, rise with stones in hand and cast them on sacrificial pyres. My world reduced to a few meters of dirt on a strange planet – a bucket; a ditch; a box within a box.

A hand touches me on the shoulder, a cup is filled from a steaming kettle. Weak and purple-olive, I pretend it's tea. I drink eagerly, allow the hot liquid to warm me, a temporary reprieve from the cold. I open my eyes to Freda opposite.

"Better, Louise?"

"Much."

89

"How's your back?"

"Fine, getting used to it." It's only half a lie. We return to our task. Freda won't admit it, but I see the strain on her face, the twitch as she stands, her once white bonnet now gray. They may be used to a hard, physical life but surely not this; yet I've not heard any complaints or harsh words, they accept it like they were born to it. I draw my strength from them. Even the children. I turn to three distant figures bent before the plow.

I STINK, A rancid nightmare aroma of stale sweat, earth, open wounds, old clothes, smoke, and scraps of food. It's only because everyone's the same that I don't stand out. Here behind the plow, my mind wanders. Henry and Cephas take to the task as if born to it. All I have to do is add my weight, keep it straight and it's good. I watch Menno and his team turn for another pass, each of their furrows arrow straight and even. Not bad for men ten years older than me and, if I believe Henry, they feel that way, too.

"Depth, depth," Cephas says.

It brings me back, the plow's angled too deep, pulls against Cephas' trace. I bear my weight down to bring the blade to the right depth. Sometimes there's a reason but often none. It's as if Cephas makes a point to lean on me, always something he's not happy with on each pass. Unlike Henry, Henry cuts me that little bit of slack.

Slack. I tug the traces, straighten Cephas up where there is no need. If he wants to take it out on anyone, it should be Peter. He's totally avoided the plow, wanders between the other groups to sometimes lift a stone, collect some wood, but mainly disappears from sight. I've tried to talk to him, get him to pitch in with us, but he stares and stays silent. I've already got one child to worry about, I don't need another.

We reach the end of the run, one down and who knows how many more left. We rotate the plow, flip the blade face over. Henry's out of harness, I'm strapped in, arm across Cephas and ready to start the run when the rain starts, a heavy, cold, windblown drizzle. The traces go slack, I turn to follow Cephas' gaze.

"This one's settling in. George's team are unhitching, and the women are heading back," Cephas says. "What do you think, Henry? Head in?"

"I don't know."

I look around at abandoned fields blanketed in gray haze, everyone clustered around the Pegasus. The drizzle is heavier, more insistent. A movement to one side catches my eye.

"Greg, do you want to get out of this?" Cephas asks.

Menno and his team start their next run, I see water cascade from his hat to his bare back. Whatever else, they're determined. I watch their steady rhythmic plod, a ghostly shadow march into the mist as drizzle strengthens to rain.

"Hey, Greg, I asked if you wanted to quit."

"No, Cephas, not while there's daylight. Henry?"

"Fine by me."

Cephas turns, leans into the run. "Let's get on with it."

Louise scowls, pulls the emergency blanket's tab. "You're an idiot, Greg Robertson."

Maybe, but I outlasted Menno. Cephas had to drag me in. I'm not physically up to them, but mentally I'm stronger. "I'm not the only one, there were five others out there."

"Shhh, keep your voice down."

I move closer. Privacy's a myth, crowded together we use the Pegasus as a dormitory. The jury-rigged partitions of packaging and plastic sheets are hardly more effective than open air. "It's got to be done, rain or no rain. Anyway, I'm not letting Menno think I'm a shirker like Peter."

"He does his share. It affects us all in different ways."

"Not Peter. No one's happy about this, but you don't see us all sitting in circles, sobbing. He should put his shoulder to the plow with the rest of us."

The emergency blanket folds. Lou dips the rag in a small cup of water, presses it aggressively into an open sore on my back. "He does what he can, and the extra muscle is needed elsewhere than the plow. Like Freda says, all work is honorable."

"Now, just what does that mean?"

"Arm up."

I lift it obediently, let her get to the welts across my side and chest.

"It means everyone has a contribution to make, as long as they make it. Even a small piece of a plan is important."

"Plan? What plan?"

"You know, this, the settlement and community."

"I didn't know we had one, just a fight to get it in the ground before we starve. Menno's got other ideas?"

"Other arm. Not Menno, Freda says it's god's plan."

"Oh." God's plan? I know Menno thinks god's in charge, but a plan? She spends most of her days with Freda and the Amish women. Could she believe it? Maybe, there was all that junk with Clara back home. "You're not buying it, are you?"

"I'm not sure, there's something about them, something…certain about everything. They're good people, Freda's been really supportive, they all have, and considering what's happened, they're so calm, so confident."

91

"Well, they've got to be, there's no choice, either do it or give up. But a plan? Tipping us out of η-space, Pen's illness? I suppose that's part of it, too?"

"You shouldn't be so close-minded."

"It's what you think that bothers me. So, what do you think? You said before that Pen's illness was my fault, so what now, part of god's plan for the Amish?"

"Oh, don't bring that up again."

"No, seriously. If you believe it's god's plan he must have given the bad genes to my dad, so Menno gets an empty planet."

"Well, it can't be all coincidence. It makes sense when you tie it all together, look at it from where we are now. Like Rachel was saying, it's all worked out, and considering she's got those two poor children, you think she'd be the first to give in. But she hasn't."

"I don't believe them, Lou. I can't accept being pieces in a plan for someone else's benefit. It's all random chance or probability, call it what you will, but it's no one's plan. Did he tell you about it?"

"Who?"

"God. Did he tell you?"

"No, don't be stupid. Of course not."

"Then who? Freda, Menno, who'd god tell?"

"Well, I don't know, Freda's never said anyone told her anything except maybe Menno. She said he was led to take them to Juuttua, but this planet was what god really intended for them."

"That's my worry. One minute someone thinks it's god telling them what to do, the next they tell everyone else what to do. How can you tell what's Menno and what's god?"

"You think he's lying. You think he's manipulating everyone including Freda just to get what he wants?"

"I don't know, well, probably not. Menno's different, they all are, but they've not done anything strange. He's put in as much as anyone, without him we'd be in more trouble than we are now. Don't misunderstand me, I don't share his beliefs, but I respect him."

"And me?"

I stare at her. It's never crossed my mind, all the things she got into with Clara I'd seen as games, little explorations that had no real meaning, no substance. I'd never seen her take any of it seriously, never thought about what it might mean if she did.

"Greg? Do you respect me even if I don't think what you think, share your beliefs?"

"I've never had to think about it, it's never been an issue. I don't know how I'd manage if you turned Amish."

"Who said anything about turning Amish? I just keep an open mind, try to understand them. They've got something, god or whatever, but it shows. You should try it some time, try harder to understand people. Like Peter. You know his kids and partner were on Juuttua? We're here but he's never going to see his again. Ever. Think about that."

"I didn't know."

"You should try to look into people, not just at them. Now hold still while I finish this off, I want to get some rest."

She continues across my chest. The day's work overtakes me, tiredness rises on a tide of guilt. She's worked as long as me, as hard as me, and she tends my wounds? I open one eye, watch her hand around the wet rag. Small flecks of orange make a final desperate stand on cracked, ragged fingernails, lines in her knuckles and fingers etched in jet black bas-relief.

"Lou?"

"Uh huh."

"I respect and admire you more than you can imagine."

"I know. Greg?"

"Yes."

"You're still an idiot. Now shut up and let me rest."

Chapter Seventeen

Greg

A DAY LOST, a whole day when we can least afford it. I try to scrape the filth from my jumper and straighten it out. Menno's counted the days, declared today to be the seventh one here. Sunday. And Henry tells me every second Sunday requires this. It's surreal; divine service under an alien sky both intrigues and amuses me. I need to pull back a bit, take Lou's advice and at least try to understand them. If it's important to them, it's important to me. Or at least I should pretend it is.

Pen twists and pulls, pushes her bonnet higher. A fold of dark brown hair cascades over her left eye down to her chin. "This thing's never gonna sit right."

"Hold still." How did Lou do this? I bundle her hair, jam the bonnet on and tie it off with a solid double knot. Not the prettiest, but it's not coming off.

Pen grimaces, makes choking sounds. "It hurts."

"No, it doesn't. Stop complaining."

"Why don't you have one?"

"You'd have to ask Henry or Menno. Now give me your hand, we've got to go."

"I'm not a kid!"

"You've been demoted until you stop complaining. Now come on." We walk over to where Lou stands with Kelli, Freda, and Henry. Further on boxes and crates are laid out with military precision, two lines to the left, two lines to the right, and between them Menno, somber beneath that hat, arms clasped behind his back. Our gazes meet, Menno nods in return.

Freda bends, reties Pen's bonnet with a bow. She's rewarded with a smile; Pen pokes her tongue at me. They move off arm in arm. Kelli hesitates, whispers to Henry then hurries after them.

"It means a lot to him you being here, Greg, but he won't show it," Henry says.

"Anything to keep the peace. Last minute tips?"

"Follow along quietly and don't talk to the women. We're at the back, so don't worry, no one will notice. I'll translate."

"Translate?"

"The service is in PennDutch, prayers and hymns in German."

"This is going to be an interesting few hours."

"Okay, come on, follow me."

Henry leads me into the group of men. Men I've eaten with, sweated and strained in the dirt with, greet me one by one with solid handshakes into their community of belief from our shared community of toil. Menno greets each man in the same fashion – a handshake, a nod, a mumbled welcome. We move to his right, settle in at the back. The women file past Menno, oldest to youngest, sit to his left on the crates in the same order.

Henry opens a small black object to reveal thick, dark text on a cream background. I lean across, tap one finger on the text twice. Nothing happens.

"It's not a screen, it's our hymnbook, the Ausbund. It's printed on paper. These are old, go back before my grandparents."

"I can't read it."

"It's German. Quiet, it's started."

Menno removes his hat, then sits on a vacant box in the middle of the front row. The quiet deepens, even the children still, silent, expectant.

"Eins drei eins," from the second row, followed by a rustle of pages.

The same voice, a rich deep baritone rises and falls, draws out one syllable then one word slowly, carefully, gently; and then, as it pauses to draw breath, is joined by the rest of the Amish. No accompaniment, no conductor or instrument, they continue without a voice out of step, a line garbled, a word out of tune. There's a depth, shared strength as if the hymn is an anthem, a challenge thrown by these strangers to the new world as the hairs on the back of my neck rise. Henry's translation, soft in my ear, is nearly lost:

> "O God Father, we praise you
> And your goodness exalt,
> Which you, O Lord, so graciously
> Have manifested to us anew…"

They fall silent, the echoes fade as we kneel where we are, heads bowed, locked in our own thoughts or prayers. What would I pray for if I believed? Rescue to Juuttua? Time to be reset? Crops to grow and harvest to come?

Cephas stands, shuffles his feet. "Second Corinthians Chapter twelve verse nine, my grace is sufficient for thee; for my strength is made perfect in weakness."

Cephas sits as quickly as he stood. Menno walks a little uncertainly to the space between the men and women, his gaze fixed on the crates at the far end. He speaks slowly, clearly, as if he searches out and confirms each word, hands clasped in front as he stands rigid on the spot.

"What's he saying, Henry?"

"Shhh. It's nothing, the usual stuff, how unworthy he is, apologizing for his inability and wishing someone else would do it."

"Really?"

"Yeah, he means it, he's also got to show it so that – hold on, he's started."

"More than a year ago, we placed our trust in God to seek a home free from the world, to raise our children in the way He intended, to give them the living hope we have. God's plan for us was a surprise to those we left behind. Now we too, creatures of vanity and pride, are surprised He leads us here and not to Juuttua."

He pauses as if unsure.

"This place is empty, harsh, unwelcoming, of little hope and few prospects. We have ourselves, each other and what we brought with us, our weaknesses and inabilities plain in the face of this part of God's creation."

He lifts his gaze deliberately, searchingly from one person to the next, to come to rest on me. "But it is in our weakness we see His grace, in our shortcomings and inability His strength. Where we see only desolation and despair, He brings hope and life. In our small minds we cannot hope to understand His plan, His plan for all of us, His hand guiding us whether we acknowledge it or not."

Menno turns. "Centuries ago, our fathers were persecuted for their faith. Martyred and outcast, they journeyed to America to escape persecution. As they, so have we. As God led them, so He leads us. In our ignorance we looked to Juuttua, in His wisdom He brought us here. Our faithfulness and obedience have been rewarded. Where we sought distance, He gifts us separation. Where we pray against temptation, He banishes the deceiver. Where we desire a new start, He brings a new dawn, this Neueanbruch we stand upon to mold, to build a gmay obedient and faithful to Him."

Menno turns to the Pegasus. A solitary figure sits at the hatch, legs over the side. "Some say the world has come with us, but this, too, is God's plan. No one knows the heart of man and no one has the right of judgment except God Himself. We remember Dirk Wellems, who saved the lives of those who would burn him at the stake; Jesus Himself helped sinners. The gmay is one thing, Neueanbruch another. They are here because God has brought them."

Menno sits, the married men rise one by one to echo his sentiments, his beliefs.

"At least it's got a name now," Henry says.

"What has?"

"This place. Neueanbruch. Means 'new dawn' or 'new advent'."

Neueanbruch. It doesn't sit right, doesn't feel good. They assume it's empty, but we've only scratched the surface. I kneel as Menno leads us in prayer. The morning wash hasn't shifted the dirt from under my nails or from the abrasions on my fingers. Is it god's or Menno's plan for me to be a farmer? I'm being herded again, someone or something else pulls the strings while I dance. I'm getting paranoid – it is what it is, and I have a choice, farm or starve. His beliefs aren't mine and he's made no demands, no threats, only help.

The congregation divides – men, women and older children move one way, everyone else heads back to the Pegasus. Pen stays, sits by herself on the boxes.

I move over to Menno. "Thank you. I've never been to one before."

"It seemed impolite not to invite your family. Usually outsiders do not get asked. Henry was able to translate for you?"

"Well enough." I look past Menno to the group of adults. "I have a question if you have a few seconds."

"That is the gmay meeting, they will wait."

"That's the question. You said the gmay is one thing, the community another. What do you mean?"

"The gmay is our church, those who are baptized, committed to it and our doctrine. No one is born into it. A person must choose, it is up to them."

"And that's why you left, to come here? They were choosing not to?"

"Yes, that is perhaps a little simple, but true."

"And the community?"

"The community is all of our families, gmay or not, who live together. We are the community, Neueanbruch, yourselves included. Back on Earth or Juuttua you would not be, you would be English, outsiders, the world. Here, God has placed you in our community, as part of us."

"Are you sure? You know we don't share your beliefs, your dress, even the language is different."

"There is no question. God knows your heart, has placed you in our community. We do not need you to join the gmay, adopt our doctrine or ordnung. That is for each of you to decide or not to decide as you wish. Up to now, things have been without trouble between us?"

"Yes, of course, although I admit I'm not made for farming."

"None of us are horses, Greg. The bridle hurts us as well, but it is what God has given us, so we accept it with His grace. Now, I think I must attend to the gmay."

I watch him walk off. The ramrod straight back fails to hide his tiredness. Maybe a day of rest's a good idea, a chance to recharge and reset. Maybe it will be fine, maybe it's fatigue that sets me on edge. One way or another it will work out. I turn, walk with Pen to the Pegasus.

"Dad, Mister Menno's weird. He's nice, isn't he?"

"Yes, I think they all are. But I don't know about the beards, maybe I should grow one."

"Bad idea, way bad."

I stop, look to the meeting. They stand in a circle, Menno at the center in earnest discussion. Occasionally a face will turn, look furtively at me, and as quickly turn back to Menno. Pen fidgets with her bonnet.

"You can take that off now, the meeting's over."

"It's okay, I think I like it."

Sleep. Rest. A mild dry day needs no extra inducement, Rachel's find in the hold simply adds to the impetus. Whoever it was on Juuttua who freighted in a carton of tinned soup was thanked by all of us; it made our one meal complete, each of us torpid on thin gruel that on Earth may or may not pass for dishwater, but here feels like a banquet. We lie or sit scattered in small groups to talk about nothing or snore away the afternoon.

From my perch on the rock I see Lou, Pen, and Freda to one side of the Pegasus, Rachel and her two children asleep to the other. I stretch, reposition myself, careful not to disturb Kelli or her buzzsaw snores. She fell asleep next to Henry, but somehow managed to work one knee into my back.

Henry yawns, holds out a crushed blue box. "Smoke?"

"No thanks, I don't."

"Good, I've few enough anyway."

"Never seen you with one before."

"Trying to stretch them out." He points to the Pegasus. "They don't like it, so I smoke in private, try not to antagonize Mom."

"Seems there's a few things they don't like."

Henry pinches the end of the cigarette. It lights, he takes a long draw then sends a column of gray to meet the overcast. "Oh, there's the odd couple of thousand, but that's all for the members, not outsiders like us."

"You aren't part of them?"

"No, never was. Never got through the classes, never got baptized."

"Must've been tough with your dad in charge."

"Father wasn't minister when I left. It would've been worse if I'd been baptised. Wouldn't be allowed to see, speak to or visit any of them."

"Why?"

"Break the rules often enough and they cut you off totally. At least I can still see them, although I didn't expect this much."

"Why'd you leave, they try and force you?"

"I wanted to keep learning, reading, finding out things. At home, it was school until eighth grade then that's the end of it – learn to be a farmer, join the gmay, get married, have kids, and make them do the same. I didn't want that, so I left." He holds his cigarette out between forefinger and thumb, studies it intently. "And look at me now. Ironic, isn't it?"

"Menno said he doesn't want us to be part of the church if we don't want. You don't think he'd try, all that talk of god's plan and all that?"

"No, Father's stubborn at times but he doesn't go back on his word. Don't misunderstand them. Ask directly and they'll say you should, that their way is the only way and even then, there's no guarantee. But they'll never force you, it's not their way, it's not his way, and it wouldn't build the community he wants."

"You mean the one god wants, the plan god told Menno about?"

"Oh no, god's not talked to him. None of them believes that happens. They'd cut Father out of the gmay instantly if he even thought it."

"So, what's this plan he goes on about? Everyone seems to agree with him."

"It's the guidelines and rules for living that go with the Bible, the ordnung of the gmay. They cover everything: clothes, customs, what tech or machines they can use, even how they appear. Wondered why they all have long beards but no moustaches? It's an ordnung."

"So, he's going to follow a plan to live here like they lived on Earth?"

"Yeah, basically. They'll make a farming community, one you could have found as far back as the ancient times, the 1700s. And they'll do it, too, he can grow crops in rock. He had the best farm in the gmay before I left."

Kelli stirs, sits up. "He seems to know what he's doing. He's got sixty people who agree with him, and an empty planet to work with. Guess we're all going to be farmers, Greg."

"That's what bothers me."

"There's not much we can do about it. If we don't farm, we don't eat."

"It's not the farming, it's the notion we're alone. I get no one's looking for us, but we don't know the planet's empty."

"But Peter and Louise checked for signals and you went out to look with Henry. It's empty."

"We only did twenty or so kilometres out, then the same back on a different route," Henry says. "You're thinking about the mountains, aren't you, Greg?"

Kelli points behind the Pegasus. "What, those things? They're impossible."

"No, not those ones, Kell, the others. When we got to the end of the first day, we saw mountains on the horizon, smaller ones far away."

"We could see all the way to them and back and there was nothing and nobody there. But we don't know what's on the other side. Me and Henry will have to have a look, and if Menno's building his dreams on an empty planet, the sooner the better."

"So," Henry asks, "about two weeks there and back? Then what, a week looking around? I'm not convinced now's the right time."

"It's not. The fields need to be plowed and we're the animals, so there's no choice. But once that's done, what's next? Stick the seeds in, then sit back and watch? They won't miss us then."

"Sounds reasonable, it's long enough to wait. I heard Cephas tell Lester it could be another three to four weeks to finish plowing."

Four weeks? I'll be an exhausted wreck by then, but it is what it is. "Okay, four weeks it is. You and me, unless you want other company."

Kelli holds up her hands in mock horror. "Oh, no you don't, I saw your feet when you got back last time. I can wait with Louise."

Lou. I keep forgetting. But she'll be fine, it's only three weeks.

Chapter Eighteen

Louise

HE'S ON THE rock with them when he should be here with me. Even when there's time, he's got none for me. What does he think about this morning? The service was strange, but why did I feel part of it? Penny twists, squashes her face into my ribs, bonnet over her nose. Freda hands the water to me. "So, you've only the one child?"

"Yes, even by herself she's a handful. We only applied for one, a brother or sister would be good, but it's impossible. We'd need more income, a bigger fee. You have three?"

"No, six."

"Six? Three's the legal limit."

"There's exemptions for us, but I would have liked more. We both had seven brothers and sisters. Like most of the gmay, our families are smaller than our parents'."

"Must be difficult keeping six in line."

"Getting them ready on Sundays can be a trial, but their chores help. If they get too much, I send them off to Mary's or Ida's for a few hours, or they send me theirs if they need time."

"What, to someone else's building without you with them? You're not worried what could happen if you can't see them?"

"Why would I? The gmay's safe, God takes care of them. It's the world that's dangerous, not us."

"I had fits when Penny used to visit in the apartments. I'd have the full cover track and feed bots live to my link all the time."

"That's the world for you."

"I panicked the first days here when I couldn't track her, but now it seems normal."

"It should be. Children should be able to run around safely, parents shouldn't have to worry."

"Another part of god's plan?"

"No, just how it should be."

"You've always been farmers?"

"Back to my great grandparents, yes, as best we're able. It was getting harder though, more and more gave up the land for other work."

"Everything I've seen, all your equipment, there's no machinery, no bots. They'd make it easier, wouldn't they. I mean, to keep farming?"

"No doubt, but it would take us away from the simple, plain life. If it could, or the gmay believes it could, we won't use it."

"What about vidscreens, live links?"

"No, they bring the world into the home. Anyway, who needs that when I have my friends and family? How do you feel now your…link doesn't work?"

"A little lost. It was all there, the cross-feeds and shares, all my friends in my head when I needed them. It's too quiet now."

"You miss it then, not your friends, but that thing in your head?"

"Yes, of course."

"So, who was in charge, you or it?"

The answer's obvious, but then again, I never turned it off, too scared to miss that one piece of gossip or news I couldn't live without.

"You see? How long has Penny had hers?"

"Barely two months, even then not fully activated."

"Perhaps it's for the best."

"So, how do you explain the threeship? You had no problems with that."

"It's not the thing itself but what it does to us that matters. It's how it's used, what it leads to. The threeship's not good or bad, the same way a plow's not evil or holy. Travelling in this had a purpose that was correct, but to own it or travel in it just to travel is another thing." Freda shifts, tucks her dress back in below her knees. "Like everything else. Who's the master and who's the servant. There's only room for one master and that's God."

"Sounds simple."

"It does at that, although there are things you take on faith. Like zips, buttons, and hooks. We can use buttons and hooks, but the ordnung says no zips. I've never understood why, but there must be a reason, so I accept it."

"Well, Menno could change it if he wanted to."

"No, no one's in charge, the gmay works together on everything. Menno's the only minister now, so he has to preach at the meetings and do other things that…well, that take up a lot of time. He's a servant like all of us, the only difference is that the lot fell to him. Nobody wants that, nobody."

"Why? I'd think it's an important, responsible role."

"Nobody seeks anything for themselves, Louise, pride's a subtle sin." She turns, eyes moist. "He can't quit, he's minister for life, even if he lives to a hundred fifty. He has to provide for his family, take care of the souls God has given him, and prepare for every second Sunday. He takes the cares of the gmay upon him, he's always free for any of them any time of night or day as counselor, adjudicator, judge, or support."

I put my hand on her shoulder.

"He's aged ten years in the past two, he gets little sleep and no rest and when he does, he's too tired for me or the children. He can't tell me what goes on and he's like all Amish men, keeps his feelings and hurt hidden between him and God. As much as any Amish man doesn't want the lot, his wife wants it less." She turns, gives a near-convincing smile. "Anyway, God doesn't give anyone a burden they cannot carry. As much as he was chosen, his family was chosen."

"He must be strong."

"Oh no, he's like us all, weak and helpless. He just doesn't show it. Solid and stable outside, but inside he really cares."

Amy Lehmann shakes, the blanket slides to her feet. I stand, reach to put it back. Freda takes the other side: "He really wants what's best for all of us, believe me."

Chapter Nineteen

Henry

IT'S A RELIEF – after three weeks on that damned plow, up and down, back and forth, even a change is a holiday. I stare out over turned earth to the harrow team; Menno, Cephas and Greg drag it slowly, methodically along to carve furrows into which seeds are planted. Behind them, backs bent, come the rest, shuffling three to each furrow; one to plant, one to backfill, one to compact. It's a minor miracle we're at this point but there's no confusion – once this field is planted out, there's the next; and the next.

It takes its toll, I've joined a short list of the injured who, in other circumstances, would be side-lined for a few days. Here it's impossible, there's no time for more than a shift to lighter work for a day then back into it, hopefully recuperated. I gently rotate my left arm, look ruefully at the crude splint along my finger. The pain of the break was only matched by re-setting my dislocated shoulder, but that's nothing compared to how the injuries were obtained. If I'd been injured by the plow or rocks I could live with it, but to fall out of the Pegasus half asleep on the way to the toilet? Hardly pioneer stuff. When, or rather if, the history of this world is written, will that be remembered to my lasting shame?

"Can we get on with this, Henry?"

Her eyes are the same as that first day, if stressed and tired. At least now they're my constant companions. I'm surprised how easy it was to fall into this with her. Back on Earth, I'd be one of thousands with no hope, but here I am, here she is.

Kell grins, flicks violet grass across my nose. "If you could stop ogling for one minute, we can finish it. Unless you prefer Menno's company to mine?"

"No, I just got distracted."

"That I could see."

I gather up the next bundle of twigs and hold them together, ends against the ground as Kell ties them with fibrous violet grass. I straighten, take the small bundle a few yards and deposit it on the pile. Thatch. One of an unknown number of things we don't have and can't fashion from the threeship; like buildings, places to sleep, store tools and, hopefully, seed and food. Rooms need roofs and this will have to do, at least for a while. I turn, pick up the next bundle and crouch.

"You look tired, Henry."

"You would, too, if each time you went to the toilet, you broke a finger." I see her drooped shoulders, tilted head as she fiddles with the next grass tie. "How'd you sleep last night?"

Kell shrugs.

I drop the twigs, crouch lower. "Did you get any sleep?"

"A little."

"How little?"

"Not much, I don't know, a few hours."

"You still worrying, or is it the dreams?"

"Both, you know."

"We'll get through. Father knows what he's doing. You've got to trust a bit, try not to worry."

"It's not that."

"What, then?"

"When I close my eyes or try to sleep, I see them."

"Who?"

"Joseph and Amy."

"Well, of course you can, they're outside all day and sleep next to us."

"No, when I woke, before anyone." She sits, knees drawn tight under her chin. "I was first awake after η-space, everyone else still in stasis when I went to the lower deck and saw them. They waited for me, watched me get off the ladder, stared at me until Peter revived. Then they stopped, just went and stopped."

"No, that's impossible."

"They did. They looked at me. They know, I saw it in their eyes, they know."

"Know what?"

"What I did to them, that I'm to blame."

"What, you turned them like that and destroyed the spindleship?"

"I must have. I was last to go into stasis, it was my responsibility to make sure everything and everyone was fine, and I failed. They're like that because of me."

"No, you couldn't have. I mean all the automatics, the AI, the other ships. You couldn't have done it."

"I must have missed something, done something, even by accident I must have. No one else was awake, no one else could have."

"Come on. Didn't you tell me how wonderful the threeship was, how good the AI and all the fail-safes were?"

"Well, yes, I did."

"And you told me no matter what I or anyone else did, we couldn't get the AI or the ship into trouble."

"Yes, but…"

"So, even if you wanted to, you couldn't have."

"Maybe. But it doesn't help, that flight and everyone on it was my responsibility. I was senior steward, I failed, and they're my proof."

"Sometimes, no matter what, things happen. You're not to blame, no one is, it's just one of those things, a random event."

"But I still feel it. I can't escape it. When I'm busy, I don't think about it. But the moment I'm not, I see Joseph and Amy staring at me, watching me, accusing me.

When I sleep, all I dream about is people dying in η-space. Horrible, awful deaths. I can't sleep or relax until I'm so drained, I collapse."

"Maybe we've got to get your mind off those things, get you to wind down without thinking about it."

"And how do you suggest I do that?"

A stab of pain shoots through my left shoulder, I see the rock bounce high over Kell's head and skip across the field. I stand and turn in time to dodge the next one. Twenty meters away one boy tackles another, sends the pair of them to the ground in a flurry of kicks and punches. I curse vehemently then run towards them.

The two boys are locked together, neither one lands anything other than insults and curses, although by the looks of things, there has been some earlier success. I can't drag them apart; I'm content to wait for them to tire but it gets ugly, the one on top grabs a rock and raises it above his head. I send my foot into the boy's back, knock the wind out and sit as heavily as I can on the pair of them. I'm rewarded by grunts, attempts to dislodge me.

"Daniel! Aaron! Break it up." A feeble kick by one boy, a few rabbit punches from the other and I lean in, bear down with my knee on Aaron's shoulder. "I told you to quit it."

Daniel gets both arms free, tries to bench-press up. Another hand comes into view, bends Daniel's arm back to his neck. "Okay, okay, I'll quit," Daniel says.

I turn. Kell's beside me, clearly in control: "Self-defense technique. They teach you before you fly."

"I see, remind me never to get on your bad side." I look down. "If we let you get up, no more trouble, promise?"

They sit apart after a quick, mumbled agreement. No real damage, nothing out of the ordinary for a pair of fourteen-year-olds.

"What happened? You first, Aaron."

"He tripped me up, twice."

"And you, Daniel?"

"He stole my twigs."

"They weren't yours, I put them –"

"I put them there, I know 'cause –"

"You're lying, they were mine. I already had –"

"Shut up or I'll take this to your parents. All this is over a bunch of twigs?"

Daniel nods, Aaron shakes his head.

"What else, Aaron?"

Aaron hesitates, slides away from Daniel. "Last night, Daniel took more food than me, I got one bowl, he got two. It's not right they get more."

"We don't, no one does," Daniel says.

"I told you to shut it, Daniel. Last night, Aaron, you got your family's meal?"

"Yes."

"How many people in Daniel's family, including Mister and Mrs. Wagner?"

"I think nine in all."

"And yours?"

"Six."

"One of them's a baby, can't eat yet?"

"Yeah."

"So, you think maybe Daniel's family might need more food than yours if everyone gets the same?"

"I guess."

"You think Mrs. Lehmann's dumb enough to give out the wrong amount?"

Aaron examines his shoes. "No, no, she wouldn't."

I turn to Daniel. "What's the idea of throwing rocks?"

"I was trying to stop him."

"You know you nearly hit me twice?"

"No."

"What were you going to do with the one I caught you with?"

"Gonna hit him good, I was."

"You remember Cain and Abel?" Clearly they both do, we've all been told that Bible story. Not that I believe it, not now anyway, but it serves a purpose. "You would've killed him, then god would've cursed you forever."

I let the boys absorb it. Everyone's tense and drained. We all act strange, but at least the adults work it out, control themselves. But these two and the other kids? One slip up, one stupid moment could be a disaster.

I give them both a cold stare. "You're a pair of bloody idiots."

Their eyes widen. I smile to myself. Swearing's unknown to the Amish, the sole preserve of the English. At least they'll remember. "Both of you take ten minutes off, ask each other's forgiveness, then come back. Right?"

"Yes, yes, sir," they reply as they hurry off.

With Amish kids, it's easy, there's still built-in respect, Bible teaching. Any others, it wouldn't have worked.

"I never knew they fight like that, Henry."

"They don't. We're all on edge and nearly done in, so it's got to crack somewhere."

"You seem to be doing okay."

"Me? Seems to be is right. I've got my own problems."

"You've not said."

"It's not like we've had time."

"Well, we've got some now."

"It's nothing new or dramatic, Kell. It just looks like I'll be living close to them forever. I'm still getting used to the idea."

"You're not too happy being marooned?"

"Not totally, but there are some positives."

106

"Like?"

"Well, if you come closer, I'll explain."

Chapter Twenty

Greg

"FOUR OF PICKLES, three of jam, in the other cargo node, freeze-dried…"

The words wash over me; I tune the conversation out, the odd smile or nod of encouragement my only contribution. It's important to know how much food we have, but if it's pickles, canned tomato, or caviar, what's the difference? The only real question is how much each until the crops come in. If they're on time. Big if.

Another Sunday, an 'off service' Sunday but the day of rest remains sacrosanct. A chance to recharge, rest and plan. So, here we sit to dissect the final inventory, the final count of what we do and don't have. After four weeks, I'm convinced I'm no farmer and never will be, no matter how much these people try to encourage me.

I look around the circle. The same people I met the day I woke up have changed, some subtly, some dramatically. Everyone looks thinner, tired, and worn. Grime's the new black, a baleful, uniform tribal marker of shared experience. I see deeper changes evident in eyes and behavior, variations misplaced in a self-defined uniform community; or, perhaps, that reinforce their humanity.

There's a wariness when they talk with me, an outwardly cordial and friendly demeanor that, as the weeks tick along, is supplanted by caution. Not that there's open hostility or anger, but it's like I'm out of the club or being kept deliberately at a distance; so I'm always on edge, a touch defensive. For reasons I can't fathom, Cephas is the worst. Perhaps the first days on the plow together did it; my weakness was clear, but I pushed through.

Everyone now looks to Menno with a touch of deference. As much as Henry might not think it, Menno's clearly their leader. Whether by design or default, I don't know, but it's simply the case. As for Menno himself, it seems as he grows physically weaker, the inner man grows stronger, more determined, as if it's all a test of faith or stamina.

Kelli was a worry early on but now she and Henry are close, they find some solace in each other, partial recompense for what is lost. The shock of being marooned, the separation and uncertainty of his children and partner not knowing if he was dead or alive hit Peter hard. He's pulled inside himself, withdrawn to a shadow even as he finally starts to throw his weight in; as much as all of us have tried, he refuses to engage. Pen on the other hand seems more at home here than back on Earth. She's fitted in with the Amish kids, shown a maturity I never suspected was there.

Which leaves Lou. She sits beside me, locked in earnest conversation with Freda. They're nearly inseparable, they spend all day working together and most

108

of the evening in each other's company. I never imagined her able to stand, let alone function, in an open space, yet by some miracle, Freda helps her do it. Freda's clearly good for her, but I can't help but worry. Lou's always taken some joy in thinking herself 'spiritually open', whatever the hell that means.

It's gone quiet, Cephas stares at me. "We were wanting your thoughts about rationing."

"I thought we were."

"Yes, but now it's going to be stricter."

"How much stricter?"

"If we keep eating like we have, perhaps it will last three weeks. The trouble is the first crop will be twelve to fourteen weeks, sowing to harvest." Cephas holds a small tin in his hand, thumb on the top, little finger on the bottom. "This would be three days' ration per person for twelve weeks, give or take. So, any ideas would be welcome."

I turn to Menno. "How much food will the first harvest give?"

"That one acre? Usually one acre feeds one person for a year, but that is not one crop. Divided among us, it would last for five days, ten if we stretch it."

"Then the rest?"

"Another five weeks to plant from now, so it could all be ready in nineteen, twenty weeks. By the time we finish we will have tilled enough land for a year plus seed stock."

"If all goes well."

"God willing."

"God willing indeed, Menno, but if it takes fourteen weeks, we're two weeks short, and if the main crop's late or something happens, that's more trouble."

"So?"

"We should cut the ration lower, plan for fourteen weeks as insurance in case the first harvest's late."

There's a series of sharp gasps. Henry grabs my shoulder. "Greg, the Amish don't believe in insurance."

"What?"

"Insurance is an expression of lack of faith in God, one that we will have no truck with," Menno's voice cuts above the hubbub.

"You said it could take fourteen weeks, so it's just being prepared. I can't see the issue."

"The issue is that God will take care of us, so there is no need to insure in any way other than to be good stewards with what we have."

"That's all I mean, we've got to be careful and smart. We hardly know anything about this place, how the crops might go. We don't even know what season it is, if it even has seasons."

"It is moving to spring."

"What?"

109

"Spring. I feel Neueanbruch is coming to spring."

"What? God tell you that this morning, Menno?"

"No, He did not, but it is plain if you open your eyes."

"How can you be sure. I mean how can you –"

Lou turns to me, brow furrowed. "Because he's a farmer, Greg."

"But that was on Earth, Lou, and this isn't Earth, in case you haven't noticed."

"What does that matter? It's the same isn't it, stick a seed in the ground and wait. How much farming have you done before this?"

"But to say it's spring's ridiculous."

Lou shakes her head, turns back to Freda. "It doesn't matter, Greg. Let it go."

"What would you have us do, Greg, wait one year until we see it to satisfy you?" Menno asks. "We have no choice, if you choose not to believe me, it is up to you."

"I don't. You could be right or wrong, but in any case we should prepare for the worst. It would be prudent to plan on fourteen weeks. That's not being faithless, it's being sensible, using your own estimate."

"Then fourteen weeks it is. I suspect the difference in rations will not be all that great anyway."

Cephas holds up the tin again. "About three-quarters each, for three days."

"Do the children need as much as the adults? Back home Pen didn't."

"I don't think so, but it makes it difficult if we do it that way." Cephas picks up a jar; the tin fits easily in his hand, the jar extends out top and bottom. "It will be hard enough working out how it goes, how to divide it when nothing's the same size."

"And that's forgetting what's in them. Does a jar of jam equal a tin of soup?"

Cephas passes me the tin. "No idea, Greg, it's just another problem."

I study the label carefully. "And what would a week of these prune things do? Who knows?"

"It is best if Rachel coordinates the food, cooks communally. To make it easier. The boys could keep hunting, get more of those things they found."

"I wonder what other bounty God has left for us here. We have not looked, perhaps there are fish in the waters," Menno says.

"Henry and I plan to find out, maybe next week go out to that mountain range and look for what we can use rather than other people."

"I think it unwise. We cannot afford it."

"Why? The heavy work's over, the fields are turned and you've only the one harrow. It's not vital we're here."

"There is more than enough work to do, everyone is needed. We cannot afford to lose one, let alone two."

Lou grabs my arm. "Listen to him, Greg, he knows what he's doing. You don't."

"It seems to me that planting's where it gets easier, not harder."

"Greg, please, shut up. You're embarrassing me."

"There is more than you think, Greg, from planting to harvest, and between there is work and more work," Menno says.

"Surely not that much, just sit back and watch it grow? Doesn't sound too hard to me."

"We have no fertilizer, no pesticides. We will have to tend it all by hand. And build storage, start on shelter. There is no such thing as down time."

"And I suppose after harvest it all starts again?"

"That is what God gave us, the way it has always been, a life on the land."

"So that's it, Menno? As far as you're concerned, there's no time now and there never will be, it's an endless cycle and you think the whole planet's like the tiny piece Henry and I saw?"

"Neueanbruch is empty, God's gift to us, ours to work, which means hard work and no time to go off on pointless exercises to confirm what we already know."

"That's a pretty blinkered view, even from you."

Lou's fingers dig into my arm; if her nails were intact, she'd draw blood. "Don't insult him, you're making a fool of yourself."

"He cannot insult me, Louise, I do not have pride to be wounded. We have different perspectives, and I am trying to help him see the practicalities of his situation."

"And I don't mean to be insulting. There could be things out there we can use or might help us survive that we don't know about. I need to satisfy my curiosity sooner or later because until I do, I won't be able to settle into the kind of life you're mapping out."

"You do not want to be part of our community?"

"No. Yes. I mean, look. I've never wanted to be a farmer, I never met one until I met you. I'm not good at it but if it's what I have to do, I have to know the whole planet's like this."

"I understand. Not all Amish are farmers by choice or desire, we have members who have other trades. The physical nature of our work serves a purpose in our faith, it is not the other way around."

The small circle of bonnets and hats nod.

"But you are ahead of yourself, Greg. It is not about the next twenty or forty years of your life but the immediate survival of your family. The only time when your trip is possible, barely possible, is between planting and harvest. If it helps settle your mind. Any other time is out of the question."

"I need to do it. And it will benefit everyone. So, after the planting?"

"Yes."

"And Henry?"

"If he wants to. We do not control him or you."

I stand, brush off my pants. I stare at Menno with what I hope is my impassive, calm, poker face. I'm boxed in. Again. He's right and he's wrong, he's taken the moral high ground and the group with him. Why do I feel like I'm asking for permission?

"Fine. I'll wait four, five weeks until planting's done."

"And back in good time for harvest?"

"Of course."

I turn my back and walk off.

Chapter Twenty-One

Greg

NO MATTER HOW the day goes, I look forward to it, to stretch out and rest rather than curl, lie, or hang across a row of chairs. With one cargo node half empty, the landing site's a jumble of odds and sods, ironmongery. The upside is the newly liberated space into which half of us shifted. The dismembered seats make relatively soft bedding, space and chairs for outside.

Tonight, I go to sleep early, climb into the Pegasus as the frost descends so I can stay away from all of them and simmer down. I pull my hands into the jumper's sleeves, wriggle close to the hull, plant my feet against the bulkhead. The sky darkens; in a few minutes it will be black, lit up later as the stars arrive, but it is no matter – I'll sleep through it all. We can't reset the clear hull, I don't want it opaque, I find the confines of the Pegasus claustrophobic.

I close my eyes and try to make sense of the day. I'm being manipulated, boxed into decisions and actions I don't agree with, a situation I found myself in my entire life. Why do I feel the need to lash out now, break through it even if I can't, to try to make them know how I feel? I know Menno's right on at least one point, but it still doesn't change my desire to fight for the hell of it. Damned shame I didn't do that back at Uni with Santosh, how would my life have played out if I had? That particular 'what if' haunted me for decades, it's about time I put it to bed and act rather than dwell on the past. I sigh, shift until my hips find the right place, back to the hull as tiredness overtakes me.

It's Lou I can't understand, she might like them but where was she when I needed backup? She's supposed to be on my side, isn't she? The questions repeat themselves as I slip away.

It might be her body against me, the familiar scent of her breath or warmth that signals my unconscious she's here, but it is undoubtedly the finger poked deliberately and firmly into my side that rouses me. I keep my eyes shut, press against the hull as I brush her hand away.

"I said, are you awake?"

"No."

"Don't lie. We need to talk."

"Tomorrow. Tired."

Another poke, another failed attempt to move away. "No, now. You've got some explaining to do."

I crack open my eyes. In the darkness, I barely make out her face. I drape one arm across her waist. It's removed forcefully.

"Stop that, I'm serious."

113

"Explain what?"

"What you did in front of everyone. What's the idea?"

"It was just a difference of opinion."

"But the way you went at him? Seriously?"

"So maybe I need to be a little more forthright, opinionated. It's about time I was."

"You've been getting more aggressive since that idiot at the spaceport."

"I wouldn't call it that."

"I would. Menno's a good man, he wants what's best for all of us."

"And I'm not?"

"I'm not saying that, but he knows what he's talking about and it would be smart to listen to him."

"He doesn't, Lou, he's deluded or kidding himself."

"You shouldn't put him down because he's different, because they have beliefs you don't."

"I don't, as long as he doesn't try to jam it down my throat, I'm fine. No one else has gone more than thirty minutes away and he's giving the planet a name, saying it's empty and made for them? He doesn't know, you don't know, and I won't know until I take another look."

"Oh, that's it, you're peeved 'cause he doesn't want you two to run off again."

"Of course I am. He's not my leader or minister or..."

"Shhh."

"...or whatever they call it, and I don't see why I need anyone's permission when it's in our best interests."

"But he's doing that, too. Freda says he could grow anything anywhere he's that good. It's just his manner to say things direct."

"I've met his type before. They say it's all best for you when they take advantage, but once you're no use anymore, it's finished. Don't forget where our friends went when we needed them for Pen."

"That's not right, not everyone ran. Some stuck it out right to the end. You've got to let go of the paranoia, think about us, me, Penny."

"That's exactly what I'm doing."

"Which is what Menno's doing."

"And that's what worries me. He's planning a life for us based on the way they live. I won't do it. I don't want to be boxed in by people or jobs or cities or anything like before. I hate what I was, what I had to do and I'm not going to anymore. It's not for me and it's not for you or Pen."

She's quiet, I can feel her breathe but there's nothing else. "Lou?" The silence lengthens, broken only by a chorus of gentle snores. "Lou, did you hear me?"

"Yes. Yes, I did. I don't agree with you. For me and Penny it could, I mean, it might be a good place."

"Seriously?"

"I wouldn't have gone near them on Earth but here I feel connected and welcome. I can be me and not worry about how they're linked socially or professionally or who they gossip to. I never really had a family as a kid, but you've no idea how bad it was. I tried to give Penny what I didn't have, it was impossible before but now, with them, maybe I can. Do you know they let their kids visit each other, alone, by themselves? I never dreamt anyone could do that. But they do."

"You think so? They don't even try to educate them. How do you think Pen's going to take that? Can you make a call based on a few weeks?"

"You have. You love this place, all the empty and quiet and cold. You probably want it to stay that way, no one to touch it or spoil it."

"You could be right."

"I know I am. Remember Angie from your squad? I e-lunched with her once."

"And?"

"You know what they called you? The 'wire flier', because of all those jaunts you'd take above the grid. The squad tracked you, had a betting pool on when you'd go and for how long."

"They did? I never knew."

"She thought you were crazy. Like the rest of them. Like I do."

It stings. "Lou."

"What?"

"Earlier, in front of them, you didn't back me up, you took their side. Why?"

"Apart from you being wrong and making an idiot of yourself? You're changing and I don't like it, you're getting further and further away from me while everyone else gets closer. It's easier to talk to Freda than you now. Goodnight."

She rolls over, moves away to leave a small, but distinct, gap between us. As the cold seeps in I fall asleep, catch part of a whispered conversation: "Mum, why does Dad hate Menno?"

"I don't know if he does, Penny. He just thinks he's better than him."

"Is he?"

"Maybe, maybe not. Depends."

"Mahlon says I should pray for him."

"Uh-huh."

"Should I?"

"It can't hurt, I guess. Now go to sleep."

Chapter Twenty-Two

Louise

I ADJUST THE shoulder strap, help the seed bag sit gently on my stomach then resume my slow, legs apart waddle along the furrow. A handful of seed dribbles into the valley as my feet slide along the peaks. Freda follows, collapses the soil back in, tamps it down. It's monotonous, boring work; but it's vital we get it right. I concentrate, keep a steady pace, deposit the exact amount of seed.

Since sunrise we've been here, the sun behind a perpetual overcast barely warm enough to chase off the evening cold. Freda's unusually quiet, speaks only when we change over at the end of each furrow. It suits me, the usual daydreams of food and warm baths replaced by re-runs of last night's argument with Greg. I haven't laid eyes on him today. Perhaps he's plowing somewhere, it doesn't matter.

The end of the furrow comes suddenly, jars of water sit to one side. I take the seed bag off, turn to swap it for the mattock.

"Perhaps a break, Louise?"

"Great idea." I flop down. Just like being pregnant, my back screams. At least I won't have nine straight months of it. We sit in silence and rest, stare at nothing until Freda seems to reach a decision. She puts her jar down, turns to me. "Last night I couldn't help hear you and Greg."

"Oh."

"It's hard not to, there's so little privacy. Normally I block it out, but if you need to talk, I'm here."

"How much did you hear?"

"Everything."

"Are there things Menno doesn't know about you?"

"I don't think so. It's hard to hide, the gmay's small. They talk among themselves about themselves, so he would know, like I do about him."

"There's things Greg doesn't know about me, about my past. I've tried but he can be insular and uninterested, so I gave up." I tug my jumper over my hands. "When I was young, home wasn't a nice place. My dad loved Mum, but she didn't, not quite the same way at least. She had lots of uncles and cousins she spent time with, and Dad drank more and more as I got older. It wasn't until later I put two and two together."

"You must've found that hard."

"At the time I thought it was normal. By the time I found out it wasn't, I didn't have a family anymore."

"What happened to them?"

116

"I don't know. I was taken away, my brother and sister as well. I've not heard of any of them since."

"I can't imagine that. My family's scattered but we still keep in touch. And the gmay's like an extended family, not exactly, but close enough. You must have had friends, some support where you lived?"

"Some, but it's different, everyone's a bit wary. Having Greg in Enforcement didn't help."

"Maybe there's a bright side to all this. You might not have wanted it, but you're stuck with us. That might give you a little support."

"It already feels good, and I know Penny's getting on, but I'll always feel like an outsider."

"Why? No one's pushing you away."

"Does god punish you for doing bad things?"

"Eventually yes, but if you mean now, then I don't think so."

"I had a friend, she believed the universe ran on karma. You get back what you put in, you know, good for good, bad for bad. Eventually, anyway."

"Sounds like reaping what you sow, but honestly, if we were all punished for the bad we've done, we'd all be grease spots. Why do you ask?"

"I think it's my fault we're here."

"How? You can't be serious."

"It's karma or god's punishment and it's caught all of you up in it. A few years back we found out Penny was seriously ill and…"

I tell her the whole story, not an emotion-laced torrent but a calm, business-like recital from the first diagnosis through Greg's meeting with Santosh, then that woman with Jonathon. It doesn't take long. The silence after I finish drags on, planting forgotten.

"It sounds like you had no choice. It's not a thing I'd want to go through. Anyway, you're looking at it the wrong way."

"How?"

"Perhaps your 'karma' was Juuttua, a place you didn't want. Neueanbruch may be a positive, you being caught up with us."

"I've never thought of that."

"It's just perspective. Why does it bother you? We can't change the past."

"It's what Menno said the other day, about the community and us being part of it. Would you still want us if we were responsible for stranding you here?"

"Of course. If you told Menno, he might even thank you."

It nearly drags a smile out of me. "You could be right. This place is made for him."

"It seems so. Greg, I think not."

"It is, Freda, he's starting to love it but he's different, he's no farmer and there's no place here for Enforcement. He's changing and I'm not sure where we're heading."

117

"The only thing you can be sure of is that it's going to change everyone in ways you don't expect. It's wonderful to watch each other change over a lifetime."

"Yes, but children grow old too quick, go and lead their own lives before you know it."

"I wasn't talking about children, I was talking about husbands and wives."

"But you said a lifetime."

"Well yes, that's how long you marry for."

"No."

"No?"

"No, I've never heard of such a thing. Not nowadays, anyway. Who does?"

"We do, we all do. You don't?"

"No one does. Marriage contract is ten years plus two renewals up to thirty years, long enough to bring up a child properly. I mean seriously, who could spend a hundred years married to the same person?"

"I could, Menno could, we all will. How long have you and Greg been married?"

"We're into our second contract cycle, about twelve years in total."

"So, in eighteen years?"

"It would be finished, we'd go our own way."

"It's a strange, worldly thing that is, and not one for me." Freda stands, hoists the seed bag over her shoulder. "It's not God's way and not good for children."

I heft the mattock ready to turn sod over seeds. "Anyway, it's irrelevant, that life's gone. It's not like I can replace Greg."

"Would you want to?"

I mull it over for the rest of the day, play with it like chewing gum. Technically, we aren't contracted now. But do I want it to end? Do I want it to continue? By sundown, I still haven't reached an answer.

Chapter Twenty-Three

Menno

EIGHT BOXES AROUND another pretend to be chairs around a table. It matters little, a home is not judged by the greatness of furniture but by the hearts it contains. To my right sits Henry, around us my five other children. It is as it should be, and again Neueanbruch proves itself the place I know it to be.

Henry rubs his forearm.

"What is the matter?"

"A cut, Father. Nothing really."

"Let me see."

Henry rolls up his sleeve to show a ten centimeter gash weeping clear fluid.

"When did you do that?"

"About a fortnight ago on the plow."

"And you have left it untreated?"

"No, I've seen to it as best I can. It doesn't want to heal."

"Perhaps some salt water, cover it up?"

"Yeah, maybe."

Freda returns with the day's meal, sets the paltry assortment down. Orva fidgets, my youngest as usual unable or unwilling to be quiet. Freda clasps Orva's hands together in her lap. I lower my head, lead my family in silent prayer.

"Reach and help yourself."

The traditional invitation is all well and good when the table is full, but here, now, it is tinged with irony. One jar catches my hunger's attention, Freda's home-canned beef. I control myself, do not move; Henry and Freda likewise. The children pitch in. Only Luke seems aware of the number of mouths, the amount of food, the impossible implied statistic. He tries to be restrained, as restrained as a sixteen-year-old can be.

Only when the children's assault is finished do I lean in, take a spoon of pickled cabbage and one of strawberry jam as my portion. At least there is water in abundance, enough to fill an empty stomach. I make a show and savor each mouthful, lean back as if I have finished off a suckling pig. I conjure up a barely adequate belch and smile. Freda gives me a strange look that accepts and exposes my charade; all these years and there is nothing I can get past her, nothing she does not see.

I lower my head, lead the silent prayer that marks the end of the meal.

"Orva, Elizabeth, Isaac, you are excused to your chores," such as they are, little make-times to keep habits for later when they will be needed. "Mahlon, Luke, return the containers to Mrs. Lehmann and then you are both excused."

Contented peace suffuses me, covers up the continual demands of my stomach. It is as it should be, my family intact at table, wife to one side, eldest son to the other. Admittedly Henry is only partly back, but time is on my side. "It is good to have you share a meal with us, Henry."

"There's not many options around here. It's not as if I was a complete stranger before."

"You were never there when I was at home, even when we were planning to move, you seldom stayed."

Henry toys with a cup, spins it, stares at it intently. His actions remind me of my father. "You never made it easy. I couldn't let myself get chained."

"It was for your own good."

"But it wasn't what I needed. If I wasn't supposed to think, why was I given this mind? To sit, to farm, to be stifled and then shunned when I eventually broke?"

"No. That would never happen."

"Of course it would. The ordnung chafed at me day and night, and if I joined the gmay, I would have let all of you down. At least this way I can keep in touch."

"You know it is up to each person, their own conscience. Nobody would force you to join."

"There's no way you wouldn't have, especially after the lot fell to you. The minister's eldest son not part of the gmay? Impossible."

"That is not true. I would never have done that."

"Why?"

"Because before you were born, I saw what becomes of it."

Freda turns to me. "You've never mentioned such a thing."

Neueanbruch is changing me: I am talkative, open, more ready to speak than listen. Is it bad or simply what needs to be? What do I make of it, how do I use it wisely? There is silence, Freda and Henry wait for me to continue.

"When I was Mahlon's age, when Bishop Jesse was a baby, our families were neighbors. His father was a stern man, our minister, and I was close to his son, Timothy. Timothy was quiet, easily shoved around, the sort that would churn things over, things would brew inside him for weeks on end. When he turned seventeen his father pushed him to join the gmay, told him again and again that if he did not, he would lead other children astray, make his father's words in the gmay weak and ineffective."

"The Sunday he was baptized, he told me he did not want to do it; he wanted to wait, see if it was right for him, but because of his father he did it anyway. For a while it looked like everything had worked out. But then the shouting started, the arguments. Timothy could not stay clear of the ordnung for one minute, and each time his father came down harder, more demanding. He could not leave, he had no money, no job, no place to go. The longer he stayed the worse things got."

I pause, no one speaks. After all this time the memory is still raw, the images vivid; I take a deep breath, calm myself and continue.

"Jesse, his mother and baby sister visited with us that day. Late in the afternoon, after they left, we heard the screams. Timothy had taken an axe, killed his father and six of his brothers and sisters, then hung himself. His mother walked in as he pushed off the stool, swinging right in front of her."

"They had only been buried six weeks when she drowned herself. We looked through her things, read the note Timothy left her, tried to make sense of it all. The gmay broke apart. Everyone sold up and left. Jesse and the baby were all that remained of the family, they had a cousin at our old gmay, so my family took them there. We never went back."

"You never said, no one's ever mentioned any of this," Henry says.

"I had no need, and Jesse may have tried to forget. It is not something to be remembered."

"If I'd known, understood, it might have been different."

"Perhaps, perhaps not. I would never force you, but I will not cease praying for you, trying to bring you back."

"If you had talked to me instead of being so stiff..."

"And if you had listened instead of turning your face? But it is the rod for our backs, we do not talk, no man does among us for fear of pride, fear of showing anything other than humility. Even fathers to sons."

"Or sons to fathers."

"In this place I feel it change, things are different. A new world, new challenges, new bridges for old."

"A new way of thinking, too."

"In what way?"

"For the gmay, the ordnung. What use are injunctions to live apart from the world when there is no world?"

"It is our faith, our guidebook, the wisdom of the gmay. I will not toss them aside as an old rag. First the ordnung, then the Martyrs Mirror. What next, the Bible? Impossible."

"That's not what I mean. Why make the ordnung heavier? Is it better to follow ten rules or ten thousand?"

"Would it change your mind and keep you with us?"

"I don't know. But the wall would be a little lower."

Henry stands, walks away.

"You should have told us years ago," Freda says.

"Perhaps. I have not felt comfortable until now. The time was right."

"He'll come back to us, Menno, I believe it."

"As do I, but the company he keeps worries me."

"Greg?"

"He could be a good farmer, he has the strength of will and mind, could even be on the fringe of the community. But he does not respect our beliefs. The closer Henry is to him the harder it will be. Then there are the rest."

"It's hard on them. We have the gmay, each other, our lives with God. They left everything behind and lost it all."

"I know, even so Louise does not have the same influence or make the same noises as Greg. You and she have spent a lot of time together, you know that."

"She's said nothing against us, she has her issues but nothing of concern. We talked about her place in the community, there's hope she'll fit in."

"I do not want to abandon these people. They are as much my responsibility as the gmay. But the chance to make this place what it should be? I cannot let that slip."

"Would they be the world, in the community but no temptation to the children?"

"No. Simply not living the right way is worry enough, they do not have to bring anything other than their disbelief to be a threat."

"So, where does that leave you? If he doesn't fit or at least doesn't work against us? And it's not only Greg, there's Kelli and Peter."

"I have not forgotten."

"What if he doesn't change?"

"I will not turn them away. It is not the right thing to do. They cannot survive without us and we need them. It is later that worries me."

"Why, when there's every hope God works on him to the good?"

"If it does not happen, if it is the same two or three years away when we are established, then perhaps it must be as it was going to be, us and the world outside. As it was on Earth, as it would be on Juuttua."

"Henry and Kelli are close. If they stay that way and he doesn't return, would you turn him away?"

"No, he has been given back. I will not lose him again."

"What of the gmay? Louise is close to Ida and Mae, and Rachel grows attached to Penny for what she's done for Joseph and Amy."

"Only Cephas and Nathan have said anything. They are wary, Nathan for his children and Cephas for those he is yet to have."

Mahlon and Luke walk toward us, each carries a small leather clad book. I nod, rise, motion Freda to do the same.

"Devotions, then sleep. Conversation can wait."

"God will take care of it."

"In the meantime, prayer and work. In any event, it is not my decision, it is the gmay's."

Chapter Twenty-Four

Henry

I'M SHAKEN AWAKE, open my eyes to Mahlon's silhouette. Is it already three hours? It doesn't matter, there's no way to know; anyhow, sleep's a fickle and fleeting friend. I stand, give my brother a hug, then make my way across. The air is crisp, the stars bright and steady, the threeship cold against the still background of Neueanbruch. My eyes have adjusted, improved over the weeks, yet all I want to see deserts me. All else pales away. I make sure my clothes are correct, climb into the cargo node.

I nod a greeting to Mary Aylmer. She nods back from her seat. I can't risk talk, can't trust my voice not to catch, stumble or worse. If Mary wishes to, then perhaps, until then silence will do. I cross to one of two identical, hastily fashioned boxes. She looks peaceful in the faint starlight, calm, asleep after a long day of play; the illusion is shattered by the awkward lie of her neck, small indentations, missing hair to one side. The emptiness steals up within me to ask for tears I have exhausted, answers to questions I do not want. Half of me lives in shocked, enveloping silence; half screams to run to the faith I turned my back on for any scrap of hope. I am left marooned, nowhere with nothing. Seven years is too young, a cruel and senseless end to a life of promise and expectation before it could be glimpsed. Elizabeth, my darling sister, why?

I move a few steps to the second box that holds Emily Aylmer. In death, as in life, they are inseparable; if it weren't for that, Elizabeth might still be alive. Somehow, they'd gotten into the threeship's cargo node, opened the upper door then slipped to their deaths. It was no one's fault, everyone's fault. Everyone doubts, wonders if we should have kept a closer eye, sealed the cargo node, whatever. Both families blame themselves, forgive the other, cling to faith that it's all in god's hands. As now their daughters.

I sit, numb from two days and nights vigil. Tomorrow the funeral. Tiredness upon emptiness, I fight to keep my eyes open.

"Do you think there will be kind weather tomorrow?"

"Perhaps so, Mrs. Aylmer, the mornings seem drier."

"Emily never liked getting wet."

"I'll make sure she's dry."

The morning comes, as it must, to carry my sister to the edge of the trees, the place we settled on. I'm at the rear, one arm across Cephas beside me, the other on Nathan in front as four of us carry Elizabeth along. I am pulled in, the strength and acceptance of the gmay shared freely, openly with me. My grief is their grief, but their certitude can't cross the barrier to me no matter how I crave it. Together, with the Aylmers, we are encircled by the gmay, two coffins, and Father, Kelli and the others on the fringe. I rejoin my family; Mom leans on me, tears enough for us all. Grief weighs her eyes to rest in elongated bags, tiredness etches in lost sleep. She's aged years in days, drawn and stooped as if the wind's sucked from her. I pull her close, tighten my arm as if to stop her following her daughter into the grave. I remind myself to be the dutiful son, the reliable son, play the game and take the face of the Amish son, if only to help her.

"The kingdom of heaven is promised to the little children, Henry, for her, for Emily."

"I know, she will never know evil, never know temptation." I stumble over the words even as I speak them.

"I'd rather see her called home than grow up, fall into sin and be lost forever." She means it, yet the tightness of her hand in mine and the heaving of her chest betrays the lie, the injustice of a mother burying her child. "I will not lose you."

"I know."

"No, Henry Stoll, hear me. I will not lose you."

I can't lie, I can't promise what's not within me. I kiss the top of her head. Older. When did she become this short, frail thing beside me? Where's the strong woman who would start before we rose and not stop until we were asleep? Has this stolen her from me?

Father coughs, motions us to prayer. I lower my head, hunt in vain for the right words, words I was taught and memorized, but instead come up with hate and venom. I try to banish them from my mind, silently plead my father to begin, drown out the empty in my mind and heart.

His amen sounds out. I lift my head to see my grandfather's eyes wear my father's face. The strength is gone, peeks out as a question, a vulnerability and uncertainty there for an instant while his guard's down.

"The Lord has given, the Lord has taken away. Blessed be the name of the Lord," he begins; and the rest is lost to me, a drone from other times, words that bring no solace. He finishes quickly, without haste, and I am lowered into Elizabeth's grave after her, feet astride her coffin to take spade after spade of dirt from Cephas, lay it gently, precisely down so it makes no noise, that she is respected as she is committed to the ground. Her grave filled, I move to Emily's.

We regard the two small mounds in silence. Father walks over, stands between myself and Isaac Aylmer, places one hand on each of our shoulders. We respond, reach out to others in turn until every man, woman and child are linked, a physical reminder of shared pain, shared suffering, shared destiny. He calls us to the Lord's Prayer, and we respond, join the incantation as one, voices soft then rise, grow strong, soar into the mountains and plains. The normal dedication of obedience and acceptance of god's will is more, an affirmation to assert the faith of the gmay upon Neueanbruch, that their will shall be imposed and they will not be broken.

One by one they disperse, until I am left with my family. We tarry a while, turn, make our way to the threeship. Halfway back, Father stops, turns to face the younger children. "You know there is no reason for us to come here again."

"Why?" asks Mahlon.

"She is not there, she is in Heaven. One day, one day long from now, we will all be together again."

Chapter Twenty-Five

Greg

"YOU OKAY, GREG?"

I look up into Lou's face; her hair's always in a bun now, tucked under a soiled bonnet. I take my finger out of my mouth carefully, hide it behind my palm as I drop my hand to my lap. "Yeah, think I had something stuck in my teeth."

"One way to get another meal."

"You're okay? I mean, out here by yourself?"

"A bit, I can manage if I can see someone. Thanks for noticing." She straightens, lifts the buckets. "Have to go, get more water."

I watch her walk to Pen then set off for the stream. A slight chill catches me from the inside, she's a little aloof, more formal as if she plays a role not a life. I'm too tired to think why and I can't get enthusiastic about anything. I'm an automaton driven to do what I must to get by, get the planting done so I can go. Anyway, I've got my own problems.

I bring my finger back, watch in weird distraction as a few crimson drops fall to the ground. My tongue finds the spot in my mouth, I swear I feel the tooth move as I run my tongue over the top. Add it to the list, Greg, add it to the list. I look around, everyone's head down doing one thing or another; only the youngest aren't out here laboring all day, every day, slowly but surely grinding themselves into dust. I lift my shirt, rub my hand across my side. It emerges thinly coated with translucent red-yellow as it has done all week. I stand, roll my jumper back over my shirt, return to Cephas and the rock.

He doesn't see me. I'm practically beside him as he swivels his head left-right and spits. I watch a rose-colored tadpole soar away. He's said nothing, none of them have, maybe my problems aren't mine alone. I get down on my knees, scrabble in the dirt. At least now, there's a mattock in my hands.

"What color?"

One thing about them, they're direct and have no sense of tact. There's an obsessive interest in the color of everything coming out of everyone. "Sunny yellow, egg yolk."

"You should drink more water."

"Can't, saving it for my first bath."

I don't even get a grunt in response. They have no sense of humor. How'd Henry make it out with his intact?

It takes us the better part of an hour to clear around it, undermine the edges as much as we can. Roughly cigar shaped and twice as long as a man it lies

126

impassively, daylight under both ends. We tried once to shift it and nearly broke our backs in the process.

"We have to get rid of it?" I ask.

"No choice, it's right in the middle."

"Can't lift it by hand, too smooth."

"Perhaps if we modify the plow harness, get a few more people?"

"Might work."

Cephas returns a few minutes later with harnesses, help, and a sheet of threeship skin. We pass the harness under one end of the boulder, then across our shoulders. Menno and Henry are at the other end, mattocks wedged under it. Mahlon stands in front, threeship skin in hand.

Cephas grabs my shoulder. "When I say, backs straight and push with your legs, we only need daylight to slip the skin under it. One, two, three, go."

I didn't know anything could be that heavy, I think my knees are going to buckle when Cephas calls the okay. I sink down, the boulder settles with a rattle and crack on the threeship skin; the five of us drag the boulder out and away. Nearly spent we lie against it. Three weeks ago, it would have been easier, we were stronger, but now I'm drained before I begin. Too much work, not enough food; I don't know if I'll be strong enough to go on soon.

Henry points off to one side. "Some old friends have come for a look."

Three bison crest the rise and meander in our general direction. My stomach comes up with the idea a split second before my brain. "Hey, Henry, do you think –"

"I'm way ahead of you." He goes to the harnesses, unbuckles the traces, and tosses one to me. "Which one, Greg?"

"Might as well try for the biggest. Any idea how?"

"I thought you had a plan."

"You were the farmer."

"Farmer maybe, animal catcher, no."

I hear the crunch of grass in mouth, the smells and grunts of feeding animals. I slip the trace through its buckle, make a loop and small leash. I move closer. The bison favors me with a short glance.

"Hope that one's docile, Greg."

"Not as much as I do."

Mouth full of grass, it lifts its head as I drape the loop around its neck. It gives me one glance, turns to see the leash in my hand and resumes grazing. I turn and shrug at Henry; he shrugs back. A small crowd behind him nods.

I move two steps ahead of it until the leash is horizontal, then give a gentle tug. It takes one step, stops as the leash slackens. I walk slowly, keep the leash taut; the bison follows.

Henry shakes his head. "That's crazy. Are they all like that?"

"Only one way to find out."

Within minutes, Henry has another in tow. Behind us, the other grazes contentedly.

"What do we do now?" Henry asks.

"I've no idea. Menno, have you ever done this?"

"Butchered an animal? Of course, but not one this big. Perhaps it is the same."

"We can't do it here, and three at once may not be a good idea."

"Yes, only one and closer is better. There are other things we can use them for. If we tether the leader, the other will stay."

"But which one is it?"

"If you take yours to the left and Henry takes his to the right, we will see."

We set off, Henry with two bison in tow. Pen bounces along beside me.

"Can I have a ride?"

"No, it might be dangerous."

"But Betsy looks cute!"

"Who's Betsy?"

"She is."

"Don't get too attached, you know what's going to happen."

"What?"

"Betsy's, I mean, she's going to be dinner."

"Really?"

"Yes, she's not a pet."

"I still want a ride."

"The answer's still no."

"Can I drive?"

It's hopeless. I hand over the leash, watch her lead it like a pet dog. Henry takes his two between the Pegasus and the trees, Cephas follows with a crudely fashioned stake and a coil of rope. As we near the Pegasus, I take over from Pen. Menno rushes ahead, stands in a small group with an assortment of business-like knives, pots and pans.

"You do not have to watch, English, if it will make you uncomfortable."

"No thanks, Menno, I'm fine."

"Good."

I hold the leash tight, stand my ground.

Menno hefts an axe, feels its weight and grip, turns the blunt edge forwards. "It needs to be done quickly, not prolong the pain. If you could raise the beast's head?"

I lift the leash, the bison's head follows. Menno brings the axe down above its eyes. It impacts with a crack – the beast falls, tearing the leash from my hands. Menno flips the axe over and with three strikes severs head from body, sending dark violet blood over my shoes.

"Every piece of the animal is of use," Menno says, "nothing is wasted. Except the blood. That we are unprepared for."

I help butcher it, fascinated as piece after piece, layer after layer is flensed, examined, then hurried away. I watch Orva wrap a length of intestine around her neck and follow her brother away.

"The children seem used to this."

"It's a natural part of life, simply the way it is," Henry says, one hand on the bison's foot as the other chops at its knee. "She's fine. From about five, we start to kill chickens for dinner." He straightens, pulls the shank free and hands it to Pen. "That one to Mrs. Lehman, kid. Anyway, it's best to know where food comes from, not think it's from a slot or a bot and that's it."

It's nearly too much, I'm going to explode but, like the rest of them, I try to cram more in. Weeks living out of strictly rationed jars and tins, hunger tied down by self-control and group pressure, goes up in a puff of bison-flavored smoke. We barely manage to stop ourselves eating the meat raw, wait until it's barely cooked to descend on it.

I add to the chorus of self-satisfied belches. Amazing what a little food can do, how small things quickly change how you feel. I wipe my hands on my trousers, mix dirt and grease on both, then run my fingers through my tangled beard in case any scraps caught hold. Cephas does likewise opposite; for all the minor irritations, he still manages a smile, a nod. He's a grot, barely recognizable. Hair longer, unkempt beard, filth-caked skin and clothes, he isn't the worst; but for the dresses, I can't tell the men from the women. I look at myself with new eyes, don't like what I see. Or smell.

I go into the Pegasus, emerge with a set of stupidly ill-suited clothes I brought from Earth. "I've had enough."

"Of?"

"Smelling like something dropped out of an animal's rear end, Henry."

"Oh."

"I'm going for a bath, wash my clothes, see what it's like to be human. I'll be out past the third bend downstream, so if nudity offends, don't go there."

"What about soap?"

"Doesn't matter, I'll scrape myself with sand or rocks, whatever."

Henry laughs. "Hang on, I'm coming, too. Let me get a change."

Everyone's on their feet, in and out of the Pegasus. Freda points one finger and serious eyes at me. "The women and children will be upstream. Keep your distance."

I raise both hands in mock surrender. Henry grabs me.

"Ready?"

We passed the spot I had in mind when we came back from our walk. I make my way to it, Henry and Cephas beside me, men and boys strung out behind.

It's not far, I'm naked by the time I reach the edge. I put my clean clothes on the ground, hold tight to my dirties and jump as far as I can to hit the ice-cold water in a ball. A series of yelps and splashes announce the arrival of the others. I move to the far side, slap my clothes hard against the rocks; one dip in the water, three slaps again and again. I'm rewarded by chocolate brown, brick red and caramel rivulets. Satisfied, I move to the other side, throw my wet clothes to the ground, then sink my hand into the silt. I pull it back full of coarse red-black gravel, slap it on my forearm and rasp it back and forth. It's sandpaper, scours and tears against my filth-encrusted skin. I drop my arm into the water, rinse it to reveal clean, fresh, olive-brown skin then repeat the process over the rest of my body. Except my back. That I can't manage; I try to scrape it on the rocks when Henry comes over, grabs my shoulders and spins me around.

"Here, let me do that." Hands like buckets silt me, drive it into my back in a circular, deliberate motion. Henry pushes me under, sluices it off my back. "Return the favor?"

"Yeah, fine."

I turn and face him as he turns away. I've adopted the same behavior I'd been taught at the Enforcement sauna; don't stare, don't compare, don't comment. I break all three rules immediately. An elongated wound festers across Henry's chest, ends in a series of huge purple-black bruises.

"How long you had that, Henry?"

"What?"

"Across your chest. The gash."

"It's nothing, hardly notice it."

"Be serious, it's at least thirty centimeters long."

"Since we started using the harness, maybe three, four weeks, I don't know."

I straighten with hands full of silt, Henry's back to me. I stare nonplussed, it's crisscrossed by broad lines of raw skin punctuated with bruises, cuts and welts. I slap on the silt, work it in. "Your back's a mess."

"Yours isn't much better, I can't tell where the bruises end and the skin starts. Are yours healing?"

"Not that I can tell. I thought maybe it was because I didn't get out much before, but I'm worried if you've got the same problem."

"Father's got some cuts and bruises that won't go away."

We wade across to Menno who sits half submerged, deep in conversation with Cephas. They stand and face us. Menno's torso's a mass of bruises and inflamed scratches, the inside of his arm's laced with red welts; below his collarbone, three parallel cuts glisten bright red. Cephas bears a wide band of blisters down and across his chest, his left arm above the elbow blue-black and puffed; a hole large enough for my thumb weeps yellow on his upper thigh.

"Greg's cuts and bruises don't heal either."

"Cephas and I, we have found that out about ours."

130

"And the others?"

"I have not asked."

"Perhaps we should."

The men and boys join us, we stand in a rough circle, take stock of our bodies and what they aren't doing. Everyone talks at once, everyone a patchwork of welts and bruises.

"Why?"

"I don't know, Henry."

"Perhaps it's something in the water, the air?"

"No, Neueanbruch's a gift, it cannot be."

"We're not used to working this hard, this long without horses for plow and harrow."

"I'm always tired, hungry, maybe that's part of it."

"Then the meat tonight will help?"

"Has anyone's wife or child complained, have the same problem?"

Lester lifts his head. "Not that she says, but Rachel burned her arm that first week and as far as I can tell, it's no better."

Cephas starts to make his way out. "We should go back and ask."

Everyone's in the same boat. We sit around the fire, clean and refreshed, dry our clothes, swap descriptions of bruises, cuts and abrasions that can't or won't heal. The women have suffered more, although I wasn't aware of it; how can I be when they cover themselves from wrist to ankle and make a virtue out of stoicism?

"So, it's not normal for farmers, Menno, and I've never heard of cuts and bruises taking so long to heal."

"Yes, there should at least be a start but there clearly is none. And we are all affected."

I shake my head. "Then why, and how much worse can it get?"

"It is what happens when women do men's work, are forced to step out of the natural order of things."

I'm not surprised by the nods and murmurs around me, only the slight nod of agreement from Lou that stops as I glance her way.

"Perhaps they're less used to being farm animals than we are, Menno."

"That is what I said."

It's not. I let it go. "What about the children?"

A chorus of 'Nos' resound.

I turn to Lou. "Any ideas? You used to work in a medical center."

"No, I wasn't a doctor or a nurse."

"Kelli, you must have some training, you and Peter."

"A bit, but only how to stop bleeding, call the parameds for help. Nothing more."

"I didn't do more than Kelli, just learned to apply first aid kits," adds Peter.

"So, no one has any idea apart from being tired and hungry, unused to the work?"

"Perhaps it will sort itself out after the last field is plowed, the first harvest in," Cephas says.

"When things settle down a bit?"

"Yes, Greg, when the normal rhythm of life comes back. We have bison that may pull a plow or harrow, what is left from that one animal today may feed us for four, maybe five days. One or two more and we may have food enough to last."

"You could be right."

"You should worry less. The injuries will sort themselves out. It's all part of God's plan."

"I'm not so sure."

"What?"

"That it's god's plan. I don't see it that way."

"How then? You're quick to say what it isn't, but not what you think it is."

They look at me, wait to hear from me, each one so certain when all I have is doubt. It makes me tense, defensive, argumentative. "That's the issue, Cephas, it's all questions to me. From where I sit, we had two options, live or die, dropped on a planet at random from η-space. That we lived for a start is long odds, all the rest has to be chance, even luck if you want to call it that."

"Or a miracle, God's hand guiding each step. There is no such thing as luck."

"I agree, luck doesn't exist. It's all randomness, how the probabilities fall." I point to the paddocks, green peach fuzz of young shoots visible in the early evening light. "Even that ridiculous probability is randomness and nothing more."

"Because you don't believe does not make it any less true that God's in charge of your life and ours."

"I don't accept that and even if it were, I wouldn't. All my life other people have been in control of me and I won't have it, all it's ever done is bring trouble."

"That's where you are wrong. It all works for the good, everything leads where He wants us to go."

"Really, Cephas? You'd have me believe everything that put my backside on the Pegasus was god making sure I'd get here?"

"Of course. We cannot see it at the time but yes, it is true."

"So, my daughter's illness, my father's genes I inherited, what those sharks had me do for the money? That was god?"

"If so, then yes, like everything else in your life and ours."

"No. That makes your god a puppet master, playing with lives and shoving this way and that, no better than the idiots who did that to me. You want to believe that, you want a god who's a vindictive user that screws people around, you can have it, it's not for me."

"You do not understand, Greg, it is not like that. He wants only what is best for us, knows it even if we do not."

132

"Maybe you'd better ask Elizabeth and Emily what they think about that." I regret it even as I say it. The words echo out to the mountains, their stony countenances reflected in those around me. It's cruel and tactless, but I mean it; I want it to tear at these people as they try to tie me down.

They don't say a word, but quietly melt away. One or two look at me, eyes filled with sadness, even pity. I try to mumble an apology of sorts, mouth silent inanities to the fire. A hand rests on my shoulder.

"Don't worry, they don't take offence easily, particularly from an outsider."

Henry moves off, leaves me alone with Lou and the night.

Chapter Twenty-Six

Louise

THEY LEAVE US alone, nothing from the threeship but snores, nothing above but dark. Greg hasn't said a thing, hasn't moved his eyes from the fire since Henry left. He's more a stranger than ever, not the person I committed to, not the father of my child, not the reliable easy-going man I knew. I should be angry, I should be livid at his cruelty, his callousness to parents whose children are still warm in their graves. But I'm not, I've gone past that; I have no anger left, rather a cold rational accounting of options and arguments devoid of all emotion, all pity. It scares me, it's a place I seldom go, a path that invariably leads to pain.

It's over a week since our last fight. We talked since, but with polite guardedness that was never there before; and Freda's question still plays in my mind, no answer when years ago it would have been simple reflex. I want to talk but don't want to see him; I follow his gaze to the embers. "That was cruel."

"I know, I knew it as I said it."

"But you didn't stop. What if it was reversed, if it'd been Penny that was killed?"

"I'd be livid, shattered too, I guess."

"You're lucky they are what they are. Kelli and Henry, I don't know what they'll make of it. Then there's Penny."

"Pen?"

"She was there, she heard you. You don't act the way you taught her, she sees you changing, keeps asking me about you and what's going on."

"She's not said."

"She wouldn't, she adores you but she's frightened, doesn't understand what's going on. Like me."

"Make it three of us."

"You're getting worse. I can understand frustration, but you're not a cruel man, not that I remember, anyway."

"I'm not, but when they start with that stuff, I can't wear it. I can't accept it's all laid out beforehand. It gets to me, I get scared."

"Scared?"

"Yeah, scared. I'm not an idiot, Lou, I know what's going to happen, how we have to survive. I thought earlier if I could see, know this place was empty and was all there could be for us, I could settle down and do whatever to survive. The more I think, the more I know I'm kidding myself. I don't know if I can do it."

"And that justifies what you said?"

"No, but it's the why. All I can see is thirty, forty years of the same, of planting and god's plan and on and on."

"It's not like there's a choice. If it wasn't for them, we'd be dead. If it had been the other threeship, we'd have nothing, starved to death or eaten each other long ago."

"Don't you think I know it? It doesn't help, I can't rationalize it like that."

"What's there to rationalize? They've shared everything with us, asked nothing, and tried to help us fit in. What's your problem with that?"

"It's the constant push, being shoved around again."

"So, what do you do? We need them to survive and I think they need us. What's left, wander off and hope?"

"I don't know. I know I've changed, part's deliberate and part's natural, like it's the right time. It might not be fair on you or Pen, but it is what it is, and I don't want to stop it."

"You drag me out here and the first thing you do is abandon me, then you go and start turning my friends against me? Can't you at least be considerate for my sake?"

"I spent my life biting my tongue on Earth, being the nice, reliable, quiet guy and look where it got me. It's about time I turned it on its head."

"But now, here, of all places?"

"This isn't the start. I had enough after Santosh finished with me, I needed to change how I spoke, say what I thought rather than what people wanted to hear."

"If it was only about you, I'd understand, maybe even think it's good, but it's not. It's about the three of us, and like it or not that's how it works. Everything you do rubs off on how they look at me and Penny."

"You'd have me live a lie to keep them happy, pull back to what I was to keep the peace? Is that it?"

"You need to put your family first, put me first, your daughter. Do what you have to, to keep us alive and together. If that's what you want."

"You really think we can do it, live with them and everything they are, bring Pen up in the middle of it all?"

"Yes. Each day I ask myself and each day I'm more certain, more convinced. I can't take on their beliefs, but living like they do? It's not much of a choice, but if it was, it's one I'd take."

"Why? Their whole existence centers on how they see god telling them to be."

"It's simple and honest, it's safe, I don't have to worry what Penny's doing, where or who she's with."

"She gets what you never had."

"Exactly."

"And you? What about these open spaces? They're farmers, it's a life outdoors, not inside."

"It's getting better. I still don't like it, but I can function. One day, maybe it will be gone, but even if it doesn't, I can manage."

"I'm not the only one who's changed."

"Maybe. But maybe I haven't changed, and you haven't noticed. When's the last time we spent all day every day together, seven days a week?"

"I can't think when."

"Neither can I. Maybe it's not new, maybe it's who we always were, and I've never seen it before." I've no more left; I'm empty, poured out. As much as I've asked him, the question turns back to me. What do I want? Do I want this family, this him? I know the answer, but I deny its existence, suppress it, bury it deep inside me.

All the stars are gone, a cold breeze starts in, smells of dank. I stand, pull my sleeves down. He hasn't moved, eyes fixed ahead, arms crossed.

"You're right in a way. Menno and the others were looking for something and they've found it. I think I may have found something, too. You're still looking." I walk to the threeship; a cold rain starts as I look back. His head's on his knees, forehead on forearms as mist and breeze extinguish the embers, send him back into the night. I turn, rejoin the others.

Chapter Twenty-Seven

Henry

THANKFULLY, THE WEATHER'S changed. Although the cold days and bitter nights remain, the rain stays away in the morning. Even with all the extra clothes and emergency blankets I'm taking with us, we'll end up soaked, but at least for a few hours we'll be dry.

Next to the bison yard, I lift my right foot onto a crate to tighten my bootstraps. The herd's grown, my beast surprised us with a calf the day after it was caught. It imprinted heavily on Orva; when not hustling milk from its mother, it follows her all day.

Kell holds out two bone-handled knives. "These the ones, Henry?"

I take one from its scabbard. "Yes, thanks."

"Think you'll need them?"

"For bushes or twigs, small animals. That's all."

"You're sure?"

"Yeah. Most dangerous thing here is the young bison if I'm between it and Orva."

"That's not how Louise sees it, she thinks there's worse than what you've seen over the next ridge."

"Where'd she get that from? Greg doesn't even want the knives."

Kell sighs, plants herself on the crate. "You haven't noticed."

"Noticed what?"

"Since the day you caught the bison, they haven't said more than five words to each other that's not an argument."

"Now that you mention it, I haven't seen them together. But it's not only her, he's not saying much to anyone."

"Well, whatever it is, there's anger in his eyes. I don't know, I can't imagine what's happened to do that."

The noise grows, wooden plugs driven home into crudely trimmed logs, kids shouting to each other as they lay thatch on the roof. The first building, a sign of permanency, settlement. I wave indiscriminately left and right. "She's probably done nothing. It could be all this, all of them."

"What?"

"I was born into it and by seventeen I'd had enough. He's been dumped in the middle of it, maybe he doesn't like what he sees."

"You feel the same?"

"A bit, but I'm reconciled to it. It's different for me, I'm family. I know what they are, what they can manage, what my options are. But he's an outsider. For him, it'll be either all in or all out someday."

137

"And me?"

"And you, and Peter and Louise and the kid. They won't push anyone away if it harms them, but once it's possible without hurt they will." I gaze to the right. Two figures stand rigid, arms crossed in stilted conversation as they look past each other. "Of course, the flip side is they'll never try it with you while I'm around. And if they do, they'll have to get rid of me, too."

"And if he goes? What happens to Louise and Penny?"

"They'd have to choose. They could stay. Or go. Who knows? Anyway, I plan to find out what Greg's thinking once and for all."

"How do you think you're going to do that?"

I smile, reach into the sling bag at my feet. I pull out a green bottle, shield it between us. Kell grabs my hand, spins it around: "You brought bourb –"

"Shhh. They hate alcohol more than smokes, you'll get me in more trouble."

"How many did you bring?"

"Four, as many as I could jam into my carry-on. They cost too much to leave behind." I shove the bottle back, pull the drawstring tight.

"And the rest?"

"Our little secret."

One of the two figures turns and waves; the other hurries away. I stand, lift the bag across my shoulder. "Looks like Greg's ready to go." We share a quick kiss. "Two weeks at most. Don't worry if I'm longer, I'll be fine."

"I know. Anyway, if you're not, I've got three bottles to console myself with."

"Don't be too sure, you don't know where I hid them."

I'm barely halfway to Greg before Father and Mom intercept me. Father's stern faced. "Two weeks, Henry, two weeks only on this folly, then I need both of you back here for what really matters."

I look over his shoulder to a field of knee-high green shoots. "You're positive?"

"It may look as if it grows well, but it is not as strong as it should be. It will yield less than we thought, we cannot allow a single grain to rot for lack of effort. You will be needed in four weeks definitely, two weeks possibly."

"We've barely enough food for two weeks, so there's not much choice."

"Take care with Greg."

"I will, I'll keep an eye on him."

"That is not what I mean. What he says, what he does, it is still of the world no matter what you think."

"We've been through this, I'm not part of the gmay."

"But one day you will be."

"No, I've told you. You're still the stubborn old man that made me leave."

"And you the unteachable, pride filled son."

138

Mom puts one arm on Father, one on me. "Not now. Henry, you'll be careful, and you, Menno, will not rebuild walls."

I hang my head, bring it up to meet my father's eyes. She's my weak spot and she knows it. Fortunately, she's also Father's. I hold out my hand. "I promise I'll take care. And two weeks, I'll do my best."

He grips it, vice-like as always. "I know. We will pray for you. Both."

I hug Mom; she holds me for a moment or two, lets go reluctantly. "Go, come back and settle. Please."

We set off along the path we trod nine weeks before. Once wild grasses, violet-red growth on an unfamiliar blood red planet, now green shoots stand separate, alien trespassers for which we have broken the sod, poured in our blood and sweat to graft into the soil. A jarring clash of the familiar and unfamiliar.

I am between worlds, of both the new and the old, part owned, part visitor, wholly unsure. Whatever I am, whatever I was, whatever this planet is.

The Myths of the Children of Sha'ntwoy

Descent From the Stars

The daughters and sons of Sha'ntwoy and Kert'ankway prospered and filled the world; and in filling the world the Nothing within them grew. In looking to themselves and the lands and the animals, saw they only questions reflected upon the Nothing.

They said in their hearts, 'We will seek out Kert'ankway in the All', so built they wings of fire to the stars. Seeing empty they bought fullness; seeing desolation they bought life; and found they their sisters and brothers, and amongst them answers. Yet for each answer two questions were found; and in each new heart met they the Nothing. As they grew, the Nothing grew greater.

In their hearts and minds they cried, 'We have erred, we have not sought Sha'ntwoy with all that we are', and turned from their wings of fire to a terrible magic, to travel the All as one and search that which lies between the All and the Nothing. Then stood they across the All as masters in their minds and children in their hearts, for as answers grew, the questions grew greater; and the Nothing multiplied within their spirits. And Sha'ntwoy remained hidden.

In those days arose a great and wise leader, troubled in her heart as the Nothing weighed heavily upon her, within her people. She took herself to the highest peak of Mortantoy to fast and meditate, and upon the twelfth night of the twelfth cycle at the twelfth hour did Sha'ntwoy come to her, asking, 'What better is there for my daughters than to rest from their labor and enjoy the time I have given them? And what better for my sons than to cease their striving and rejoice in the love of their youth? What more for my children than to build peace and stillness?'

From the peak she descended, the words of Sha'ntwoy received with joy by her people. And took they the answers they learned from the All and turned their lands into fertile gardens that they should no longer toil. And took they the sun and caused it to burn orange that its days would be long and gentle. And took they the sun and the moons and the land and sent it to the edge of the All that it should be hid from the other children of Sha'ntwoy and Kert'ankway.

To the orange children, the daughters and sons of Sha'ntwoy and Kert'ankway, are given the songs of the past.

Chapter Twenty-Eight

Greg

I FEEL BETTER the instant the Pegasus disappears below the low rise, taking the settlement and its continual chatter with it. Henry doesn't want to talk and I'm not in the mood, so we continue locked in our own thoughts. The empty quiet's a magnet; I'm sure Henry feels it, maybe even Menno does. But no one understands the way the empty drains the negative from me, fills me with a peace and sense of place, a calm intoxication. It's impossible for me to frame the words, get the meaning across.

We make good time, although not as fast as I'd hoped. We reach the hill around midday and keep on, make a beeline for the white-capped peaks on the horizon. For the better part of two days, we traverse silent grasslands at a steady, rhythmic pace.

We bed down in an open plain, silver emergency blankets as waterproof onesies. The familiar mist rain's no problem. It's only an exceptionally cold night that brings morning frost and ice to concern me. I finish half of my daily food ration, reseal the container and return it to the bag acting as my pillow.

"Stretching it out already?"

"Yes, Henry, like you."

"Any particular reason?"

"We're slower than last time. No matter what, I'm going to see what's on the other side of that range."

"I guess it'll be two weeks to get there."

"That's what I was thinking."

"Four weeks, then?"

"Plus a quick look at the other side, four weeks minimum."

"That'll make Father happy."

"What does? I didn't promise him, and I won't be missed."

"I said I'd try, but it's fine. I don't think he can get any more disappointed with me."

"You think so?"

"Bad example to my brothers and sisters, minister's renegade son? There's not much worse for him, have to stand up in front of them, tell them how to live when his own son doesn't listen."

"Did you keep in touch when you left?"

"Only with Mom. I used to watch the fields from the road. Once a month or so I'd dash home when he was out, visit a while, then go. I never talked to him but it's not like I could before."

"He never tried to come after you?"

"Never, but each time I visited, Mom tried to talk me into coming back. He would've been surprised, I was closer than he knew."

"Oh?"

"You know what started it all?"

"No."

"One book, that's all, one book. I was eleven when I realized life was going to be dirt, kids and gmay. I didn't like it but didn't know any other thing existed. One day, Father needed help with some paperwork, so we went to a firm in the city. Father goes into an office, leaves me at Reception. One of the people took pity on this weird, scared Amish boy I guess, so they gave me a present, an old battered book. I had to hide it, keep it out of sight. Father would've burned it if he knew."

"Honestly? What sort of book was it?"

"A story about a man, a whale, and revenge. I've still got it with me."

"Doesn't sound evil."

"It's not, but it's not the Bible or the Martyrs Mirror, so they see it as the Devil's, a waste of time. It got me hungry, kicked off my imagination. Once I read it, I needed more, and I wasn't going to get that at home." Henry tightens his hood. "If it wasn't for that book, they might not be here. The person that gave the book to me, when I left, I went to live with her family. I ended up working in the firm she was in."

"So?"

"The day Father decided to leave Earth, he goes back to that firm. I had to hide, didn't want him to know. I spent the next year and a half getting the best deal for them, setting it up with Denae and Elliott, selling the gmay to the people on Juuttua."

"Does he know?"

"No, he thinks I was some sort of office boy. He can't know any different, Mom either. If they knew I was part of the reason they were able to leave, if it was me in the world that helped, I don't know what it would do to him."

"He might thank you."

"No, more likely it'd make him worry it's not all god, not him that made it happen."

"I won't say anything."

"Maybe it doesn't matter. We're here and not there, and he's not liable to change his mind for anything."

"Sounds like all of them from what I've seen."

"It serves their purpose, helps them stick to the ordnung."

"Another reason it gets to me. Those rules are a waste of time, they're going to get what they want regardless."

"What do you mean? They're a cornerstone of their life."

"What do the ordnung actually do, Henry?"

"Stops them adopting the ways of the world. It stops new things, things that make life too easy."

"Like the zipper versus button business Lou told me about?"

"Exactly."

"And that weird hairstyle the men have, beards but no moustaches?"

"True. Mom had a fit the first time I came back. I grew my hair long, cut off my beard – the world come back to invade the sanctuary."

"That's my point. Out here, there is no world to guard against. It's past, and barring miracles, none of us will see it again."

"To them it's not. You, me, all of us outside are a threat to them. As long as we're here, their kids are at risk, the gmay's at risk, and the ordnung keeps them safe."

"How old's Mahlon?"

"Fourteen, fifteen."

"And he's never spent time outside the Amish?"

"Not as far as I know."

"How much electricity do we have?"

"Be serious, Greg, none, you know that."

"The same goes for cars, spaceships, bots, McDs, everything from the world. None of it's here."

"No, except the things on the threeship."

"And all that's useless without power. It's just so much shiny junk."

"What's that got to do with Mahlon and the ordnung?"

"You and I know what those things are, but the Amish and their kids don't. All they have is a vague idea and rules telling them it's bad. If you ask Mahlon what a bot is, he's probably got no idea."

"So?"

"One day he'll have kids and they'll ask him where he came from, what it was like for him growing up. They might even ask why there's a rule against bots, ask what a bot is. Do you think Mahlon could make a bot to show them?"

"Of course not."

"Same thing with electricity or copters or vids. Same with all of us. I can't build a surveillance node, although I could tell you all about it. No, all Mahlon and anyone could give that kid are stories and tales, secondhand accounts. It gets even worse for Mahlon's grandkids."

"Why?"

"Because by then no-one's left who's seen them. It goes straight from fact to fairytale. His grandkids won't believe him, put it in the same place as green grass and blue skies. They can't see it or touch it, no one alive has it, it's only old people's dreams."

"But the threeship will still be here."

"Remember we're talking fifty, maybe sixty years on here. The Pegasus will be a pile of rust and mold or been broken up and used for barns or whatever. The useless tech's been abandoned, most of the tools are broken and discarded or repaired with what they can find here. And anyone who saw any of it working here or on Earth, or who even heard about it second hand, are dead and buried. Maybe on Earth you could live to a hundred forty, a hundred sixty on the outside. Here I'd be careful hoping for sixty."

"The ordnung will still be there."

"That's the problem. That and Menno's impatience."

"He's not impatient. You don't know him well enough."

"He is. The rush for god's world here, enforcing the rules? All he has to do is wait. If he did that, didn't seem so hellbent on making me conform to rules he doesn't need, things would work themselves out."

"I still don't get it. Any gmay that does that ends up dissolving sooner or later. He won't allow it."

"Look, fifty years from now, no matter what, whoever's left will be living as simple farmers. No tech, no world, no nothing. Exactly as Menno wants. God's plan or whatever you want to call it will happen regardless. If they're lucky our descendants may have tools made from wood and scraps, perhaps use bison to plow the fields. If not, they'll dig with pointed sticks. That's why he's impatient wanting to force it. It's also why the ordnung are useless, there'll be nothing left to make rules against."

"So, all he's got to do is wait, wait and hope?"

"Not even that. It will just happen. It'll go back to what it was pre-tech or further. This world will end up exactly as Menno wants if he likes it or not."

"If it's going to happen anyway and the ordnung are irrelevant, why the problem?"

"He still enforces them and from what I've learnt, half of them apply to what you do. If they exist, they can be added to. And the only thing that would need a rule against it is me."

"It's not only you. It's all of us outside the gmay and it's inevitable."

"What is?"

"Once it's no longer about survival and the gmay thinks we can make it without them, they'll ask us to go. They might help or pitch in if we need them but there'll be no staying."

"Even for you?"

"Especially me."

"At least I'll be in good company."

The landscape changes, the plain now a long rise covered with chest-high tufts of brown-yellow bracken. It showers us with perverse pixie dust, clouds of purple-blue spores that work their way into every nook and cranny. At least the bracken gives some shelter from the ever-present drizzle.

The bracken abruptly changes to dense forest, ramrod straight trunks tower overhead crowned by an umbrella-like canopy of branches. Underneath it's dark and dry, only the patter of rain thirty meters above and the crunch of feet on leaves below to disturb the silence. The novelty of living in soaked clothes has left me after seven days of constant effort. As dark starts to slide to ink black, we drop our packs and follow them down. Henry rummages through his things, emerges with a tiny package.

"Thought you'd run out."

"Nearly."

"Can you hold on for a second?"

I make a small pile of leaf litter, put some branches on top.

"Try not to set the forest on fire, Greg."

I take his cigarette and start a fire; it settles down with a steady flame. I take off my shoes and socks, stretch them out with my clothes to soak in as much heat as possible. The smoke reminds me of coffee, drags out memories of a life now lost. I glance forlornly at today's meal, a glass of meltwater and a dollop of pickled cabbage. I laugh, regret it immediately as the wound on my side protests.

"What's up?"

"The room's not too bad, but the catering's below average."

"Ask for your money back then."

The trees start to shrink as we continue, the cold deepens, my breathing labored until we emerge dry, but hopeful, onto the plain. The forest ends as abruptly as it starts. Nothing grows ahead of us; it's stone, snow, and water as far as I can see. We are the only living things – no plants, no animals, no birds. We press on, try to avoid the ponds and rougher ground, step in each other's footprints to negotiate ankle-deep snow while ahead of us the white caps beckon. It's enough effort to keep going and keep out the cold, our dry clothes barely last an hour after we emerge; talk isn't necessary or desirable.

Maybe it's the boredom of step after squelching step; my mind plays back that last conversation with Lou, bites back into my insecurities. As if it's not enough to try and understand myself, what's happening to us? It's natural and normal, change an absolute certainty in lives ordinarily destined for one hundred fifty years, to grow apart or closer to someone else. They're thirty-year contracts, Greg, thirty years for a damned good reason. Both your parents were deep into their first contracts when they had you, lasted long enough to raise you, then separated as they should to head into their next with other people. Lou wants to go left, and I want to go right – why should it get to me? Perhaps it's early, but maybe it's like she said, we've spent an intense amount of time together fighting to keep Pen alive. What makes me think any of it's for life?

145

It's different now, different than it should be, different from what I was promised. On Earth, in eighteen years we'd happily split and find someone or something else, keep in touch superficially in case a mutual friend dies or a grandchild turns up, live happily ever apart. Here none of that holds, none of the pattern and rhythm of normal life exist. It's me, Lou, Pen, isolation. Isolation. Pen.

The cold seeps into my thighs, creeps along my trousers. I'm locked in my thoughts as I stand knee deep in snow, Henry blithely unaware. I shake myself, rush ahead to resume the plod behind him, hope he hasn't noticed.

What do I want? I question Menno's hidebound acceptance of rules from the past yet cling to this one from mine. Does it have to end in eighteen years? If it doesn't, would I want it to go on? I remember hearing about a time long ago when thirty years was a lifetime, was forever, when one partner was for life. Would Lou have chosen me back then? We both had our reasons, the attraction was mutual, but always with that thirty-year limit in mind, always knowing it had to end. I could see it growing between Lou and Clara, knew their contract cycles meshed; it was an open secret they'd partner next time around, but our thirty years were ours she kept telling me, kept promising me, so why's she getting so far from me when we've so much time left?

You're scared, Greg Robertson. For all the attraction of this place and the times you hunted out privacy on Earth, you've always known deep inside there was a place to go, people to be with if it got too much. You've never had to face yourself, be alone with what and who you are, how short you fall in your own eyes. There was always someone to anchor yourself to, tell you it doesn't matter, that you amount to something; now if she goes, what do you have? Myself. Can there be a crueler fate, a harsher judge, a more unforgiving audience? No, and at the center of it all stands one little girl too young to understand the frailty of her father, yet young enough to love unconditionally, accept me for no more reason than a random alignment of genes. To lose Lou would be one thing, but to be torn from Pen is another. I have no illusions; where Lou goes Pen will, it's the way things are, the way they should be. Regardless of what I feel. Lou may have found something but I'm still looking.

The beauty of the scoured landscape is lost on me. As Henry leads, all I see are his footprints and the back of his head. When it's my turn, I fix on the mountains, try not to walk into waist-deep drifts or creeks covered by thin layers of ice. Day and night always the rain, huge languid drops that slap onto my clothes to shear away in dozens of tiny fragments, seek out any crevice or remnant dry place. I'm chafed, the shivers add to the bloated nausea of my empty stomach, the pain in my head, the grit behind my eyes.

The broad plain changes to an immense valley floor that rises ahead, each side bordered by mountains, red-gray sentinels, the snowbound valley's eternal guardsmen. How many millennia have they stood watch until we two intruders disturbed the natural order? I feel alien, detached, an unbeliever in an ancient holy of holies, uninvited and unwelcome; yet inside me it resonates familiarity and purpose.

We sleep that night as we had many, huddled together in a small hand dug depression to ward off the cold and rain only to fail miserably. Again. Twelve nights of this and my resolve falters even as the goal seems within reach. Is it worth it to know, to see? My imagination transforms the Pegasus to paradise, a sanctuary of dry clothes, dry bed, warm fire, and food.

I wake to the first pangs of depression, rise and banish them, screaming profanities born of hate and fear, memories of vows made never to follow that path again. Henry joins in eagerly, vehemently, until we stand face to face, heads thrown back to curse the planet, the ground, challenge the universe itself to do it's damnedest. The rain continues, the cold continues, but my breast burns.

"Better, Greg?"

"Hell, yes. I needed that."

"And me. Two more days, it's nearly done."

Chapter Twenty-Nine

Greg

THE LAND WAS not told and the sky's an unbeliever. To the end of the morning the ranges crush closer, change the funnel to a gash, a two-hundred-meter-wide strip of rock and snow. Sheer cliffs block the feeble sun, the wraith wind screams and clutches my clothes, my matted hair flails my cheeks raw. Soil hardens to rock, snow to ice, flat boulders to mounds of stone; some razor sharp, some overhang ice-laden and threaten to crash down at an instant. We stumble on, slip and fall to deepen old wounds and collect new ones, hold on to each other as we plod or crawl into the teeth of the gale. I see a rise ahead, a point where the valley stops, the walls to either side perhaps fifty meters apart. I slap Henry on the chest and point. Two, maybe three hours.

The sun disappears, leaves us in a chasm of deep violet as clouds descend. Behind us black, before us the last few rays of light a red scar.

The first hits behind me, throws me violently into the ice, nearly renders me senseless. I look to Henry as the second bolt of lightning strikes ten meters beyond him. We try to run but lightning and thunder toss me from one rock face to another. I lose Henry as lightning peppers the ground, gathers into balls and shoots through the air. I struggle to my knees in a brief lull, then I'm picked up and thrown sideways into the cliff wall, slammed face first into jagged shale as my emergency blanket bursts into flames. My pack falls from my shoulders as another bolt lances into it, scours me along the rock face and back to the valley floor bloodied, face up, unable to move. The clouds are lower, pestilential against the blood-red twilight.

I watch, strangely detached, as lightning races across the base of the clouds, an insane lattice that weaves, sizzles, then hurtles down in unconstrained violence. It's only moments until one hits me; what will I smell like? Will it be like the bison, barely warmed and red? Or like the soysaus at Pen's birthday, overcooked and charred? I never have the chance to decide. A hand reaches out, drags me backwards until I look up at Henry's singed eyebrows, half of me under cover, half still assaulted by the storm.

It's not a cave, not even a hole in a rock, just an overhanging boulder that gives some protection. Water courses down one side and part of the floor to leave enough space for the two of us scrunched together in the dry. It looks like Dante's Hell; it shakes like it will fall. It feels like hours until the storm eases and I can shout to be heard.

"How'd you find this?"

"Got thrown in headfirst. I was out for a while, smashed into the rock." Henry pats his pack. "I woke up face down on this, kept my mouth above the water. Might've drowned without it."

"My pack's out there somewhere, last thing I saw it was smoking ash."

"I haven't checked mine. Hold on." He looks into his pack, stop motion accompanied by tympani. One hand stays in the pack, his other grabs mine. "Take hold and don't let go."

He guides my hand around a smooth tube, slowly brings it out. A bottle glints in the sporadic light. Henry isn't taking any chances: he puts one hand to the bottle's neck, leaves mine around the middle, and with his other twists the cap. He waves the bottle under my nose.

"Bourbon? You brought a bottle of bourbon? How?"

"Does it matter?"

"Of course not."

"I've been saving it. This might as well do. You first."

I'm not up to it. I'm gaunt, hungry, drained; I don't care. I put the bottle to my lips and take the tiniest of swigs. The fire shoots down my throat to explode out my nose as it twists my eyes out my sockets. I control my coughs long enough to grab the bottle for a second shot.

"Wow, how old is that?"

Henry makes sense on his fourth attempt. "Forty years when I got it."

"Smooth."

"Yeah, real smooth."

"You finished?"

We work our way through a quarter of the bottle as tempest subsides to violent storm. I'm warmed through, the bits that hurt the most detach from my mind, which blithely refuses to acknowledge any notions of pain or discomfort. Part of me wants to go relieve myself, part of me knows this will hurt like hell tomorrow; but that's later and right now I'm detached, warm, fuzzy and talkative, good even, maybe carefree.

I help myself to another. "Maybe save some for later, Henry, for the way back?"

"Good idea. Can't take it home though, upset Mom if she knows."

"There's no risk of that."

"Nearly perfect, need a bison steak to make it complete."

"Yeah, beats pickled cabbage. Don't know how much I can take, last week it was all Rachel gave us."

"Did you try to swap it?"

"No, what do you mean?"

"You don't have to take what's given. Isaac and Mahlon change it if it's the same, and if Mrs. Lehmann won't, they trade with someone else. We never get the same food twice in a row."

"There I was thinking you're all acceptance and stoicism. Didn't think there was any cunning in you lot."

"If you look hard, it's clear. Sometimes it comes looking for you."

The wind shifts, drives the rain across us; droplets accumulate on the collection of icicles on the lip of the rock.

"Hey, Greg."

"Yeah?"

"That thing you said the other day, about it all turning into farmland one day. You really think that?"

"I'd bet on it."

"Not the farm bit, but it all being here when our grandkids are running round, you know, lasting that long."

"Yeah. Come back in a million years, they'll still be here."

"Why? You don't believe in all that plan stuff."

"Why are we still alive? We drop out of η-space and just happen to land on a planet that is habitable? No, Kelli's got faith in what the AI did but no one really knows. So, we're alive when we should be dead and for me it ends there. Dead or alive, heads or tails, black or white, it's all random chance; this time we won. I figure if we won, that everything else will work out. But..."

"But what?"

"But everything. You drink the water and don't die. We breathe the air and it's okay. Menno sticks seed in the ground and it grows, we eat the animals instead of them eating us. All the stories about ancient Earth have animals that kill, bugs and viruses that cripple, poisons in the air, water, and food. Each planet we've colonized, it's the same thing. Don't forget the ice worms of Juuttua."

"Maybe this place is different. Maybe only the weather's bad."

"I can't buy that. We'd have to be the luckiest people in the universe to drop onto a place without problems. I think the rest of this place is where the problems start, where the things that can kill us are. It's out here it'll balance up. I have to believe it."

"Why?"

"Simple. If it's all good and great, then Menno's right, it's made for us. That I can't accept, it's not possible."

"It could be."

"What? I thought you'd walked out on them."

"Father and the gmay yes, but that doesn't mean I can't believe in god or that. I don't think he's right, but I didn't totally throw god away. I've been with Mennonites all the time since, it's the ordnung and the restrictions that made me go, not any disbelief in god."

"So, you think god's done all this?"

"A personal plan and a planet made for us? Not one bit, we're not that special. Since we found η-space, we've colonized hundreds of worlds – no god,

150

just planets, plants, animals, and nothing else. Maybe god exists, maybe not, but I know it's not the one Father goes on about. It's something else, and I don't even know if I'd recognize it if I saw it."

"You had me worried for a second there."

"It's hard for me. I had eighteen years with them day in day out and only a couple outside. There's still things that are habit, still automatic, it'll take time."

"I guess."

"You've never dabbled in religion, have you?"

"Me? Never."

"Louise?"

"Perhaps, maybe, she says she has an open mind, so I guess so. You'd best ask her." The wind picks up, Henry shifts back against my side. Jarring memories of Lou surface, she hasn't been that close to me in weeks. "Any chance of getting the bottle out again?"

"Oh yeah, sure."

I pull a long swig after him, cradle the bottle. I close my eyes; how much more do I have to drink until it knocks me out?

I think I've had another, the bottle's not in my hands and Henry's a long way off. I feel the warmth from his leg pressed next to mine. Everything's telegraphed outwards, this little cleft stretches to forever. I'm an observer in my own body, detached, my mind watches my mouth and body go on undirected as I sit back and start to slide away. It's funny and sad, and it's nice to talk to someone.

"How are you and Louise? Kell's worried."

Which one? The Lou I dated, the marriage contract, or Pen's mum? She had those fake green cat eyes when I met her, red hair and ridiculous Ray Bans. Stupid glasses over wonderful eyes, why's Kelli interested in her eyes, she has her own, but aren't hers Henry's, too?

"I'm happy you and her are Kelli and you."

"We are too, thanks, but you and Louise?"

There's another voice somewhere else saying what's in my mind. Henry's voice talks to it and it's good, I don't want to talk much about Lou, she's not too happy with me...

"...she's happier with Freda, she talks to her."

"Oh, I didn't –"

"You know, she says she's found it. She wants to stay at home with the farmers, but I can't grow a beard. She blames me even if Pen doesn't, but it's my fault."

"Why's it your fault?"

"She's alive."

"Well sometimes kids aren't planned."

151

My hands feel funny, there's a drip from the roof bouncing off my eyes to my hands but they sting saltwater. "What could I do? She was going to die, and I didn't want her to."

"The kid's dying?"

"Money, so much money, but it's worthless. Didn't want the money. I had what I...had what they wanted, and that made me one of them."

"Who?"

"Jonathon, now he's not bad, he could help. Not his fault he's Miss Xi's, a hard woman she is."

"Who?"

"Kumara's nasty. Old friend I could trust? Oh, no, just bad, evil, don't remember whose ass they hung out to dry. We all did it, and who'd they throw under the bus? Me, that's who."

"Did what?"

"'Keep it shut', they said, 'we'll take care of it', but no, all that money they get off, hang it all on me. One set of questions, just one and I'm kicked out? No more books, no Uni, no nothing, and they act like it's my fault. Then he's back like I owe him, die or go, no choice and she blames me. She said yes, too, it's half her. It wasn't only me, so why blame me, would you blame me? She says she doesn't, but she does. Pen's better alive than dead, yes?"

"Of course she is."

The voices fade and it's good, I'm tired, the light's a red blip inside my eyelids, I can't trust them at all...

"...can't trust anyone, not after that, no more..."

From the left a hand reaches out, grabs the knotted rope of my hair, forces me to arch back, feet planted firm body bowed and stressed, eyes forward, silent. From the right a crudely formed knife, its pitted and roughhewn blade exudes primal danger. My hair is pulled tighter, higher, I balance on the balls of my feet, calves tightly strung and back erect. The staff falls at my side as both arms stretch out, reach out.

The knife rises, hesitates momentarily as the hand tightens its grip then descends quickly, deliberately to the nape of my exposed neck.

My eyes are torn open, impotent screams into the teeth of the raging tempest return to me, knives of ice-cold rain hammer my nakedness as I stand outside the cleft in a maelstrom of light and noise. I'm in a column of lightning, it crackles and fizzes with energy that burns my skin, pulls my head back to see the column punch through the clouds to the star saturated night. I'm frozen, I can't fall or run or cower, just stand as stone and scream. With a flash the column soars, the cloud retakes the night and I drop, my beard sizzles and spurts as my face hits the icy surface. It's all I can do to crawl back to the cleft, curl up on my discarded clothes and try to sleep.

Chapter Thirty

Greg

"OKAY, I'LL LEAD first."

Morning. Henry's got the pack across his shoulder, the clouds have risen to take the worst of the wind and rain with them. The bitter cold remains as do the visions of last night. Was it real or imagined, the product of a tired mind? I have no way to know, no evidence other than what I thought it may have been; I say nothing. Today holds the promise of the end, to see what lies beyond the mountains. I can see the end of the rise an hour, maybe two, away.

Henry sets off upslope in his long loping gait, eyes fixed on the horizon; I follow, eyes down, to place my feet where he trod. It's no hard task, my foot easily fits inside the crater-like depressions he leaves. Five steps and the snow is smooth rock, two more and I look down, see a gouge as broad as my hand and deep as my thumb around me, a perfect circle as wide as my outstretched arms seared into the rock. Henry continues, I drop to one knee. It's smooth walled and rounded; tiny globs fold from the outside edge as if a giant finger has scooped a circle in yellow-ochre ice-cream. Outside the circle a tiny smear of red ice holds a few twisted strands of brown hair. I stand, resume my march. He hasn't noticed, hasn't broken stride; I say nothing, keep my own counsel.

The dull red glow is overhead, so it must be midday. I lean down, help Henry scale a small rock face. It's not a cliff or even a ledge; in Enforcement, I would've jumped up and grabbed the top for an easy pull up. Now, here, it's a major effort. He flops face down, exhausted beside me. "Thanks, Greg."

"Ready?"

Henry sits up, starts to stand. "Wow, what's that?"

I turn. The mountains on each side are barely ten meters apart, the ground between them flat. The clouds start to break up halfway to the horizon to reveal a clear, ruddy sky. Across the sky a faint thin band of blue and green shimmers, an arc truncated by the mountains ahead. I stand, the arc remains steady.

"Rainbow?" Henry asks.

"Strangest I've seen. Shouldn't it have all the colors?"

"Might work differently here. Seems pretty thin."

"I haven't seen one before, not back at the Pegasus or up here. You'd think we'd have seen one with all that rain."

"One way to find out, let's go have a look."

It's easy going, we walk side by side, eager now the end's in sight. The wind's gradually drowned by the crash of water, I'm convinced we're approaching a ledge; perhaps water cascades along a twin of the valley we've traversed.

154

We come upon the ledge suddenly. The arc spreads from horizon to horizon; it reclines as if being pushed aside. Beneath it, far away, a series of white jagged teeth protrude.

"That's too big for a rainbow, Henry."

"It must reach around the planet. They're rings, faint rings."

"No, can't be. We should have seen them."

"How? They look lopsided, we'd never see them through the clouds."

I look along the cliff face, get a true sense of scale as my eyes follow smooth basalt walls. The mountains disappear above us into cloud; broad torrents of water hurl themselves into the abyss in front of me to fall first as shafts of water, then broad watery vines as the winds and gravity work on them, to disappear as fine mist into cloud far below. I catch glimpses of ground under the clouds, a randomly broken patchwork quilt of red-brown, violet, and purple. I try to make some sense of it, reconcile it to the rest of the planet, when I become aware of Henry's hand on my sleeve.

"Greg! Greg, concentrate, will you? We're saved."

I follow his outstretched finger. Far below us, a quarter of the way to the horizon, two thin columns of gray-white smoke rise.

I'm certain it's from somebody. The columns remain steady for ten minutes as we stare at them, pencil lines drawn neatly and precisely from the ground. There's no movement, no change to indicate an uncontrolled blaze.

"Definitely artificial. Somebody's sending that up."

"You could sound more enthusiastic, Greg. We're saved, we can get off this planet. No more scrabbling in the dirt, rotten food, stress from the gmay, it's over."

I don't want to crush his optimism. I think it's what I want, too, but it all seems a long way off. I have doubts and worries and I'm not in the mood to keep them to myself. "First things first. We have to find out who or what they are before we go booking tickets. You forget, we didn't find any signals, so maybe these people can't send us back."

"Maybe Peter missed them, maybe the threeship was broken and couldn't pick them up."

"Perhaps. How far away do you think that smoke is?"

"A day, maybe two at the most."

"Given what we've been through, that's optimistic, but assume you're right, it's two days. What about getting down?"

We'd not looked straight down, simply side to side then along the rock face. I step cautiously to the ledge. It's vertiginous, a sheer face of worn rock and fissures that plummets through the clouds below. It's at least five hundred levels. "That's got to be over a thousand meters, Henry, and I didn't bring any climbing gear."

155

"Maybe we can signal them, start a fire or something."

"With what? I don't think ice burns, and compared to the light show last night, nothing we do will make any difference." I take a good look to both sides. The ledge is one huge slab; the right looks like it's been smoothed onto the rock face, the left abuts the cliff at right angles, the last meter a jagged tooth. I walk over, the jagged tooth transformed to a slope that runs down and away. "Henry, look at this."

"Look at what?"

"It's a ramp down the face of the cliff. It goes behind that first waterfall, keeps going the other side."

If I strain, I can make out where it doubles back towards us. What I mistook earlier for a colored band in the rock is a ramp descending into the mist and then, presumably, the valley floor.

"There's our way, then."

"And another day."

"We could go back, tell the others first."

I turn back to the black sky, mountains, and frozen landscape as I wipe the rain from my face. "I don't fancy that again straight away. In case you've forgotten, we've lost half our food. We might not have enough to get back, but if we can get some down there, we'll be fine. The other thing is they might not believe us."

"What?"

"If we go back empty-handed, they might not believe us. It could be months until we get back, go down and get help, and I don't know what state we'll be in. What if the crops fail or something happens?"

"So, we go now, find out, then go back?"

"Yes, the extra days don't matter, it's a case of making contact and getting out of here. But not now, it's getting dark and it's a long way to the bottom if you fall." The clouds start to descend, ominous gray splotches appear then disappear as they had last night.

"Sounds good, but let's try to get settled. I don't want a repeat of last night."

"There's an overhang ten meters back."

It's spacious, I can stretch out and still be well inside the cleft.

"Greg?"

"Yeah."

"We ought to sleep in turns, you know, so one of us is awake all the time."

"Why?"

"The ramp. What if someone comes up and we're both asleep?"

I hadn't thought about it, but I don't feel worried. The ramp's clearly been there for ages, if someone was going to come up, they would've by now. "Fair enough. I'll go first."

156

Chapter Thirty-One

Menno

IT IS THE MORNINGS that grow on me. My body clock has adjusted, I manage to be up an hour or two before everyone else. Precious time given the calls and clamor, time I am thankful for.

My boots crunch on grass as I make my way to the forest. No light but stars and dull early morning, no encircling city or constant rumble, it is as close to Eden as I can imagine. I pass between its thick trunks, frond-like branches a canopy above my head. A time for quiet contemplation and prayer, cold to sharpen my mind, peace to sharpen my soul. The perfect place to prepare for the day, reconnect to the almighty and center myself.

The forest is never still. In the early hours when sound travels clearly, further, I hear small scurries and hops as some creatures start their day and others end it. This morning is no exception, the gentle tap of rain on the canopy adds to the symphony. I turn left along a new path in the undergrowth; carved by my morning sojourns it leads to a small clearing dominated by a single, massive tree. Four circuits in silent contemplation and prayer will bring me back to the threeship in time to start the day.

A rhythmic creak rises; it is gentle and metronomic, new. I stop, it continues; as I resume my walk, it grows. Through the final line of trees, the sky lightens, starts to cast shadows. The creaking is distinct, it comes from the clearing. Perhaps a new type of animal, a broken branch, I am unsure. I realize the source is in front of me; I see it yet fail to comprehend.

Halfway up the tree, partly obscured on the far side it swings, groans as it describes a slow arc. They are familiar, legs and shoes lifeless passengers on a pendulum secured by a looped cord of seatbelts around his neck. Peter.

He has no family here; they wait for him at a place he will never reach. He was not of the gmay and none seem to know if he had any shred of faith or belief, yet it seems wrong to make a hole in the ground and cast him away like so much rubbish. For months he has been part of our lives, it seems right he be treated in death as in life, one of our own by God's hand. Perhaps to him it would be irrelevant, but for those of us left, it matters.

The others take little convincing. Once again I find myself watching vigil over a hastily fashioned coffin as I struggle to understand why, order my mind to the words I will say at the graveside, words that will be harder to find this time. There is no comfort. The gmay will understand. The others? Perhaps not.

Death is no stranger to me; suicide is another matter. How deep must the pain have run to make him do this, to throw God's gift of life back at Him? How

157

did we miss the signs, the withdrawal, the quietness? We have our families with us, we look inward to ourselves and not out to those who need us. I failed you Peter, as I failed myself and God.

"Hello, Menno."

Kelli stands outlined against the fire. I have not seen her since Cephas and I cut Peter down and brought him back; she has spent her time with Freda and Louise.

"Is it time for you to take over?"

"Not quite, I thought I'd sit for a while with you. If it's okay."

"Of course."

Kelli walks to the coffin, fiddles with Peter's shirt. "He always had that top clasp done up, felt out of uniform if it wasn't." She sits with an uncertain smile. "I put his holo of Daniel and the boys in his shirt pocket. That's allowed, isn't it? I mean, if he can't go home, at least they can rest with him?"

It is a typically useless English gesture. Peter is dead, the holo inanimate, and neither will profit by the other. The gesture is for herself and herself alone. She punishes herself, perhaps guilt drives her.

"Of course, he would appreciate it."

"What happens to him now?"

"We wait until morning, then commit him to the ground as we did Elizabeth and Emily."

"No, that's not what I mean. I mean him, Menno, not his body but him. What happens to him?"

"The same as for us all. He will face God as his judge."

"And then?"

"It is not for me to say. God will decide."

"But you know where you will go."

"No, that is not the case. It is solely up to God, we have no absolute assurance. We place our hope in His justice and mercy."

Kelli's head drops, she slumps. "So, he's dead and there's no hope."

"I cannot say that, it is not up to me."

"Well, I knew him, and I don't think his life would measure up to what you say. It's no comfort."

She wants me to give her what I cannot, a salve or fix for her pain. I cannot offer any magic incantations or rites, prayers to chase after the dead and boot him into heaven. It is typical, no thought to what matters when the chance is there and then hopeless striving when it is too late. Yet for all that, I wish I had something for her, even the smallest scrap of consolation. "We make our own choices, end the same way, face the same God. As much as we care for anyone, in death we stand alone before God. It is why we stand together while we are alive."

"Does Henry think that, too?"

"Henry? You would have to ask him. I can no more speak for Henry than I can for Peter." I turn to leave. "I am sorry I cannot make it easier on you. If it is of any comfort, it is no easier for me. Sometimes having faith makes things hurt that much more."

"Thanks. I didn't mean you don't feel anything."

"I know, but it can seem that way. Death to us is a natural, expected part of life. As Jesus said, we let the dead bury the dead and the living continue on. Goodnight, Kelli."

I find my way to the threeship easily, even the clamber through the ink black interior now no trouble. I take off my shoes and outer clothes, slide under the blanket next to Freda.

As usual she waits for me. Her voice is soft and measured, her concern clear. "Have you settled on what you will say tomorrow?"

"No. It will come at the time."

The gentle buzz of the children's sleep cocoons me. There is no other place I would be, I would change nothing, not even bring Elizabeth back if I could. I would take the pain from Freda, but knowing at least one child rests eternally with God is greater comfort than any can know.

All I said to Kelli was truth, my conviction and the teaching of the gmay; yet for all that, the knot in my stomach knows Peter is lost for eternity even as I hope desperately that by some miracle he is not. It is an English attitude, a worldly attitude that creeps into me. "I failed him, Freda. It is all that is in my heart."

"What more could we have done? He was not part of us and drew himself away. Each of us had us all in their prayers."

"Yet here we are, and everyone is my spiritual responsibility. I cannot avoid that."

"They aren't. Only the gmay, and even there each is ultimately responsible to themselves, each household under headship. Peter was never yours."

She is right. Within the gmay my duty is clear, but outside I have none, other than being a light to the world. I have lost sight of the boundary, blurred the separation between gmay and world as it dwells with us. "We have worked hard together, perhaps I have presumed too much."

"They've been with us continually night and day and we've treated them as part of us. You had no choice, they had no choice. For the gmay it has been good, we are closer and more of one mind than I have ever known. As hard as it may be for us with them, it may be harder for them with us."

"For Greg, perhaps, the others I do not know."

"God willing a few more seasons, some help and teaching and they can stand by themselves."

"That worries me, Freda. We were sixty-six, now we are sixty-one, fifty-six of us and five of them. Anything could happen. Who knows what their influence on the gmay could be? If we lose five or six more, can the gmay survive? What of their spiritual health?"

"Then you must do what you have to, what you were chosen for. God chose you to shepherd his flock, to lead it. Do you doubt it?"

"Of course not."

"The gmay followed willingly when you led them from Earth?"

"Yes, they did."

"So, continue to lead them, protect them, be the servant you were chosen to be. The gmay is your responsibility, not the others."

"We should not turn them away."

"Yet we must be separate from them and them from us. Perhaps we need to be reminded, the gmay encouraged."

"Peter still troubles me."

"You know there is nothing you can do. We all failed him. It should make us more resolved."

She is, as she has always been, the perfect foil. Wherever I am weak, she is strong; where doubt casts a shadow, she holds the light of faith. I move closer, surrender to sleep.

The area is too familiar. A slit hole lies next to two small mounds. There has not been enough time for the dirt to settle, the grasses and weeds to start their assault to reclaim what was rudely excavated then lovingly replaced. Everyone is here out of respect for a man few of us talked to and, perhaps, no one really knew. The hope tinged sadness that possessed them last time yields to resigned anguish. They know, teaching or no teaching, tradition or none, where Peter is. Can they see the anger in me, the hatred of what drove him, the fear another is lost? Freda knows, Cephas perhaps. To the rest, I am no more than Menno, minister, shepherd of the gmay.

The words spill out easily. I listen, detached and curious, thankful the language of belief carries me through. It is simple enough. It is not about the deceased, the lifeless husk of flesh being returned to the dust. If this was Earth, they would eulogize him, talk of what he did, or who he was, or the gaps left raw and bleeding that will never heal. After all, what more do the English have, where is their hope? A waste of time, a vain attempt to blur the vision from the truth, something the gmay neither seeks nor condones.

"...Lord gives and the Lord takes away..."

For us it is about hope, about a living hope before a just and merciful God, not the vanities of a life lived and lost.

"...continue in the ways of the Lord God and His..."

Kelli knew him best but does not weep; held fast between Louise and Freda she waits expectantly for comfort over his death. Her eyes tell me she understands dimly, starts to grasp that comfort is held out for the living as the living, and not for the memory of the dead.

"…hope founded on God's word, our gmay…"

We must draw the circle tight, attend to our own salvation. I cannot undo what is done yet the lesson is clear and simple.

"…in the world but not of it, a peculiar people called…"

Their eyes have not left mine all throughout, Freda watches knowingly, Kelli and Louise quiet, thoughtful. My voice is stilled by the brush of soil on thatch. Cephas leads the Lord's Prayer, his voice measured, subdued. Finished, they walk away, leave my shadow to fall across freshly turned soil.

Death of the body is inevitable, natural. I will not allow a single soul from the gmay to depart unprepared for God. I am resolved; if it means difficult decisions or choices, I am prepared.

Chapter Thirty-Two

Greg

"TAKE IT SLOWLY and stay against the wall."

Henry's fifty meters ahead on the other side of the waterfall. A final check makes sure my rolled-up trouser legs are secure; I crawl forward on all fours.

It's stupendous. I never imagined water this powerful; a five-meter-thick sheet hurtles over the path, barely clears my head as it dives into the abyss. Hard against the wall, I crawl through wrist-deep ice water as the wind tries to tear me from my precarious hold and dash me to certain death below. It's an eternity until Henry reaches out and drags me clear.

We rest, I have to shout to be heard. "We'll need to go back through it on the switchback."

"Should be all mist by then."

"Did you see any others from up top?"

"Maybe a few small ones."

"Thank goodness. Hopefully there's a different way back."

"We're making good time. You right to go?"

Going downhill's easier than the route up. Except for the waterfall the path is uncluttered, relatively free of ice and scree, wide enough for two of us to walk side by side. We have to keep an eye on our pace, not get too confident or go too fast. One trip, one misplaced step, and it's all over.

We reach the first switchback by midmorning. The path stops at a small flat area, tall steps hewn into rock lead to the switchback heading down. Henry stands at the top, gazes back along the path. "We might be a third of the way. It's hard to be sure, I can't see through the cloud."

"If we're off this cliff tonight, I'll be happy. I don't want to sleep with that drop next to me."

Henry makes his way down the stairs. "The steps are huge, Greg, they're nearly a meter deep."

"Could make it easier." I move onto the second step, hurriedly lean face in. "Hey, you could've told me about the angle."

"Sorry, they're all bowed in the middle."

"The dip in the middle's fine but they slope back to front. I nearly slipped off."

"I didn't notice. It's only at the front, the back's flat."

"All that water and ice takes its toll."

Henry rubs one hand over a step. "Polished smooth, too. Well, we know for later."

We set off down the path. I'm on the outside edge, I don't look down, try to keep my eyes straight ahead. We haven't gone far when I decide to look back up and see how far down we've come. I stop Henry with one arm. I'd assumed the path was cut into the cliff face. A neat line of stone extends about two meters out from the cliff and runs back up into the cloud. Precise joints are clearly visible every five meters or so along the smooth underside.

I point up, his gaze follows. "It's all stone slabs stuck into the cliff."

Henry shakes his head. "Walking on a cut's one thing, but on a cantilevered slab?"

"It must be strong enough, it hasn't broken yet."

"Yet. Any idea how thick it is?"

I crane my neck as far as I dare. The black slab above refuses to give me a clue. I lie down, crawl to the edge. "Just a second, I'll see."

I twist my head out and down, stare at the path intently. I close my eyes, shake my head and look again. I pinch the slab between thumb and forefinger, stand and poke my hand at Henry's face. My thumb nearly touches my finger.

"Stop trying to scare me, Greg."

"I swear, this is the thickest point."

"Two mills? That's all that's between me and the ground?"

"Seems so." I lift my foot and bring it down as heavily as I can. No sound, no vibration, no crack. I start to repeat the dose rapidly. "Must be an advanced composite of some –"

Henry's backed up, flat against the rock. "Do you mind not doing that?"

"Sorry, does it bother you?"

"Of course it does."

"Can't see why. You went through η-space and the Pegasus' walls were only two thou thick."

"That's different."

"How?"

"I knew who made that, I don't know who made this."

"It looks like they knew what they were doing, it should be fine. If it helps, I could try to dislodge one, maybe dig away at a slab where it meets the cliff and find out how it's attached."

"Don't even think about it."

I look up at the nearest slab. I think I see a thin crimson thread of sky where the slab meets the cliff; the thread extends back along the others into the distance. A product of a tired mind or overactive imagination, I suppose.

I turn back to Henry, he seems to have settled down. "Are you going to be okay, Henry?"

"I think so. You're not worried, are you?"

"No. If it was going to go, it would have already. Anyway, we've been on it the last few hours and haven't died yet."

Henry starts to nervously edge his way down. "Just one favor?"

"Anything."

163

"Can I stay on the inside?"

The dull glow in the overcast is halfway to the horizon as we reach the bottom. It's warmer and drier than back at the Pegasus. I stand at the edge of an ethereal forest of elongated, egg-shaped boulders. Each is covered in peach-yellow lichen fur, stunted and twisted orange-trunked trees scattered liberally among them like oversized bonsai. Henry's behind me, above the canopy.

"I see each of the big ones has six smaller ones, but I don't know what you mean, Greg."

I'm on a small ledge a few meters below him. A set of broad steps expand out and down in front of me to a small clearing. "You can't see it from there, come down here."

Each of the larger boulders has three smaller ones in front, three more behind. From my viewpoint they line up in radials, hundreds of large ones taller than either of us, six times as many smaller ones. All aimed at me. Or, more correctly, at the one waist-high boulder I lean against. It, unlike its brethren, is bare and solitary, a general inspecting an army at attention. A path leads away from the clearing. We step down and start along it.

As we move past the forest of boulders, the land changes again. The grasses are lower, denser and lighter than those near the Pegasus. Groves of trees are dotted about, some with garish flowers, others with bloated pods that pull down the ends of the branches, some with distorted bulges along their length. The ground has a soft springy feel that gives way easily, my fingers warmed by cloying, fragrant soil. The air's a cold, humid blanket wrapped rich in scents, some pleasing, a few gut-wrenchingly awful, all new and unknown.

"Pity we didn't end up landing here, Greg, might've been much easier."

"Or at least warmer."

"What do you think they'll be like?"

"Who?"

"The people. What do you think, Westies or Osties?"

I hadn't thought about it. Race means nothing, the genetic pool's so mixed that for all practical purposes there is no such thing. All that's left is a slight tendency for some people to have a greater chance of thick black hair than the others. Everything else is common property, able to spring up anywhere anytime, and so much the better. I'm a prime example. If I were born six hundred years ago my Nordic blonde mother would've been lynched. "No idea, Henry. It doesn't matter as long as we can get a ride."

"They'll more likely be Osties, they colonize more rapidly and widely."

"Hopefully we find out before dark."

We come to another intersection.

"Which way, Greg?"

"Straight ahead, keep to the wider path."

Orange. Orange and big. We come around a tight bend and she appears in front of us, perhaps thirty meters away. I don't know why I think it's a she, but she feels like it. We freeze, she keeps coming then stops in front of us. She's a good twenty centimeters taller than me, solid hard body partly covered by a basic tunic, her skin a uniform burnt orange covered in fine multi-colored hairs, a translucent shimmering pelt. I fight the urge to reach out and pet her.

She nods at me, I nod back. She lets out a short burst of unintelligible sound from her triangular slit mouth.

"Hello, I'm Greg. This is Henry."

She tilts her head to one side, a long thick ponytail of purple hair sways behind her. I think she smiles as her lower two mouth parts angle up; I smile back. She reaches behind her for a container, pulls off the top, takes a long draft. Her hands are huge, long sinuous fingers with an extra knuckle and pale apricot undersides. Six digits to each, four fingers, two opposable thumbs. She offers the container to me in one hand, I grab it in both, my fingers touch hers and feel cold soak through. I drink deeply, hand the container to Henry who does likewise, hands it back to her.

She points one arm down the path the way we are headed, lets off another short burst of sound and walks away.

"What the heck was that, Greg?"

"I've no idea, but she's not human."

"Must be, there's nothing but humans."

"Maybe she's a mutant, maybe the first one ever found."

"You and your luck again. Whatever she was, she wasn't much use."

"The water was welcome, and she showed us where to go."

"Unless she's sending us into a trap."

"I get the feeling if she wanted, she could have killed us on the spot. We're not exactly intimidating."

Henry looks self-consciously at his torn, soiled clothes, tugs carefully where his shirt sticks to his wounds. "Okay then, let's do as we're told. We were going that way, anyway."

We hardly move off when I see them. A knot of six, two taller than the last one, they all move with the same ease and economy of effort. If anything, these ones are more solid than the last.

"Maybe this is trouble, should I get the knife?" Henry asks.

I don't feel threatened by them; something inside me says they're different but the same, there's nothing to be worried about. But if we start with drawn knives, then what happens? No, the water, like she did, it feels right. "No, Henry, it's going to be fine, just give me the water."

"What?"

"The water, give it to me."

They stop, line abreast in front of us. I lean back to see their faces; the nearest one stares at me through piercing yellow eyes. It's another she, I feel it in my bones.

I nod slowly; all six return it. I unscrew the cap from the water jar and hold it up. "Greg." I take a small sip, hand it to Henry. "Copy me."

He touches the jar briefly to his lips then hands it back. "Henry."

I hold the jar out to yellow eyes. She puts the jar to her mouth, pauses, then meticulously pronounces a single word: "Te'eltwofo."

She passes the jar around; her companions each speak a single word. Each word is different. Names, they must be names. She hands the empty jar back.

"Hello, Te'eltwofo."

Her eyes widen, head tilts to one side. "Gre'eeg. Hinry."

Before I can respond, her right hand brings up a long, thinly tapered knife pointed straight at me. I feel Henry tense as I stiffen, Te'eltwofo smiles to expose three rows of perfectly formed pale yellow teeth.

She moves closer, leans down until her hands nearly touch my chest. "Gre'eeg."

Chapter Thirty-Three

Greg

I'M NOT SURE what to do. I feel no threat as she towers over me. Henry's close, his breath heavy at my side. Te'eltwofo's companions are silent, fixed in place. Her face holds no menace, yet her face isn't human, so how can I know? I can't, so I do all that I am able, hold her gaze, hope I am right.

She raises one thumb of her left hand then lowers the tip of the blade down, allows the weight of the knife to slowly dig its way in. She lifts the knife, a thick ruby drop poised on her thumb, offers the knife to me hilt first.

I take it. It's a thing of beauty, heavy yet perfectly balanced; I rotate it, watch the narrow blade disappear as it goes edge on, admire the workmanship in the gentle wave of the double edge. I raise my thumb, place the tip of the blade on it as I loosen my grip. My thumb is air, no pain or sensation the blade sinks deep before I can tighten my grip. A few drops of crimson follow the blade out. Te'eltwofo's companion takes the blade from my grasp.

Her eyes lock to mine. She moves her thumb to mine, rolls it until the two drops of blood mingle, run down our thumbs and fall to the ground. With her right hand she covers both our thumbs; I lay mine on top of hers.

She holds me in suffocating embrace as her companions break into an excited high-pitched babble, a jumble of noise, slaps, and cinnamon sweat.

The eight of us continue, Henry and I flanked on each side by three of them. As we walk, they point to a flower, grass, or rock outcrop and chirp excitedly. Te'eltwofo is the worst, every few minutes a 'Gre'eeg' this or 'Hinry' that. We try to mimic them but only succeed in drawing confused glances or broad smiles. They, on the other hand, come close to our words on their first attempt.

I struggle to keep pace. For every two strides they take, I use three; they seem to enjoy it. "They're friendly enough, Henry."

"Fit, too. You notice they've no vehicle?"

"No marks on the ground either."

"Could be they haven't any comms devices."

"So, we'd still be stuck?"

"Maybe." Henry looks at the one nearest him. "Well, Shu'urtana here seems like good company." A group of bison push through nearby foliage. "Shu'urtana. Bison. Bison."

"Beesun, Hinry." Shu'urtana responds after a brief pause, follows it with a series of clicks and pops.

Henry tries to repeat the sounds. All six stare wide-eyed and mouths open, then dissolve into deep-throated sounds like laughter. Shu'urtana grabs Henry's head in both hands and wiggles it left-right. "I wish I knew what the joke was."

"I think you are."

"Obviously my pronunciation's worse than his."

"His? You mean Shu'urtana's?"

"Yes, who else?"

"How do you know he's a he?"

"I just do, like you know Te'eltwofo's a girl. You can't tell?"

"I haven't thought about it. Now that you mention it, yes, I think you're right. He's probably the only male."

"They're the only adults, the other four are children, maybe teenagers."

The walk lets me better observe our hosts. Their skin is not quite the deep orange I first thought, the dark translucent fuzz lends an overall ruddy orange hue, apricot tinged palms, under their fingers and in the folds of their skin. They're not uniform. Te'eltwofo is closer to grapefruit and Shu'urtana light mandarin, their companions shades between. Te'eltwofo's hands are soft, free of calluses, dirt or scratches, broad fingernails clean and unbroken as if hard toil's a stranger.

Their hair is long and straight, held by small bands or elaborate plaits but always in one strand, always straight behind. Each wears a simple one-piece tunic. Sandals on the feet, an odd bracelet or two and a sling bag across one shoulder complete their clothing. They look like they travel light, I assume they live nearby. I'm surprised when, as the sun touches the horizon, they take us into a small outcrop of ferns and start to settle on the grass.

"Looks like this is it for the night."

"Better than the mountain. Eat now or tomorrow?"

"Now, I'm hungry. What's left?"

Henry drops his hand into his sack. Six pairs of wide set eyes watch him bring out a familiar bottle.

"That's it?"

"No, we've got to get back, so we should keep the rest."

"It would be polite to share."

"Of course, but after us."

I take a small swig after Henry. Shu'urtana grabs the bottle eagerly, sniffs, passes it on untouched. The other four do the same. Te'eltwofo gives me a crooked grin. I'm convinced she knows exactly what it is.

I hold my thumb and forefinger about a centimeter apart. "Easy Te'eltwofo, this much."

She places one thumb under the bottle and her second halfway up, where the bourbon stops. She drains it in one swallow.

168

"Remind me never to try and out-drink you." I bundle my jumper behind my head. "It's warm, it'll be a novelty not to be rained on."

Henry winces as he takes his off. "Yeah, I think I've had this on forever."

"What is it?"

"My side." Henry pulls up his shirt. I bend to look with six broad orange faces. The gash glistens red-yellow raw as if new, not weeks old. "Still not healed. Not much I can do."

A rapid discussion between the others ends as one disappears into the dusk. Shu'urtana leans in, gently touches the wound with forefinger and thumb then pulls them apart to watch a small strand of pus bridge the gap.

"Ugly, isn't it? Been like that for ages," Henry says.

The other one returns with a thick needle-like leaf, rolls it up from one end. A yellow-violet mucus emerges. Shu'urtana takes a large drop, smears it across Henry's wound until a wide band obscures the gash.

"What does it feel like?"

"Nothing. It was cold, then I lost all feeling."

"I read somewhere Old Earth plants had some use as medicines."

"Could be the same here."

"Can't hurt."

"Easy for you to say, you're not the lab rat."

It's warm, even cozy. My desire to sleep fights my curiosity as Te'eltwofo hands me a soft purple ball. She has its twin in one hand, squeezes it until it splits then peels off half the rind. She points to the rind then her mouth and shakes her head. She repeats the dose, smears her armpit with the inner face of the rind and tosses it away.

I try to imitate her, struggle with one hand, succeed with two. I rub the rind over my pit to receive a sharp sting followed by coolness. Perhaps antiseptic, perhaps perfumed sap, it won't cover two weeks walking.

The slurps stop, the six of them wait expectantly for me. The pale blue inner flesh doesn't appeal, the slimy fibrous lump gently oozes violet juice. I bite and chew. It's a strange texture, melted ice-cream and over-cooked soba noodles, toothy resistance as I munch my way through it. Aniseed, licorice, parmesan and caramel work their way across my taste buds to be chased away by strange and delightful new ones. I swallow reluctantly.

"What's it like?"

I ignore Henry and take a second deep bite, slurp the flesh down as fast as I can. I pause briefly to belch, my stomach unused to the fruit's richness. The slurps around me resume with gusto, Te'eltwofo nods as she tears off another strip. I reluctantly hand my fruit to Henry. "That's amazing. There's no way we'll finish one, never mind two."

The sky is clear, the faint daytime rings now brightly lit multi-colored bands that straddle the horizon. It hasn't cooled in the clearing, yet the shimmer of wetness and breeze betrays a cold night. They all sleep save Te'eltwofo and myself; we sit in silence and feel the planet breathe. If the Pegasus at night is quiet, here the planet's a living beast, faint beat of wings in air, rustle of grasses, gentle tumble of water over rock. I ache for rest but even more for the cleansing communion of the dark.

A faint flicker in the distance catches my eye, streaks of blue-white fire. I see the cliff face, the mountains to either side obscured by heavy cloud. From the forest of stone past us clear sky; mountain to Pegasus black thunderheads. Lightning multiplies, the narrow ledge lit as neon in rain. I see the path down, a black zigzag across the face of the cliff, fancy it extends past the mountain tops, above the cloud.

Te'eltwofo stirs. She says something reverently under her breath, turns to repeat it to me with hope and desire, then closes her eyes.

A name helps, it always does. It rolls around in my mind jumbled with everything else from today. But a name is only a label, not the thing itself and even of that I'm unsure. Does she mean the mountain? The lightning? Perhaps the cloud? I can't tell, I have no way to ask. The warmth conspires with soft ground to win me over; I give in, rest my head against a large foot. She will use the word again. Then I will know. Then I will understand what Mortantoy is.

I wake to the novelty of sun on my face and a mild breeze, a clear pink sky rather than a dull glow forced through recalcitrant layers of cloud. I'm rested and in a better mood than I can remember, so I stay on my back and listen to the world awaken. The sun is blotted out by an orange eclipse. Te'eltwofo chirps at me then moves away.

"Morning, Greg. Mother's in a rush."

"How long you been up, Henry?"

"Maybe half an hour. I had no choice, I ended up using Shu'urtana as a pillow last night."

We squat with them in a small circle. Half a dozen flat black slates sit in the middle; small bowls on each rock and click as they steam away.

"They seem keen."

"Been at it since they got up. They've got breakfast going, you'll be interested in this."

"Two meals in a day? Too right I'm interested."

"No, not that. Remember how warm and dry it was last night? I found out why."

"So?"

"Shu'urtana showed me. You see the black slate under the bowls? They used them last night, like heaters."

"Must have a good power source. Solar cells or batteries?"

"Nothing. Can't see any switches or ports."

Te'eltwofo lifts a bowl, places it in front of me. She stretches to pick up the slate.

"No, you'll burn yourself!"

She grabs the slate firmly, favors me with a curious gaze. There's no reaction, her hand's wrapped tight. I point to the slate; she casually drops it into my hands. There's nothing, no heat, no cold, only smoothness and weight. It's rectangular, black, perhaps as thick as my little finger.

"Looks like the stuff on the path down the mountain. Where's the touch pad?"

"Can't see a thing, there isn't one."

"So, how's it work?"

"Maybe induction, perhaps the bowl's special."

I put the slate down and place the bowl on top. It bubbles immediately. I take the bowl off, it stops. I put it back on, it starts again.

Shu'urtana waggles his fingers at me, lifts his bowl to his lips and back again several times. Clearly playing with my food is not encouraged. I shrug and reach for the bowl; I miss and put my hand flat on the slate. I look down. The bowl bubbles away merrily, my hand beside it safe and cold.

"Definitely induction, Henry, safe as you like. Nice and compact too."

Shu'urtana crouches, shifts his gaze from the bowl to my hands to my eyes and back again. He places two thumbs firmly on my hand, holds it down. With his other he takes the bowl off the slate and pours gray-white gruel across my fingers. The gruel on my fingers is warm and soft; where it touches the slate, it spits and bubbles fiercely. Shu'urtana brings his other hand back, dribbles water over my hand; it washes the gruel from my fingers onto the slate to be hissed and steamed away. In seconds the slate is clean, no hint of gruel or water save a few remnants in the hairs on my fingers. Through it all my fingers feel nothing, I see no damage, no mark, no redness. Shu'urtana points to my bowl, my mouth, then moves away.

"I've never seen anything like it."

"Wonder what else it does?"

"If they've got this, maybe they've got more surprises back home."

"A comm link, maybe a ship?"

"Hopefully, Henry."

Our path takes us along a river, a broad meander dense with reeds and pads, occasional rock outcrops and small sand banks. We happily tramp and eat as Te'eltwofo tries to tell us what each thing is. After a few hours, they grow more excited, more exuberant. We round a bend, Shu'urtana yammers and extends one hand.

"Hey, Greg, is that what we saw from the mountain?"

171

"I think so. Looks like a settlement, maybe their home."

"Do you have a plan for when we get there?"

"What for?"

"Finding help."

"I assume they'll take us to whoever's in charge."

"One thing."

"What?"

"Can we make sure we don't get split? I don't know how I'd track you down if we did."

"Good idea. Doesn't look like the biggest place I've seen, but who knows?"

We meet others in pairs or groups; they stop, chat to Te'eltwofo, offer us water and unintelligible greetings. They never seem surprised to see us, none stay to examine or interrogate the strange, five-digited short creatures we are. It's a good omen if a different species is an ordinary thing to them; if they've seen others there should be a comms device close by, perhaps a spaceport further on.

The village resolves itself into a loosely grouped collection of colored, sinuous roofs. Some have walls on all sides, some one or two but the majority have none, their insides clearly visible. Like screen walls in our old pod applied to standalone houses. Our companions leave one by one until it's the four of us at the far edge of the village. We stop at the last two houses, Shu'urtana heads to the left, Te'eltwofo motions us to follow her to the right. It's like the others, a roof suspended in mid-air, contents and occupants on full display. The scale is appropriate, everything overly large and distorted yet at the same time retains a delicateness. A figure stands and watches our approach from inside; a shorter figure to one side and an even shorter one, knee high, peers from behind the larger one's tunic. Mine, Amish, or Te'eltwofo's, families look the same.

The shorter one bursts from the house in a babble of noise and crash tackles Te'eltwofo. She joins in the child's chatter and points to me, then Henry, then hands the child her sling bag. The child runs off into the house to dance around the larger figure inside. I see their mouths move, no sound reaches me.

Te'eltwofo steps inside. I lift my foot and I'm taken from the cool quiet of an afternoon to a house filled with children's noise and the aromas of spice, warmth, and sleep. It's a switch, off then on, that catches me unawares. Henry stops and looks around, I balance myself back across the threshold half in, half out, one ear to the house and one to the outside world. Sure enough, I feel the cool breeze's gentle rustle on one side, noise and warmth on the other; neither encroaches.

Chapter Thirty-Four

Louise

IT'S THE FIRST time I hear laughter. There's been nothing to laugh or smile about, not with the hand-to-mouth struggle to survive, not when the first shoots broke through. Now, even with all the uncertainties and setbacks, it feels like there's hope, a chance or, as Menno says, testament to god's faithfulness.

The wind is different, the harsh rasp through native grasses replaced by a swish through shoulder-high corn. It's a beautiful, confused picture, a field of dark green stalks topped with yellow-brown husks under a blood-red sky. Greg should be here to see this, eat the first meal from the soil, help with the harvest. I don't miss him, not like the way I used to before, but that surprises me less and less as each day passes. I'm curious rather than concerned, I miss the familiar sound and sight of him, but not Greg himself. It only confirms what I've decided. They're two weeks late, they should be back soon. Perhaps today, like I thought yesterday.

Cubes of dark purple plop into the hash. The bitter root's barely edible raw but, when cooked, is close to sweet potato. If you use your imagination. Freda cradles my hand, guides the spatula around the rim. "Fold it back in, Louise. Keeps it from lumping up."

I've nearly got the hang of it, but there's no doubt an open fire is a poor second to the autorange; at least with that, Greg split the cooking with me. Not here, and not that I mind, it mainly comes down to Rachel. The optimism's rubbed off on her, she swears the children's eyes follow her and Amy once squeezed her hand. I have my doubts, but I'd rather keep my mouth shut than crush her hope.

Freda takes another heavily laden bowl to Kelli. "And one for you. Are you alright?"

"Huh? Yes, Freda, I'm fine, just lost in thought."

"About?"

Kelli nods to the green fields. "This. Peter would've loved to see it."

"He didn't seem like a farmer."

"He wasn't, but he had a sense of family, a need to belong. It might have helped if he saw it. It felt bleak to him before, well, you know. I let him down, didn't try hard enough to help him."

"Most of us think the same way but he kept himself to himself. I can't recall much said between us."

"He was always quiet. Well, he was when I worked with him, but that's no excuse. I can't help thinking what'll happen when Henry gets back."

"What do you mean?"

"If they find somebody and we get rescued, what do I say to Peter's husband? How do I explain he killed himself and I didn't see it coming?"

"None of us did, any of us would have done anything to stop it. I'm sure his family will understand."

"I can't help thinking about the three of them waiting, not knowing, hoping one day Peter will come home. How long are they going to suffer?"

The hash simmers, a yellow-purple patchwork of lazy bubbles that expand then sedately settle back with a self-satisfied pfffftt. I watch detached as small craters appear, one after the other as I bore my gaze into the side of the pot; my vision blurs, clears, blurs again in time with the craters. "A lifetime, lifetimes never knowing."

"What's that?"

I keep my head down, locked to the rhythm of crater and blur. I've had time to accept it, for my mind to come to grips with how long and what it means; but it still feels raw, a barely healed wound torn open when Peter hung himself. "He knew it was hopeless, already dead to each other, children and grandchildren dead before they were alive."

"What?"

"There's nothing you could have done, Kelli, not you or Henry, or Greg or Menno or anyone. It's not your fault, even if he'd not made me promise, there's nothing you could have done."

The spoon's taken from me. I look up to see Kelli crouched in front of me, concerned. "What are you talking about?"

"He said everyone would give up, lie down and die, so we didn't tell."

"Tell what?"

"How long we took getting here."

"It's no secret, a few days maybe."

"It's a lie, Kelli. It was four hundred years, not three days. Four hundred years."

"No. That's not funny. It can't be."

"It's what Peter said, something about subjective for three days but really four hundred years."

Kelli's ashen-faced, Freda looks confused: "Is it possible, Kelli, could it be that long?"

Kelli grabs my shoulders, moves closer. "Where did Peter get the time from?"

"From the AI, it was on the screen. I saw the numbers, but I didn't understand them."

"What exactly did it say?"

"Four hundred forty-eight and a bit years. Objective something. I think."

Kelli sits heavily, stares into space. "If the AI said it, Freda, then it's true."

Freda joins her, the cooking forgotten. "But so long, we can't live that long, can we?"

174

"It's a trick of η-space. It's everywhere and everywhen, time works differently there," Kelli says.

"It's why he didn't say, why he made me promise. He knew his husband and kids had already died, and their kids and their kids, too."

"He wore that by himself?"

"We both did. I had Penny but he had no one. He felt he had no reason to survive, nothing and nobody to live for."

"He still should have said. It wasn't right not to tell us."

"Then what, have all of us feel the same way? How long would it have been until we actually tried to survive instead of giving up?"

"We would've made it through together, we haven't given up yet and we wouldn't have if we knew."

"No, it festers, plays on your mind, doesn't really sink in until you're alone at night with your own thoughts. Do you know what his last words to me were?"

"No, what?"

"One day a few weeks before he, well, a few weeks before, he told me he'd worked it out, if they all lived it was nearly six generations dead. He said he wouldn't even be a distant memory to them. Try and imagine what we'd have been like, all of us trying to survive and come to grips with it."

I see it in her eyes; it's only words, a fact, not truth. "I can't."

"You must have family, Kelli, somebody close or special."

"No, there's no one, I mean, no one back there. My parents lost touch when they started new cycles and I'm an only child."

"Workmates, friends? You must have friends."

"Well, of course. The other crews, the guys at home, they keep in touch."

"Can you see their faces?"

"Most, it's been a while."

"They're all dead, every one. All of them dust, the dust itself smashed to nothing. Even the memory of them is gone, you might be the only one in the universe who even knows their names, who they were."

Reality bites; Kelli turns away, chin on chest, eyes screwed tight.

"You could've been gentler," Freda says.

"No, Freda, I'm making a point. It hurts like hell, but for Peter it destroyed him, and there was nothing any of us could have done. Absolutely nothing."

"But you knew and you managed."

"Barely. I left Earth forever, I was never going back, so I accepted I'd never see any of them again. But it still gets to me. The world I knew is gone and if I have a choice I don't want to be rescued."

"Why?"

"Because I'm four hundred eighty years old! What's Juuttua or Earth or any of it like now? Can you imagine how different it is, how much it's changed for better or worse? I can't. All I know is the universe has moved on and I haven't. If I went back it would be like dumping an ancient from the age of radio into our world. No, thank you."

We sit in silence as each of us try to imagine change, adjustment, a futile wrestle to drag ourselves four hundred years forwards when every reference point, every anchor, is gone or unrecognizable. I don't like the quiet, the brooding. "So, no matter what Greg or Henry find, I'm not going back. Menno's staying put, Freda?"

"We all are, why should we leave?"

"Good. Penny likes it and she's safer than she ever was on Earth. I feel like I belong, so I'm not going anywhere. If your invitation's still open."

"Of course it is. But what about Greg?"

"I don't know. There's two things that might be a problem, he might feel differently than I do. Would that be an issue?"

"It's strange, but these are strange days. It's up to the two of you, if you and Penny stay and he doesn't want to, it would be unusual for a married couple."

"We're not married."

"You said you were halfway through the other day."

"That's what I thought, but we're not. We got married under Earth law, we had thirty years and that ended hundreds of years ago. We can't extend it, it's not allowed."

"But this is Neueanbruch. It's not Earth, so why keep to it?"

"We never thought about an extension. Even if it were possible, Freda, it won't work out. Whatever Neueanbruch is, it's changed both of us and not in the same way."

"Have you told him?"

"No, not about how long it's been, but about us otherwise, well, yes, perhaps not straight or direct but yes, I have."

"And he said?"

"Nothing, as usual. But I can read him well enough to know."

"You must understand no one will marry you if you leave him. God doesn't allow us to marry someone who used to be married."

"That's no problem, Freda, I've never been defined by who is or isn't sharing my bed."

"You said there was another thing. I can guess, it's clear he doesn't believe."

"That's true but it's the rules, he won't stay and be controlled by them."

"The rules are meant for the gmay, they don't apply to him. You'd have to be baptized for it to be so."

"Then why'd you say even in a community they exist?"

"You know we left Earth to keep the children away from the world. That's what the rules do, they set the boundary. If you and Greg stayed close, lived by them as best you could, we'd manage. But if you didn't and say, used electric lights or smoked or drank, then you'd be the world and we'd have to keep our distance. We couldn't let you be part of our community."

"That doesn't seem hard, we've lived together for a while and it's been fine."

"As it should be in future. We are the world now, there's not much influence to guard against. Only what's in our hearts, and we can't control what's in yours."

Kelli turns, face drawn. "So, why is Henry so adamant, Freda?"

"He was nearly a part of the gmay. He wanted to read and learn more, so he left, the world lured him away as others get lured by different things."

"Am I a lure? You know Henry and I are, I mean, we're seeing each other, what does that make me?"

"I'm not blind. What goes for Lou goes for you. As for you and Henry, well, whatever that is it's up to the two of you."

"Then it looks like I'll stay around, too."

"Good, I hoped you would. You see it's not so difficult, we're not that harsh." Freda stands, smiles at me. "And don't worry about not saying anything about the time. I'll let the gmay know and you'll see, it will make no difference to them. The world was dead to us before we left. Neueanbruch is perfect, four hundred years into the future or not. Now, if the two of you will mind the pots, I'll see if Cephas has any more of that purple root."

As I watch Freda walk away, I feel lighter, relieved to have told someone rather than keep it a dirty secret. Greg's another matter, I didn't think it through until I said it. I finally have the answer to Freda's question.

"They're all gone, aren't they?" Kelli asks.

"Everyone, everything."

"Maybe you're right, maybe it's best we're never found. I don't know if I'd like to go back and not understand anything."

"I had a friend once, she said as long as one person remembers then they're never really gone. The trick is to never forget."

Chapter Thirty-Five

Menno

"AFTER THE SERVICE, the gmay needs to talk."

"Of course, Cephas, there is always something."

"No, Menno, this time it's a particular thing. And only the married men and women."

Cephas resumes his seat, leaves me curious and no wiser. After each service we meet as a gmay to discuss any matter, big or small. There is no need to seek permission, least of all mine. He is a thinker, that one, hardly rushes headlong but waits and weighs up his options.

I cast my gaze around as the last one takes their seat. Neueanbruch is alive with harvest and planting, a barn of badly trimmed lumber sprouts from the ground. Perhaps that is it, with the space to build we should start on the homes. We have outgrown the threeship, moved beyond the vital necessity and novelty of close living to where patience is being tested.

The time flies, a service of thanks and hope to lift hearts and minds from weariness. Kelli was attentive, the closer she is the better for Henry. Henry, wherever he is. Four weeks or more overdue, he is in God's hands, but prayer notwithstanding I worry. While he is alive there is hope, while anyone lives there is, even for Louise or Penny. Or Greg.

The others return to the threeship, leave the gmay to ourselves. Though eager, none will start the discussion but will wait until an older man speaks. In the larger gmays that would mean another; here it is me.

"Cephas said there was a specific thing we should discuss. I think I know what it is, and the time is right to do so."

"We were hesitant at first, waiting until we knew it wasn't pride or impatience but that we thought alike," Lester says.

"We have spent too long living in that vessel, it is the right time to build our community. The barn will soon be finished, so then to houses I agree."

"It's not houses."

"Then what is it, Lester?"

"There are two things. The gmay lacks a deacon, it is too much for you to bear alone. We should have a selection and First Communion."

"It has been on my mind as well, but when?"

"In eight weeks, it will be Easter, as near as we can figure."

"Easter plus four hundred fifty years?"

"Yes, it would be appropriate."

"Then, of course it will be then. What is the second thing?"

"We are worried for the gmay and our children."

"Why?"

"We followed you to live on Juuttua, to give our children the right life. Here on Neueanbruch it can be better than we dared hope –"

"But," Omar breaks in, "we have brought the world with us, and it resides with us. We would not do it on Juuttua, did not do it on Earth, and should not do so here."

"At the beginning it was necessary for us and for them," Lester continues, "but not now. The soil seems good, the weather bearable if a little cold, and there is nothing of concern on Neueanbruch. No one will starve and no one need be at risk. Before it would not have been right or Christian to ask the English to leave but now it is, we could help them set up away from us, even check on them sometimes, but leave they must."

"Does all the gmay feel this way?"

They all nod.

"If they cannot or will not live by the ordnung at a minimum, then they must. It's no different than when our children become adults, a choice needs to be made," Lester says.

"Would it surprise you if some have already agreed?" Freda asks.

"It would, I've not heard."

"Kelli and Lou have, and Penny too. None say they wish to join the gmay but that is surely no issue?"

"They are not our concern, Freda. My children, all of us pray for them. It is her husband, and Henry for that matter, that are our worry."

"She is not married anymore."

"She is divorced? How?"

"No, Lester, not divorced. It is the world's limit to marriage, they are given thirty years and no more. By any measure they have not been married for hundreds of years."

"Has she considered that she can never remarry?"

"She has, it makes no difference to her."

Rachel Lehmann lifts her head. "Then it makes no difference to us. She is not asking to be part of the gmay, merely to stay with us; I see no reason to deny her. Or Penny and Kelli for that matter."

There is a murmur of assent. Cephas fingers his beard, a nervous habit from youth he never conquered. "Which leaves Henry and Greg. Can we discuss Henry? It is difficult for me. I love him as we all do, and I know Lester's sons look to him. That's part of our concern."

"Speak openly, Cephas."

"He left once, Menno, and that puts ideas in young children's minds. When we learned he was coming to Juuttua, we rejoiced, we thought at least that tie would remain and one day he would return. Yet he's brought the world back with him and the children listen to him, especially the older boys. They watch him,

179

they pick up his speech, his attitude. If they doubt, if they start to falter, that is where they will look, not to us. And you know what that means."

"You know I do. You know, as does everyone, about my family. Do not forget my boys, they look to their brother and he has not tried to change or dissuade them."

"Yet. Can we be sure that time won't come? He tries to hide his smoking, yet we smell it on him, and he has used profanities already with Nathan's son."

"To be fair," Nathan says, "Aaron and Daniel were fighting with rocks and could've done serious harm. Henry shouldn't be held to the same standards as we are."

"That's the point, Nathan. He reacted as the world would, not as God would have us, and that is how he will react the next time and the time after that." Cephas turns to John. "And you said Daniel repeated his words?"

"Only the once and not after but yes, he did."

"There is the heart of the matter. It has already started and as much as it is a concern for Mae and I wanting to start a family, it should be more for you with children."

"So, what do you suggest, Cephas, I should send Henry away?" Freda asks. "All I want is what every mother wants, for him to be home and safe. You fear for your unborn children, so surely you understand how much more I fear for him."

"We don't want him so far that he starves or never sees you. No, there's no need for anyone not to prosper on Neueanbruch, we'd help set him up, even help him farm if we must, but if he can't abide by the ordnung at least while around us and our children, he must not stay."

"I agree," Rachel says. "I've lost two, but I have two others to protect."

"Could you trade one away to save the other, Rachel? No," Freda says, "and neither can I. There are few enough of us as it is, I cannot cut him off utterly as any of you couldn't to your children."

I am torn, my duty to those God has entrusted to me against my duty to the child God has given me. Forty something young souls on one hand and one precious one on the other, even so there is a piece missing. I can no more control Henry than I can the wind, I have lost sight of the heart of Henry's actions now and on Earth. I am startled by the quiet, nineteen pairs of eyes wait expectantly for me.

"We forget it was Henry who left my home, not my home that left Henry. As much as we may not want the world with us, he may desire us even less."

"I hadn't considered it," Cephas says.

"We have been so busy working together we have forgotten many things. Henry may be waiting for the chance to move away. That was his plan for Juuttua, so why would it change for Neueanbruch?"

"It would be impossible by himself, perhaps with our help he will be able."

"As I thought, and as it would have been for any of us stranded alone with a group of English. But I cannot close the door on him, lock out the prodigal son, as I would never ask you to do for one of your own. Remember, he was never baptized into the gmay, so he cannot be shunned."

"That's not what we ask for, Menno."

"I know, Cephas, but it bears remembering."

"So, what do you intend?"

"I will speak with him when he returns. If he still has a mind to be apart, there is no problem. If he wishes to stay, he must understand and work within the ordnung. Either way it will be resolved. And I am mindful of the responsibilities I have to the gmay. Of those I have never lost sight."

"Which leaves Greg. On this the gmay feels as one, Menno. As soon as we are able, he must leave us. His influence is noticeable, but it is his complete lack of faith, his attitude that cannot remain among us. You of all of us should be concerned, he and Henry are close, and his influence will keep Henry away."

"Cephas is right," Nathan says, "and that's not all. He's irresponsible and does not fulfill his duty to the community."

"How? He pulled the plow with us, helped to plant, even though he has never been a farmer. How is that irresponsible?"

"Where is he now? Where has he been these weeks while we've been planting and harvesting and building? Leading Henry on a wild goose chase when we could have used two more pairs of hands."

"He waited until the first fields were in hand, until the crop was started and he might be spared. Unlike us, he only has his family and now not even that, I can understand his desire for rescue, to go back to the world he belongs to. That the seeking is in vain I have no doubt, he will find nothing, Neueanbruch is empty."

"And how long did he promise to be, two weeks? It's more than double that now."

"I know, Nathan."

"Even if I can understand his desire, even if I put it to restlessness and misplaced hope, he has still broken his word and avoided his responsibilities. Continually. It is not the example I want for my children."

"And what of the things he says," Cephas says, "questioning God's plan, doubting before all that Elizabeth and Emily are with God? This we cannot have among us."

"I hear, Cephas, I think as you. Does anyone feel otherwise?" No one speaks, no one avoids my eyes as I search theirs. "Then it is settled. But I will ask him once, directly, when he returns. As I will ask Henry."

"We will build him a house, see to his fields and help when he needs it, but he must not be close at hand."

"One day away, perhaps? Close enough for help, far enough to be separate? He will still want to see his child, we cannot send him so far that it is impossible.

181

And even if the world deems their marriage over, something may remain with Louise."

"What if you talk to him and he will neither submit nor move away? What then?"

"By the world's standards, he is not stupid or insensitive. I do not think it will happen. Like Henry he may be keen to leave but cannot survive without help, help we must offer and give as he needs."

"We should pray God's help and strength for you, for us all."

"And for Henry and Greg, and their safe return. They are alone making their way home through an empty world."

Chapter Thirty-Six

Henry

I'VE GROWN USED to the domestic normality of family life with orange skinned giants. The moment we ran into them we're taken in like long lost cousins, slotted into family and village as if we always belonged. It might be age difference or how we look at things, Greg's less surprised and seemed instantly at home. 'Why wouldn't they?' he asked the second night as we tossed it around. 'There's nothing to fear from us and maybe we bring in a little excitement.' Perhaps.

I play with my breakfast, sort the chunks into similar colored piles as the children do, watch Greg and Te'eltwofo try to engage in meaningful conversation. We gave up trying to learn their language, the clicks and pops impossible, gentle changes in nuance lost to us. They, on the other hand, took to English readily and are halfway towards a form of pidgin. Another year, maybe two, and they will be as good as us.

I finish my food, set the spoon down on the counter. Dish, spoon, and counter disappear. Amazing the first time, it now just simply is. Like walls that aren't walls, furniture that appears only when you need it. The equal and more of anything back on Earth but not as prominent or as visible; it hangs in the background in elegant simplicity.

Regardless, I'm glad it's our last day. Something has surfaced in me, a need that teases the edge of my mind. Family. I miss them more than I hate the restrictions of the gmay, a tug of war inside me that wavers between cutting them off totally or crawling back. It was Greg who opened the door, gave me an out. If there is no world to guard against, the ordnung are irrelevant.

I move outside, sit on the grass beside Te'eltwofo and an array of bark and leaves as she holds class. She grabs a frond, waves it at Greg as she pulls up my shirt. A pink scar stands proud where a gash had been.

"Cut. Spread. Good."

"Okay, saw that one," Greg says. "It looks like the ferns halfway back, Henry."

She picks up a deep blue branch, effortlessly plucks two leaves and hands one to me. She grabs hers by each end, tries and fails to break it. I try with mine, fail miserably.

"Unbreakable?" Greg asks.

"Maybe, you give it a try."

"See what you mean."

Te'eltwofo hands over the branch, I remove a leaf with no effort. "How many of these things has she shown you, Greg?"

"Dozens, everything from soap to these leaves. Wish I had more time, something to record it on. Some of the things look familiar but others I've not seen."

"Anything more on contacting someone?"

"No, but I'm sure they know what I mean. There's no going home."

Te'eltwofo points back to her house. "Gre'eeg home."

"Te'eltwofo home. No Greg home." Greg points past the village. "Greg home. Henry home."

"No. Mortantoy."

"There's that word again, Greg. Have you figured out what it means?"

"No, she just says it each time I point back to the mountains. Could mean anything."

"Could it be the name for the whole place?"

"No idea. You could ask."

There's a patch of bare earth to one side. I wipe my hand over it and erase Greg's latest base twelve math lesson, scrawl three stick figures. Greg and Te'eltwofo crane their necks.

"Greg. Henry. Te'eltwofo."

Te'eltwofo scrubs out the last figure, re-draws it so it's obviously taller than the other two. "Te'eltwofo."

"Okay, if it makes you happy. Greg, Henry, Te'eltwofo." I point to the nearby roofs, draw a series of triangles near the figures. A little further away I scrawl a mountain, a flat line for a plain, and a square on top of that for the threeship. "Greg. Henry. Home."

Te'eltwofo shakes her head. "No. Mortantoy."

I put my finger on the mountain. "Mortantoy?"

"Mortantoy."

I move my finger to the plain. "Mortantoy?"

"Mortantoy."

I move my finger past the plain. "Mortantoy."

"No." Te'eltwofo scratches a circle around the mountain and plain. "Mortantoy. No Te'eltwofo. No Shu'urtana."

"It's the whole thing and they don't want anything to do with it," Greg says.

"Can't say I blame them. Do you think they don't want us there?"

Greg taps the square. "Te'eltwofo. Greg. Henry. Home."

Her face hardens. "Mortantoy. No home." Her finger moves to the plain. "Home. Gre'eeg, Hinry, yes no yes."

I stab the plain and mountain repeatedly in succession. "Yes. No. Yes. No."

She looks at me the same way she does her youngest child. She reaches a decision, taps the square. "Hinry. Gre'eeg. Yes." She taps the top of the mountain. "Hinry. Gre'eeg. No."

"Well, that's clear. Hopefully we won't get kicked out, Greg."

"I doubt it. If they don't like going up, they won't come near us."

By now we've attracted a small group of onlookers. We're still a curiosity even if the novelty has worn off.

I draw a large circle, a ball with the stick figures, mountain, and village balanced on top. I wave my arms, tap the circle, the ground either side of me, swing my arms again. I point to the circle, look as confused as I can make myself, then repeat it.

Te'eltwofo touches the circle. "Sha'Kert. Sha'Kert."

"Sha'Kert?"

"Yes."

I point to the mountains, then the circle. "Mortantoy. Sha'Kert."

"Yes."

"See how far you can take it, Henry."

"Okay, let's see. Maybe this?" I erase the scene in the dirt and draw a circle. "Sha'Kert."

I add a much larger circle slightly away from the first. I point to it, then to the sun behind the morning overcast. I grab Te'eltwofo's hand and guide it to the circles. I let go, she hesitates then stabs the ground twice next to the first circle, adds a wavy line around it. "Must be the two moons and rings, Greg."

I'm sure she's finished, but she adds another circle between the sun and Sha'Kert, half the size of the sun. She points directly away from Mortantoy.

"What's that? Another sun or planet? Why haven't we seen it?" Greg draws circles in the air near Sha'Kert to mimic the moons' orbits. He traces the orbit of Sha'Kert around the sun. Te'eltwofo shakes her head, grabs Greg's hand to orbit Sha'Kert around the other circle. She shifts his hand, draws the other circle orbiting the sun.

Greg repeats the orbits by himself. "Te'eltwofo. Sha'Kert? Yes?"

"Yes."

"So, Sha'Kert orbits around another sun or planet that orbits the sun we see?"

"Seems so, Henry."

I draw a large circle off to the far side, place ten dots in a line away from it. I point to the third dot, then to Greg. "Greg. Henry. Home. Earth."

"Urth? Hinry, Gre'eeg home?"

"Yes, Shu'urtana, Earth." I make a long arc from Earth to Sha'Kert, point to both ends. "Henry, Greg, home?"

I realize in short order they don't understand.

"Draw a spacecraft, Henry."

"Fine, but what does an η-ship look like?"

"Make it simple, maybe a threeship?"

It sounds good but even a threeship's beyond me. I settle for a bullet shaped affair with a tail of exhaust gas. For good measure I give it wings. The chatter stops. I look up, meet stony-faced silence. "What's wrong? Shu'urtana?"

185

One by one they stride away until we're left with Shu'urtana and Te'eltwofo, both silent, heads hung.

"Greg, what's going on?"

"No idea. We must have offended them."

"How? With that?"

Shu'urtana points to the drawing. "No."

Te'eltwofo stands, grinds the threeship into the dust with one foot. "No Hinry. No Gre'eeg. No Te'eltwofo."

I wipe the ground smooth, leave no trace. "No Greg. No Henry."

Te'eltwofo and Shu'urtana relax and move to the house, beckon us after them.

"They don't want to know about space travel."

"I'd say they don't have any comms either, Henry."

"Or they don't want us to know about it."

"They seemed pretty upset."

"Yeah, but they got over it quick."

"Only when we promised we wouldn't try."

"Easy promise to keep. No ship, no comms."

"That's that, they know what a ship is, they know what we're asking. There's no rescue. This is it, Henry."

"At least the neighbors are friendly."

"For now. What else don't we know that might be a problem?"

By next morning it's forgotten. The whole village watches us leave, the pack they give me feels like everyone's contributed. Food and water for the trip but more importantly small plants, roots carefully wrapped, the start of a small garden of medicine and food. I feel sleek, weeks of good food has put flesh on my bones, flesh that bears scars instead of open wounds. Shu'urtana mended our clothes, small tears covered by knitted fiber, dull Amish black and gray shot through with olive and deep blue. Te'eltwofo gives us a slate, no larger than the palm of my hand. Glad as I am to head back, concerned over what Kell and Mom must be thinking with both of us overdue, Greg's hesitant.

"You don't want to go back?"

"Part of me wants to hang around, learn more." Greg pats his stomach, runs a hand down one arm. "It's done us good being here, it would do everyone good."

We easily keep pace with Shu'urtana and Te'eltwofo along the river. "How you feeling?" Greg asks.

"Good. I think we're doing twice the speed we came in at."

"That much?"

"Maybe more. At this rate it might only take a week to get back."

"They need to come here. It's simpler, easier, we'd be better off. If there's no chance of rescue we need to act like it."

"I don't think they will."

"They think it's better suffering?"

"Maybe, but there's other reasons."

"Like?"

It worries me, all this time with the gmay and Greg still doesn't understand? Maybe it's hard for an outsider but they've told him directly and he still misses it. The world is the world, regardless if it smokes or drinks or has orange skin and twelve fingers. No one will come here, not to stay or visit. "Reasons. Anyway, you'll be back."

"Depends. Trade maybe, curiosity for sure, but I can't make a choice without Lou."

We come to the edge of the boulder forest in the early afternoon. Shu'urtana and Te'eltwofo stop, point ahead. "Mortantoy. Te'eltwofo, Shu'urtana. No."

"Too late to take it on anyway, Henry. What say we wait until tomorrow?"

I lower my pack to the ground. "I don't want to face those storms at night. Maybe with an early start we'll miss them."

The night is clear, the rings a delicate jewel. It's a peaceful place, I'll come back, bring Kell. I'm assuming I'd be welcome, what if I'm not, if all they're doing is making sure we leave? We've broken a taboo with the drawing, the only thing that got them close to upset with us. We promised not to try but I've not apologized or tried to make amends. It's ingrained habit. There's no dirt, no sand, so I hold the rind of half a fruit in one hand and a stick in the other. I straighten my back, eyes nearly level with Te'eltwofo's and Shu'urtana's chins.

I hold the rind and scrawl a bullet shape, try to get it close to the one from the other day. I've only learned two words in their tongue; hopefully I'll get it right. I hold the rind at arm's length. From the corner of my eye I know I have their attention.

"Te'eltwofo, Shu'urtana," then carefully I try their whistle and pop that means sorry.

Greg takes the rind, repeats my words, hands it back. I hurl the rind as far as I can into the night.

Shu'urtana places a thumb on top of mine. "Hinry. Sister."

Shu'urtana moves to Greg, Te'eltwofo takes his place next to me. "Hinry sister, sister Te'eltwofo." She points up, past the rings into the infinite. "Sorry no Urth. Sha'Kert Hinry home. Sha'Kert Gre'eeg home."

I smile at her. "Henry no sorry no Earth. Henry no sorry Sha'Kert home." An impulse takes me, a feeling I blurt out without a thought. "Henry sister Sha'Kert. Sha'Kert sister Henry."

Te'eltwofo goes quiet; if she were human, I swear she holds back tears. She envelops my face in her massive hands and draws close. "Yes Hinry. Sha'Kert sister. Hinry sister. Gre'eeg sister. Shu'urtana sister. Te'eltwofo sister."

We push hard the next day, put as much distance behind us until early evening finds us far down the valley. It rains hard, the sky's a black menace but the lightning's behind us. An overhang to one side offers some protection, so we settle down for the night.

The slate throws bright light to a hard ink-black circle around us. Inside no trace of dark, outside no trace of light. It's effective if a little too bright. The light dims to a warm pearl glow.

"How'd you manage that, Henry?"

"No idea, I was just thinking it was too bright."

"Shame you can't get it to heat the place up."

"Yeah, Shu'urtana knew how to– hey, how'd I do that?"

"Same way as the lights, I guess. Be careful what you ask for, crank it up any higher, it'll be an oven."

"This thing could be a surveillance node, for all we know."

"I wouldn't be surprised, everything about them is different."

"Of course, they're not human. How much different can you get than that?"

"That's not what I mean. Have you stopped to think who they are?"

"No, what could I learn in two weeks, Greg?"

"Think about it. How much industry did we see?"

"None, but it means nothing, it could be somewhere else."

"Perhaps, but did you see anyone do any work other than gather food?"

"No, can't say that I did."

"Did you see anything broken, anything being repaired apart from clothes?"

"No. Come to think of it I didn't see anything thrown away or worn out."

"See what I mean? We know some names and a little bit about them, but we don't know who they are."

"I can't see the problem. They're not like us, not like anything I've heard of, so why shouldn't they be strange?"

"We're here for life and I'd like to know more about who I'm here with. I can't ask them and I don't want to accidentally offend them like we did the other day."

"It was only a picture in the dirt."

"Well, it got me thinking."

"And?"

"I think they're leftovers."

"Leftovers?"

"Yes, leftovers. All the things they use, from this slate to the house walls to the ramp up the cliff, who made it all, who put it here?"

"They did."

"How? They don't make or repair anything as far as I can tell."

"So, who did?"

"Hold on and let me finish. We didn't see any planes or spaceships, did we?"

"No."

"And Shu'urtana wasn't confused when we drew Earth?"

"No."

"But they knew what a spaceship was when they saw it, right? They had to know, the reaction was so strong."

"I guess. No, you're right. But how could they?"

"Just the same as your Amish could, like the ordnung in a thousand years."

"The bots?"

"Exactly. Te'eltwofo had no idea what it was you drew, it's only a picture to her, a picture with a bad meaning."

"So, they had them before?"

"Maybe, I'm not sure. They've got things they can't make or repair, things way too advanced for them. And a hatred of spacecraft even though they don't know what they are. I've got two theories. It could be they came here like us, some sort of accident a long time ago. Everything they have is from then, they don't have the means to make it and the accident is now an ancient evil myth."

"The second option?"

"They're the last of a dying civilization. They don't know how to make their technology but use the crumbs. Space travel is an awful reminder of what they once were and can never again be."

"You could be right."

"Maybe I am, maybe I'm not, I've got no way to prove it."

"Which gets back to my point. I can't see the problem either way, or the difference it makes."

"Maybe nothing more than making me comfortable, Henry. I'd hate to think they're lying or hiding help from us."

"I can't imagine it, it doesn't feel right."

"In the end, maybe there's not a lot of technology they can share. A limited supply and no way of making more? I don't think they'll be too keen."

"It won't be a problem. I can't see the gmay breaking down doors to get these things."

"Really? It's been hard on them, faith or no faith in a plan, surely anything that helps would be welcome?"

"Me, I'd take whatever's on offer. Father and the gmay, well, I guess you'll have to ask them."

"That's what I intend to do."

"We'll tell them everything?"

"You think we shouldn't?"

"No, but don't count on anyone being too eager."

A few drops of clear blue juice lodge themselves on my cheek. Greg smiles sheepishly, mumbles a vague apology.

"At least they won't resist the fruits and trees."

I'm eager to get back to Kell, tell her what we found. I know what Menno and the gmay will think but that's another thing. I push Greg harder; the closer we get the less enthusiastic he becomes. I always seem to doze off before him, wake up after him, as if he's anxious not to lose a minute of wakefulness. I stop, drink a little water. "You're slowing again, Greg. Rediscovering blisters, are we?"

"Hardly. Just enjoying it, looking around. It's still growing on me."

"You fell in love with it the moment you stepped out of the threeship. Not what I'd expect from a city type."

"Did I tell you how much I hated the city? Probably not. But you're right, it feels like Sha'Kert's home and I was stranded on Earth, not the other way round."

"Guess it explains why you don't want to go back."

"What does?"

"How you feel, Sha'Kert, the threeship."

"It feels wrong, like it doesn't belong."

"You sure you're not putting what you feel back onto it?"

"No, I don't think so. Even if Menno and everyone was gone, if it were the five of us, it still wouldn't feel right."

"You sound like Te'eltwofo and that whole Mortantoy thing."

"Before we found them, I felt it, it's stronger now. Maybe knowing it's their planet makes me feel more like an outsider, an alien."

The land becomes familiar, a small rise in the distance signals the threeship and home. An hour, maybe a little more.

"Have you thought how we're going to tell them, Henry?"

"No."

"We might want to have a plan."

"Why?"

"Some might be disappointed, and if they hear it second hand, there'll be mistakes."

"So?"

"What about we sit them all down, tell everyone at the same time?"

"And not say anything before?"

"Exactly, otherwise we'll find ourselves repeating the whole thing over again and again. It'll take hours, anyway."

"It won't hurt to have support. If it's only one of us, they may not believe it."

"Or not want to."

"Either way. Okay, we'll do it that way."

We top the rise, threeship and fields in front of us. When we left I looked back, thought how ordered and solid it appeared. Now it seems ramshackle, fragile, temporary. Perhaps out of place.

Chapter Thirty-Seven

Greg

IT'S GOOD TO hold her, six weeks feels like forever. Welcoming but hesitant, the quick peck and rapid release are strange, out of my experience. "We were starting to worry."

"Sorry, Lou, it couldn't be helped. Anyway, nothing could happen with Henry there."

The grip around my waist doesn't waver, it never has and I hope it never will. "Did you bring me a present?"

Maybe I spoiled her before, but it doesn't bother me. I'm prepared. I reach into my pack and pull out a fist-sized blue fruit. "I've got some other things for later, but this is for now. Don't eat the skin, Pen, open it up and get into the flesh inside."

Lou stares hungrily at the fruit.

"And share with your mother. If you like it, I'll let you take care of the plant it grows on."

She nods vigorously, juice runs down her chin as she reluctantly hands it to Lou.

Lou's cheekbones are more prominent than I recall, fingers playing with the fruit thinner and dirtier. I glance at the crowd around Henry then back to Lou. Did we look like that, gaunt creatures casting furtive gazes? Perhaps we still bear some passing resemblance, but food and rest have done wonders. The back of her hand still suppurates. I pull the frond from my pack. "Give me your hand."

I roll the frond, pick up the sap with one finger and rub it across her wound, gently work it in.

"What's that?"

"It helps it heal. We've both used it, it's good stuff."

"How did you find it?"

"It's a long story. Henry and I, we thought we'd tell everyone tonight, make sure no one misses out."

"Good idea, English. We should not waste daylight with idle talk."

"Hello, Cephas."

"God's provenance has brought you back safely. There's much to do, harvest has started."

He strides towards the fields, a line of people in his wake.

"He's that busy?"

"We all are, Greg. We could've used you," Lou says.

"A farmer's life is never dull, there's always something to do."

192

"Seriously, the first field's nearly in and the second one's ready. Lester says if it stays out it rots, so it has to come in soon."

"The lean-tos are coming along well."

"We're storing food in some of them." Lou adjusts her jumper then moves off. "Have to go, I'll see you tonight."

I'm about to follow when Menno comes over. "Thank you for bringing Henry safely back, English."

There it is again, that word. English. What did Henry say, it's used for outsiders? I try to think when Menno went from Greg to English and I can't. I've probably always been an outsider to him, maybe I always will be. Another little difference, a line drawn between us. As if one's needed.

"Good to see you too, Menno."

"You will help gather the harvest with Lester?"

"Of course, I'll just put the pack away."

He follows Cephas, leaves me with Henry and Kelli.

"Some welcome."

"Well, I'm glad to see you both back."

"Thanks, Kelli. They always like this, Henry?"

"Pretty much. No one stands on ceremony or small talk. A day, a month, a year, the greeting's pretty much the same."

The rest of the day passes in silent labor. I have to give them their due, the crop's grown; yet it seems a little stunted, a touch underdone. Maybe the soil is lacking, the air wrong, the light too strange. I say as much to Lester as Ruth puts an empty basket down, takes a full one away.

"Not the best it's true," Lester replies, "but here and there it's good. Those ones we'll keep for seed stock. All land's a little different, each plot has its own way with the seed. You need to know the land well, English, we haven't had time for that."

"Is it as much as you'd thought?"

"No, it is perhaps a third short."

"More will need to be planted?"

"More will need to be planted, of course."

"...so here, we're hard up against one end of a valley with these mountains behind us, forest to one side and sea on the other. We followed the valley to where it ends, narrows right down to a cliff. How far was the cliff, Greg?"

"Not sure, but it took the best part of a week to come back and nearly two to get there."

"You would have run out of food," Kelli says.

"Nearly, we held back a bit thinking there'd only be one chance to have a look." We sit around the fire, a wisp of smoke twists in the evening breeze. We decided to go through it bit by bit, give them chapter and verse. No one says anything, asks anything, only Kelli seems curious.

"So, what Henry's getting to is that the land and weather down this end is far better than up the other. It's all violent wind, rain, thunder and lightning all night, as far as we can tell."

"Three weeks there and back but you were gone nearly six. Did you get lost or trapped?"

"Neither. At the bottom of the cliff, there's a huge plain. We had a look, it was a long way down, maybe five or six hundred levels. We got up and down using the stairs."

"Stairs?"

"Yes, stairs. And good ones, not stones, not a few cracks in the right place. Henry and I were on rock stairs set into the cliff, mainly a long, sloping ramp and switchbacks."

"So, there's someone there, someone made them?"

"Yes."

"Did you meet them?"

"Maybe not the ones who built the stairs, but we did meet somebody."

"So, there's other people here?"

"Yes and no, the thing is they're not people," Henry says.

"What do you mean 'not people'? Everyone's people, I've never heard of anywhere not having people. There's nothing else."

"There are here, Kell. Orange, huge round faces, twelve fingers and toes and all taller than me."

It causes a ruckus, everyone's suddenly interested, talks at once, fires questions at us.

"What are they like?"

"Are they friendly?"

"Why didn't you bring one back?"

The questions keep coming, Henry and I struggle to keep up. Eventually they settle down; I see curiosity and interest in some faces, concern in all. "Henry and I, we still can't speak their language, maybe two or three words, but they have more of ours. One thing we know for certain, they don't have comms devices or spacecraft."

"That much does not change anything. We knew we were on Neueanbruch for good before, this is confirmation."

"It changes everything, Menno. For a start, it's not Neueanbruch, it's Sha'Kert. Then there's the question of who owns it. Te'eltwofo was here first, it's theirs and we're trespassers."

"It is as much ours as theirs, God brought us here and everything is His to give. I do not see any of them here. If they do not want to be here all the better, we will bother no one and no one will bother us."

194

Rachel shakes her head. "I don't want them near the children, filling their heads with ideas and strange beliefs. We should have nothing to do with them."

"We didn't learn much about what they did or didn't believe did we, Henry?" I don't give him a chance to answer. "This place is taboo to them. They know Henry and I are here, but not all this. At the very least we need to try and talk to them."

"No, not at all. They are still the world even if they are orange, and we will not go out of our way to see them or be with them. If they come up here, if it is not as taboo as you say, then we will greet them as any other of God's creatures. This is Neueanbruch, God's plan for us, and here we stay."

A rustle of approval sweeps around the circle.

I can't believe it. I could understand if there was a threat but there is none, quite the opposite. Perhaps I'm not taking the right line. "There's so much they know that we don't, things about Sha'Kert and foods and medicinal plants. We've only scratched the surface, Menno, I'm sure there's more. You've seen how our cuts and bruises have healed, the weight we've put on? Surely you can't ignore that?"

"It is clear it has helped you both. The plants you brought back will be put to good use, but it changes nothing."

"You'd throw away the chance to learn more, help the community heal and prosper?"

"God asks us to grow where we are planted, it changes nothing."

"Even if they can help us with the work, the farming?" I reach into my bag, put the slate on the ground. "They have things that can make it simpler, easier than dragging rocks and dirt by hand in the dark." I concentrate; light and heat envelops the camp. "This is a small thing, heat and light whenever you need it, there's others that cook, that –"

"Turn it off."

"What?"

"Turn it off, English."

"Why? It's what this place needs."

"Humor him, Greg, just for a bit," Henry says.

I think it off, plunge the camp back into firelight and cold. "Okay, Henry, if you think so."

Menno stands. "That is why we left Earth, what we do not want and cannot allow. It is the world, the easy path, the way to destruction. We will have nothing to do with it, or any of its kind, or any of those you saw who gave it to you."

Everyone walks away until only Henry and Menno remain. "The gmay will have nothing to do with anyone who use it or brings anything like it to us," Menno says. "There is no place here for those things, those ideas, or anyone associated with them."

I watch Menno walk away. I turn to Henry. "You tried to warn me, you knew this would happen."

"Would it have made any difference?"

"No. I didn't understand how stubborn your father was."

"Not only him, it's all of them."

"I still don't get it, Henry. They use a threeship to travel across the universe, comms tech to call for help, but can't accept a light they really need?"

"They're full of contradictions, I still don't understand them."

"Could they get violent?"

"I don't think so. The Amish are pacifists. If Shu'urtana turned up and needed food, they would feed him."

"Can they coexist?"

"No. If they set up house here, the gmay would pack up and move."

"They won't take any help, advice, tools?"

"Absolutely not. Father's probably dreaming up fresh ordnung against it now."

"That's it, then."

"That's it."

"Blinkered arrogant fools the lot of them."

"They'd say the same about us if it wasn't thought judgmental. Father's probably harder than most, he's watched the gmay fade away bit by bit, person by person."

"If he loosened up maybe they wouldn't go, you might have stayed."

"Then what is he? He is what he is, what they are. It's archaic, unreasoning, inflexible, and frustrating, but there's a lot of good in them. If the threeship had been full of normal farmers, whatever they are, would you have been treated better?"

Would I? I look down past the barn door trousers to the boots Nathan gave me. They'd literally given me the shirt from their backs, the food from their mouths, held nothing back. What would my old Enforcement buddies have done in their place? "No, probably not. But whatever good there is gets washed over by everything else."

"Now maybe you understand me better. It's not a life for everyone, not one for me. People either stay with the gmay for life or leave before they reach twenty. I'll tell you this, it also works the other way. Every so often an outsider will join the gmay."

"Really? Must be rare."

"It is. There's one here."

"What?"

"Cephas Miller. Turned up when he was nineteen and stayed. He was one of the first to agree to shift to Juuttua."

"I hadn't imagined anyone would do that. Lou's told me she likes them, and I guess I can understand how someone thinks like that, but to go all the way and

196

turn your back on it all, give up the life you've lived for something so radically different? It's hard to understand."

"And that's exactly Father's problem with me, his problem with anyone walking away. You're more alike than you think."

"Then neither of us will change, neither of us will fully understand the other."

"Even with the best intentions, even if you both gave way a little, you'd always be at each other."

"That's no way to live. For either of us. If I thought before I'd stay in the community, it's not possible now."

"You'd end up going sooner or later and in the meantime it'd be difficult. You can't pretend to keep the peace."

"Don't I know it. It's not so bad, I can go out to the sea by the mouth of the river. Lou and Pen will like it, I can take them to see Te'eltwofo, maybe stay a while. What about you?"

"I wasn't going to stay with them anyway, just close enough not to lose touch. I might end up as your neighbor."

"That wouldn't be a bad thing."

"Then there's Kell, I don't want to be far from her."

"Have you talked to her?"

"Not since we got back. Just a quick word then back to work."

"Any idea how she'd react, what she'd think?"

"No. What about Lou?"

What about Lou? The cracks between us feel like a chasm. But we've more than ten years left, it's time enough to heal, to work things out. She's built relationships here, substitutes for ones left behind on Earth; I know how she feels about the people, the community. It's obvious. "I'm sure she'll want to stay close. But I haven't had a chance to ask."

"That's going to make it tricky."

"We'll work it out, we'll find a spot that suits us both, the river mouth's close enough for her and far enough for me."

"I think I'll go find Kell, see what she thinks."

"I'm going to soak up some more warmth then turn in."

"You're not going to light up the slate?"

"No, I've stirred the nest enough for one night."

197

Chapter Thirty-Eight

Menno

HE NEARLY KNOCKS me off my feet as he rounds the threeship. Always in a hurry, a rush in and out of this and that as if haste can make the meaningless valued. The way of the English, now the way of my son.

"Sorry, Father."

"We need to talk."

"About?"

"The future."

"I knew you wouldn't like it, but it can't be helped, it is what it is."

"That does not matter, the world is the world no matter the color of its skin. While you were away the gmay met. They are worried."

"I'm grateful for their concern."

"It was not about your safety. It was about what happens now."

"And what, exactly, is supposed to happen?"

"Where you will stay. They are concerned. As am I."

"About?"

"Your example to their children, your influence. You know what they are worried about, you were with us long enough to understand."

"And you? What do you think?"

"I agree with them, your example is worldly. It is not what we want. Do not forget I have to look to your brothers' salvation."

"It's always the way with you, everyone else then me at the end. If you'd put the effort into your family, into me, then maybe I never would've left."

"Perhaps I am not the best of fathers, but I always put my family first."

"No! It was always the ordnung, the gmay, putting chains around me. You knew I could never join the gmay, but that didn't mean I had to leave home."

"Then why did you?"

"You. You just wouldn't cut me any slack, expected me to act like all of them. All I wanted was to read, to learn, and you wouldn't even let me do that."

"But it is a fruitless waste of time. All you need is God's word."

"That's my point. You remember Ben Lutz?"

"I do, he left to join the Mennonites."

"I stayed with his family. None of his children disappeared. You know why? Because he understood them enough to make allowances. Because he loves them."

"It is not right to accuse me, even if you feel it. I love all of you. I know I am not outwardly affectionate, but I have done everything to keep you safe, bring you up the right way without fear or want."

198

"Maybe that's the issue, you kept doing things, the farm, the house, the gmay, the neighbors, all the time more away than near."

"But we talked, we talked all the time."

"You did, not me, not really talked or listened. It was always across a table or behind a Bible. We've talked more, really talked, since we landed here."

I know it is true, but it is the way my father brought me up, the way it has always been. A child is a serious responsibility, a difficult one, a boy particularly, and there is no room for frivolity or laxness. "If it was that bad for you, why did you follow us? You said you promised your mother but that does not seem enough."

"Isn't it obvious? You're my family. I still need you, all of you, even if I can't live with you."

"Your mother, your mother and I, we will not stop praying for you, to bring you into the gmay. We will not be whole until then."

"I can live with that, but you need to accept it will never happen."

"If I can never?"

"At least try, or pretend while I'm around."

"Even if I do, the gmay will not. That is why I need to talk to you."

"I guess they don't want me near. Tell them they worry for nothing, as much as they don't want me, I want them less. You forget I turned my back on them and on you."

"You know they are not heartless or cruel."

"Perhaps, perhaps not. I've learned more about people away from the gmay than near it. But that's nothing, I wasn't going to live with them or you on Juuttua and I'm not going to here."

"Where will you go?"

"Not far, maybe a day away. Close enough to visit."

"We will help you set up your farm, run it if needed."

"What, me a farmer? All I need is to plant the seedlings I brought back and wait. A few trips to Shu'urtana to get some more and I'll be fine."

"It is your choice."

"It always has been."

Henry moves off as I continue toward the fire. Greg is there, I sit opposite him across the dying embers. I do not know him, understand how he thinks or what drives him. Do I care, would it make any difference? Tonight, now, not at all. He said he found others; as distant as he may be from them, I am from him. It is a gulf I do not want to cross, cannot understand let alone accept, whatever his beliefs and truths tell him. In nearly fifty years of life I have never spent this long in the company of the English, to see and feel their impact, their strangeness. It is not something I wish to continue.

Perhaps by the world's standards he is a good man, and as God commands I love him as I am told to love all people; yet I must do what I promised and for that I know I will get only one response. Has he spoken with his wife, has she told him what Freda told me? He could be wounded, vulnerable or even irrational; to ask for a commitment or decision now is perhaps not right, not fair, but it has to be done. I know it is necessary; I take no delight in it.

"You didn't seem too happy with what we found, Menno."

"What you found is beyond my control. It is only what it means to us and what we do or do not do that matters."

"I know you're serious about having nothing to do with them. It's not how I think."

"That much is clear."

"I don't understand you, even talking with Henry hasn't helped."

"Would you be surprised if I said the same of you?"

"No. Why, Menno?"

"Why what?"

"Why the total shut down? Even if I don't understand, I see your strong beliefs, your sense of purpose. I know it gives all of you strength and hope. Without it maybe all of us would be dead. But simply refusing it's, it's like pretending none of it exists. But it does."

"It is a threat to our way of life, the way –"

"The way god intends you to live, I know. But back on Earth you had to deal with us, the...what do you call me, that's right, the English. I was the world there, too, wasn't I?"

"Yes, you were and yes, when we had to we did, but as little as possible."

"Why can't you meet them, at least be a neighbor?"

"This Neueanbruch is our last hope. I watched the gmay on Earth bled of its youth, pulled into the world. Ours is one of the last, I led them here for our faith to survive."

"I've seen Te'eltwofo, stayed with her people. They're no threat."

"I cannot afford the risk. We did not wake up one morning and jump on a threeship on a whim. It took years of prayer and organization, years of being questioned and doubted and even accused of destroying our community. Do you know we are only half of our original number? We could be all that is left, the last gmay. I will not risk its destruction."

"Aren't you tired? We've no animals save a few bison to use in the fields, your work is never-ending from sunup to sundown. Even if you don't want to know them or talk to them, they could have things that might help, might make it easier."

"That is why we cannot. It will destroy us."

"You want to live your lives as slaves?"

200

"It is you who are the slave, Greg, a slave to yourself, your desires, your fears. Yes, if you put it that way, we do want to work like that, it is how God wants us to live. We had the chance before the fall to live idly, but once Adam sinned the curse was to toil ceaselessly. In a while we will understand Neueanbruch, tame the land and be wiser with the planting, but the work will not stop. Idleness, simple pleasure-seeking moves us away from God and that I will not allow."

"And that is what your rules, your ordnung protect?"

"Yes. To you English it is always confusing, a mystery why such and such is banned, a color on a buggy, a hem too thick or thin. All of it is to protect, to avoid idleness or vanity or self. Even if the reasons are lost to us or seem vague, they remain, the wisdom and love of our fathers to watch over us."

"It's your choice, Menno, it can never be mine."

"That I know, and it is why the gmay, why I have a request."

"A request?"

"You understand why we choose to live as we do?"

"A bit."

"That it means separation from the world?"

"That much, as you say, is clear."

"So, you know that to us you, Penny, Louise, all of you are part of the world."

"It's obvious."

"Then my request should be no surprise. It is a simple one. If you can live by the ordnung, obey them and not spread dissent, then you can stay with us. If you cannot, if it is too much, we wish you to leave."

"You're kicking us out?"

"I have to think of the gmay first. It would not have been possible earlier, you could not survive on your own so we accepted what we were given. Now it has changed, if you go you will survive, and we will help you as much as you need."

"Leaving will hurt Lou and Pen deeply."

He does not know, he thinks I talk about his family. It is you alone, Greg, and you have no idea. "You have not spoken to them?"

"Not really since I got back. Why?"

"Perhaps you need to discuss it. As a family."

"You know what our answer will be. Maybe it's been hard on your people having us around, but it works both ways."

"It can wait until tomorrow, until Sunday. Time to settle, to think about what is best."

"I have one question."

"What?"

"What do *you* want me to do?"

I stand, put my hands in my pockets and look at him. What do *I* want? The gmay is my first and only concern but that will not be enough for him. Yes, I have

201

an opinion, as bad as it is to have any. "Put yourself in my shoes, with my faith, my God, my family, my children, my gmay. What would you want?"

I turn, walk away before he can respond. I have an urgent need for security, for a pair of arms and eyes that see me as protector, not executioner.

HENRY WARNED ME, I prepared for the inevitability of it, but he still got to me. I sit mute and watch Menno disappear behind the Pegasus.

We weren't going to stay anyway. I'm going to take Lou and Pen and leave, and all I had to do was tell Menno. Tell Menno. But I didn't, he got in first, put it to me as if he gave me the choice, a crumb from his table to a dog. Boxed in again, even as I crack open the lid I'm put back in, made to feel like I live only by another's grace.

It's the tale of my life until I left Earth, a procession of faces and people that despite my best or worst efforts patronized me, ran my life to suit them then, emasculated, cast me away on a whim. I've started to shift it, bit by bit since I bluffed myself to believe I could convince Miss Xi to let us go, up to Te'eltwofo and that knife, going with my gut and not wondering. And I go and let Menno do this.

There's no point beating myself up. I stir the embers, bring a weak flame back. I've changed and I like it. Sha'Kert is good for me, good for my family, and I know it beyond any shadow of doubt. And the gmay? Menno? How do I feel about them?

My anger subsides, replaced by pity. Sha'Kert, a new planet, a new start, a chance to draw a line under the past and all our failures; yet they want to graft their dead past onto my living future.

No. As for me and my family we will not be shackled to them. I stand, let the fire die. I have to find Lou, tell her we will leave. Soon.

I LIE BREATHLESS in her arms; her eyes hold me captive as I hope they always will. Neueanbruch, Sha'Kert, Earth, or Juuttua; it is utterly irrelevant, my home is here and I intend it to stay that way.

"You've gone quiet again," Kell says.

"Sorry, I got...distracted."

"You were going to say something in their language."

"It's hard, I only managed two words and I'm only sure of one." I concentrate, let out a shrill series of whistles and pops.

Kell raises her eyebrows. "That's different."

202

"See what I mean? And that's only one word, 'sorry'. When they talk it's like music, music of whistles and trumpets."

"Well, it's an appropriate word for you. What was his name?"

"Shu'urtana."

"I'd like to meet him one day."

"You'd enjoy it, but I'd have to go with you."

"Why?"

"It's a long, dangerous trip, you might get lost and Shu'urtana, I mean he's a single guy and –"

"Henry Stoll, are you jealous?"

"Well no, I mean yes, yes I could be."

"So you should, you need to bring your A-game if you want to keep me."

"I've been doing fine up to now, haven't I?"

"Perhaps, but don't take it for granted. What else did you find?"

"That's pretty much it. No one's said much about what went on here, apart from Peter's suicide. I still can't believe it. Why'd he do it?"

"He knew how long we really took to get here."

"What do you mean 'really'?"

"We thought it took three days, Peter and Lou found out it was nearly four hundred and fifty years, they didn't tell us straight away. Lou only said 'cause she felt guilty about it after Peter died."

"It's right, it's possible?"

"Yes, it's right. Peter couldn't manage."

"Does anyone else know?"

"Everyone except you and Greg."

"How'd they take it?"

"Like they found out it was Wednesday not Thursday. They didn't seem bothered, as if it didn't matter."

"How about you?"

"I had a bit of trouble, everyone's gone and all that, but I'm okay now. There's not much I can do about it anyway, except get on and make sure I don't lose anyone else."

"I don't think that's an issue."

"Not for us, but it will be for Greg."

"Greg? Why?"

"When Lou told me, she said that it meant their marriage contract was over. She doesn't want to extend. I thought they were having problems, but I didn't know how much."

"Well, Greg wants all three of them to set up near the ocean. Maybe he's got a different opinion."

"It doesn't matter. If it's over, it's over no matter what he thinks. Lou's told Freda she's staying. She's not going anywhere, Henry."

203

"What about you?"

"What about me?"

"Will you stay with them?"

"Nothing's changed, it's like I said, we stay together."

"Even if it's to Shu'urtana's village, the far plains?"

"Even there, it makes no difference."

"I've nearly made my mind up to go to the ocean, close but not too close. If it's okay with you."

"Of course it is, I'll come with you, but on one condition."

"Which is?"

"If you want to do something more than live together, I don't want that thirty-year contract rubbish. I've talked to Freda and listened to the others and I want a lifetime. I don't want to know when it will end, don't want some sort of business arrangement to bring up kids then dance off in different directions into the sunset."

"Good, I couldn't have it any other way."

"Really?"

"That part of the Amish I can't get out of me. Once we get set up, once there's a roof and a bed, we'll do it."

"Then it's settled. Just keep seeing things my way and we'll have a wonderful life."

I laugh. "Yes dear, of course I will."

"And do you mind moving your hand? I'm not finished yet and it's distracting."

"Sorry."

"Don't be, just hold the thought for later. Do you think Greg's got any idea about Lou?"

"No, he hasn't spoken to her."

"So he still thinks they're a family. I saw Menno head that way a while ago, maybe he'll say something."

"I'm sure of it. If the gmay sent Father to me, they sent him to Greg."

"So, Menno tells him to get lost because the gmay don't want him, then Lou tells him to get lost because they're not married and she's staying here. What do you think he'll do?"

"I don't know."

"He'll feel like an outcast and a stranger, like Peter."

"You think he'd kill himself?"

"I don't know, but I didn't see it coming with Peter and if Greg, I mean if he did, I couldn't handle it. We must be able to do something."

"I'll make sure I work near him, stay close. But we can't tell anyone, especially not the gmay."

"You don't think they'd let him do it to get rid of him?"

"No, to them suicide's a sin, a straight ride to Hell, they'd try to intervene. That would make it worse. It's got to be only the two of us."

"What if he goes off to Te'eltwofo?"

"I don't know, it's too far to keep tabs on him."

"You'll have to go with him."

"I'll have to go with him?"

"For a while, until he's safe. He'd think you're making a point. And you've got a reason to come back he'll understand."

"I could be gone for months."

"I know it'd be hard, but even if he doesn't need you, if he's perfectly fine and it's only my stupid fear, can we afford not to?"

"No, of course not. I'd never forgive myself."

"Then it's settled, if it comes to it, you'll go with him. For a while."

"Father's going to be upset, Mom might make it hard for you."

"Don't worry. If it happens, I'll tell them a few days later. They should understand, shouldn't they?"

"Maybe."

Chapter Thirty-Nine

Louise

I FIND HIM wandering in front of the threeship. There are a few seats lying around, we choose two and sit. Greg reclines, stares up as the stars slowly rise: "I'm surprised you're out here by yourself, Lou."

"Like Freda says, the boxes are still there, only bigger."

"We haven't talked since I got back. You might've hung around."

"There's things that need doing, things they rely on me for. I stayed as long as I could, I heard it all."

"I thought they'd be happy. Guess I was wrong."

"Everyone hoped you'd find nothing, that Neueanbruch was empty."

"And you?"

"As much as anyone."

"Why? I can imagine you coping, but wanting to stay? There's nothing here for you, no friends or network to be linked into."

"You're not the only one who's changed. I need to tell you something Greg, that day Peter and I..." I tell him about the ship's AI, the four hundred and fifty years, Peter's suicide. He doesn't believe me at first, perhaps it's too outrageous, but he quickly comes round.

"He must have felt abandoned, totally alone," Greg says.

"He had no one, nobody at all."

"It's hard to accept it's all gone. How'd everyone take it?"

"Kelli was shaken but she's fine now, for everyone else it didn't matter. Well, maybe not quite that, more like it was simply the way it was."

"And you?"

Me? Finding out, having to keep it to myself knowing we're alone in time, cut off like no one ever has been with no chance of rescue or return; and then you desert me? It crushed Peter utterly, if it wasn't for Penny and Freda, I might've done the same and you stand cynically apart, threaten the support I need? "There's nothing I can do so I think I'm okay, at least there's no secret to tear at me. It's hard to imagine everyone's gone, I know it but every so often I hear Clara nattering away at me."

"It makes no difference to me, my parents are long dead and you know I wasn't close to anyone. It'd be nice to know how the kids in our pod turned out."

"The apartment's probably forty levels under now."

"Bet the Punisher's still there."

"I don't need her anymore, not with all this."

"When we get set up there'll be no more farming for us, at least the heavy stuff, the plants will grow well in the place I've picked out. We'll go see Te'eltwofo, I'm sure you and Pen will like her."

"We're not coming with you."

"That's okay, you don't have to, the journey's hard, you can always wait until I get back."

"You haven't thought it through, the four hundred years, us."

"Well yes, technically we're ancient, but I don't feel older."

I've accepted it, wanted it even as our relationship faltered and we shifted further away from each other but I hesitate; to think it is one thing, to actually say it will somehow make it real. It's still going to hurt. "The contract, our marriage. It ended four hundred years ago."

"What?"

"It's over, Greg, it's finished."

"It can't be, we're nowhere near our thirty years yet."

"It's been over for four centuries and you know there's no extension. Thirty years is thirty years."

"No, no it's not. We've been, well, asleep or something all the time so it can't count. Pen's not even a teenager."

"Greg, listen to me. It's over. Finished. It might be sudden to you, but we both knew it wasn't forever." I see it in his eyes, pain, disbelief, anger; my own are reflected in his, the same emotions overlaid with cold certitude.

"You've had months to think about this."

"Ever since Peter and I found out."

"It's a new planet, a new start, we don't have to play by the rules. We can extend, or simply disregard them."

I can't bring myself to reply, he has that look on his face, the one he had years ago when Santosh hung him out to dry, loaded the blame for all of them onto him. Betrayal. Disempowerment. Impotence.

We stare at each other in silence. His hazel eyes start to glaze over, his gaze drops; he's suddenly tired, fragile.

"You've made up your mind. It's over, isn't it?"

"Yes."

"No extensions, no nothing."

"That's right."

"If it had been days, not centuries, would you still feel the same?"

"I've asked myself that a hundred times and the answer's always the same. Yes, yes, I would."

"Have we changed that much, grown so far apart?"

I look away to the universe above. It terrifies me but I love it, love how I can be in the open and not be reduced to a quivering heap. Only here, only on Neueanbruch. "You said this place grows on you, changes you, well it's worked itself into me. You know I blamed you for Penny's disease, the whole mess that got us here? I don't now, in fact I'm happy about it all, happy I'm stranded here. How much time did we spend together, just the two of us, before we came here?"

"I'm not sure, not that much, there was always something else."

"I've had time to think, it's become clearer here without all that noise and activity around. We started to drift apart the day we first got contracted. Always kids, pod, work, friends, anything and everything chewing time until all we got were the scraps. Like friends."

"How so?"

"Freda, Rachel, all of them don't vid over or link in the net, they've never gone to McDsGlass or anywhere like that. They talk, they visit each other and spend time together, real time. It's a real community, real people, not occasional faces."

"The family you wanted, the one you didn't have."

He knows me well enough to think that's the reason, not deep enough to know it isn't. Not entirely anyway. He never understands when I try to tell him, how can he when his parents loved each other, gave him a safe home? "No, I had what I had and I'm not stupid enough to try and substitute for it. It's what it is, it's good, but the reason's deeper. Penny."

"She wants to stay?"

"Maybe, I haven't asked her. But she will and I'll see she does. I never had the family you had, I know we tried with Penny but she could never have the life I wanted her to have. How could it be normal when I tracked her all the time, bot feeds and coverage, always on guard and checking, worrying. She felt it, too, even if she didn't say."

"The old man?"

"Of course the old man! You have that happen when you're seven and you'd be terrified each time you can't see her."

"I know, I'm sorry, I didn't mean anything."

"It doesn't change the point. These people, this community can give her what I never could, a safe, honest life as a kid. It's what's best for her and me. It's what I want."

"Without me."

"She needs you, Greg, every kid needs both their parents. But I don't. Look at this place, at you, us. Life here is all day every day together, back home it was different, back to front. Mostly apart, always something else when we're together, no time for us. I don't really know you, we've gone in different directions, we're too far apart. And yes, even if we still had eighteen years to go, I'd still be asking, still doing this. I'd rather it end now than we part later hating each other."

"I can change, try harder to make it work."

"No, you can't. It's not right and you'd only end up worse than you are. I'm not moving away, not going to the sea or halfway, I'm staying right here with Penny.

How long do you think you can last, how long can you pretend? You can't live a lie. Neither can I."

His silence is harder than anything he could say. I feel the knowledge percolate through him, emotions slosh back and forth as his inner voice rages. I've been there, gone through it all over and over to always come back to the same conclusion whether driven by logic, tears or anger, always back to the same point. Thirty years is still supposed to be thirty years and somehow I'll always feel cheated. I've had time to accept it, wallpaper over the cracks so it looks like I have control. He's had none.

He stands, looks down. "I better get my grip, find a place to bed down."

"You don't have to, it's late, you could tomorrow."

"No, it's best I do it now."

"Greg."

"Yes?"

"Don't forget you have a daughter. Whatever happens, don't forget about Penny."

I watch him go into the threeship, re-emerge, then without a backwards glance stride into the forest.

I BARELY HOLD it together, take my satchel and grip from behind Pen and plod off into the night anywhere, anywhere but there. My legs take me where they want as the voices in my head scream hate, pain, anger, despair; failure upon boxed-in failure. Boxed by CLN3-R, Jonathon, Santosh, Miss Xi, Cephas, Menno, and now Lou – each in control, each one twisting my life to where I don't know what I don't want. I don't turn, don't care where I go, my legs follow the path as my brain fights my heart, sling bag smacks my back, grip hacks through grasses and brush as they, too, turn against me.

I come to a clearing, my legs throw me face down into mossy grass to yell into the sod, curse everything under the stars. Used, leached dry then spat out when it suits them, they'd strip my skin and self-respect as a trophy and nail the bastard thing to the wall? All lost, everything locked into Lou and Pen now taken from me. 'Don't forget you have a daughter'? The fuck I can but I know how it turns out, how a man goes from father to myth to byword in a child's life when he's not there. She'll be one of them, Lou already is, and I'm on the outer.

Shock and anger soak into the ground in exchange for emptiness, chews away my heart to leave it filled with nothing. I sit, look up to a single tree in the middle of the clearing lit by starlight, a gentle breeze above my breath. My eyes adjust, I catch sight of a cloth strap tied to a branch, one end crudely cut in haste, the other dug into the wood as if it bore a heavy load.

The Pegasus' belt, Peter's tree, I laugh at the irony of an empty living man staring at the nothing left by an empty dead one. Is this how you felt, how it consumed you when it was all torn away without the chance to fight back? You poor sod, I laughed at you, wondered at your weakness when all the time we're the same, the same boxes, the same chains.

Transfixed on the branch my grip slides to the ground, breaks open, the clatter an obscene assault on the quiet. My past spills out, the useless essentials of an Enforcement life: biochip drives, bot enhancer, comms link, all worthless glittering toys.

It stares back at me, gray with menace, a singular expression of place and authority from a lost world. I pick it up, feel the cold metal handgrip, ribbed dischargers, pitiless bore. A person, a tree, a threeship it doesn't matter, each are as nothing before it. I slide my finger along the accumulator and it springs to life with a soft iridescent glow. I hold it in both hands, caress it as I once caressed Lou. One push, one tiny movement and that would be it; no pain, no noise, on then off, here then not, life then nothing.

Why not, why not simply embrace the loss and close the circle? Maybe Peter was the only sane one, to accept what was inevitable, leave it behind to add his absence to the absence already there. It would be cleaner than hanging, instantaneous, and I can't miss, the wide beam will take me and half the clearing. The wind picks up, twin moons a pair of malevolent bloodshot eyes scud across the sky to watch, wait, accuse; there's no place for you with her, no place with them, be done with it and finish it now.

My finger knows its way to the safety and the weapon's alive. I swore I'd never use it, die rather than take someone else's future away. Does it matter when it's my own, when the guilt and shame of the act is absolved by the act itself? The barrel's cold, the taste of plastic and metal heavy as my teeth bite, the gun perversely elongated as it leers before me shaking. My gaze follows its length to the open grip, to a half-hidden picture strip. Strangers stare out, a man, a woman, a child. Who are you, do I know you? Part of me understands, part of me is lost.

The gun shuts down, overrides kick in before it overheats. I let it fall, pick up the strip and hold it close. It's Lou, Pen and you, my mind tells me, but her eyes and my heart deny it. This is not the Lou that walked away from you, this one's eyes shine bright yet are tinged with emptiness, uncertainty, fear. I look closer and the mask emerges, the set of her mouth, the tilt of her face, the best disguise ninety-nine percent truth. The Lou at the Pegasus has no mask; she's outgrown it and with it her need for me, the desire to hide behind pretenses of convention or pity. Whatever she has found completes her, and I am no part of it.

I stare out to my older self; the bullet-proof façade laughs, sees through the histrionics and my heart to judge its future self. I look back to emptiness and self-hate under a surface tissue of lies, futile attempts to succeed, tacit cooperation as I let others run my race and plot my course. I am still he, I am still nothing wrapped in my shell; I have started to chip at the pieces, pull away the scaffolding only to bind anger in its place. As much as Sha'Kert is a new start, a new chance, the old Greg lives; and the old Greg will hide or conform, turn away from the truth and take the easy way out each time.

Pen stares up, complicated, guileless, young enough to trust. We said we loved her and she never doubted; I said she wouldn't die and she believed. What will she learn if I kill myself, how will she face the inevitable disasters of life? Do I want a legacy of betrayal, pain and desertion as my only gift to her?

The clouds roll back to claim the night, the gun waits patiently at my feet. It pulls me, anchors me to the old world, the old Greg, the old solutions. This world doesn't know me, makes no demand but to survive, to be, to try what few can and walk away from the ruins of what was and reset my life; or squander the chance and pollute the future with my past.

I put the strip in my sling bag, take the grip and the gun, walk a few steps and put them down. I activate the accumulator, select the right cycle and return. A brief pause, a ball of searing yellow light, and I draw the line under my old self.

The last link to the old Greg remains, and with time she will forget that early life. As for me it starts now, this minute, a chance to rediscover myself.

The rain starts, I ask for dry and heat and I lie down, the drops move left and right to leave me under the gentle caress of cool night scents. I'm drained, empty and tired, but the nothing has a companion that slowly fills the space as it pulls me to sleep. All I can think of, all I can hope and dream, is to lose myself in this place.

FREDA WAITS FOR me, the children asleep around her. I barely make her out in the faint light. "Did you talk to them?" she asks.

"Yes."

"How was it?"

"Harder than I thought. It was right but, even so, difficult."

"What did Henry say?"

"Many things. He cannot break his promise to you or his feelings towards the gmay. He will be near but not among us. At least he will be close, we will see him."

"What else?"

"We talked about us."

"Us?"

"No, Henry and I."

"And?"

"He said…I am not the best father to him."

211

"Oh."

She is silent, it is unlike her. When we are alone, she hardly keeps her voice, only when uncertain or as she tries to dance between words. I grow more uncomfortable as the silence lengthens. "Say what is on your mind."

"Every boy pushes against his father, it is simply how it is."

"But?"

"Have you thought there may be some truth in it?"

"His words pierced but they were true. I did my best, I did as my father and that is my error. I forced Henry away as my father did David."

"As long as Henry's not lost, there's hope for the two of you. He could have ignored you and stayed on Earth, but he came with us. He's keeping the bridge open, Menno, it's up to us to cross it."

"I did not see it that way."

"Then there's Mahlon, Luke, Orva, and Isaac. If we erred with Henry, we should take more care with them."

I look behind her to the darkness, to the forest and the mountains beyond. A yellow flash comes and goes near the horizon. Here one instant, gone the next, it is like all life; time is short, opportunities few. "I cannot lose any more, not a single one. I realized a truth tonight."

"What?"

"We are the last of our faith. If no one followed us, if they all remained, four centuries is enough to remove them all."

"Then Neueanbruch is a greater gift, and the burden to survive and prosper clearer."

"And to protect the traditions of our fathers. We must transplant our way of living from the old world to the new."

"So, what of Greg?"

"He holds to what he believes, and his opinions have not changed. He sees his future away from us and with those he met. He said he will speak his mind Sunday."

"It is best for all of us if he goes, he will do nobody any good if he stays."

"That much I made clear. I took no pleasure in it, less so as he does not know about Louise or the time."

"He hasn't spoken to her?"

"Not when we talked. He does not hide his emotions well, he was surprised and angered by our rejection of what he found and our request. I tried to explain why, but I doubt he understands."

"When he talks to Louise there may be more he will not understand. What will you do if he asks to remain? He may think he can reconcile with her or keep Penny if he does."

I know what I must do. There is no choice. "The gmay comes first. If he asks, I must deny him. If he insists, I will deny him again. If he stays against all this, we will remove ourselves from him, leave him to those he met."

Chapter Forty

Greg

I WAKE TO low, mumbled incantations. Menno wanders past locked in some ancient ritual, loops around the tree a few times then goes back the way he came. He's oblivious to my presence or chooses not to acknowledge me. Either way, I'm warm and dry and he's clearly chilled and wet. The temptation's to stay here and put it off, but it must be done before Pen finds out from anyone else.

I wait until the sky's light then head back, emerge from the tree line and catch sight of her upslope, two seated figures nearby. It's the Lehman children, ever since the accident they've been inseparable, like triplets.

Pen hugs me enthusiastically. "Hi, Dad. Wow, you're warm and dry, where'd you sleep?"

"In the forest. I used Te'eltwofo's present. Here, give it a try."

She plays with it for a few minutes. I take it back and sit. "The plants look good. I knew you could take care of them."

"I picked a spot so the bison don't eat them, but I'll make a wall from rocks to keep the babies out."

"Sounds like a lot of work."

"No, it's easy with three of us."

"Who's helping you?"

"They are."

"They who?"

"Amy and Joseph."

"Pen, you know they can't."

"They're getting better."

"What?"

"It's a secret, you can't tell anyone."

"You know they can't get better. It's like you told me at the spaceport, wake up in η-space and that's it forever."

"But here's different. Watch."

The two children stare downslope, wide-eyed and unmoving. Pen crouches in front of them. "Amy, Joseph. Look at Dad."

Their heads turn to look straight into my eyes. My blood runs cold as the hairs on my arm stand on end. I raise my hand and gave them a hesitant wave. They respond with nods and wan smiles, then turn back.

"Have you told anyone?"

"Nobody, just you."

"Not even the Lehmans?"

"'Specially not."

214

"Why'd you show me?"

"You're different. None of the other old people will understand."

"Understand what?"

"How they're getting better."

"No one's ever recovered from η-space. What did you do?"

"Nothing. It's Sha'Kert."

It takes a second to register. She's only heard it once, last night, from me. She says it exactly like Te'eltwofo. "Say it again, the name of this place."

"Sha'Kert."

"Where'd you learn to say it like that?"

"Nowhere. It feels right, how she wants it to be said."

"Who wants it to be said?"

"She does. No one wants their name said wrong."

"It told you?"

"No, it feels right. Like you feel it a bit."

"What do you feel?"

She shrugs. "Stuff. Good stuff, just think about things and feel it. I gotta concentrate though, it's easier now and I'm getting better."

"And you think it helps Amy and Joseph?"

"I suppose. I reckon they feel it more 'cause their heads are empty. Like empty bots, fill them up with stuff."

"Does it ever give you bad feelings, things I wouldn't like?"

"Nope. Only about telling Mum or anyone, like it's a bad idea."

"Except me?"

"You're okay."

"What about Kelli and Henry?"

"Maybe, one day, not now."

"What about Menno, Mister and Mrs. Lehman?"

"Nope, never."

"And the other children?"

"Don't have to, they feel it, too."

She'd always had an active imagination but never an imaginary friend. Or planet. She never had the need on Earth, anything she'd come up with there was always something on the net and if not, the AIs filled the gap. Here there's none of that. Maybe it's her way of coping, it seems harmless enough. Amy and Joseph are another matter, but it could simply be Sha'Kert itself. It had impacted me dramatically, as it had Lou, why not those two? Yet the way she said Sha'Kert doesn't fit. A fluke maybe, perhaps coincidence and nothing more – I dismiss the thought. "That's a good idea, keep it a secret between us and the other kids. Promise me you won't tell Menno or any of the others."

"That's easy. I won't, no one else will. Dad?"

"Yes?"

"Can people get trapped by what they think?"

"Yes, sometimes worse than prison, some people never escape."

"I think that's why I can't tell them. They'll never understand, they're really scared and want the wrong things. That's what Sha'Kert feels, anyway."

"Sha'Kert might be right, honey."

"Dad?"

"Yes?"

"You and Mum aren't married anymore, are you?"

"Where'd you hear that?"

"Mahlon told me, heard Menno and Freda talk about it."

"Does your mum know he told you?"

"No. But it's true, isn't it?"

"Yes, honey, it is. I was going to tell you."

"It's 'cause we took too long to get here, right?"

"It doesn't mean we don't love you, or your mum and I aren't friends."

"I know all that, they teach us that at school. It means you're leaving."

It's a statement not a question. Maybe I haven't even told myself, but knowing's not acceptance. I pull her close. "Yes, I think I am. I only ever argue with Menno and Cephas and all of them. It's not they're bad people but we're too different. I can't live with them, Pen, and I can't live with your mum. You know you have to stay with her, don't you?"

Her sniffling settles down a touch. "I know that, I know all of it."

"Your mum would feel awkward having me around. I have to go, maybe spend some time with Te'eltwofo."

"You won't forget me?"

"No! How could I? I'll come visit, it might be a while at first, but I'll visit you."

"You won't."

"Won't what?"

"You won't ever come visit."

"Oh no, I will, I promise. Have I ever broken a promise?"

"You don't understand. You're meant to never come back. You don't have a choice, it's just the way it is." She turns to face me. No tears, clear-eyed, serious beyond her years. "It's okay, I'll be fine with Mum. It's where I need to be. You have to go, and you'll never ever come back. It's what you need to do, so don't worry, it will all work out."

She stands, takes Amy and Joseph by the hand as Menno's call to Sunday service floats across. "It's Sha'Kert, Dad. She'll take care of all of us. It'll only hurt for a bit."

FREDA AND HENRY catch me as I come out of the threeship.

216

"Louise, did you talk to Greg?"

"Yes, Freda, last night."

"How did he take it?"

"Better than I thought."

"Did he say what he was going to do?"

"Why are you so interested?"

"Cephas and the men saw Menno earlier. You know the gmay isn't comfortable with him after what he and Henry found. They've made a decision."

"About?"

"They're not going to let Greg stay, at this morning's service they're going to ask him to leave."

"Chances are he won't stay, anyway."

"They're scared, I've not seen them this way before and I admit I'm the same."

"Scared of Greg?"

"We know he's going to get with these others, and we don't want a part of it. They're going to shun him."

Henry's eyes widen, he turns to her. "He can't do that! The ordnung don't allow it."

"They added to the ordnung this morning, Henry. Menno's the only minister, so it's done and that's that."

"It's not for anyone outside the gmay."

"No matter, the men met and –"

"It's not right and Father knows it. Why'd he do it?"

"He thinks we're the last gmay. He told them we're all that's left and each one's grown harsher. They want to fight to keep the gmay intact."

I don't understand it, Henry's upset and Freda seems embarrassed. "Can you two stop it? Henry, what does shun mean?"

"It's when they ban everyone in the gmay from having anything to do with someone. They can't eat with them, talk with them, work with them, help them, or anything," Henry says.

"They do that to people who disagree?"

"It's worse than you think."

"How can it be worse?"

"They won't lift a finger to help him or even recognize he exists. He's totally alone until he comes crawling back to beg forgiveness."

"That's cruel. He may think differently but he's not a bad man. What about when he visits to see Penny, everyone's going to turn their backs and pretend he doesn't exist? Is that what you'll do, Freda?"

Her mouth moves but no sound comes out. She meets my eyes briefly then looks down. Henry puts a hand on my shoulder: "Don't be too hard on her, she's got no choice. If she disobeys then the gmay will shun her as well. Same for everyone. I've seen husbands shunned, totally cut off from wives and family."

"What about you, Henry, will you do it?"

"Never. I'll not turn my back on him. Neither will Kell."

"At least he has some friends."

Freda's quiet; she looks at the ground, Henry, anywhere but me. "What about me, Freda, when he visits and we talk or eat together, will you shun me?"

"No, it shouldn't come to that."

"It's not right, I didn't think you could be so heartless. He may not be my husband and he might not even be my friend, but I'll not abandon him like that."

"Mom, I've got to talk to Father, it's wrong," Henry says.

"You know he won't budge. All the men are behind him, you'll only make trouble for yourself, Henry."

"I've got to try. He doesn't listen to me now, the worst he can do is not listen more."

They move off towards Menno as he calls for morning service.

"Henry?"

"Yes, Louise?"

"If Menno won't change, if you can't and they do this, will you –"

"Don't worry. I won't let him go alone."

Penny wanders over to me. "We better go, Mum, Menno's starting."

"We need to talk first, Penny."

"About what?"

"You, me, Dad."

"Oh, the not being married thing. Know already."

"Who told you?"

"Dad did."

"What did he say?"

"Stuff."

"And you?"

"More stuff."

"Penny it's not a game, I'm serious. I need to know how you feel. So?"

"So what?"

"How do you feel about me and Dad not being together?"

"I don't like it but it's okay, you both love me. But you're both stupid."

"Because?"

"At school they said it's thirty years to make sure I don't grow up wrong and I'm not even halfway yet."

"Maybe we are stupid."

"No maybe. But I still love you. Both. Just."

"That's good. You'll be all right, you know, we all will."

"I know."

"You do?"

"Yes, you don't?"

"Yes, I wanted to make sure you did."

"Well, I do. And Dad said he's moving away, and I told him that was okay, too."

"So, you know everything and it's all okay?"

"Pretty much."

It's like I'm calmly picking over the corpse of my marriage with Clara, not my child. Has she matured that much? Have I been so self-obsessed I haven't seen it? "Well, there's one thing you don't know. About this morning, about Menno."

"He's going to kick Dad out."

"How do you know? I only found out a minute ago."

"Nobody notices us kids, everyone acts like we're not there, but we know what goes on. Mahlon heard Menno and Cephas and Nathan this morning, so he told me."

"What else do you hear?"

"Everything."

"We'll talk about that later, but right now it's your dad I'm worried about. And you."

"I'm okay, like I said it's all okay."

"Your dad doesn't know what's going to happen. It will be a surprise."

"A bad one."

"He won't be ready, won't have time to pack. They'll make him go straight away." I move back to the threeship, pull out an empty flight carry-all. "I can't do this, they'll see me, but they won't notice you. You do want to help, don't you?"

"Yes."

"Good. When Menno starts talking, they all pay attention to him. When he starts, I want you to fill this with food, things that will last your dad a while, okay?"

"Isn't that stealing?"

"Ah, no, not really."

She looks crestfallen.

"Well okay, it is."

"Good, it's punishment."

"Yes, punishment. Once you've filled it wait here and when you see Dad leave, go after him and give it to him."

"What about Henry?"

"What about Henry?"

"Orva heard Henry and Kelli last night, she's sending Henry to make sure Dad doesn't do something stupid."

219

She's my own little surveillance bot. What doesn't she hear? I should pay more attention to her, stop playing mother all the time. "Get another bag, fill it for Henry. Now go, Menno's starting."

Chapter Forty-One

Greg

PEN'S WORDS ECHO in my head. She's full of surprises, this the latest and largest in a long line. I can't help feeling it's role reversal, or more like a meeting of equals. With everything that's happened, the push to survive and get a toehold, I lost track of her. She's done a lot of growing and the place obviously suits her; it shouldn't surprise me, it seems to suit most of us in entirely different ways.

A small group gathers around Menno, Freda and Henry in animated discussion, Lou to one side, Pen on the grass next to the Pegasus. I should hate Menno, hate them all with every bone in my body; no matter how hard I try, I can't. I don't feel anger or betrayal, no need to rail against those who try to put me in a box, force my will. I can't raise any emotion except faint disappointment, sorrow-tinged hope they will come to their senses and at least try to adapt to Sha'Kert, learn from Te'eltwofo. Can they survive if they don't? I'm not as sure as I was, but I know I won't be here to see them prosper or perish. Pen is right and wrong; I will see her again, perhaps many years from now, but see her I will. And Lou? I can't bring myself to think.

They start, a long sonorous hymn in the still air, a monotonous dirge carries unintelligible sound to me. Faces start to turn, heads shake as it continues. I know Menno expects my answer; clearly I am already the main topic of the meeting. Should I walk away, make it clean and simple? Curiosity wins me over, a plow makes an enticing seat. I wander over and sit, give Menno a smile and a wave as he starts his sermon.

"…a new world, added to the ordnung…"

Henry sits next to me, whispers conspiratorially. "I'm sorry, they won't listen to me."

"I don't know what you mean, but thanks anyway."

"I'm talking about them kicking you out."

"They can't, I'm going anyway."

"…discipline to all, the 1632 Dodrecht…"

"They want to shun you, totally cut you off."

"You said they only did that to members."

"Father's put a new ordnung in place just for you."

"Fine, if that's what they want."

"…principles. Titus asks us to…"

"Fine? It doesn't bother you?"

"No. One way or another I'm not staying, so what's the difference?"

"You know Louise and the kid are staying? Have you thought about that?"

"Of course I have. Look, Menno might think he knows her but once she's made her mind up, that's that. Ordnung or no ordnung, she'll play the game only as long as she wants to."

"...avoid them that cause division..."

"She's playing a game with Menno?"

"Not that I know, but if Menno's god told her himself not to see me and she wanted to, then she'd ignore him."

"She wants to see you, then."

"I don't think so. It's over and that's the way it is, but I'll see Pen every so often."

"...last gmay in creation, the sole remnant living how God..."

"He believes that, Henry?"

"Totally. You're looking at the last Amish in the universe and the man chosen to lead them."

"Sounds like Moses."

"Someone warned me about this."

"...we cannot afford. I have asked him twice if he..."

"What are you going to do, Greg?"

"I'll wait until he's said his piece."

"Then?"

"I'll say mine and walk away."

"...we are to have nothing to do with him so we and our children may not become defiled, do not partake of his sins. Paul commands us to put away the wicked person, not keep their company, and to withdraw ourselves from them."

Cephas takes Menno's place, stares at me coldly. "This is to protect the gmay. Only when united and consistent, we ensure your influence is not felt on us or our children. You helped us establish Neueanbruch yet you did not lend all your effort and will to the task. We need to set an example of humility, submission and industriousness, in all of which you fall short."

"Your way of life," Menno continues, "your beliefs and actions are wicked. We must separate you from us, mark and avoid you, as you have rejected us and the way of living we value and are charged by God to continue. Maybe you wish to turn from your way of life and try to live among us. If you do, ask now, pray forgiveness before we deny you our fellowship."

Menno sits as the meeting falls silent. I walk to stand in their midst. Slowly, to make sure I miss no one, I look each in the eye, hold briefly then move on. No one flinches, none looks away. As Henry said, ears closed, minds made up, decision made.

A flicker of anger rises, a tiny flame of resentment for my life again chained by others. As fast as it rises, it falls as understanding dawns. These are not pioneers trying to continue their way of life in the face of enormous odds, but uneasy and frightened people that cling to an isolating tradition. It is all they know, all they can dream, to live by and conform to the authority of long dead texts. As much as Menno feels I am my own captor, they are slaves to their own fears.

My chains remain but slowly, deliberately, I remove them. For Menno, for all his people, their chains hold fast. I look to Menno and start to speak. "Some of what you've said I don't understand, but I understand enough to know you are wrong and misguided. You spoke openly about me, I give you the respect of the same."

I remove the clothes they gave me, stand barefoot and bare-chested in tattered Earth trousers. "You accuse me of being idle, not pulling my weight or putting effort into building this place. It's true I'm no farmer, and perhaps I am less able than the weakest of you, yet my body bears the same scars."

I pick up the discarded clothes and place them on Cephas' lap. "Perhaps you think me a thief for wearing these. I give them back if it makes you feel justified, and for the food you gave in return, I give you the plants from Te'eltwofo. I hope they feed you for many years to come."

Cephas opens his mouth, I point my finger at him and shake my head. "All this you bring up now. You never said much before, only when I wanted to go and explore Sha'Kert and even then I listened, I respected you and I waited. You talk of respect, where is the respect in what you are doing?"

"Greg, it is not –"

"I have never heard any of you interrupt another when they speak, Menno. You would do me the courtesy of the same."

He sits.

"You say you are the last of your kind, it may well be true. You say Sha'Kert is god's gift to you; that I don't believe – it's clearly not empty and not yours, although no other human has ever set foot here. Be that as it may, accident or god or neither, Sha'Kert is a new start for us all, a chance to be something other and hopefully better than we were, a chance to make new lives, new traditions, new futures. But you want to impose the old on it, shackle it with the rules and life that whittled your community to nothing on Earth? There is no world to shut out, in four centuries they should have found us, but they haven't. What does that tell you?"

Menno rises to stare at me, nose to nose. "Greg, you do not understand, you never will. You are too ready to cast off the past as useless, disregard our fathers. The ordnung, the Bible, it is all timeless, perfect, the voice of God to all mankind. Regardless if it is now or four centuries or forty centuries, it remains true. You talk of a new start, you had best look to yourself, you are still what you were."

"No, I'm changing. I should hate you, what you think you can do to me, it's what I would have felt before. But now all I can do is worry for you, pity the chance you're letting slip through your fear and ignorance. Tell me, if Sha'Kert is truly god's gift, then everything on it must be as well. So Te'eltwofo, Shu'urtana, all of them shouldn't be ignored but welcomed and encouraged, to help you. Is it right to cast god's gift back in his face?"

He stays silent, lips a rigid scar.

"So. And you, Cephas, you worry about my influence, how my words or actions can corrupt your children. It's strange to me, strange that your faith is so weak. What sort of faith is it if it's not strong enough to withstand my presence?"

A stir goes through them, a flicker of anger through Cephas' eyes until they return to the Amish passivity I've come to know. I feel no joy; it's confirmation of their fragility and fear. And of mine.

"All of which doesn't matter. Your faith is yours, not mine. It's not my place to change you, nor yours mine."

I feel inside my satchel, make sure everything is there. I settle the strap on my shoulder. "You don't have the right to shun me. I know it's only for those of your church, not those outside it. It's an act of desperation, Menno, one I'm sure no one else in your position on Earth would try. For what it's worth I reject it utterly, I have no reason to repent or return, only reason to change more. It's also unnecessary. Like I said last night, nothing can change my mind."

From the corner of my eye, I see Pen emerge from the Pegasus, Mahlon in tow, arms laden. "Sha'Kert will change all of us and I intend to see where it takes me. I'm leaving, I won't be back to visit any of you, but I will return to see Pen, keep an eye on her. If Henry could slip past you to see Freda, it should be easy enough."

I walk to the edge of the circle, stop and turn. "Look at it this way. You can keep your consciences clean, your hands blood free. I'm shunning you."

I leave as fast as I can. The wind picks up, the deep overcast foretells rain. I make the top of the rise and, without a backward glance, move down the other side. "Hello, Pen."

Mahlon's behind her, arms full. "You'll need these for the trip."

I poke my nose into Mahlon's bag. "Food? Whose idea was this?"

"Mum's," Pen says.

"Thanks, but it's a bit much, isn't it?"

"Not for two of you."

"Two?"

Henry grabs a bag as he walks past. "Yes, two. Don't just stand there."

"You're coming?"

"No, I'm here for fun. Don't be stupid, of course I am."

Henry turns to Mahlon. "You and the kid better get back before they work out who's missing."

Pen reaches up, gives me another hug. "Take care, Dad, I love you."

"I love you, too. I'll be back to see you one day."

"No, you won't." She scurries off after Mahlon.

"Ready, Greg?"
"Of course, let's go."

The Myths of the Children of Sha'ntwoy

The Place Beyond the All

Hear, daughters of Sha'ntwoy, sons of Kert'ankway, the orange children, keepers of songs:

The children of Sha'ntwoy and Kert'ankway ceased their labors, their toil, and in joy and quietness lived with the land and the garden.

In their hearts the Nothing slept. Their minds stilled to leave the gift of Sha'ntwoy, her peace in their spirits, and from their lives the Nothing receded. Yet were their lives as the snows upon Mortantoy, appearing strong bright for a season, then to leave, depart to be replaced by another, for the Nothing to awake.

There was a man in those days who loved the love of his youth with all his heart; to his love gave he four daughters upright and beautiful, her joy and peace. Yet it was that one winter they died, she and her daughters all, and in their place in his heart the Nothing raged until the man was consumed.

And he took himself to the highest peak of Mortantoy, to the sacred place where Sha'ntwoy appeared, and cursed he Sha'ntwoy and Kert'ankway, crying, 'Would a mother despise the bed in which her daughter was conceived? Would a father steal the love of his son's youth? Yet would you bring the Nothing to your children without cause!'

And Sha'ntwoy appeared to him and reproached him. 'Would the cloth tell the weaver its pattern, or the word demand of the poet her mind? What are you to question me?'

And the man stood, saying, 'Does not the just ruler cherish her subjects? What is this life you give if it only prolongs the pain?'

And Sha'ntwoy mourned for her son's grief, for the Nothing in his heart where his love for her had been. And she saw the desire of his heart had been to dwell with her, as was that of all her children.

And Sha'ntwoy and Kert'ankway touched their hearts to his; and through him knew they loss.

'Come, let us talk as sisters,' Sha'ntwoy called, and she prepared a place Beyond the All where her daughters and sons could dwell. And Kert'ankway created the bridge from the All to the place Beyond the All, and in the hearts of their children the knowing of the way. And the man put aside the knowing of the wings of fire, the terrible magic, and all the answers known. And as he, so also the orange children. And they counted it no loss.

And Kert'ankway raised up the peaks of Mortantoy and the lands around, that they should for all time be covered in snow as a sign.

But for the man's daughters and the love of his youth could Sha'ntwoy do nothing. They that the Nothing claims are its own.

To the orange children, the daughters and sons of Sha'ntwoy and Kert'ankway, are given the songs of the past.

Part III: Sha'Kert

Chapter Forty-Two

Greg

HENRY WANTS TO talk. I know it, I feel his eyes bore into my shoulders as we make our way along the path, the expectant tilt of his head as we rest, disappointed resignation when we resume in silence. He's smart enough to keep quiet, stupid enough to want to break it. I haven't even processed it properly yet. How am I supposed to make sense of it to him?

One instant I'm convinced it's a kaleidoscopic nightmare, a thirty-six-hour flurry of insane activity that tore me from them. Images of Lou, Pen, Te'eltwofo, my gun, the night rain, a sea of vengeful bonnets assault me, rattle around in my mind before rationality returns and I accept the natural outcome of a set of circumstances that could have no other end. They pitch back and forth, struggle to claim the title of the one truth – to either send me back from fear of what I've lost or run headlong from it in hope of what I'll gain.

Our progress has a metronomic quality, the crunch-swish of footfall, the hiss-suck of breath enfolds me. The longer it is, the farther away I get, the less Neueanbruch sits in my mind, the greater Sha'Kert grows. I imagine her a whisper, a faint presence close yet out of reach. I motion Henry to lead, allow my subconscious to follow and my mind to wander, float, or roam as it wishes. I have no desire for him to see the occasional shudder as emotion rises above rationality.

Late afternoon lulls me into a trance, my body moves as my mind sits back and referees the turmoil. Of course it's going to hurt. Back on Earth there are ways to transition; grown children, friends to celebrate, the arms of lovers who wait for the day. There's an adultness about it, shared knowledge and acceptance, a celebration of what had been and what won't become stale. This reeks of the knee-jerk selfish breakups of centuries past. No, that's hardly fair and certainly wrong. Hundreds of years or a decade, our contract wouldn't have made it; here, on Earth, or Juuttua. Lou's had more time to process it and work it through by herself.

Without me, really; that's the proper description, without me. She's right, we had no time together on Earth and our time here was no remedy; if we hadn't had to fight for Pen, lived that following year in a dream with her alive, the outcome would've been the same. Rationalizing it won't help, a scab on a wound simply lets the wound heal itself. Time and rest, Greg, rest and time.

"I'm beat, Henry. Let's stop here."

"Sounds good but there's not much shelter."

I look around. We've emerged from the forest onto the cold plain where snow-covered ground turns to slush under drizzle. I see a large patch of bare rock to the left. "It's fine, I've got the slate."

I sit, think of warmth, dryness and protection. Nothing happens. I take the slate out and concentrate. The air warms, the rain falls left and right, wind dies to a zephyr.

"Must be low on power."

"Could be."

Henry pulls out a fist-sized yellow disc, snaps it in two, hands half to me. It tastes vaguely familiar but nearly breaks my teeth. He seems to have the same problem.

"This is?"

"Supposed to be bread. Kell said they've nothing to make it rise."

"Uh huh."

"It should last a week or more."

"Maybe longer. Makes leaving easier."

"You haven't said much all day."

"I said enough this morning. What else is there? It's not like it'll change anything."

"You don't want to, I mean, you don't regret it?"

"No. I loved her, and I think we were happy for a while, so I can't walk away cold. It'll take time not to feel cheated out of the rest of our years."

"So, what's next?"

"I didn't think much beyond going. Guess I'll see what happens when I see Te'eltwofo. I'm not sure if I want a lot of company."

"It's not like they'll chew your ear off, they're not fluent yet and I don't think we'll ever get it."

"It's not that. All my life I felt like others were in control. I've broken it, put it to one side, so I want time to work it through, find out what it is I want without anyone's influence."

"So, why go near them? You could've easily stayed by the ocean."

"I'm drawn there, and I know I can't survive here by myself. Down there I can, I can find food and it's warmer. But there's another thing."

"Which is?"

"Sha'Kert's theirs. I've at least got to go ask them or tell them."

"You know Te'eltwofo said we're Sha'Kert's sisters?"

"Yes, but that was when we're up here where they don't go. It's different if I go to them, maybe they won't be as happy about it."

"Can't see it being an issue."

"I'm also someone without a home, Henry. Before I was a visitor, a guest or novelty. Now it's different, they might not be happy to have me as a refugee." I look at the rock-hard disc in my hand. I hand it back, swap it for a drink of water. The bourbon label's intact. "You'll need to look after that, only one in existence."

"Funny how the mundane's precious. I don't think they'll care about the food as long as the jars come back. Kell was saying Ruth used to be a bit of a potter before; she's been scrabbling in the river looking for clay."

"Heading backwards already. Guess it doesn't matter, they'll be fine."

"All of them? What about Louise and the kid?"

What about them? Lou was always going to be fine once she had friends, support and community. I've never been enough for her, wasn't what she wanted or needed; I was simply another part of her orbit. And Pen? I don't know. I can't reconcile the Pen of our last conversation to the child I watched grow. Out of the three of us she'll probably come out best. "I wouldn't worry too much, Henry. They're tougher than you think."

I lie down, try to find a place that doesn't feel like rock, or at least a contour that can fool me into thinking it's comfortable. I roll into a depression, my hips and shoulders mold into it, cradled and relaxed; a stone mattress. Henry's silhouetted against distant lightning, arms around his knees.

"Greg?"

"Yes."

"Are you going to miss anything?"

"Apart from Pen? No, I don't think so."

"I mean from Earth. The time hasn't really sunk into me yet."

"Don't know, haven't thought."

"Guess there's no more cigarettes."

"Probably, they've tried get rid of them for centuries." I yawn, it's surprisingly comfortable, if only that little spur near my leg was...ahh, that's better. "You know you're destroying valuable ancient artifacts, Henry?"

"Always was an expensive habit."

"Coffee."

"What?"

"What I'll miss. Coffee."

"Nothing else?"

"Not a thing."

"Out of everything Earth had, all the people, cities, all of it, just coffee? You can't be serious."

"I am. Earth feels dead to me. No, not quite, maybe more like a bad dream. It's already fading, Henry, like it wasn't really there. Except the coffee, that I'll miss."

"I'll miss books. I was going to read them all, learn everything I could but now I've only got one."

"It's not enough."

"Can't be, how many times can I read Moby Dick?"

"I saw a whale once."

"Where?"

"Natural Science Museum. Nice big one, you could walk through its mouth, see it from the inside. They had all the extinct ones there, elephants, lions, even a chimp or two. Just like us."

"Museum pieces?"

"Yeah, gone but not missed. You'll see, give it ten years Earth won't even be a vague memory."

"Probably for the best if there's no going back."

"Exactly." I close my eyes and sink into Sha'Kert, imagine myself enfolded in her grasp. "No going back."

Nearly but not quite, a zephyr carries the whisper, *nearly but not quite.*

Chapter Forty-Three

Henry

WE PAUSE AT the boulder forest. I assume we're heading to Te'eltwofo. Greg hasn't said anything more on the subject.

"Where now?"

He stops rummaging around, looks up. "I can't take any of this stuff, Henry."

"Why?"

"Don't want to owe them anything, you know, clean break."

"Don't be stupid, you've earned it. Anyway, it's part of a Juuttua cargo consignment. Kell's signed for it."

He puts a hunting knife and a multi-tool on the ground. "Oh, well in that case, these will be enough."

"At least take the shirt. It's mine, it's a bit big but it's a present, okay?"

"Thanks."

"So where?"

"Where what?"

"Where are we going?"

"The village, find Te'eltwofo."

"You remember the way?"

He points directly away from me. "Follow the wide path. I think."

We walk for perhaps three hours, then come to an intersection. Greg stops, hesitates, turns left. "Just a quick look."

We end up on a grassy bank beside a lake. I can't see the other side; perhaps it's elongated, perhaps it runs out to an ocean, I don't know. Greg seems pleased with himself.

"This will do nicely."

"You're not going to Te'eltwofo's?"

"Not to stay. This is the place for me."

I look around. Nicely situated, peaceful even. It's certainly isolated, we've seen no one all day, heard nothing. "It's a little out of the way."

"It's what, maybe two hours to Te'eltwofo's, four back to the cliff? Far enough for peace and quiet, close enough in case."

I sit and watch the wind play on the water's surface, the strange ballet as insects above the water try to snare those below it. He sits a short way off, back against a tree.

"We'll stay here tonight, the light's starting to fade. Tomorrow we'll see if Te'eltwofo's around, if it's okay."

Greg tries his best to explain but fails spectacularly. Te'eltwofo seems stuck on our home being near the threeship. Jab, counter jab; home, no home. It wears my patience and Te'eltwofo's frustrated.

"Let me try something different, Greg."

"Fine, you can't do any worse."

I add some stick figures in the dirt near the crude scribble of the threeship, then two more slightly apart. I point at the group, then the two apart. "Sisters. Greg. Henry. Sisters. Home."

"Sisters yes. Gre'eeg Hinry sisters," Te'eltwofo says.

"That's right, up till the other day. Watch." I draw a line between the group and the two, point alternately at them. "Sisters. Greg no sisters." I shove Greg to the ground as hard as I can. "Greg no home. Greg no sisters. Greg no home."

Te'eltwofo pulls Greg to his feet, touches thumbs. "Gre'eeg home Te'eltwofo. Hinry home Te'eltwofo." She erases the two stick figures, re-draws them next to her village with a wide circle around the lot. "Home."

It's settled as far as she's concerned.

Greg takes out the slate, screws his face tight like he's freezing and clasps his arms. He puts the slate in front of her. "Broken."

Te'eltwofo stares, no reaction at all. Greg taps the slate as if trying to wake it. No change in Te'eltwofo, if anything she looks amused as Greg continues to tap the slate, pretend to be cold, tap it again. We try everything we can think of over the next half hour, but nothing works. There's no sign from Te'eltwofo that she understands as she watches us madly flail away.

Shu'urtana wanders over, a young child in tow. The child stares transfixed at the slate. An opaque roof appears above our heads; it flickers then wobbles drunkenly. I duck to avoid being hit, the only thing that reaches me are gales of laughter, and Shu'urtana's thumps on my back. Eventually, the child's persistence pays off; the opaque roof hovers at the right height, stable, the air beneath warm and gentle. Shu'urtana and the child hurry away happy and excited.

"I think we got it wrong, Greg."

"How so?"

I pick up the slate, spin it in my hands. "It's not low on power, it's gone to level two."

"Perhaps it gets harder the more you use it, to train you."

"What for? So you can use it better?"

"Maybe, or maybe so you can do more with it."

"Hold on, I'll give it a try. Tell me when you feel it." I look at the slate, concentrate, wish for cool. The faintest breath of chill air caresses us.

"Impressive. Bet their kids do better in the womb."

Te'eltwofo watches intently.

233

"That's alright, I've a lot of catching up to do." I concentrate, perhaps being more specific will help. Greg smirks as he waits for the next fizzer; I'd like nothing better than to get it freezing, wipe the smile off his face.

I no sooner think it than an icy blast flattens him. Greg pulls himself back onto his haunches and shivers, looks at me from under hoar-frosted eyebrows. Te'eltwofo's beside herself.

"Okay, Henry, I feel it already."

"Sorry, I thought –"

"Well, don't think it again, okay?"

Chapter Forty-Four

Greg

"I'LL ADMIT THAT for peace and quiet, you picked a good place," Henry says.

I look behind him to the first dusting of snow. I concentrate, try to lift the temperature near me without changing his. It wavers hot-cold then settles. Four months here, four months practice and I can get it right with just a little effort.

"I know they come this way, but I've not seen any of them."

"They might understand you more than you think, Greg."

"Possibly. Anyway, it's working out for me."

"Do you still think of them?"

"Of course. You?"

"Yeah, Kell for sure, each day. Don't know if I'm cut out to be a hermit. I'm not like you remember, I ran away from empty into the crowd."

"I like not having to worry about anything except myself, no one watches what I'm up to or tries to change me. I've got time and space to think."

"Certainly got that." Henry stretches then turns. "I never thought you'd stay by yourself, I figured you'd want to stay in the village and get to know Te'eltwofo." He walks off, collar turned to the damp.

GREG CAN HAVE the shelter for a bit. Even in this weather, the bank's comfortable; perched on my rock, I gaze across the water. Warm and dry are good but there are times when cold is a friend, the wet a sympathetic salve to settle and re-center me.

I reach into my jumper, take the packet out. I knew it would come to this. My last cigarette stares glumly back. I light it carefully, draw the smoke in reverently to linger far too long until it seeps out. Enjoy it, Henry, make sure you remember each second; you'll never see another one.

My stupidity amazes me, making promises before I thought them through properly, if at all. That and, as Elliott once tried to explain to me, a misplaced sense of loyalty and duty, the honest man's curse. I should have put some sort of time limit on this rather than a blanket promise, then I go and compound the problem with both Kell and Louise. How long does it take until it's clear Greg's no danger to himself? He's only been better since the day he walked away.

I twirl the stickpin in my jumper, turn the threeship design one way then the other between my fingers. A keepsake, a reminder of promises made. It's fine for Greg to close the door on his past and move on, but my future lies a week behind

235

me; and if the snow is the first touch of winter here, what is it like back at the threeship?

Each day the debate, each night I sleep with it unresolved. Another day, another week he'll be fine and I can go, I say to myself. But the day never arrives, it feels no nearer than at the start.

I hold the stub for too long, drag on it until my fingers feel like they'll ignite; I reluctantly crush the life out of it. I heard others on Earth curse the fact they were everywhere when they tried to quit, the futility of going cold turkey when companies keep sending sample packs. I don't have that problem, they're finished and I simply have to get used to it.

I realize Greg's the same; no matter what he says, me being here drags it out, every minute with me is a reminder. He was never going to do anything stupid and never will. It's time I left, time to go back.

A SMALL CLOUD drifts away from him. Henry always manages it, finds another one, announces it's the last cigarette in creation then somehow finds yet one more. Always one more.

I settle back to watch the night close in. The days and nights are constantly wrapped in dark clouds, continual drizzle, and now the first snows. I've started to learn the cycle of some plants, some fruit as the cold triggers them and others start on the obvious decline to inactivity. There's always enough, not a remote chance of starvation. There's so much to learn, so many things about Sha'Kert.

Too much I realize, way too much for me alone. In months here I haven't learned much, it's like I'm fumbling around blindfolded. The simplest of things, learning when something is ready to eat, led to nights of cramps and sweats, days of uncertainty and prevarication; and that only for knowledge of a handful of the fruits and berries around us. Myths of explorers starving to death in the middle of plenty ring true. I'm not in that predicament and never will be, but the process of learning enough to move from scraping by to properly living with country promises to be long, slow, and painful.

Henry's another thing. I've grown to like my own company, perhaps not quite as much as I led him to believe, and we've started to run out of things to say. Not that we're at each other's throats for the sake of it, or that days drag into weeks of silence, but rather that conversations are short, staccato exchanges of things previously discussed or conversations past. Familiarity may indeed lead to contempt, perhaps that's where we're headed. That he needs other company I've no doubt, yet he remains with me, two outcasts together; it could be he simply needs my presence.

I roll to my side, will the temperature up and a gentle press of weight. I seem better able to work the slate when my mind is quieter, and the slate is now more than light and shelter. I've grown used to the pretense of a blanket to give better sleep and comfort.

That, I remonstrate, is the problem, Greg Robinson. The comfortable, the familiar appeals even when you know it's second best. Henry for company, a simple existence with no one to challenge or second guess; a pathway to lesser understanding. You want to know Sha'Kert, you feel drawn to her, yet you avoid those you can learn most from.

I know it, I've known it for weeks but it's only now I feel like facing it. The same groundless fear shifts to Te'eltwofo. Would they try to box me in, impose their rules on me if I decide to stay with them? What if they do, what then? Does it even matter? If I'm to know Sha'Kert, I can't stay here. I need to learn from Te'eltwofo and Shu'urtana. A hermit's life is not for me.

Tomorrow, tomorrow when I wake if I feel it's still right, I'll go. There's nothing to take, perhaps a bag, that's all. And it will be good for Henry.

"I've had a think about what we said the other day."

Henry keeps his head down, pulls berries from their stalks. They taste delicious only if picked and eaten before early morning; any later it's like eating liquid soap. "About?"

"Here, Te'eltwofo, being by myself."

"Oh. That."

"You're right, it was good for a while but it's not how I want to live. I should be with them."

"Makes sense. You're not going to learn much out here by yourself."

"I thought you'd agree."

"So?"

"So, let's go. Today."

"No point hanging around."

"It's okay with you?"

"Me? Of course."

"Good."

I look at the patchy white land, the tiny assortment of things that comprise our camp. Hardly one bag between us and the fronds we use for bedding will rot soon enough. "We could head off now, be there by midday."

Henry pops the last of the berries into his mouth. "Sooner the better. Give me five minutes to get the food together."

Henry pushes the pace, we make the intersection in no time. I start to turn left towards Te'eltwofo's village, Henry stands still.

"You all right, Henry?"

"Yeah."

"Well, come on, don't stand there."

"I'm not going that way."

"What?"

"I'm going back to the threeship."

"I'M NOT COMING with you, Greg, I'm going back."

"You can't, they kicked you out. Oh, that's it, you're going to get Kelli."

"They didn't kick me out and I'm not bringing Kell, not right away, anyway. I'm going back to her."

"You're going to live with the gmay?"

"No, I'm going to set up towards the ocean. Close enough to visit, far enough to be too far for them."

"It's a good spot."

"I'll plant it out, a few bison, fishing. No farming, I've still got the scars. You know you can come back and stay."

"No, my future's down here."

"And mine's back there. But you can visit, you know, when you see the kid."

Greg chews it over, smiles. "I intended to but somehow I don't think it'll happen."

"Why, don't want to open old wounds?"

"No, just a feeling. Before I left, I promised Pen I'd visit but she was adamant, said I never would."

"Perceptive kid."

"More than that, Henry, much more. Can you do me a favor?"

"Anything."

"When you get back, let Pen know, let all the kids know where you are, that if they need to they can get to you. Something's going on with them."

"Sure, but what do you mean? You think they're in trouble?"

"Not at all. You know I'm drawn to Sha'Kert; at times it's like it whispers to me. Well, the same's been going on with Pen and the kids. Except it's stronger, they don't have the baggage to get rid of I do."

"Does anyone else know?"

"No one, and I'm not even sure I should tell you. You can't tell anyone, not even them, okay?"

"Of course." The uncertainty has left him, Greg stands and looks at me clear eyed. He is where he needs to be; I have to go where I belong. "We'll see you one day, come down to see all of them. It might be years, I can't walk out on my promise to Mom."

"You know where I'll be, and I'm here if anyone else wants to change." He hands the slate to me. "Take this, you'll need it."

"No, I'm fine."

"Don't be stupid, Henry, take it. Te'eltwofo's probably got thousands of them tucked away, I'll get another."

I take it, put it in my bag. I hold out my hand. "I better be going. It's been a pleasure, Greg."

He pulls me into a tight, lingering hug. "Couldn't have survived, couldn't have done any of it without you. Live long enough to be an embarrassment to your grandchildren."

He steps back.

"One last thing. When you get back, tell Pen I don't hurt anymore."

With that he turns, walks off without a backward glance.

Chapter Forty-Five

Greg

I POINT TO Mortantoy. "Henry home." I point between my feet. "Greg home."

Te'eltwofo drapes an arm around my shoulders. "Gre'eeg sister. Gre'eeg home."

They seem unsurprised to see me. Shu'urtana casts an anxious glance or two up the path, a child and slate at his feet. I point to the slate then Mortantoy, turn out my pockets. "Henry, home. No."

The child scampers away. Te'eltwofo gently pulls at the holes in my trousers to be rewarded by tearing fabric. I left the Pegasus with them as an act of defiance; now it looks more like an act of stupidity.

"I know, I know. They're the only pair I have."

She shouts to the child's back, waves one hand in an arc from Shu'urtana's clearing to her own. "Gre'eeg home? Gre'eeg home."

It's flat, grassed, with trees to the far side. I walk about fifty meters away, halfway between her home and the trees. "Here. Home."

The child returns arms laden, hands a slate to Te'eltwofo. She places it on the ground, moves back to Shu'urtana. They talk rapidly, the child smiles, nods once then closes her eyes.

A five-meter circle of grass flattens, knits together, the ground rises a few centimeters. Some more chatter and an opaque disc forms four meters over the raised ground. It wobbles, phases in and out, then settles down. Two rectangles rise and mold themselves to an oversized chair and bed, suitable for Te'eltwofo perhaps, but I'd be lost in them. Shu'urtana whispers to the child, the bed and chair assume the correct proportions.

"Gre'eeg home."

"Thank you, Te'eltwofo. Impressive display."

The child leaves, Shu'urtana holds up the bundle she gave him, a smaller duplicate of their tunic-like clothes. Te'eltwofo tugs at my trousers.

"Okay, okay, I get the idea."

I pull the tab and the tattered ribbons fall away. Te'eltwofo points to my underwear.

"These as well?"

Shu'urtana loses patience and slices them with his knife. The rag joins the others at my feet, my nakedness a source of much interest; they talk excitedly and point, examine me. I try to get the tunic from Shu'urtana, but he holds it away from me as Te'eltwofo reaches out and down with one hand.

"No, Te'eltwofo! Greg Mortantoy, Greg Mortantoy."

It pulls her up immediately. Shu'urtana laughs and tosses the tunic to me. I hurriedly slip it over my head, the sides meet and seal. Shu'urtana gives me a slap on the back; Te'eltwofo's in front, hands wide apart.

"Mortantoy," Te'eltwofo says, then holds her thumbs barely a centimeter apart. "Gre'eeg. Gre'eeg no Mortantoy," provoking more laughter from Shu'urtana.

Life in the village has its own rhythm. Food is plentiful and easily found, even under deep snow, there are no buildings to maintain, animals to tend, shops to fill. Nobody seems to have a job or trade of any sort, yet the days don't idly waste by. Life is centered on children and community, an endless series of social and communal activities balanced by jealously guarded early morning solitude. Even the children; perhaps it keeps them balanced, young, I've not seen a decrepit or aged one yet.

I participate eagerly; I'm here to learn and they start me on it after two days. The first morning Te'eltwofo rouses me, takes me in the cold pre-dawn air to a rock that overlooks a small, iced over river. We sit, legs dangle over the edge.

Te'eltwofo puts two fingers to her lips. "Gre'eeg no. Te'eltwofo no." She wiggles violently, stops. "No." She touches her eyes, ears, head. "Gre'eeg yes. Te'eltwofo yes," turns and ignores me for the next two hours.

I sit silent and still; after an hour the conversation in my head dies. I slowly become aware of myself, legs on the rock, air as it makes its way through my mouth to my lungs and out again, the faint pulse behind my head as my blood runs its race. The land reveals more, detail rises even as it falls away in favor of something else on the edge of awareness. Again, the whisper; a close, vague presence grows in the interstice between noise and self as my mind empties. Too soon, Te'eltwofo takes me back to the village.

The next two days she wakes me; the next two days I am awake to greet her; on the fifth day she points me towards the rock as she goes elsewhere. I am alone to pursue my own solitude, my first steps into village life.

I start to learn their names, see the subtle differences between individuals – Shu'urtana's not-quite symmetrical eyes, Te'eltwofo's delicately long fingers, her neighbour Ker'paano's pronounced chin. Whatever I teach Te'eltwofo is transmitted to the rest of them. On the one hand it's good, I have no problems with communication, even if it's still pidgin; on the other hand, no matter how hard I try, I am now 'Gre'eeg' to all of them.

The spring thaw, gentle warm air, and the return of the birds puts more energy in everyone's step. I find myself on the shoreline with the village, another communal sports day, I suppose; it seems to be their main preoccupation. That and eating. I sit with Te'eltwofo's and Ker'paano's families, a rowdy collection of young children or teenagers. I don't know how old any of them are, I simply guess, given their size and behavior.

Ker'paano taps me on the shoulder, points to a small group of children in waist deep water. "Gre'eeg watch. Lesson. Up long. Up best."

Six children form a rough semi-circle around one in the middle. A scrawny child to one end I recognize as Rii'tvaa, Ker'paano's youngest daughter, raises her arm. The child in the middle nods, shakes gently, then rises slowly out to hover above the surface. As the child drops unceremoniously back, Rii'tvaa lets out a gasp. Everyone on the bank makes appreciative noises, Ker'paano in the lead. "Up good."

"How?"

Te'eltwofo points to a slate a short distance away, then to her head. "This. Babies. Lesson. You."

"Me?"

"Gre'eeg lesson."

I watch as one by one the children lift their friends up with nothing more than the slate and their minds. One child slowly cartwheels above the water for twenty seconds, another barely gets their knees clear. They are all greeted with the same enthusiasm by everyone on shore. When they finish, the children turn and point to me. Before I can protest, Te'eltwofo and Ker'paano deposit me in the middle of the children.

"Up long, Gre'eeg," Te'eltwofo cackles as they leave me alone with seven smiling faces I'm sure are up to no good.

"Take it easy, treat Greg nice, okay?"

The seven raise their arms as one. I might as well give in, so I nod and hold my breath.

I lose count at twelve dunks, some from a few meters, some from surface level. It feels like the world moves away and back, each a solid smooth motion even when they send me in spinning. My shouts and flailing arms only egg them on, add to the entertainment on shore. Eventually, when they deem to finish, I stand thoroughly drenched and sand-coated to the obvious delight of their parents. It's a heck of a display and, I realize, a controlled one; again I've been taken unaware by the slate, by their technology.

"Thanks kids, that was fun," I lie as the last of the water drains from my nostrils.

Rii'tvaa gives me that weird, three-lipped pout I've grown used to from Te'eltwofo's children. "Now. Gre'eeg lesson."

"Me?"

"You. Now lesson."

The seven of them are close, gazes locked on me. They're serious, they want me to try; they must know I'll fail. Te'eltwofo said it would be a lesson, so why not? I raise my arm, look at Rii'tvaa who nods back, and wonder what to do next.

242

I concentrate on the slate with no real purpose; as the seconds drag by I become more aware of my inability. I close my eyes; I haven't trained for this, I'm able to get the temperature and the walls right in my home, but this? What am I doing here? Embarrassment threatens to drown me; right now, I want nothing more than to be back on shore between Te'eltwofo and Ker'paano, put the kids back with their parents.

I don't know what I feel first, sand under my backside or the thump on my back. I open my eyes to empty water in front, Te'eltwofo next to me, and a high-pitched babble of voices.

"Good, Gre'eeg. Lesson good," Te'eltwofo says.

"How the heck?"

She grabs my head, presses gently. "Yes, Gre'eeg. Lesson good."

Maybe it's the way it always is, first time's way too easy then it gets harder. Although more impressed, I'm warier. What more can that slate do?

Solitude slowly changes, deepens me. The presence hovers closer, barely out of reach, a whisper or feeling I'm not sure, but as I wait in the quiet, it connects somewhere inside; as it does, Sha'Kert reveals more of herself. A detail here, extra sharpness there, nothing dramatic but rather layer after layer peels away to build knowledge, awareness. I know if the blue fruit is ripe before I see the tree; I feel the brush of small birds' wings before they fly; and I know where Te'eltwofo, Shu'urtana, Ker'paano, all of them are each day. No voices, no far-seeing; a simple, sure knowledge.

I grow restless as the days warm, snow replaced by light drizzle, partial overcast for solid murk; Te'eltwofo's invitation to roam is one I can't pass. Five of us set out; Ker'paano and Shu'urtana lead, Te'eltwofo, Mii'irkentra and I follow. I think Mii'irkentra is the oldest orange person I've met, light gray thinning hair, respected by everyone in the village. It's not deference or authority but perhaps acknowledgement of age or wisdom. I feel he's here for Ker'paano's benefit; as the days pass, they walk ahead of us, lost in conversation until Shu'urtana takes his place.

At times everyone walks with eyes shut, unerringly on course without the least stumble. Again the slate's doing, yet I'm the only one who thought to bring one along. If it weren't for the slate, for the obvious signs around me day and night, I could mistake Te'eltwofo and her kind as simple hunter-gatherers who lead the easiest of lives.

We follow a river downstream through a valley, stop for the night where it suits Te'eltwofo. "Te'eltwofo?"

"Gre'eeg."

I wave one hand in a wide circle. "More people?"

"No more sisters."

I tap my chest, point behind me. "Greg people sixty-three." I tap Te'eltwofo. "How many Sha'Kert people?"

"Two hundred ninety-eight."

I cup my hands, roll them as if cradling a ball. "More people Sha'Kert?"

"No. Two hundred ninety-eight."

The others join us; we sit in a closed circle.

"Yesterday two hundred ninety-eight?"

Te'eltwofo points all four thumbs over her shoulders. "Yes. Two hundred ninety-eight."

"Always?"

Te'eltwofo creases her brows. "What always?"

I'd not taught her that word, now is as good a time as any. "Te'eltwofo. Always. Billion, billion, yesterday. Always."

"Always."

"Yes Te'eltwofo. Always. Billion, billion, tomorrow. Always."

"Always."

"Yes, always."

Shu'urtana breaks in, points behind then in front. "Always yesterday. Always tomorrow."

I point behind me, in front, then in a broad circle. "Yesterday. Today. Tomorrow. Always."

I still have no answer. "Mii'irkentra?"

"Gre'eeg."

"Sha'Kert people. Always two hundred ninety-eight?"

"Yesterday always. Tomorrow…" and he gives an all too human shrug.

Te'eltwofo points behind her, then waves her arms at the stars. "Gre'eeg people sixty-three. Gre'eeg people more?"

"Yes, more."

"Two hundred? Two thousand?"

I know what they want but my information is four centuries old. I know what Earth was, is it still there? What of the others, they weren't the same; some as populated, others empty as Juuttua, and then there's the spacefarers. There were only a hundred planets, are there more now or none? It doesn't matter, any number's as good as another. I double what was Earth's, times it by a hundred, then by ten. It will do.

"Greg people. Five hundred trillion."

"Five hundred trillion sisters? One Urth?"

"No, Te'eltwofo. One thousand Earth."

It causes an argument, one that, apparently, Mii'irkentra wins. He looks up, extends his arms, fingers spread wide. "Yesterday hundred thousand Sha'Kert. Yesterday sisters up. Sha'ntwoy no up. Sisters no up. Today no up. Today one Sha'Kert. Today sisters two hundred ninety-eight."

"Sha'ntwoy?"

"Sha'ntwoy."

"Sha'ntwoy no up? Always no up?"

Mii'irkentra puts his hand on my heart. "Always. Always no up. Sha'ntwoy lesson, no up. No up good. Up no...no..."

He struggles for the word; I know where he's going. "Mii'irkentra. No good. Bad. Bad. No good."

"Bad. Bad no good. Good no bad. Bad, good."

"Yes, Mii'irkentra. Sha'ntwoy lesson?"

"Up bad. Sha'Kert good."

They wait for me; I try to get the words right in my head. "Yesterday, sisters up. Hundred thousand Sha'Kert. Sha'ntwoy lesson. Up bad. Sisters no up. Always tomorrow one Sha'Kert. Always tomorrow no up." I take a quick breath, make an educated guess. "Sisters no up. Sha'ntwoy good. Sisters good. Sisters up. Sha'ntwoy bad. Sisters bad."

"Yes, Gre'eeg."

Mii'irkentra wanders away with Ker'paano, suddenly engaged in deep, private discussion. The light fades to a soft glow as Te'eltwofo and Shu'urtana drift off to sleep.

They are not what I thought a year ago and I'm sure they have no idea themselves. A remnant population, an advanced civilization of a hundred thousand planets reduced to one planet, this tiny remnant. Why, I have no idea, but whatever it was has been reduced to myth built around Sha'ntwoy, a deity whose favor is found only by staying put on Sha'Kert.

The slates, everything that can be done through them, must be the last tangible signs of the height of their civilization, possibly once another piece of hardware taken for granted, now Sha'ntwoy's blessing. I shouldn't be surprised, the Amish will be like this in a few generations; myth to override fact, god substituted for events, remnant metal tools and plasteel components his gifts, no one will care to know how they work. Perhaps Te'eltwofo and her people's acceptance of things as they are mirrors Menno's; accept the boundaries given, don't improve the means you have, live the way your god intends. The comparison can't be drawn too far; for these it is an open door to a welcoming people who, to this point anyway, place neither limit nor restriction on me; perhaps if that had been my experience with Menno I wouldn't be here.

Nearly but not quite; a whisper, a thought, it sinks as it rises, fades indistinct to watch, to wait.

We take our solitude together the next morning as, Mii'irkentra tries to explain, we will do for all the days left. As we sit around Ker'paano, I can't help but feel this is a design of hers, the whole thing somehow to her benefit. It's not an uneasy feeling, more one of rightness or even acknowledgement. These four are the closest I have to friends, the ones I felt connected to from the start; even Mii'irkentra, who seems to have sidled in unnoticed after that spring by the shoreline and now, at times, I'm convinced is my shadow.

Solitude starts, as always, with my mind quiet and detached. It's quicker and easier now; as I sit and close my eyes the first breath is a trigger. The grass in front of me explodes as I fall into its fractal avatar, as does Ker'paano as she fades from prominence to grow in detail. My connection to Sha'Kert is stronger, the faint knowing of where the others are shifts, sharpens, dances around me until they are a physical presence in my mind, five as one a tangible object I examine even as we sit apart.

I feel the breath scratch down Mii'irkentra's throat, scoured by years of singing; my shoulder itches as Shu'urtana's tunic shifts in the breeze, the sharpness of his shoulder blades a childhood irritant mastered and forgotten; I know the fall of Te'eltwofo's knuckles on her fingers, feel the remnant knife prick on her thumb, taste the evening meal's rind caught between her lower teeth. I do not call these things, yet they are there; oneness and separation as strong as each other.

I look out from Ker'paano to the four of me gathered around me as my heart sings, my time moves on to rejoicing, the start of my journey. I know why I am here, why my strange, dark-skinned sister is here, but she does not have the words, so she cannot hold onto it. Pity, a shame, but her time will come; as it has for me.

They help me to my feet as the sun tries to push through the overcast. Half the day passed as a second.

Te'eltwofo smiles. "Lesson good, Gre'eeg?"

"Yes, lesson good."

We resume our walk along the valley floor. I am acutely aware of Mii'irkentra and Ker'paano to the front; the dull feel of grass against legs, drizzle on bare heads if I concentrate, if I make the effort to reach out. I push myself, absorb my mind in the task as best I can to slowly, achingly, add the tiniest detail. We stop at the edge of a stream, they turn to me expectantly. I open my eyes, Mii'irkentra smiles, nods, then makes his way slowly across moss-covered rocks. I follow, disconcerted. I've walked the last three hours with my eyes closed.

We travel in what I think is a broad circle, the longer we stay out the closer Shu'urtana and Ker'paano become; for the last few days they and Mii'irkentra are a tight knit trio, engrossed in conversation and each other to our exclusion. Each day's routine starts with group solitude; it summons me to greater effort, a need for deeper concentration, focus. They encourage me, each session centered on Ker'paano to the point I'm convinced I'm linked to her; vaguely, obtusely, yet linked nonetheless.

We walk until dark, three in the lead heads bowed, pony-tails swing in locked concentration. Te'eltwofo and I examine the landscape and talk as we follow; not that there's much, a few words then hours of silence until evening is our fill. It's as I imagine it should be for anyone freed from the strangled morass of the city and released to nature; it is not to be feared, but to be embraced and desired as much as solitude, the chance to reconnect with yourself and drown the cacophony in your head with silence. Somewhere, somewhen, humanity had cast this aside for the cages I grew up in; had that been the only path open to us?

We settle as the dull splotch in the cloud hunts the horizon. It was in front of us the first few days until, now, it is behind us. We still hug the valley floor, I've no way to reference Mortantoy, but I have no doubt we're on the way back to the village. Te'eltwofo hands me the evening meal; the other three sit some distance away. "Tomorrow home," Te'eltwofo says.

"Good."

"Tomorrow home. Next tomorrow Mortantoy."

"Mortantoy?"

"Yes. Tomorrow. No Gre'eeg home. Gre'eeg Te'eltwofo home. Next tomorrow. All sisters Mortantoy." She seems insistent.

"Yes."

"Next tomorrow lesson. Mortantoy lesson."

She stares at the others as the light fades; a hint of pride and envy flashes across her face.

The village is still, empty, all homes save Ker'paano's opaque. We walk in silence to her home; she goes inside with Shu'urtana and Mii'irkentra. For the thousandth time that day Te'eltwofo presses her fingers to my lips; we walk into her home.

Welcome is brief, sincere, and silent; as soon as it starts it is over. She points to a corner; suddenly tired I fall into a deep sleep.

Chapter Forty-Six

Greg

THEY WAKE ME, wait in silence as I shake out my sleep. No food, no water, the transparent ceiling greets the first glimmer of a new day. Te'eltwofo stands close, presses her hands against my lips and shakes her head; she moves her fingers to my eyes, ears, then to rest over my heart and nods.

She arranges us as toy soldiers, I to her left, her children to her right, her partner at the far end. She takes my hand, presses my flesh; something tells me it will be held all day. Along the line hands are joined and we wait, an orange-skinned family and one interloper.

The house disappears, as do all others; each family stands hands linked, no one moves, a gentle breeze the only sound.

Mii'irkentra appears from my right, moves to the edge of the village at a slow walk. Shu'urtana and Ker'paano follow side by side, eyes fixed on Mii'irkentra, then behind them Ker'paano's family. As they pass, we fall in line. By the time we reach the edge of the village everyone is in the procession, hands linked across families. We start at a brisk walk that rises to a steady jog; hand in hand, line astern, we continue for the next three hours. We halt at the edge of the stone forest; Mortantoy towers above as the sun glowers through cloud.

Mii'irkentra turns as if to check no one is missing, then ascends the steps at the foot of the stone platform. Te'eltwofo moves us left, halts behind a large obelisk-like stone. I look forward, see a row of stones three small, one large, six small, one large repeated directly from me to the platform. Each family has fanned out, each one behind a row. I feel a push, walk towards the platform, keep pace with Ker'paano's family to my right, orange caterpillars that converge on the platform, draw near then stop when our shoulders touch. At the head of her family line, Ker'paano's eldest daughter puts her arm across my shoulder; I lift my arm to drape it across the family to my left, each linked to all through an unbroken chain of flesh.

I feel all two hundred and ninety-five as if I have a hand in each of theirs; it stretches from my mind, I know each of them feels me clearer, closer. I had a taste with the four of them, this is simply scale; of Shu'urtana and Mii'irkentra I have vague knowledge, of Ker'paano a certitude as if we embrace.

The drizzle returns, makes no difference; no one uses the slate, none seeks to shield themselves from the wet. Ker'paano turns to face her eldest daughter; Shu'urtana stands one step up behind Ker'paano; behind him Mii'irkentra solid, erect. All three raise their eyes to Mortantoy. Mii'irkentra reaches out, places his hands on Shu'urtana's shoulders; Shu'urtana puts his hands on Ker'paano, Ker'paano grasps her daughter's face in her hands.

My world explodes. I am Ker'paano, Ker'paano I, both one with everyone and everyone one with us. It's joy, music, acceptance of each by all in full knowledge of who we are, what we are. Above it all rightness, an action in its proper place and time, Ker'paano at the center, all of us a part of her and whatever is to come. At the edges something indistinct, something more, faint echoes of muted voices and minds slip in and out as tenuous links break, re-form, break again. That I only feel in part I am sure; as sure as I am that they accept me into them, that I will see Ker'paano again.

As quickly as it comes it goes. Ker'paano releases her daughter, ascends with Shu'urtana the few steps to the ledge, then turns. Without fuss or hurry Shu'urtana removes Ker'paano's tunic, leaves her naked and exposed. I know Ker'paano is female in the same way I know Te'eltwofo is; yet there's nothing about Ker'paano to indicate either way, simply a smooth, featureless orange skin from crown to toe, fingertip to fingertip. She holds her arms out beside her as Shu'urtana lifts her knotted hair in one hand, with the other a thin-bladed knife severs hair from head to join her tunic on the ground. They turn, rapidly scale the ramp to Mortantoy; we watch until they are out of sight then filter back through the stones in silence to sit around Ker'paano's family.

We keep silent vigil all afternoon. Has Ker'paano been banished for some error? Perhaps it is some rite of passage. I am unsure and even if we could talk, Te'eltwofo won't have the words to begin to tell me. I know Ker'paano was willing; I suspect Mii'irkentra is central to it all; and I am certain we are all eager conspirators. But to what end?

The afternoon drags, the sky darkens. A slight tremor brings everyone to their feet; as the tremor grows, so too the air of expectation until, in the middle of Ker'paano's family circle, a gray stone pokes its bashful head from the soil, hesitates briefly as if to gather strength, then blossoms to another perfectly formed obelisk. Pandemonium erupts, eventually settles to slaps and excited chatter as the first food and water of the day make themselves welcome.

I move to the fringe, seek a little peace in a vain attempt to understand. I'm no better off than before; is each stone one orange person or two? I try to count them, give up after I pass a thousand. It'll come, Greg, give it time, be patient. Two had gone up. One stone had risen. And it all seems expected. I sit, back to a tree, embrace my lack of understanding.

Te'eltwofo sits beside me, babbles at me. Her family join us, talk through me, perhaps forget I am the illiterate one.

"Lesson good, Gre'eeg?"

Good experience perhaps, but the lesson's lost on me. "Ker'paano home Mortantoy?"

"No. Ker'paano home Sha'ntwoy. Always." Te'eltwofo slaps the ground, points to the new obelisk. "Ker'paano. Sha'ntwoy. Always."

"Shu'urtana home Sha'ntwoy?"

Te'eltwofo points to the village. "No. Shu'urtana home. Tomorrow."

I wave my hand at Te'eltwofo's family, tap her on the chest. "Tomorrow Te'eltwofo sisters up Mortantoy? Te'eltwofo family home Sha'ntwoy?"

She breaks into a broad grin. "Yes. Lesson good, Gre'eeg. Sha'ntwoy home, all sisters home." She pushes one finger firmly into my chest. "Sha'ntwoy Gre'eeg home."

The days lengthen, I suspect summer makes her presence known. I have no way to be sure, time is an abstraction. I once marked the days, but the rhythm of the village takes its place, the cycle of solitude, socializing, regular communal meals enough to mark time's passage.

I'm quieter, more patient and receptive; my early idea of learning goals for Te'eltwofo fell away, traded for acceptance of whatever happens. In spite of this or, perhaps, as a consequence, she becomes more fluent. And as she, so too the village, to my lessening surprise.

As I quieten, Sha'Kert arises. I am now perhaps where the youngest of Te'eltwofo's children are with the slate; the ease has left, forces me to concentrate, to try, to think clearly. In solitude I win small, hard-fought gains in awareness; each time the whisper comes, when to watch was not enough, I reached out gently, carefully, to build a bridge to that presence. She waits with me now, Sha'Kert a gentle, all-pervasive companion.

I return home one morning to find Te'eltwofo waiting for me.

"Lesson, Te'eltwofo?"

"Later, Gre'eeg. Now talk."

"Talk."

She pulls my slate from behind her back. "This I take."

"You take?"

"Yes."

"For always?"

"Always. Never for Gre'eeg."

"How house? How food? You take no warm, no house, no dry. Why?"

"This for baby. Baby take. Baby use. Gre'eeg no baby. Gre'eeg no use. I take."

"But –"

She puts a finger to my lips, points to the slate. "Baby speak this. This speak Sha'Kert. Sha'Kert speak baby. Gre'eeg no baby. Gre'eeg speak Sha'Kert. Sha'Kert speak Gre'eeg. No this always."

"Yes. Te'eltwofo teach Greg."

"No. Sha'Kert teach Gre'eeg. Yesterday lesson easy. Tomorrow lesson hard. Sha'Kert lesson hard."

Left alone, I sit morosely and wait for the seat to disappear, the chill to seep in, the walls and roof to suddenly not be there. Nothing of the sort happens; the banal normality of living in a space generated by thought silently mocks me. After everything, I doubt this? I've accepted everything Te'eltwofo has told or shown me and not once has she failed me. Admittedly, I can't make sense of most of it but that's the point, to learn. I can almost hear Henry's laughter, why won't I play the game properly if I really want to learn?

I haven't thought about them for a while, there's too much to occupy me here, nothing to drive them to front of mind. My thoughts drift to Pen, wonder what she's up to, how she is. I lean back, close my eyes as a wave of tiredness creeps over me. It would be good to know, to hear her, but that's years away if, or when, she decides it's time to visit.

Not this place, never this time, Sha'Kert whispers as I balance between wakefulness and sleep.

"Even if it's never, you know I'll be okay, Dad."

"I know, but sometimes I wonder."

"We couldn't be safer, either of us, don't you see yet?"

I spring upright, eyes wide, alone in my house. Pen's no voice inside my head or imagination but clear and distinct, close. I reach out for her, call out to her in my mind; she remains quiet, her presence hidden, the limit of my reach the edge of the village. I am alone, no one in sight, yet Pen's voice was clear.

My surprise fades; after all, what's this other than another thing from Sha'Kert, another tantalizing glimpse to be won by hard work and persistence? The more I think, the greater their technology seems; what was Te'eltwofo's race like at its height, how much has been lost? Now this, like the roofs and the children playing, another lesson. I concentrate, will the room warmer and slowly, sluggishly it changes until I'm satisfied. What seemed impossible months ago, I manage; perhaps there are hard lessons to come but I will learn.

The seasons blend into each other, lessons with Te'eltwofo change. She has no need of my instruction, she speaks well enough. Now we simply sit and talk, yet the time she set aside for me stays between us, perhaps Mii'irkentra and Shu'urtana join us, more for my benefit than hers. I defocus my eyes, seek her presence from the two hundred and ninety-six others; of all hers is the strongest, the clearest. This, too, test and extension; I feel her a short distance away with Shu'urtana as I know they feel me.

I've tried to reach out to Pen. As much as Mortantoy is a soaring physical barrier, it looms impenetrable in my mind. Cold rain closes in, I think myself warm and dry in its midst and wander off.

I sit, watch a small, yellow-black striped bird flitting deliberately between flowers, huge orange-yellow upended trumpets. The bird hovers, folds its front wings to hang beak down, then descends briefly until it resurfaces streaked in buff pollen. It rights itself, then moves off to its next suitor. I've never grown tired of them; I'm all the more impressed as they only appear in heavy rain.

"I have question, Gre'eeg."

She always does and unfailingly gives notice; as if any is needed. "Yes, Te'eltwofo."

"Children. How Urth teach children? Urth talk children?"

"No. Earth no talk children. People give lesson."

"Sha'Kert give lesson. Day. Night. Always. Urth people give children lesson always?"

"No. People teach half day. Not always. Give lesson school."

"School?"

"Lesson home school."

"All Sha'Kert school. Always lesson."

"Always day night?"

"Always. End Mortantoy."

"Earth lesson end twenty, thirty years."

"Then Mortantoy?"

"No. No Earth Mortantoy."

"Why lesson? No Mortantoy, no lesson."

"Lesson for after school."

"Sha'Kert lesson end. Sisters go Mortantoy, go Sha'ntwoy. Sha'ntwoy teach."

"Always teach?"

"Always teach."

We watch the birds feed, dance in and out of vine-covered bushes as they search for flowers. Three hover in front of a particularly overgrown area that barely covers an outcrop of large, untouched blooms. It amuses me for a while to watch the birds bounce back after unsuccessful attempts to break through, yet the longer they persist the more I imagine them frustrated and tired. I reach out with my mind and move the vines aside, gratified as the birds plunge again and again into the flowers then drunkenly fly away, leave tan-colored smoke in their wake.

Shu'urtana turns to me. "Sha'Kert teach Gre'eeg good. Gre'eeg not baby. Gre'eeg child."

I'm deflated. I've spent years with them, thought my progress was great; but they're right.

Shu'urtana seems sympathetic, reaches over to tap me on the forehead. "Baby new. Child new. Sha'Kert lesson quick. Gre'eeg old. Here old. Lesson slow. Sha'Kert teach slow. More Sha'Kert teach Gre'eeg, more quick lesson Gre'eeg."

"All Sha'Kert baby lesson quick?"

"All baby. All children. Sha'Kert teach quick." He stands, turns to leave. "Gre'eeg children. Sha'Kert teach quick. Sha'Kert lesson good."

Chapter Forty-Seven

Greg

MY TOES SKID, a tenuous grip lost then regained as I find the crevice in the moss-encrusted rock. I balance spreadeagled centimeters above cold, crystal clear water. Waves of silt, pebbles and lichen crawl along the riverbed as small pieces of detritus flow downstream beneath me, somewhere in the meter and a half before the bottom.

Fishing. Te'eltwofo's so excited she drags me along like an empty sack; with Shu'urtana and Mii'irkentra we make a group of four. Meat of any sort isn't in their diet, I can't recall fish in the five years I've been with them.

"Once in year only, one day only. No children, no babies, you old enough. Just," Shu'urtana says.

They start a fire when we reach the riverbank; two holes filled with grasses and branches let out a thick oily black smoke, then settle to two pencil-thin columns of dark gray as branches turn to coals. Te'eltwofo shows me what we're after; a long, deep ochre eel-fish that lazily progresses along the riverbed. We watch a small school pass by, I lift the largest and slowest out and hold it in mid-air. Te'eltwofo scowls, breaks my grip, and returns it to the river.

"Not with mind, not that one." She lifts a second specimen out, rotates it in front of me. "Only these, only with silver here and here. Only one, like this. You do not take. They give. Watch."

She releases it, jumps to a rock in the middle of the river. Her other foot stretches out to a second rock then she lets herself fall forward, balanced by one hand on a small boulder under her chest. She waits, stares straight down, and slowly extends her free hand into the river to emerge with the larger cousin of the eel-fish she'd thrown back minutes before. She rejoins me on the bank, hands her catch to Mii'irkentra with a self-satisfied air.

"Wait, listen, take gently."

Every eel-fish on Sha'Kert hates me, that I know. I sense my three companions as they sit and watch, I know exactly where the eel-fish are. Worse still, I know they know where I am and how far I can reach; the steady flash of ochre and silver barely far enough away to be safe mocks me. All I see is my own face staring back in frustration.

I have no mirrors, no cause to look at myself, and it takes a few seconds to reconcile what looks back to what looks down. The straggly beard and knotted rope of hair is no surprise, the end tied off orange people style as Shu'urtana had shown me. My skin is loose around my cheeks and neck, as if the spring has left the flesh to simply hang in place. Above my tunic the welts and cuts from my days at the Pegasus are healed, not to the faint pink scars I expected but to dark

253

orange lines that blend to my skin. As the scars so my life, blended to Sha'Kert and Te'eltwofo to the point where Greg from Earth is replaced by Gre'eeg from Sha'Kert. Yet not fully, so much remains it can only be skin deep, so many apparent contradictions, like this.

None of them hunt. I've never seen them eat meat. No one fights anything except their own inner being, the only struggle is with the self. So why this, why the age limit, why the need to hunt on a planet that always gives?

I allow the end of my hair to dip below the surface, open my mind to Sha'Kert as I narrow my awareness to the river. I stare at myself through a hundred eyes, watch my arm slowly submerge from the rocks around me. Fifty minds ask if I know why they are here.

Do you understand the need to remove the old, the weak, the infirm when time demands?

Perhaps.

The fifty call for balance through Sha'Kert; that everything must...even I as part of two hundred and ninety-eight...that to leave is not to die. A form presses itself to me; I walk to Te'eltwofo, hand her the gift.

We cook them whole, savor each mouthful. It's disconcerting, a hard slap to know what I eat gave itself to me after our minds touched. Conflicted hardly covers my emotions, I'm thankful this is once a year; if they were regular meat eaters the guilt would be insurmountable. The thought of the bison returns.

"Te'eltwofo, do orange people hunt bison?"

"Who are bison?"

I form an image in my mind, relax and open up to Sha'Kert. Te'eltwofo brightens instantly.

"Those? Once. No more."

"We did, on Mortantoy."

"I know."

"They might still be eating them."

"Yes."

"Are they like these, giving themselves?"

"Could you take them if they did not?"

"No."

"You have your answer."

I slowly pick the eel-fish bones clean, its wide set eyes stare back expectantly, wait for a gourmet's verdict. I can't bring myself to suck the skull empty. I place it down, Shu'urtana plucks it up instantly. He has no such reservations.

"It feels strange, to have it all linked then to kill and eat it."

"Why? Want it not to, then do?" Te'eltwofo asks.

"No, but knowing it knows makes it personal."

"This why no children. Only grown people. Is next lesson."

"What?"

"When end not matters. This to Sha'ntwoy."

"You mean death is nothing?"

"No. Yes. I cannot tell in your language. You will not learn it yet."

Mii'irkentra raises three fingers. "When this soon end, orange people go Mortantoy for Kert'ankway," lowering one finger, "other people go other for Kert'ankway or," with a serious air, "no Kert'ankway go the Nothing."

"So, Ker'paano go Mortantoy."

"Go Kert'ankway, Gre'eeg."

"So, Ker'paano dead."

"No. Ker'paano go Kert'ankway."

Mii'irkentra doesn't get it. I point to the bones at our feet. "Fish dead. Ker'paano dead."

"No. Fish go the Nothing, Ker'paano go Kert'ankway."

"So, Ker'paano not dead?"

"Yes."

"Kert'ankway home Mortantoy. Ker'paano home Mortantoy?"

"No. Kert'ankway home Mortantoy. Ker'paano other home. Ker'paano go other home."

"Ker'paano not sick, not old. Why Ker'paano go?"

"Right time, time go."

"Who told her?"

"Sha'Kert. Sha'Kert call her. One day call all. One day call you."

"Me?"

Mii'irkentra lies back, places his head on Shu'urtana's chest. "Yes, Gre'eeg. Sha'Kert always was call you."

Te'eltwofo studies me intently from the corner of her eyes. I move next to her: "Kert'ankway. Is she your god?"

"What is god?"

I try to think clearly but all I come up with is Menno and a tribe of judgmental bonnets. I try harder, banish one stereotype for another. It will have to do.

"He is not that."

"So, what is he?"

"Kert'ankway take us home, to Sha'ntwoy."

"So, Sha'ntwoy is god?"

"She is not. They are where we from. They are where we go."

"Where is that, what is it?"

"You do not have words. I cannot tell, Sha'Kert cannot tell. Only Sha'ntwoy can."

"So, the only way I can know where Sha'ntwoy is, is to go to Sha'ntwoy?"

"Yes."

"And the only way to Sha'ntwoy is Kert'ankway?"

"Yes."

"And the only way to Kert'ankway is Mortantoy?"

"No."

"No?"

"Not you. Listen Mii'irkentra. Mortantoy for us."

"So, how do I go to him?"

"Sha'Kert knows, I not."

"I could go to Mortantoy, go right to the top."

"He will not be there."

"But he will for you, when it's your time?"

"Yes."

"So, I could follow you."

"No. Kert'ankway Mortantoy for me, other for you. Sha'Kert not call me without you."

"Why?"

She smiles like I'm an idiot child, remains stubbornly silent.

She's right, your ignorance hides understanding.

I know no one will tell me. Not directly anyway. "Do you have any stories, help me understand?"

"Yes, many, but…"

"I won't understand because I don't have the words?"

"Sorry."

"You can't change one or two, help me understand?"

"There are simple for children, they are something."

She starts haltingly, warms to the prose of life from sorrow, scattered children, orange people alone. She grows loud, the three as one sing the ache of a separated people, joy in solitude, grief that sways the heavens, a pact to trade lordship of the universe for a place, a home, a promise.

It is both truth and lie; a broad brush to obscure meaning, for the youngest, a signpost to fuller truth to come.

"It helps?" Te'eltwofo asks.

"A little."

"It can be no more now."

"What do they ask in return?"

"Nothing."

"Nothing?"

"Sha'Kert teach, they wait. Is enough."

"No one has ever turned away, not done as Sha'Kert teaches?"

"No. It is they or the Nothing, so why? No one force, no one turn, no one close ears."

"It works well for you."

"For everyone."

"What would you…what would Sha'Kert do, if someone not do as Sha'Kert teaches?"

"No one has. No one will. Sha'Kert talk from when born, how can we ignore?"

"But if someone did?"

"Nothing."

"Nothing?"

"You talk for you to Sha'Kert. I do not. If you not talk Sha'Kert I do nothing. It is for you to do. Or not do. It is not for me."

"I would leave, be sent away."

"Why?"

"Others see me, not listen, maybe be like me."

"Gre'eeg, you not listen Sha'Kert?"

"No. I hear Sha'Kert, I feel Sha'Kert. A little, no shouts but whispers."

"Sha'Kert hurts, says bad to you?"

"No."

"Then why ask?"

"When home on Mortantoy, people said god talks to them in a book. I did not hear or agree, so they sent me away."

"You worry we do same."

"Yes, one day. If I do wrong, or bad, or think different."

"We do not. We are sisters. Always for us. Gre'eeg home, Te'eltwofo home. Always."

Mii'irkentra stirs. "No one ask, no one send, only Sha'Kert, only Kert'ankway."

"What?"

"Each all, you, Sha'Kert call once, Kert'ankway ask once. Everyone."

"Everyone?"

"Everyone. Hinry, Gre'eeg family, all sisters."

"And others? People on Mortantoy?"

"Sisters yes, others maybe. Ones listen book not hear Sha'Kert, not hear call."

"Same call Ker'paano, same call Greg?"

"No, one call, one sister, one different."

"How do you know when Sha'Kert calls?"

"You will know. All sisters know."

Sha'Kert bubbles away at the edge of my mind as I fall asleep: *Truth in part, yet you see through a glass darkly, and that as a shadow faint.*

As the others drift back to the afternoon's sleep, she remains with me: *As Ker'paano at Mortantoy, these three sisters will know when I call, as will all the orange children, as they will when I call you.*

But called to what and for what reason? They know, Sha'Kert knows, but no one tells me.

I watch my nightmare unfold, a disinterested observer, the scene far removed, fear overlain with anticipation, expectation. A hundred pairs of eyes resolve themselves to deep brown, a sea of Pens stare up at my nakedness as I stare at myself staring down. This time the hand is orange.

I look past meter high snow as naked trees scratch dull pregnant clouds. Midday as dark as night, cold to sear my heart if I let it, Sha'Kert wraps herself in winter. As bad as it is here, what is it like back at the Pegasus?

"Not worry, Gre'eeg," Te'eltwofo says.

"They don't know how to do these things."

"Still. I know."

My mind easily touches and knows all here but Mortantoy remains a barrier I can't scale no matter how hard I try. What my mind can't grasp my feet tried; and failed. Sha'Kert is insistent.

Now, here, the world ends for you at the foot of Mortantoy.

"If only I could see."

Not for you. That way is the past, fear, desire. This you know.

"I know."

I bring up the heat and light, feel Te'eltwofo do the same fifty meters away in her home. Shu'urtana's mind ticks over, touches ours as he sleeps. Lou would love it, makes the net look prehistoric.

"How much longer is winter?"

"Seven years. Always. Seven years good, seven years bad," Te'eltwofo says.

"Six more years of this?"

"No."

"No?"

"This start, not bad. More bad next six years. Weather bad, lessons good."

"Lessons hard."

"Always. Good lesson always hard. So. Gre'eeg try. Try again. Try hard."

I see it in my mind's eye. Blue, ovoid, soft skin puckered with myriad small dents, stalk cut neatly at one end, torpid violet sap that refuses to fall. I rotate it, feel the gentle give of firm flesh, the sour sweet smell so strong I nearly salivate.

"Yes, Gre'eeg. Take from mind to real."

Like warm, house, knowing where your sisters are. It is all the same. I will it firmly but not aggressively, the image fades from my mind as a shape rolls against my foot. I open my eyes to a perfect blue fruit in front of me, a miniature no larger than my thumb.

I pick it up, pop it in my mouth. "Well, it tastes right."

"Better to make one good size than a hundred tiny."

258

"Try again?"

"Yes, Gre'eeg."

The empty rinds stare back, they and my distended stomach testament to success. I sweep a loose crumb from my knee, a small piece of Earth created here. Te'eltwofo had no concept of a jam doughnut but easily copied it as I brought it to reality. Hers lies discarded, one bite taken and thrown away in disgust. I finished mine out of stubbornness, stodgy sweet dough correct but unwelcome.

"Now you are middle child, Gre'eeg."

"An older child does this?"

"And more, as you will."

"You still pick fruit, fish, talk when you can do this. Why?"

"Same as talk and think, go or walk, carry or lift. Each has purpose, meaning. Stop one, forget how, stop other."

"Forget what?"

"Everything. Body lazy, body not work. Body lazy, mind lazy. Mind lazy, mind not work."

"That happens often?"

"Sometimes always, children first learn yes. Think 'good Sha'Kert lesson', body lazy then Sha'Kert give best lesson. Lesson only once."

"Did you learn lesson, Te'eltwofo when –"

It's an explosion, a burst of light and pain that dies rapidly to a black hole of fear, despair and horror as Rii'tvaa falls from sight, draws me in as her presence is crushed out of existence and they become two hundred and ninety-six. I am pulled to her, one instant in my house the next with the others as we look down on the snow-laden branch across Rii'tvaa's face that leaves only surprised and lifeless eyes to gaze back. Te'eltwofo reaches out for her, tries to connect in disbelief at what is no longer there and finds nothing, less than nothing. Seconds they stand and try, reach, until the realization filters through.

It begins as a howl, a low guttural keening that smashes through faces twisted in pain, builds to tortured screams that shake the ground, drive me to my knees head in hands to cower, try to bury myself in the soil. Their minds open uninhibited, unrestrained grief assaults me, unutterable loss and emptiness given full voice to cry death without redemption, life without purpose, past without future as Sha'Kert bays through us all. I'm caught, reflect emotion that is mine, ours, join the chorus in heart and mind until my voice cracks, my mind overloads, and the world turns black.

Chapter Forty-Eight

Greg

I WAKE WHERE I fell. No one has moved, voices and minds stilled for deeper, greater despair in an all-consuming void. Te'eltwofo's face is a death mask, knees pulled rigid beneath her chin, children cling limpet-like.

"How, Te'eltwofo? She could have held it off, pushed."

"Maybe not see. No matter. Same whatever."

I move my leg, I'm rewarded by cramps and pain. My mouth is sticky. "How long?"

"Three days."

"I can't remember."

"Sorry."

"I didn't feel this with Ker'paano."

"Different."

"Rii'tvaa go Kert'ankway, then go Sha'ntwoy?"

Te'eltwofo crushes her eyes shut, her back shakes. "No. Not go Sha'ntwoy. Go the Nothing."

"Why Sha'ntwoy reject Rii'tvaa?"

Te'eltwofo helps me to my feet. A path clears in the snow as we head away.

"What now?"

"Family goodbye Rii'tvaa then home."

"Will they pray Sha'ntwoy for Rii'tvaa, bury her?"

"No pray, no bury. Same whatever."

"They can't leave her lying there. It's not right."

She pulls me aside, lets the others pass. Alone, she takes me back to Rii'tvaa, points to her. "Empty. This go the Nothing, not Sha'ntwoy."

"Is this what happened with Ker'paano? Did Shu'urtana kill her on Mortantoy and leave the birds to pick over her bones?"

"No. Ker'paano home Sha'ntwoy. Rii'tvaa home the Nothing."

"They're both dead, Te'eltwofo, you can't treat them like the eel-fish. You can't."

"Rii'tvaa, eel-fish, same whatever, nothing, no fix."

"Then what was all that about? If it's the same, why mourn Rii'tvaa and be happy for Ker'paano?"

She grabs me, looks down with barely concealed pain. I feel her mind fight to stay controlled, calm. Mixed with anger and emptiness for Rii'tvaa, there's fear and dread hopelessness for me.

"Gre'eeg no learn only lesson! Te'eltwofo teach. Shu'urtana teach. Sha'Kert teach. All teach. Why Gre'eeg no learn?"

260

"Learn what?"

"Ker'paano no die, Ker'paano live Sha'ntwoy. Rii'tvaa die. Rii'tvaa no home. Rii'tvaa go Nothing. No Rii'tvaa. No Rii'tvaa always."

She turns, shudders. "Where go Gre'eeg?"

They pull closer, each subdued contact earnest yet tender, Rii'tvaa a scar to be gently healed. As much as they watch each other they look over me, Te'eltwofo's concern magnified in each of them unobtrusively, delicately, deeply. I've seen death enough, mourning and loss, yet nothing writ as large as theirs. Is it simply the barrier of missing words, or is it that different? I am sure it's the latter, their absolute conviction she's gone completely, lost to a promise untaken. With Ker'paano their hopes exceed the Amish; with Rii'tvaa their despair greater than any I know; and they fear as much for me.

My solitudes stretch to consume most of my days, hours on frozen ground slowly build me. There are no simple answers, the orange people as all people are a bundle of contradictions, individuals who conform less and less to what I think they are. I need to see Mortantoy; more to the point Mortantoy when Ker'paano went. I can't, but someone had. I reach out to Shu'urtana.

"Gre'eeg yes."

"Shu'urtana, talk private?"

"Yes."

Our minds close off the others as we become indistinct to them. "I need to ask a question, maybe a bad one."

"No question bad, only answer."

"This one maybe. About Mortantoy. About Ker'paano."

"Yes."

"You stayed until she go to Kert'ankway?"

"Yes."

"How did she leave?"

"I cannot tell. We do not have words."

Another dead end, another frustration.

"Can you try? Even if I can't understand –"

"No, not your words. Our words. I do not have words to tell."

"You are not allowed?"

"No. We do not have words. I show, you see through me?"

"Yes."

He thinks back, our minds linked, I see that day through his eyes, look along a narrow ridge that plunges through cloud to a valley far below. Long shadows play, the first flash of lightning from gathering storms, an arc of darkness on the horizon, a distant glint of sunset on metal. We are beyond them, beyond it all. Ker'paano stands in front of me, a lone figure on a platform of thin black on the roof of the world, the last step up Mortantoy. She turns and smiles. It is time.

261

Behind her, the sky loses definition, becomes fuzzy and indistinct. It is both there and not there, here and gone at the same time, fluxed to a state my mind cannot accept let alone describe. Ker'paano turns but does not move, her shape narrows until she is a black line, an infinitely thin marker against an unknowable background. The ends contract to the middle until a dot remains, then that too goes to leave the restored sky alone to stare back. She is gone. I turn and start my way down.

"See Kert'ankway, Gre'eeg. I have no words, you have no words."

"Yes, thank you. Same all orange people?"

"Same always."

"No one told me."

"You did not ask."

"Even Sha'Kert not tell me."

"Sha'Kert, Shu'urtana not tell child. Gre'eeg not child now."

We walk atop new snowfall to solitude the next day. Even with constant mental companionship there is something indefinably attractive to physical presence. There's a difference to one of them today, a faint blur or overlap of presence I've not felt before. "She has baby. Start yesterday, Gre'eeg," Te'eltwofo says.

"So that's two I feel in one?"

"No, yes. Little later two, now one and little. Baby name Ees'tyaro."

"Already? Only conceived yesterday."

"All important, age no matter. Ees'tyaro important. We are two hundred ninety-eight."

I do a quick count, include Ees'tyaro. Te'eltwofo's wrong.

"There's only two hundred and ninety-seven of you."

"No. We Gre'eeg, we are two hundred ninety-eight."

"I am you?"

"Always."

"When did you decide that?"

"I did not. You did."

I feel my hair sway, catch sight of smooth skinned hands on my tunic. I've looked like a miniature version of Te'eltwofo for years, but my heart stood a little apart, slightly aloof as I clung to my humanity. Now it's raised it sloughs off as if it never happened, never mattered, Earth the alien world and Sha'Kert home. There are still bits missing, questions unanswered, but it doesn't matter; gaps are relegated to afterthought, afterthought to irrelevance. I am of them, one of them, and I can't recall making the choice. "Rii'tvaa."

"Rii'tvaa?"

"When I decided. I guess."

"Gre'eeg lesson slow, always slow."

Sha'Kert is clearer, as if a deathly-still frozen landscape removes background noise, lets her voice travel further, clearer. It's all one lesson, one long lesson as layer after layer has been peeled back to expose the next then the next, pared down to some central kernel of truth, an immutable fact that still lies in wait to be discovered. At its heart patience, slow deconstruction of fear and desire and assumption until I am ready; for Te'eltwofo and her children no such process, born to it as blank canvasses as, I had come to realize, were Pen and the children back at the Pegasus. I know why I can't reach past Mortantoy, why I never will, why it is right. I feel no bitterness or grudging acceptance; only peace for something that simply is. As much as Sha'Kert closed that side of Mortantoy to me, the world this side of Mortantoy will forever be unknown to Menno and the other Amish.

It's my turn for lunch; Te'eltwofo waits patiently. I allow a crack of sub-zero to seep in as a reminder, concentrate, then produce two bowls of steaming broth. I recall our first meal together, the charade of the slates, the progression to mind, then this generation *ex nihilo* that I have nearly mastered. Shelter, food, healing, communication, community at a thought through Sha'Kert.

Nearly but no, you lift the corner of the curtain, but the window remains closed. Always a taste, a gentle touch to bring me on, prick my curiosity and encourage. "We would have run away screaming."

Te'eltwofo favors me with a quizzical stare.

"If you had done this when we first met, made food appear, shelter and walls and warmth and light from nothing. It would have been too much for us."

"Now?"

"Normal, right. But not ordinary."

"Normal? Not always. Normal now."

"I know what you are, Te'eltwofo."

"No secret. Te'eltwofo daughter of Sha'ntwoy and Kert'ankway. As you."

"Yes, but long ago your ancestors left you here, why I don't know, but they left you with Sha'Kert, with all this, as a remnant. It's all you say it is but more, more that's hidden from you."

Sha'Kert smirks, patient, parent to child. *Yes?*

It's a question with no acceptance, a hint of challenge, a goad to jump the gap. "They left you with Sha'Kert, to control and keep you, keep us at two hundred ninety-eight until, until…Kert'ankway and I don't know what."

"Nearly but no."

Am I real to you?

"Yes, of course."

"If Kert'ankway calls Gre'eeg, if Sha'Kert calls, you go?"

"Yes, to know, yes I would. Shu'urtana showed Ker'paano to me."

"Mii'irkentra say three ways to go. Kert'ankway, the Nothing, others." She points to the bowl in front of her. "You need Sha'Kert for make this?"

"Yes."

"Nearly but no."

Panic rises like a flood then stops, dragged into place. I can't feel Sha'Kert, can't sense my sisters. Te'eltwofo stares at me intently; the planet remains frozen. Sha'Kert is gone. I am alone.

Te'eltwofo points to her bowl. "Hungry. Make again."

"I can't. I need Sha'Kert."

"I give slate when baby. I take slate and give Sha'Kert when child. Now I take Sha'Kert. Hungry. Make again."

Her eyes challenge me, dare me, plead with me. I call on all I've learned, years of solitude, practice, to call what isn't into existence, control my mind and ignore my senses. I picture it, feel it, imagine it, examine it from atoms to whole then call it to be. A second bowl joins Te'eltwofo's first.

Te'eltwofo leans in, taps my temples. "Sha'Kert now here. Always." She raises one arm to the sky, her gaze lifts. "Gre'eeg no three ways. Gre'eeg four ways. Warm is food. Food is shelter. Shelter is warm. All same to make, mind make to real. Big fruit, small fruit. Same. Small roof, big roof. Same. Bowl, house, planet. Same. Daughters of Sha'ntwoy and Kert'ankway not left behind. We choose to stay."

One second the sky is empty, the next an Enforcement η—ship hovers barely ten meters above us. Its a-gravs shake the ground, exhaust plumes tear ice-laden branches from trees, sear the earth to smoking charcoal. A boarding chute touches down in front of me; I can read the stencils, smell the scorch marks of re-entry on the fuselage.

"We stay. We choose. Gre'eeg choose. Stay. Or go. Choose. Now."

I could stand, walk to the chute, rise into the η—ship and go and no one would stop me. Three hours to Earth, three hours to anywhere in the universe. But never back here. Everything is silent, Sha'Kert stilled. The η—ship hovers, its drives hum, the Enforcement insignia calls me back to my past.

"Nothing forgotten if go, all remain. Shelter, warm, fruit. Gre'eeg all still make if go."

The myth is real, what they turned their backs on. Any time, any second, they can go and stand as masters over the universe. And they choose not to.

Their choice.

Now mine.

"Gre'eeg daughter of Sha'ntwoy and Kert'ankway. I choose. I stay." The η—ship snaps out of existence. Two hundred and ninety-seven return, Sha'Kert floods back, and I glimpse a presence beyond Mortantoy.

Te'eltwofo stands, walks away. "Lesson finished, Gre'eeg."

"Until next."

"No. No more lessons. Last lesson."

She stops, grins. I know her pride and joy; in her, in Sha'Kert, in equal measure.

"Te'eltwofo no remnant. Te'eltwofo an heir."

Chapter Forty-Nine

Greg

WARM IS FOOD. Food is shelter. Shelter is warm.

Te'eltwofo's words have bounced around in my head for the last two years, constant companions to lay out the edge of the possible and define the absolute impossible logic of it all. It's limitless, Mortantoy my only boundary.

Once it sunk in and took root, I indulged in orgiastic daydreams that would make Botticelli weep with envy and Caligula blush until, accompanied by Te'eltwofo's wry amusement and the patient humor of Sha'Kert, it dawned on me. Being able to have anything means the best place for me is to have as little as possible. My tunic, my companions; they are more than enough. Once pared back, all that remains is peace, community, stillness.

Yet for all I've learned, everything I've seen, for all the answers given, a greater question remains. Why? Te'eltwofo's no help when I ask; Sha'Kert's also silent. Only Mii'irkentra offers any response, his half-serious 'why not?' infuriatingly obtuse. As far as I can tell, as far as my link with Sha'Kert takes me there is no reason, there is no purpose but to keep us comfortable and amused until the day we go to Kert'ankway.

Nearly but not quite. All of this designed, made only for your pleasure, for two hundred and ninety-eight of you?

Perhaps they overshot, gave too much and made it too dangerous to do anything except stay. What if I had this power when I found out about Pen's CLN3-R, when I found out what friends I really had, where I stood in the order of things? What then? A small task to cure her, hardly more than I do now to scrape the fats from my arteries, to go in and re-sequence her genes, then give her a leg up on the world. A thought here and her brain's firing at 150 per cent; a touch there and all bias to disease is gone; a mere glance and my flesh and blood's supergirl, no mere renaissance woman but the renaissance itself, true *homo deus*. Change her, bend them all to my will to reap a trillion-fold the crushing restrictions I believed delivered to me. A tyrant the world could never imagine, never dislodge, never placate.

And with two hundred ninety-seven companions I sit here, able to crush and mold the universe to our wills. For that alone the trade makes sense, the restriction to Sha'Kert; yet they gave me the option to go, ability intact. It was no option then, even less so now; the more I learn the less inclined I am to leave until, as master of those abilities, I have become a willing partner in Sha'ntwoy's promise to put away leaving, to stay, simply to be.

I pull myself out of my reverie, concentrate on the task at hand: for all I've learned, I'm still a clumsy oaf; the sickeningly bent middle finger and shattered bone that pierces my flesh are obvious and fresh reminders. Abilities or not, Sha'Kert in her sixth year of winter is not to be discounted. Nothing moves, nothing gives, nothing grows but the blue fruit that burst forth snap-frozen from their trees. How cold it is I have no idea, but if Shu'urtana's children as they urinate frozen sculptures of green-yellow ice are anything to go by, I have no desire to know. That each and every surface is rock hard, slippery, and unforgiving of the slightest lapse in concentration I have evidence enough.

I hold my hand out, send the bone back to knit with its other half then, satisfied, fold and seal the skin along its length. Once done, I shape my finger to lie with the others straight and true. I lift my other hand to compare; the color isn't right, I darken it a touch then, pleased with my handiwork, lower them. I'm not quick enough. I glimpse the shake as they fall, the butterfly shimmer I've had for months. I ignore it, pretend it's nothing, that what I don't see isn't there. Like I ignore the flaps of skin on my legs and arms; ribs like xylophone keys; stomach that sticks to my backbone. Rest eludes me, sleep a mere memory. I'm wasting away in a land of plenty.

My nightmare has returned, a vengeful companion who screams at me day and night, faces and voices of orange people; Lou, Pen, Menno to bring the blade down; a sea of bonnets and barn door pants slide to lines then pop out of existence and fold through η-space to start over again. In days as waking vision, it hangs at the edge of my mind ready to spring if I dare relax; at night it overtakes me, banishes sleep and solitude. I manage to cage it, hide it from them until now, until my clumsiness snaps my finger and the barriers drop as I heal myself. My carefully massaged avatar slips away, replaced by reality; there is no place to hide an open mind. It doesn't take Te'eltwofo long. "Gre'eeg, what is this?"

"Nightmares, bad visions."

"Tell me what."

"It's hard, it changes but it's mostly the same."

"Let us see through your eyes."

I open my mind and relax; the nightmare returns with violence, thrusts me back arched onto my toes on the edge of flaking cracked rock, naked as a six-fingered hand savagely yanks my hair back, its orange twin balancing a knife skillfully, carefully sliding against the nape of my neck to send it slashing up...and it is gone, replaced by clamoring, Mii'irkentra at the center, Te'eltwofo's concern replaced by hope.

"This is what follows you from your endless city of gray?" Mii'irkentra asks.

"Since years before I left."

"Always the same?"

"No, sometimes, but different."

"You stand in its way, stop seeing clearly. Do you want to see?"

"See what?"

"Truth."

As quickly as Mii'irkentra thinks it, the nightmare returns crystal clear, day replaced by burning cold morning. Naked, I stand arched on the rock, Te'eltwofo pulls my hair up in one hand as the other closes on the knife, Mii'irkentra beside her. Below me, hand in hand arrayed in ranks, my sisters stand and stare, hope, rejoice, encourage as behind me, Mortantoy clothes herself in lightning and cloud. One instant I am me, the next I am Ker'paano staring down at me from the peak of Mortantoy; I flip back, forth, back again. The vision flees.

You have learned all you can from these ones. All you can from yourself. All but the last from me.

"You understand what it is," Mii'irkentra says, an assessment rather than a question.

"I am as Ker'paano, I stand in her path different yet the same."

"Two paths, Gre'eeg, one path for the orange people."

"One path for the others."

"Our children have our songs, myths to help learn; when we know all, it is time for our song to be sung, time for the call."

"And me?"

"You had the dream. You have it no more. There is only one thing more."

"What?"

"You know, you have always known."

I'm ready. It's what I've come for, the last piece of the puzzle. I lock eyes with Mii'irkentra, draw breath.

"Sha'Kert! I am."

I hear her strong, low, irresistible as she weaves among us, soaks my heart and mind with one solitary word.

"Come."

Chapter Fifty

Louise

SHE'S BEAUTIFUL. PERHAPS it's the way with all babies, they trigger that thing inside to make you want to hold them, care for them, watch them grow safe and strong. Maternal instinct. No one told me it could skip generations, even bloodlines. Ever since Cephas and Mae's first, I've wanted this, needed it, no matter how hard it is outside, this is hope, beautiful hope.

Mahlon kisses her forehead, moves through the skins over the doorway to the day's work. He'll make a good father, there's more Freda in him than Menno; softness under the stiff exterior makes him a partner not an autocrat. He wouldn't have been Penny's first choice on Earth but here, now, it's right. A smile flicks across my face. You can't hide what you are, jammed together like this; all of us in the longhouse when it's dark, working together outside when it's light, there's no room for secrets. What did Menno call us, The Outpost? Perhaps isolation binds you tighter.

A small burble reminds me not to let my mind wander, a gentle kick from inside papoose wrappings reasserts her central place. Yes, you are beautiful and yes, like everything else, this place changes us. Your slightly too oval face, the faint orange pallor of your skin – it's all in keeping here, still beautiful, still right. I shift in my seat, my foot clips the cup, sending hot tea soaking through the dirt floor. Amy's up and refilled it nearly before it happens.

She stands, walks with Joseph to the skins. "Time for us to join the others."

They follow Mahlon, leave us alone.

In the middle of it all, miracles, little inside big: a miracle we survived, two miracles returned from near catatonic and this, the mundane, everyday miracle of life. She seems happy wrapped in her silver-blue cocoon. I look closer, recognize the fabric as one of Greg's old shirts. He should be here, should hold his granddaughter, should be with me, with Penny.

"What's that, Mum?"

"Sorry, I didn't realize I was talking." I hand her back carefully. My hands aren't what they used to be; to fumble a stone is one thing, this child another. "I was thinking your dad should be here to see her."

"Yes, I suppose so. It's been ages since you mentioned him."

"Doesn't mean he hasn't been on my mind."

"You haven't said anything."

"There's not much to say."

"We could've gone with him."

"No, I had to think about us, where we'd best get by. He had no idea what he was getting into, I thought we had a better chance here."

269

The child starts to cry, Penny puts her to her breast. Her ribcage teases her flesh, too thin as we all are, balanced on the cusp; always barely enough, never quite full, Neueanbruch begrudgingly admits our survival, not our comfort.

"You miss him, Mum?"

"Of course. Not only him, all of them."

"How long has it been?"

"Freda and the rest? Four, maybe five years. I haven't set foot near the threeship since, I don't know how many's left. And Henry and Kelli make it worse, here one minute gone the next. I'm the last one."

"Last one what?"

"Last adult who remembers Earth without being Amish. The oldest woman here, alone even with all of you."

"No, you're not, you've got us."

"And you've got Mahlon and your daughter. It's just the way things go."

Joseph pokes his head inside, takes away a small woven grass mat.

"I've never quite believed it."

"What?"

"Amy and Joseph. They shouldn't have recovered, now they're like this? I'm glad Rachel lived long enough to see it."

Penny smirks, that self-satisfied grin when she has a secret.

"What?"

"What do you mean?"

"The grin."

"Oh, it's this place, you've known all along how it changes you, some more than others. Depends if you fight it or not."

"You sound like your father."

"Joseph and Amy could fight the least, so it worked for them the most. Menno, well he's never going to listen."

"Maybe I accept it, I've got no choice, anything more I don't know. Well, perhaps. It's taken years to feel okay by myself outside, to stop fighting." Sometimes she's my daughter, other times, I'm not so sure; a stranger perhaps, or more rightly an allotrope seems to take hold of her. Like now, barely twenty but with depth and calm that was never remotely part of her.

"Sometimes that's it, Mum, simply letting go. When you're quiet it can get a word in here, a thought there, a feeling perhaps." She looks up. "They didn't say, but you know where they went."

"He was always going to take Kelli to see. Once Freda died, he had nothing to keep him here."

"Only a question of when."

"Well, he must have been keen, build all of this, stick it out over the rough years then go."

270

I look back through the house, along walls and open thatch dividers that separate sleeping areas from the great room. A longhouse, it had been Henry's idea, big enough for thirty I'd thought him mad when there were only four of us. But as the children filtered over, Luke then Mahlon then Nathan then Sara's until we were twenty-five, I wondered at his foresight. Now, with the twelve of us, the space feels empty, the grass bedding in that one alcove forlorn yet poetic. He came here with nothing, left the same way.

Nearly. The slate sits untouched where Henry put it years ago, waiting patiently in the center of the great room. One piece of alien technology, one gift that saved us through the worst years. Warmth, protection, I'd never mastered it but thankfully the children had. "Do you think they'll be alright without it, Penny?"

"I'm sure. It's not too bad now, even if that last part's as rough as he made out. Could never understand Menno's attitude, simply refusing it when they needed it the most."

"Don't underestimate faith. No matter what he was, he stuck by his principles."

"And that got him what, his wife and half the gmay dead?"

"He'd say they weren't lost."

"He'd be wrong. Mahlon hasn't forgiven him and probably never will."

"Have you forgiven him? Or me?"

"You had nothing to do with it."

"Not that, your father."

"What for?"

"I sent him away. Menno or no Menno, he would've stayed if I kept the contract. He picked this spot out, started to make plans."

"It was never going to happen."

"No, seriously, it was. That night he came back he told me all about it, what he would build, if I'd be fine with it."

"Mum, the moment we got here, he was going to go. I saw the way he looked when he jumped out the Pegasus, how this place hooked him before he even knew it. If it was only the three of us, he'd still be gone, it's the way it was always going to be. There's nothing to forgive."

"He never liked the city, jammed onto the levels with everyone else. As much as I hated the open, he hated the closed." It still gets to me, all these years and protestations of how tough and independent I am, it still aches, ached as I watched Henry and Kelli grow closer, more so when I think too long about Penny and Mahlon. Maybe it's different when there's only a few, when you're thrust closer and closer unable to escape to the distraction of a hundred friends, a thousand acquaintances, a million data streams. It doesn't bear thinking about. It is simply what it is, how it turned out. It was the right decision then, and with my daughter and granddaughter alive in front of me, I know it.

271

"Everyone changes, well nearly everyone if they let it. Some quicker than others, some on the inside. Dad was just quicker than most."

"Do you think he's alright?"

"I know he is. When Henry left him, he was fine, he said the orange people were friendly enough."

We lapse into silence, Penny slowly rocks the baby to sleep; I enjoy a brief respite, let my leg warm a little before I head out. It never set right, crude splints conspired with my pain-laced directions to make a poor remedy. The occasional ache and discomfort are a small price. I shift, move my weight a little, deliberately tarry.

"Don't worry about me, Mum, I'm going to be fine."

"It's alright, just a little more heat before I'm out."

"That's not what I mean and you know it. The baby's healthy, I'm healthy, Mahlon's good and we'll survive. You can let go."

"Is it that obvious?"

"Only to me. You might not say much but I see the way you stare into space. It's okay, I understand."

"You were still young, I had to take care of you. Now, maybe next year, once it's all settled, I can."

"Why?"

"I have to know, I need to find out what happened to him, where he went."

"It's a long way, two weeks or more from what Henry said. You can't want to face that because you're curious."

"Did you say anything to him the last time?"

"A little."

"What?"

"I can't exactly remember, probably 'I love you' or 'goodbye' or something. Why?"

"After we crashed, we never seemed to talk, always argued, and the last words we said to each other weren't good. It's not the way it's supposed to be, it should end better. I feel guilty, Penny."

"It's a long way there and back to patch things over."

"I'm not coming back."

She doesn't react, keeps rocking her baby, Madonna and child. I half expected calm acceptance, while part of me secretly hoped she'd beg me to stay. When she looks at me, she seems happy, as if I've accepted a choice she's made for me.

"When did you decide?"

"I don't think I did, it's a feeling, a thought that's been with me for a while. Like I know I'll go and not come back, as if something's out there pulling me."

"You're sure it's not someone?"

"No, Greg's, well, I guess he's part of the reason, maybe an excuse."

272

"We'll miss you."

"A bit. You have your own family now, you'll be fine." I stand slowly, lean on the branch that serves as my walking stick. "I'm no cripple and I'm getting stronger, even if I rely on this."

"Would you like company?"

"What?"

"Not permanently, just the way there. Next year would suit, if the weather holds, we can go with you. Mahlon and I've talked with Amy and Joseph, it's about time we met the neighbors."

Chapter Fifty-One

Greg

"WHAT DO I do?"

We walk for two days, Te'eltwofo and I together, Mii'irkentra and Shu'urtana a little behind. It feels familiar as we weave along the path we took with Ker'paano, yet it's clothed in solid hard white, still and silent. We make no sound, travel in unbroken silence; our minds speak, yet even in that there's an economy, a reticence.

"You will know. Mii'irkentra will lead; where he cannot I will; where I cannot you will alone. Be. Calm. Open. Is enough," Te'eltwofo says.

Commitment is one thing, knowledge another. I've no fear about what's to come, only curiosity; am I to be like Ker'paano and simply slide over, or is it something else entirely?

"Gre'eeg first other. You do not know, we do not know. Yet."

"You have no tales, no stories of what it is?"

"It is the place prepared outside the All. That alone."

"One place, two paths."

"One place, all sisters."

Sleep isn't easy. The others are childlike; they switch from on to off at will while I keep watch over the stars, my sisters' thoughts in their rest a gentle wave on the shores of my mind, Sha'Kert in the background laced with anticipation, eager welcome. When sleep comes it is short, uninterrupted, deep. I am still gaunt, yet I feel younger, stronger, my mind clear and quick. Deep, unassailable calm has returned to confirm the rightness of my decision, the time, my path.

We sit the fourth evening on a bluff, sun to our backs, ocean in front; rose-tinted ice near the horizon gives way to languid waves. Here and there flaws in the surface wink or glow, some send rainbows into the air, others cast jeweled rods across the surface. Sha'Kert still surprises me, still has secrets she's chosen not to show. My sisters are rapt. Soon I will leave all this, what I know, what I don't, and with it Te'eltwofo and the others. What do I really know of them, how much of them have I seen? Nine years feels like a lifetime yet what of before, what of that? It is as I've seen it, details or events perhaps different but the essence of their lives the same. Village. Sha'Kert. Family. Life. To know part is to know all.

You are the mystery, all they know is you among them and your dreaming.

I've never seen it that way, never considered their curiosity may outweigh mine; and what have they seen? My time with them is not my life before; a hard line separates them, a line I turned my back on the day I walked away from Neueanbruch. I've not meant to hide it, I'm not ashamed of what I was; for me it is the divider between the death of old Greg and the birth of the new. But have I shown them less than the truth by this omission, somehow changed a pact of openness to one-sided honesty?

Te'eltwofo's knee pushes me, the familiar, eager wiggle comfort as she eats. Theirs is a different, narrower, concept of privacy. With each linked to each other and Sha'Kert, there can be none. Each minute of each day in everyone's mind, the others move in the background, each experience and every thought open to all; after a lifetime no one is unknown, all are bound together. There is no two hundred ninety-eight, simply one; less part of me.

They loom large in my mind. I've concentrated, my thoughts the equivalent of a loud conversation that draws them in. I'm overwhelmed by an urge to share, to tear down the walls of memory and send it all to them complete, unvarnished, instantly.

"Nearly but no, Gre'eeg. Not right, not now," Mii'irkentra says.

"Why?"

"Yes see others feel others all day, all lives. Story not finished before go Kert'ankway. Not give before. Give then, like Ker'paano."

"Ker'paano did? I was there, I didn't hear."

"That then, this now. Then baby, now sister. Now different."

"How?"

"Not for me to tell, not for us to show."

A small bluff makes itself known, a tiny finger of land I'm drawn to. "This is only for you. We wait," Mii'irkentra says.

A path leads away. I stand, follow it along one side of the bluff; to the other lie a half dozen low buildings evenly spaced between the path and the edge.

I walk along the path, resist a strong urge to look as flashes of lurid color in the first building nearly pull me in. As I progress the buildings become plainer, dilapidated, start to miss walls, roofs, flooring until, at the end, there is only a small, cleared patch of land.

I stop, stare across an unbroken expanse of ice ahead of me.

The first building glints in the sunlight. I rushed past it, thought there was more. Why?

Nearly but no, always too anxious, too impatient.

I laugh, retrace my steps. It had tried to draw me in, entice me, and I resisted. Not this time.

There is no hesitation as I step inside. The sole room is circular, soft light and gentle breeze from above. Colors shift, pastel eddies swirl and play in random patterns across the walls, faint enough to look at, strong enough to play across my skin.

The room fades to black, the colors brighten, coalesce to a rapidly spinning ball. It shimmers then changes to a perfect, if overly large, rendition of a blue fruit. I wait for the next change, for the image to transform itself; nothing happens. I sit and look at it; it rotates end over end as the minutes drag on.

"So. It's a picture of a fruit."

The room responds from nowhere and everywhere, a clear two-toned pop-whistle.

"Yes, that's what Te'eltwofo calls it."

Again, the two-toned pop-whistle.

"Fruit."

Pop. Whistle.

It seems insistent. I never managed to speak the orange people's language, it's too different and nuanced; not having three independently hinged jaws is also no small hindrance. But, it seems, the room has other ideas.

"Okay, if you insist."

Pop. Whistle.

I concentrate, think it through and speak. In my mind it's pop whistle, to my ears click pffttt.

A small tingle of satisfaction filters across me, the room clearly happy with the effort, if a little disappointed with the outcome.

Pop. Whistle.

I try again and, as I am about to speak, my tongue shifts by itself, wraps across my palette to snap out and down as I draw breath.

Pop. Whistle.

Perfect. I've never dreamt of doing it that way, it's a near physical impossibility; yet here I am and there it is. Even if it is only one word. The tingle of satisfaction grows. I know it's the room that frames the word; no matter. I wrap my tongue and try again.

Pffttt szzz.

Close but still wrong. I try again, and again, sometimes by myself, occasionally with the room in control, usually together until, fifteen minutes later, I have it. We sing pop whistle back and forth as the image dances and sways, as the trickle of satisfaction grows.

The fruit shimmers, changes to a dull red sun.

Bzzt. Whistle. Pop.

I lose track of time; there's no day or night, only awake or sleep, learn or rest. Word follows word follows word, words for all I've seen at the village, words for all I'd seen with them, all their names in their tongue. Weird, mouth-numbing gyrations produce lyrical sound that paints objects rather than mere labels. And more, the very act of calling them by their true name changes my perception, calls their place and relationship, attribute and being.

The word bison conjures only a large, docile shaggy creature to mind; now, in their language, layers of meaning peel away with sound, the animal's relationship to Sha'Kert and all in it, its beauty and strength, its place and rightness, the feel of its back under my legs, muscles across shoulders.

Each building digs deeper, challenges and builds me. Only when one judges my progress to be right does the next become whole and active, missing walls or features restored as and only when I graduate from one to the other. In the second the words are joined to sentences; in another sentences to conversation; the fifth pushes me from the obvious to the nuanced until, when I emerge, I'm unable to talk or think in English, my mother tongue stripped as I ascend to the language of the orange people, my people.

I sit in the cleared patch that marks the last building. I wait. They won't be rushed, and neither will I. The world around me is different, changed by language as language changes me. I thought it complex and deep before; now infinitely more so, each facet fractal upon infinite fractal of meaning, depth, consequence. I replay conversations with Te'eltwofo and Mii'irkentra in my head, compare what was said to what I understood; the loss of meaning is stupendous, even mind to mind. How I managed surprises me; their patience with me, an imbecile in their midst, is overpowering.

The world fades to black, three figures approach to form a circle of four. One stands to sing the creation myth, the tale now clear. A universe from nothing, one seed of life in chaos to start it all, send out life in infinite variety yet joined at the base, the corner stone, the orange people, the crux. She sits as the song fades into me, another rises, draws me into the despair and futility of having seen it all, known it all; the realization every breath is useless and puerile, every end a beginning in eternal repetition until, in a moment of insight, that to be is enough, has and always will be enough, to self-exile behind a gas giant around a sullen red sun at the edge of the All. The last cries of the despair of life itself, to curse the beginning because of the end, vanity loaded onto the irrelevance of days like summer flowers, bright shining for a moment then gone, irreplaceable loss until, even as this barrier is removed, Sha'Kert came to be; to send all that was to myth and legend, all that follows simply an antechamber to that Beyond the All, a place to live, to grow, to wait.

The last note hangs pregnant, the three face me expectantly. A song to be added to songs, tale to myth, or simply a final word – I do not know. I rise, open my mouth to drag out my heart; a life of continual failure on Earth as I placed my trust again and again in people to have it lost, the gradual decline and erosion of it all to that one moment of choice to throw my life away or not, to my arrival at this point of acceptance and peace. I finish as I started, in quiet patience.

One stands, smiles. "We have no need of this now," with which the bluff dissolves to leave me standing next to Te'eltwofo in dull evening light.

"Now, when it is time for your story to be shared, it will be as it should be."

"And I will truly know you, Te'eltwofo, as I will all my sisters."

We return to the village, I stay with Te'eltwofo this last night. I am Ker'paano, to follow the ritual with my adoptive family, my sisters. I hear what I missed with Ker'paano, stillness of voice belies the songs in their minds, a joyous chorus to clothe me, send me to restful peace then, before the sun rises, gently wake me to the day.

Chapter Fifty-Two

Greg

WE LEAVE THE village in silent procession, Te'eltwofo and Mii'irkentra flank me, Te'eltwofo's eldest daughter, Paa'eyaya, leads the families in line behind. I pass memories without a sideways glance – the sea of the first lesson, the shoreline Henry and I shared, the place Te'eltwofo and I met. Mortantoy towers above, her face ice to split the dull claret sky as we climb those first three steps. I turn to face the stone forest, pick out Ker'paano's obelisk as the family lines move closer, hand in hand until Paa'eyaya's breath condenses on my beard. She waits, one hand back, one arm across her neighbor, part of an orange daisy chain of flesh and blood. All eyes lock on mine expectantly, and with their eyes, their minds. I sense Mii'irkentra raise his face to Mortantoy, bring his hands solidly onto Te'eltwofo; she lifts her eyes in response, her hands like giant's on my shoulders.

Sha'Kert courses through me clear, powerful, she and another pull at me, fill me with ten thousand minds, ten thousand orange sisters call and resonate through my body as I shake, try to steady myself. I lift my hands, my mind a dam, the gates to what lies behind, what lies ahead. I reach out to Paa'eyaya, move my hands towards her cheeks as the power surges, the presence grows, eagerness in Sha'Kert. I strip my mind bare, banish barriers and inhibitions, dark places brought into light, past as present as future I grasp her face; I cease to be Greg, I simply am.

Two hundred ninety-seven are seared into me and I into them; every aspect, every nuance indelibly stamped, never to diminish, never to fade. Ten thousand minds rush through me, family lines unbroken from the dawn of Sha'Kert now reach, touch, connect. I know them all, their children, their families, their lives, their names, their faces carved into me. Each one stood here, was called here, looked out on their sisters as I; each name a stone, each stone a sister, each sister calls me, waits for me, needs me.

My hands fall, the ten thousand recede but are not gone; those in front remain inside me never to be lost. I am Greg, I am Gre'eeg, I am more.

Te'eltwofo catches me, one arm under me as shaking threatens to overtake me; her other thrusts a staff into my hand. I steady myself, gaze out; I am one, I am two hundred and ninety-eight, I am ten thousand; I am Sha'Kert, I am sister, I am. Nothing of me is hidden from them, nothing of them from me; and we are more because of it.

Te'eltwofo has the knife, I am stone as she cuts the tunic from me. I make no effort to hide my flesh from the cold; exposed steel-blue skin, old scars and hair rise to meet the chill. Naked my soul, naked my body, naked my mind; as ten thousand, so one, soon others. I lift myself on my toes, search for where my stone will rise, a gap far to one side; I am the harbinger, my line to grow next to Te'eltwofo's.

She lifts my hair gently, caress of the blade along my neck, lightness of cut. My hair joins my tunic. The trail up Mortantoy leads to the left; we move down to the right between a cleft in the rocks, leave my sisters to wait in silence. The path is wide and clear. Te'eltwofo leads, I follow.

A day, a night, another day we walk without rest, we make arrow straight for the horizon. The land is unfamiliar, flat and monotonous, the snap of grass underfoot a reminder it's a frozen world. Day and night the rings hover above us, the moons chase each other across the sky, our voices and minds are stilled. To the end of the second day I turn; footprints carved into the plain lead away, all else a bald white unbroken expanse from horizon to horizon; Mortantoy hides from our view. I am sure the sun traces a different arc, but I have nothing to gauge it against; we are alone on a sea of ice, if having the minds of ten thousand with me can be called alone.

I close my eyes. I sense Te'eltwofo with ease, keep pace and step, count the beat of her heart, see through her eyes if I wish. I feel two hundred ninety-seven through an opaque glass as I read their lives and thoughts as an open book; and somewhere, somewhen ten thousand more. I run Ker'paano's, Mii'irkentra's, then Te'eltwofo's family lines back through thirty, forty generations to the first, the first to stand, ascend Mortantoy and cross over; behind them a wall, no explanation, no reason, no heritage, as if one day they and Mortantoy were not then the next they were. A people appearing without history, without provenance whole and complete, unchanging. An answer, more questions, as it has always been.

As night falls a coffee-cream smear teases the horizon, a long ragged-toothed stripe hangs until it leaves with the last light. It encourages Te'eltwofo; rest and food are unnecessary encumbrances as she pushes me as I push her. Night passes quickly, anticipation rises until, at dawn, she calls a halt to our headlong race. The smear is transformed to a deep arc; bands of brown, tan, and cream across its face swirl together to run in places pure, in places a crazed lattice of color. At its center, a brittle peak glows in the morning sun. The ground before us is as that behind; plain, featureless, barren. As white as that behind us is as black before us, separated left and right cleanly and sharply as if laid by design, an unerringly straight meridian to both horizons.

Te'eltwofo points to the peak in the distance. "I have led. I can go no further. You will go alone."

"How far?"

"Perhaps one day if you are slow. Go straight, go to Kert'ankway."

"You're going home now?"

"Yes, home first. Home, then Mortantoy, then Kert'ankway."

280

"You were called?"

"Now. Once we were here, once you were here, Sha'Kert called me."

She lifts the knife from her belt, holds it out to me haft first. This time there is no hesitancy, no doubt. I take it, sink the blade into my thumb, return it to her. She does the same, we stand thumbs together, eyes locked as I feel my blood move to her, hers to mine. My sister, my family, I am part of her line. As she is of mine.

A pause, a smile, then she turns and walks away. No backwards glance, no parting gesture, no goodbyes; none are needed, there is nothing lost, nothing broken, nothing ended. The opaqueness descends as she leaves to join the others on the edge of my mind.

The black crunches underfoot as energetically as the white, frozen grass exchanged for cold sandpaper. The jagged peak seems eager to greet me, pushed forward by the coquettish gaze of another planet, the arc behind. All day it sits unmoving, grows slightly in deference to the peak. I am fixed on it, it on I, and the presence of the others recede to leave space for an unknown other. White to black the Rubicon; in my crossing, has my stone been raised at the foot of Mortantoy?

To either side the black horizon approaches to leave indolent, green oceans watch me traverse the land, move along an unwelcome intrusion that narrows with each step.

It falls away abruptly to a low, windswept projection into the ocean. Sporadic mint foam rises from both sides, betraying low cliff faces and the slow, useless battering of languid waves. I sense no one, no people or animals, no movement, no sound. A path lies in front of me, runs the length of the isthmus.

I follow the path as it changes to a series of stone steps then a small raised hummock, a waist-high cairn at its center. Smooth, cool, featureless, it stares at me. There is nothing else; behind me the black, to the front the cairn, the ocean, the peak beyond. This, whatever it is, is it.

"Hello?" I call, jolted and embarrassed at the stupidity and loudness of the word. There is no one else, there is nothing, but it should be something. I stare out as if the act itself can resolve the impasse, watch the waves' caress reinforce the inevitability of place. Head to the peak you end up here, funneled and directed; there is no other way. But why, why here?

I'm not sure how long I sit and wait. Too long, perhaps. There is no one and nothing here; it's the right place, the right time.

It's not really empty; there's the cairn. I'd rushed past it, paid it scant attention, but the path and the steps lead to it and it alone. I turn, face it. Not now the smooth top, now a small indentation graces the cairn's center, an oval depression with a small spike at one end. As with Te'eltwofo, so with this. I press my right thumb down, the spike digs deep and true. I pull my hand up, see two drops of blood form, fall. They rest briefly in the depression then soak away.

"I've been expecting you, Mister Robertson."

Chapter Fifty-Three

Greg

I TURN, STARTLED but unsurprised. An ordinary looking orange person returns my gaze; he is, if anything, shorter than usual with deep blue eyes.

He extends his hand. "Kert'ankway."

I take it. It's neither hot nor cold; there's a strange absence of substance or texture, no presence to him, no impression of mind like the others.

"Of course, who else?" I look around to an unchanged land, the sun's glint on wave crests. I didn't disappear, didn't slide to a dot then wink out. Why didn't the sky melt for me? "This is it?"

"Nearly, but not quite. You still have some questions."

"Many, but they don't seem that important."

"But you'd like some answers or, perhaps more correctly, some confirmation. We've time enough. I'll give you the easiest answer. I'm not god, or any form of superior being, for that matter."

"Then what are you?"

"A gate keeper, a pathway if you like, from the All to Beyond the All. No one gets to Sha'ntwoy without going through me. When I think they're ready."

"That's what you do, not what you are."

"I am what you see, your sister as I am to Te'eltwofo, Shu'urtana, to them all. But that's not the real question; you know what that is and now the answer."

"Who are the orange people?"

"Exactly. Who are they, Mister Robertson?"

"At first, I thought them simple hunter-gatherers, then later remnants of an advanced civilization. Before I left inheritors, custodians of what came before."

"And now the songs are yours and you truly understand?"

"They're the apex. Sha'Kert's made for them, made by them, the animals, plants, climate, the power of their minds, every aspect for and by them."

"So, if it's all for them, how did you get your abilities?"

"I don't know."

"The myths are true, even if simple. Made for children, like your fairytales, broad enough for developing minds, but as they learn, as they grow, so too the meaning."

"As I found out, now I have the language."

"So?"

The creation myth rises in my mind. Children born of Sha'ntwoy, blood from Kert'ankway. Red blood. Common blood. "We're all your daughters, Sha'ntwoy's daughters, all sisters with the same blood as a sign."

Kert'ankway smiles, nods. "The species are intimately related. Sha'Kert can develop any from either if young enough, if open enough."

"If not?"

"We don't force anyone, if they aren't, they aren't. But there are ways around most barriers if the spirit's willing, even if the consciousness is unaware. What is the first memory you have of Te'eltwofo?"

"That day on the road."

"Why did you use the knife?"

"I don't know, it seemed right."

"And have you wondered whose blood now runs through your veins? Why your skin moves to orange from black? Of course not. You are for the moment unique, both fully of Earth and Sha'Kert. As much as Sha'Kert was made for them, it is made for you. Yet this way is for you and no other."

"I'm the only one?"

"No, but each will have a different way, some as our orange children, some much different."

"And we come to you in the end."

"If they choose. If they listen."

"All of them?"

"No, only those who live after Sha'Kert was made. The Nothing claimed those who went before."

"And Rii'tvaa?"

"Rarely, but yes. If they don't have control of their minds, themselves, the language and understanding, they are not ready. For them death is truly death, as it is for Elizabeth, for Emily."

We stand together in silence, look out across frozen wastes. I have no more questions, only expectation and desire. Kert'ankway leans against the cairn; the air around him blurs, swims.

"So, am I ready?"

"Yes."

"What next?"

"Something very simple, no grand gesture or task. You've mastered yourself, your desires, your fears. Take one step forward, that's all."

"Where?"

I suddenly find myself alone; the pop bzzt pop of my question hangs unanswered in dawn's early light. Before me a black, featureless plain stretches to a horizon punctured by a deep arc; to either side a line arrow straight, black in front, white behind. I turn. Te'eltwofo's carved stone an arm's length away, her back towards me as she goes to Mortantoy. I look down, my toes fall shy of the line, feet planted in white, unsullied virgin black before me. It's all slightly out of focus, everything pulses gently.

One step. Just one.

I lift my foot, lean forward and step out.

Chapter Fifty-Four

Greg

MY FOOT SETTLES onto coarse yellow sand. I lift my head; the sand changes to shingle beach, motes lift and spiral in a gentle breeze. A dark blue ocean curves left and right to the horizon as headlands rise to steep cliffs in the distance. It's neither night nor day, the light as if under a heavy thunderstorm yet everything is clear and sharp. I realize with a start it's not red, it's silver-gray, gentle pastel colors woven in as highlights.

From horizon to zenith a pearl floats in inky blackness; its face shifts and swirls as luminous multicolored discs float across a diamond spattered background to stop, reverse, resume their course. I feel the ten thousand, sense Ker'paano and Te'eltwofo close as they watch, wait.

A furrow carved between tussocks leads away; I follow it to a small row of deckchairs that face the ocean, the pearl, dark blue waves as they caress the shore. A tuft of hair and sag of canvas on the right tell me one chair's taken; I sit next to her and watch her watch the ocean. She is ageless, holds herself like this is her first time even though she's never left. There's no sign of weariness or hubris, yet her eyes do not lie; she has seen it all, understands what she has seen, knows there is everything to come. All I sense I see; she leaves no impression of mind on me. I have no need of it; I know her, where I am. "Hello, Sha'ntwoy."

"Greg Robertson." She turns, nods. "Welcome to the place Beyond the All."

"It's been quite a journey."

She grins, laughs at some private joke. "We've waited a long time for you. Or no time at all."

The headlands flicker and settle; the pearl wobbles as if to steady itself.

"This is it?"

"It depends. Is it the place Beyond the All? Yes and no; this little bit is merely a place to meet, help settle in."

She reaches forward – the pearl falls from the sky, a searing ball of light in her open palm. "The All. The everywhere and everywhen of everything."

She takes my hand, rolls the pearl into it; with a flourish she raises it to my eyes. I feel the brush of trillions upon trillions of minds, white noise within white light.

"All the universes a ball in your hand on a deckchair on a beach in a waiting room that's hardly a speck inside Beyond the All," Sha'ntwoy says.

She lifts my hand, blows on the pearl to send it back to occupy half the sky.

"Size and scale don't matter; what worked in the All may or may not work here. By those rules this place does and doesn't exist at the same time, we may

286

or may not be here or be in some other state. It can only be outside the All but, then again, we both know there's nothing beyond everything, don't we?"

"It is what it is, and I'm here. It's the end. Isn't it?"

"If you want it then perhaps, but remember you're not dead, simply outside it all."

"And you?"

"Me? I'd have to be alive first. You know what I am. I am your sister as you are Te'eltwofo's, as she is mine. That is what matters."

"Then why? If this is no more than a place to be together, we could stay on Sha'Kert. Barring accidents or stupidity, we could last forever."

"Could you? How long is forever, do you think simply being is enough? Purpose, Greg, without purpose life is merely slow decay."

"Whose purpose, and for what?"

"What are we, what is every intelligent species in the universe to us?"

"Related, we all come from the same place, the same ancestors."

"So, what does that make us?"

"The first. The first intelligent species."

"Exactly. A billion years after the universe was, we were – seven beings of pure energy in the early super-hot, super-dense soup. We are an aberration, a confluence of near impossible conditions and probabilities that should never have arisen; yet there we were. And we were alone."

"So, you created life?"

"No. For all our knowledge and power we never created material life, or life from energy. We should have died out as the universe aged, we can't exist in a universe that harbors material life, and that life can't exist in a universe that harbors us."

"What did you do?"

"There were pockets where material life emerged early, where we could still exist. So, we learned how to manipulate matter, shift and change it across all those worlds to favor life, then watched and hoped."

"And it worked."

"Occasionally. Life rose by itself only thirty times, remained only in seven. The Vypaana, they that became the orange people, were first, we had more time to mold and accelerate them. By the time we had to leave they were barely sentient, our work incomplete. We created the three of us – Kert'ankway, Sha'Kert, and I – to exist in that universe to continue, then left."

"It still doesn't explain the why of this place."

"All seven species prospered, developed, started to colonize and grow. The Vypaana were always the most aggressive, pushed the boundaries of technology and knowledge harder. By the time they created η-space they were unassailable, but that didn't stop the others, and as their civilizations fragmented, crumbled and rebuilt in isolation, the connections dissolved. All the Vypaana could see was that their efforts made things worse, seemed pointless. So they retreated, rejected all they had achieved and lived in isolation away from it all."

"And Sha'Kert started to teach them what I was taught?"

"No. Before Sha'Kert, before the orange people, the Vypaana were decaying, looking inwards with no striving, no purpose. They crashed, stopped having children, kept dying until there were barely three hundred apathetic, disengaged ones left."

"So, it was all going to be for nothing?"

"Yes."

"Until?"

"Until one man's grief overcame him, drove him to seek us out and curse us for doing nothing, for a life we'd never given him as his daughters and wife died."

"The myth of the place Beyond the All."

"They knew us as we truly were, and as he cursed us, they all did. In the end, together with the three of us, we built this place."

"For which they gave up their wings of fire, their terrible magic."

"And more, so much more. They gave it all, their knowledge, their achievements, history, even who they were. The Vypaana ceased, the orange people came to be."

"Why didn't you share this? Everything dies, nobody wants that."

"They tried, we tried, no one would listen. They had their own beliefs, their own gods of technology or stone or self; this was a threat, a challenge to their systems and order they couldn't accept."

"But I did. If I did, surely others would?"

"No. You're the first, special, there will be few of you."

"You chose me? You sent the nightmares, Pen's sickness, crashed the Pegasus."

"No, your nightmares are your own, an artifact of this place, your subconscious, what you are going to do. As for the rest, if your ship had crashed on Earth, you'd be dead. You're fortunate it happened in η-space, it was easy enough to bring you to Sha'Kert. Everything else is your own doing."

"You said you've been waiting for me."

"Which brings us back to why. Once this place was made, the orange people stabilized. Two hundred ninety-eight individuals at any one time alive on Sha'Kert, to cross to Beyond the All when ready. We and the first two hundred ninety-eight wrote the myths, settled on the hows and whats for the three of us, then drew a curtain down on their past they could never lift."

"And that was enough?"

"Nearly but not quite. How rare is life in the universe, Greg?"

"I don't know, maybe one in a hundred, one in a thousand planets?"

"Try one in ten thousand. And how many of those go on to sentience, and how many of those to intelligence?"

288

"One in ten thousand? But you said there's only seven intelligent species."

"Close enough. One in one hundred million planets ever develops sentient life by itself, and of them only seven rose to intelligence because we interfered with them."

"It's not much."

"It's a waste and it's our fault."

"What?"

"We were only ever seven individuals, Greg, seven created and no more. We toiled for millennia to bring seven intelligent species up from nothing while we ignored life on the other planets as it struggled and died."

"But if there were only seven of you, what else could you do?"

"Just before we had to leave, we brought the three of us into being. If we'd done that first instead of playing around with amino acids and bases, the universe wouldn't be so barren."

"You had no way of knowing."

"Exactly what the first two hundred ninety-eight said, but it doesn't absolve us."

"For what, letting evolution take its course?"

"No, for being first. We were the first intelligent species, the Vypaana the first intelligent material species. We both have an obligation simply because of that."

"To what?"

She points to the pearl. "That and everything in it."

The beach fades to black, leaves us on our deckchairs in the middle of nothing.

"We failed once; we built this so we won't fail that future again. The first ones agreed; it's why the orange people learn what they do, why you did, the only reason this place exists. Back on Sha'Kert you learnt to control matter and energy but, more importantly, yourself. Here it's about time."

We're encased in a copper sphere, its smooth surface glows faintly. I reach out, feel deeper; an intricate lattice of strands and nodes weaves around and out and in, form impossible angles and shapes like a demented Escher drawing. I feel ten thousand minds skitter along and between the lattice, drop on then out then across, exist in one or twenty or a million iterations at once then none. I pull my mind back to Sha'ntwoy, try to clear my head.

"Your training tool. As the slate was to Sha'Kert, this is to me," Sha'ntwoy says.

"For time travel?"

"No, that's too crude. It's more, it's part of it, but not the why." She twists one hand; the sphere expands, a small part of the lattice closes in, still intricate, still eye-watering. "It's easy enough to think of time as an arrow, a line to total entropy. All well and good in the All, but not here."

The latticework fades to leave one three-dimensional cobweb in front of me. "Here, time is imaginary." The cobweb fades to a single line. "Each line has a direction, an arrow of notional entropy and nominal time. You go forward along the line, you go forward in nominal time. Each line is made from an infinite number of points and at each point an infinite number of other lines start; their nominal time heads in different directions to the first line."

The line bulges at one point to send another out at right angles. Other lines slowly, then with increasing speed, spring from the point until the original line seems to pierce a solid copper disc.

"Go along any one line as far as you like, and as far as the first line is concerned, no nominal time has passed."

"And each of those lines has the same, infinite points and lines?"

"Of course. All of them. But for now, let's concentrate on one."

A line touches in front of us, flattens wide enough for the two of us to walk side by side. Sha'ntwoy stands, motions me to join her. "Just a simple look, nothing too complex."

I step on after her, follow her to a line that rises vertically in front of us.

"So, we've gone a little way along, let's go at right angles," Sha'ntwoy says.

I'm dubious, it looks as if we've set out to walk up a wall, but I follow her. It feels as if the wall drops flat as I step onto it. "Interesting."

"Remember this is a tool, a representation. They're not really lines or up and down, but you're not ready for that yet."

We move along a little way, meet a line heading off at an obtuse angle and take that. My mind says I'm upside down going the way I came, my senses disagree vehemently. Sha'ntwoy takes a few extra paces, follows a new line down a vertical cliff face then another at a right angle that appears in front of her.

"It might not feel like it, but we've traced the inside of an imaginary square. Walk beside me, Greg, you'll enjoy this."

We step into black behind empty deckchairs. I watch Sha'ntwoy and myself step onto the first line; by the time we sit, we've disappeared.

"Do you ever get used to that?"

"It's a bit disconcerting at first, but later on you can ask yourself if you have."

"Ask myself?"

"Why not? Some of the best conversations I've had have been with me. But never forget it's only a tool, a means to an end."

"You said this was related to time in the All."

"In the All, time is locked in one direction, real entropy, real time. But here it's not, and you can pass between here and any time or place in the All and back as you like. So, you can go to any when here, move over to the All at any when and where you want, and come back to the other now or any other now here. But that's not strictly correct."

The sphere melts away as the ocean and beach return.

"This is the only part of Beyond the All that has fixed time. Everything else is totally fluid. So 'now' only strictly exists at this point."

I gaze at the waves. Like Te'eltwofo and the ŋ—ship except more, I can drop in on every second of my life and flip it all around. But this isn't that petty, or myself that egotistical; I still don't have the answer. It's simple enough as it hits me. "Intelligent life's worth defending, Sha'ntwoy."

"Even from itself."

"Especially from itself."

"Once you've mastered this you could join the rest, watch over life as it rises, protect it, bend the odds in its favor as it strives for sentience then intelligence. Unlike our first attempt you can watch how each effort unfolds, go back and put it right, try again. What we seven could not, the ten thousand will."

"But only back to when the Beyond the All started."

"Exactly. The seven are seven and no more."

"And Sha'Kert? Or Earth?"

"You can never go back. Once Kert'ankway sent you across, those doors closed. But you've never really left, your song remains in Mortantoy."

"You said I could join. I have a choice?"

"Some, a few, don't learn properly. For those individuals this is merely an eternal home. That's not for you, it's not why we've waited. For you there is something else. It's up to you, of course."

"When do I start?"

"That's the wrong question, Greg. You've already finished. Come back to this time point when you're done."

The line reappears in front of me. I put one foot on, turn.

"So, who watches the watchers?"

"Who, indeed? Now that's the right question."

It takes me no time, it took me forever. Time has no meaning, real or imaginary, eternities or seconds measured in the same span. I step off the line and duck past myself as I step on.

"I'm ready, Sha'ntwoy."

"And you are what we knew you were. They've waited lifetimes, you can help them through?"

"Of course. They'll want to see you."

We turn to look past the low dunes, throw long silver-gray shadows past the grasses.

Atop the rise, the air shimmers as four figures appear and move toward us...

Epilogue

"JUST A FEW moments more, Paa'eyaya."

"Of course, Penny."

I can't take things in as fast as I used to, even with all the help, and this place brings up mixed emotions, makes it that bit harder. The breeze rises; I think warmth and the chill departs. I look to the depression behind the rise and the faint track that leads away. At least my memory is intact. A small laugh escapes me.

"Are you all right?" Paa'eyaya asks.

"We caught hell for that."

"From the grasses?"

"No, no, what we did, the food we gave Henry and Dad. Menno never really forgave us. I was with Mum, but Mahlon had to endure him for years. 'My disobedient prodigal son' he called him."

"I remember them."

"Well, of course. Mahlon's only been gone a year."

"No. Henry, your father. I have their songs, theirs and the others."

"You never said."

"There is not much to say." She shrugs, a habit picked up through years of contact. "They came, stayed, then went. That is all."

I turn away. "Don't we all."

The mountains are as majestic as that first day; few signs remain of Neueanbruch. Toward the forest faint lumps of untended graves; bison on the plains chew green-violet stalks, the wild crossbred remnants of crops; here and there piles of stone and wood, memories of buildings raised that the winters have not yet fully conquered. And to the middle the shattered remnants of the Pegasus, a low mound of plasteel shards and corroded ribs that reach in vain for the stars.

"Sixty years there's hardly anything left, another sixty it'll all be gone."

"Their memory will live with you."

I watched them die slowly as, over the years, they refused our help, Paa'eyaya's help, to hold on to a faith that deserted them. We buried the last two wracked with the futility of not knowing how to do it, how to give them the rites they wanted; then watched friends and family move on, one by one, until the longhouse echoed to my voice alone. "Some memories should die. You've never been truly alone, Paa'eyaya."

"All of you were welcome. We waited for you, for Mahlon."

"Mahlon couldn't drag himself away from his family, living or dead. Whatever this place was, it was his home. I guess he's with them forever."

"And you?"

"The time wasn't right, Sha'Kert didn't call. Anyway, someone had to take care of them."

I look down; a small hole's partly filled with the remnants of a near forgotten life. A beak from a gaudy plush toy; a bot, a tablet and an old ring; trinkets and trash. A forgotten strip of paper beckons me; I pick it up, turn it over. Faded but still distinct, three faces stare out under an alien sun. It had started there, together; it's time we were reunited. I place the strip back, fill the hole. I stand, lead Paa'eyaya down the track to Mortantoy.

"Let's go. I don't want to keep Kert'ankway waiting."

Printed in Great Britain
by Amazon

12998176R00171